NO WORSE SIN

Kyla Bennett

Harvard Square Editions
New York
2015

No Worse Sin, copyright © 2014 by Kyla Bennett
Cover design by Charlotte Miller ©
www.charlottemillerdesign.com
Cover photos: © Hugoht | Dreamstime.com - Blue Morpho
Butterfly, Costa Rica Photo
© Djmobeus | Dreamstime.com - Wormhole Photo
© Monkeybusinessimages | Dreamstime.com - Silhouette Of
Romantic Couple Standing In Sea Photo

None of the material contained herein may be reproduced or
stored without permission from the author under
International and Pan-American Copyright Conventions.

Published in the United States by
Harvard Square Editions

ISBN: 978-1-941861-01-1

Harvard Square Editions web address:
www.HarvardSquareEditions.org

Printed in the United States of America

This book is a work of fiction. References to
real people, events, establishments,
organizations, or locales are intended only to
provide a sense of authenticity, and are used
fictitiously. All other characters, and all
incidents and dialogue, are drawn from the
author's imagination
and are not to be construed as real.

To Eames and Denali, who have never been, and never will be, indifferent.

"I always tell my son, 'The world is crawling with creeps and greedheads. Don't you dare grow up to be one of them.' And what I mean is: Be a responsible and caring person. Is that so hard? To be generous, not greedy. Compassionate, not indifferent. My God, is there a worse sin than indifference?"

—Honey Santana, in Carl Hiaasen's *Nature Girl*

Chapter 1

CHAOS STRUCK at 7:24 on an unseasonably warm March morning in North Bayside High School.

Not the type of chaos that you see on the news almost every month. There were no gunshots, no blood or broken bodies, no shell-shocked teenagers or weeping, frantic parents. Instead, the chaos in this Cape Cod classroom started 4,000 miles away, when a black and neon blue butterfly took flight, creating an almost imperceptible puff of air from its powdery velvet wings. And Laena Foster, who stood in the doorway of Room 103 on another continent, clutched the doorframe to withstand the reverberations of this tiny waft of tropical breeze.

The air seemed to shimmer with something foreign. Laena felt dizzy, like she was about to fall from a great height, and she had no idea why. Her mind raced and her eyes darted around the room, seeking the cause of this weird feeling. What was different? She heard none of the laughter or excited chatter that typically echoed through the room before class started. Instead, the juniors were silent, staring at Laena from their seats.

All except for one. A tan, black haired boy occupied her usual desk. He was tall. Ripped. He belatedly turned to the doorway to see who had arrived, and Laena jerked back in shock as she saw his eyes—an intense, beautiful blue. Butterfly blue. His features were chiseled—sharp planes for cheekbones, an aquiline nose, and a strong chin. She had never seen him before. And Laena knew, she *knew*, that a convoluted and chaotic chain of events had just been set in motion. Starting with the appearance of this strange boy.

"Laena, so nice of you to join us," the teacher said sarcastically, glancing at the clock. "Please, do come in and sit down. But keep this in mind: one more tardy morning, and I will have no choice but to give you detention."

The new boy was sitting at Laena's desk, next to her best friend, Sophie.

Laena remained rooted in the doorway to the classroom, ignoring the teacher, unable to speak.

The teacher sighed. "For goodness' sake, Laena, don't make Cree move—Sophie has offered to help him through his first day here. Sit in the empty seat behind him." The teacher sounded exasperated. She gestured impatiently for Laena to sit.

Laena nodded, and, head buzzing, took the vacant desk behind the boy. *Cree?* She thought. *His name is Cree?* Or had she heard wrong? As she struggled to unzip her backpack and balance her coffee on the tiny wooden school desk, the boy turned around and gave her a dazzling smile. "Sorry I took your seat," he whispered. Laena looked up and her eyes widened. Her jaw started to drop, but she closed her mouth, biting the inside of her cheek. She stared mutely at the boy. His straight dark hair partially covered one of his shocking blue eyes. He had dimples when he smiled. His voice sounded different, but she couldn't put her finger on why.

"Well, now that we are finally all here," the teacher shot a baleful glance at Laena, "I would like to introduce you to Cree McNeil. He just moved here from Alaska. Cree, welcome to Cape Cod, and to North Bayside. If you have questions, I'm sure any of the students would be happy to help you."

"Thank you, ma'am," Cree replied. Snickers from the other boys erupted throughout the room. Laena could tell that Robb Berger, the most popular boy in 11th grade, resented this good-looking stranger intruding on his territory. Laena disliked Robb. They had been in school together since kindergarten, but they were basically strangers. She considered him a stupid bully, and Robb probably didn't give Laena any thought at all. Robb elbowed his friend Greg Nelson in the ribs, jerking his chin toward Cree and snorting with laughter. The other boys followed Robb's lead, chuckling and whispering rudely.

The teacher cleared her throat and the snickering petered out. "Cree, you have quite an unusual name. Can you tell us about it?"

"Yes, ma'am." The laughter in the class increased in volume again, but Cree was either oblivious to the boys making fun of him, or he just didn't care. Cree spoke over the noise.

" 'Cree' means traveler. My parents traveled all over the country prior to my birth, and they liked the name." Laena realized he spoke with a slight accent. But it was an accent that Laena couldn't place.

"In what language...Eskimo?" Robb blurted, and students around the room twittered.

"Actually," Cree replied, twisting to the left in his seat to face Robb, "Cree is the name of a Native American tribe." Cree smiled at Robb. Robb snorted in disdain, but then shifted in his seat uneasily as Cree's gaze didn't waver. Robb feigned indifference and started flipping through his notebook.

Laena could not take her eyes off Cree. She yanked her wrinkled shirt down hastily, wishing she hadn't dressed in the dark that morning. She took a deep breath, trying to shake the unsettling feeling that the universe wavered, off kilter.

"And what brings you to the Cape?" the teacher asked, perching on the edge of her desk and smoothing her skirt over her knees.

"Work," Cree said. "I came to work, ma'am. Good-paying jobs in Alaska are hard to find these days. And because I thought it would be nice to have a change of pace, and see another part of the country."

Laena frowned. Work? Lots of her friends had after school jobs so they could have spending money for clothes and going to the movies. Cree must be their age, so why did he need a good-paying job? She wondered if his parents had been laid off, or if he needed to save money for college.

"Well, I'm sure Cape Cod is very different from Alaska," the teacher said, smiling broadly at Cree. "Okay class, let's get started. Your assignment was to finish reading *Oedipus*, and to think about whether anyone is truly responsible for his or her actions. Was *Oedipus* at fault for what happened, or was it simply the will of the Gods? Do you believe in fate? Or do humans have free will?"

Pages rustled as students skimmed through the book fruitlessly. Silence.

"Anyone?"

More rustling as kids flipped through their notebooks and studiously avoided the teacher's eyes. She sighed, exasperated.

"Laena? You can help me out here, can't you?"

Laena looked up and nodded. She had arrived late—she deserved this. "There is no such thing as fate. We have a lot of control as to how we respond to things that happen to us, although of course we don't have any control over external factors, like...earthquakes or someone else's behavior. And I guess we may not have as much free will as some people think we do. Our genes, experiences we had as young children, the way our neurons fire, even the laws of physics, all this stuff will cause us to react in a certain way that is really beyond our control. But it's not fate. What happens to us isn't the will of God. So I guess the bottom line is that I think Oedipus and his parents could have prevented what happened, so...yeah, what happened is kind of their fault."

By now the entire class was looking at Laena. Cree had turned around in his seat and was staring at her openly, a slight smile teasing his lips. Laena blushed and tried to ignore him.

The teacher pursed her lips. "So, are you saying that our biology and upbringing dictate much of what we do? That's a troubling thought."

Laena frowned. "Well, I'm not saying that free will is an illusion. We have free will, it's just tempered by science and experience."

The teacher raised her eyebrows. "Interesting interpretation. I'm not sure I agree with you, but I see where you're coming from. Good." She glanced around at the class. "Has anyone aside from Laena actually read the book?" No one answered.

Laena heard Robb mutter, "Teacher's pet." Laena cast her eyes down and sighed. She couldn't win, no matter what she did.

Laena felt Cree's gaze and glanced up, catching his eyes. He smiled openly and gave her a slight nod. "I agree with you," he whispered. He winked and turned back to the front of the class. Her face burned. Was he teasing her, or was it possible that he actually appreciated her intelligence?

Laena shook herself out of her reverie. She heard the teacher's voice but didn't hear the words. Usually Laena was able to pay attention to the teacher's droning, but not today. Instead, she found herself staring at Cree's broad back as he shifted to turn the page, the muscles rippling beneath the thin fabric of his shirt. She knew she would run into him repeatedly throughout the day. The school had only 200 students, freshmen through seniors, so it would be impossible to avoid him. How would she survive all her classes, being distracted by his presence for seven hours? Laena remembered her coffee, took a sip. Lukewarm. She sighed.

Laena knew she didn't stand a chance with someone as gorgeous and confident as Cree. Laena had friends in school, but she wasn't in the popular crowd, and she had never had a boyfriend. She was smart, too smart maybe, and she intimidated boys. At 5'2", she was shorter than most of the other girls, and she had long, sun-streaked brown curls instead of sleek, straightened hair. She didn't wear makeup, or the latest fashions. She went for comfort—jeans, tee shirts, and combat boots. People always told her that her hazel eyes were beautiful, but Laena accepted the fact that the two-inch scar slicing across her left cheek cancelled anything alluring about her. Laena knew a boy like Cree would never give her a second look, not with all the pretty girls around. So why did she feel this charge in the air? Electricity, like what you feel before a dangerous storm. Laena leaned back in her seat, unsettled. Her parents always teased her about her over-active imagination. But something weird hovered, just out of reach. This time, it was *not* her imagination.

And 4,000 miles away, the wind displaced by the butterfly's wings amplified. A still tiny current of air headed toward Cape Cod, growing stronger every second. Stronger, and more violent.

* * *

Laena discovered that Cree was in every one of her classes. Not surprising, given that there were only two classrooms of juniors in her tiny school. She sensed Cree no matter where he was, and couldn't concentrate. She did her best to ignore him, but it was impossible. A flash of his blue eyes had her daydreaming about him. And worse, a glimpse of his powerful muscles sent a jolt through her body that had her squirming in her seat. After the bell rang at the end of math, Laena rushed out of the classroom to make it to her locker and get her lunch before kids flooded the hallways. She hoped she could wolf down her sandwich and leave for the library to escape Cree's presence in the cafeteria. If he sensed her attraction to him...or, God forbid, if Robb or one of the other popular kids figured it out, the kids would torture her.

Laena sat down at her usual table at lunch and opened her bag. She always brought her own lunch to school, because she thought the school lunches were disgusting. Plus, there were very few vegetarian options, except for the school salad bar, which got boring day after day. Laena had been a vegetarian since she was four years old, a decision she made when she realized the fish she was eating had once been alive and swimming happily. The other kids used to mock her endlessly about the fact that she didn't eat meat. Singled out from the start, Laena brought her own food to birthday parties in elementary school, eating peanut butter and jelly sandwiches while other kids ate chicken nuggets. She used to take the teasing silently, but that ended her first day of high school. At lunch, Greg Nelson waved meat in her face and dared her to eat it. In response, Laena smacked his entire tray of cheeseburger and fries out of his hands. After the sound of the plate crashing to the floor had silenced the cafeteria, she responded calmly, "I don't eat murdered cows." The stunt earned Laena a trip to the principal's office, and the attention of some geeky boys who loved the fact that she had stood up to Greg. No one had teased her since.

Laena unwrapped her peanut butter sandwich and bit into it.

Sophie plopped her tray down on the table next to Laena. "*So??* What do you think?"

Laena swallowed the sticky bite of sandwich in her mouth and tried to answer. "What do I think of what?" she asked thickly.

Sophie rolled her heavily made-up eyes. "Of the new boy, silly. Cree. Isn't he a dream?" Sophie picked her fork up from her tray and poked it into a glutinous mass of spaghetti in meat sauce. "Just gorgeous! Those eyes...." She closed her own eyes in pleasure and sighed.

"Mmmm," Laena replied noncommittally, taking another bite of sandwich. She lost her appetite, and placed the sandwich back in her lunch bag, pushing the whole thing away.

Sophie eyed her suspiciously. "Laena, if you don't eat, you're gonna get sick. You're so small already. I swear," she paused to take a mouthful of spaghetti, "you are the strangest person." She shook her head, swallowing, her straight, shiny brown hair swinging. Laena pushed her own unruly curls out of her face, tucked them behind her ear, and sighed.

"I'm just not that hungry," Laena said. Other kids started sitting down at their table, chairs scraping and laughter drowning out Laena's words.

"Sophie!" squealed Catherine, a beautiful blonde girl in the 11th grade with them, "Did you get a load of the new boy?" Cat put her tray down with a clatter, giving her short, tight shirt a half-hearted tug, only calling attention to the significant section of flat, tanned midriff over her low-slung jeans. She widened her kohl-lined, blue eyes as she leaned forward. "He is *gorgeous*."

"I know, right?" Sophie replied, taking a sip of her milk. "Drop dead gorgeous."

Laena shook her head, but then felt the air sizzle. She straightened, sensing Cree's presence. Her eyes darted through the cafeteria, and sure enough, there he was, filling up a plate at the salad bar. He piled the plate high with salad and vegetables, and then glanced around for a place to sit.

"Cree! Over here!" Sophie shouted, waving her hand in the air. Cat waved as well, and squealed in excitement as Cree flashed a smile and headed their way. Laena groaned inwardly and shrank down in her chair. She couldn't sit with him, couldn't be near him. Laena felt her heart hammering, and feared that everyone would sense the physical reaction she had to him. She stood up just as he reached the table. He towered over her.

"Here, you can have my spot," Laena offered, stepping away from the chair.

Cree put his heaping plate on the table and looked down at her curiously. "Aren't you going to eat?" A chunk of his black hair fell over his face.

"I'm not very hungry," Laena replied, looking away as his glowing blue eyes drilled into hers. She hurriedly stuffed her lunch bag into her backpack. God, she had to get away. If he saw the desire in her eyes, she would be a laughingstock.

"Just salad for lunch, Cree?" Sophie said, already ignoring Laena. "The spaghetti isn't bad." She smiled charmingly and patted the chair next to her.

"I am a vegan," Cree replied, smiling. "Salad is fine." Still standing, he turned back toward Laena. "Are you sure you will not stay, Laena? I can get another chair." He spoke softly, but his words echoed through Laena's body.

"Thanks, no," she stuttered. "I have to...I have to go do something." And she turned and fled, cheeks burning. *He must think I'm a complete idiot*, she thought. She felt the heat on her face. She never got embarrassed like this. She rushed into the hallway, the cafeteria door clanking shut behind her.

Laena pushed her way into the empty bathroom across the hall and clung to the side of the sink, staring at herself in the mirror. She saw her normally pale skin, flushed, with fine beads of sweat dotting her hairline. *What the hell is wrong with me?* She turned the cold water on, cupping it in her hands, and splashed her face over and over. She grabbed some paper towels and scrubbed her face dry. How on earth could she survive the day, let alone the rest of the school year, feeling like this? She willed herself to calm down, breathing deeply. *He is just a stupid boy*, she thought, *just a boy*. She repeated it over and over in her mind, like a mantra, until her heart slowed to a somewhat normal rate and her breathing calmed. *Just a boy, like all the rest.*

She took one last deep breath. Exhaled. As if everything were back to normal. As if it wasn't going to be total freaking chaos.

* * *

Laena's heart was racing again by the time she walked toward biology. She knew the lab seat next to her was empty, and the teacher, who happened to be her father, would undoubtedly seat Cree there. Bad enough that her father taught her biology class. The kids already joked about her being the teacher's pet. If her father heard the other kids teasing her about liking Cree, she might die from embarrassment.

Could she stand sitting *next* to Cree for the next 50 minutes? She couldn't hide her attraction. *Calm down!* She berated herself. *He's nothing special.* When Laena entered the classroom, she saw Cree in front, talking to her dad. As her father glanced up, he smiled and beckoned her over.

"Laena, I hear you've met Cree?" he asked, throwing an arm around Cree's broad shoulders. Her father, a good-looking man with straight light brown hair going gray, a perpetual five o'clock shadow, and gray-blue eyes, smiled with obvious pleasure. Cree stood at least four or five inches taller than her father.

She smiled and nodded, still not trusting her voice to speak.

"Good, good. I'm going to seat Cree next to you. I think he'll be just fine in this class, but you can give him help if he needs any."

"No problem," Laena said. Her voice sounded rusty. Cree rewarded her with another blinding smile, and followed her to their lab table.

"Thanks," Cree said, touching her elbow lightly. A tingling sensation ignited where he had touched her, and then traveled to the pit of her stomach. They both sat down at the well-worn soapstone table, moving their chairs in, scraping the linoleum noisily. "So," Cree said, "your father says biology is your best subject. But you sure did a good job in English this morning."

Laena smiled weakly, and then realized she really should make an effort to be friendlier. "I guess it helps to be raised by two scientists," she conceded. "Science is definitely my favorite."

Cree laughed. "I would think so. Your dad told me your mom does research at CCOL." He pronounced the acronym correctly—*cee-col*—and Laena wondered if he had heard about it before her dad brought it up. CCOL, or the Cape Cod Oceanographic Laboratory, was a famous east coast research lab located on the Cape, but she doubted whether it was well known in Alaska. She nodded and smiled, but he kept staring at her, and she squirmed uncomfortably.

"Ummm...is something wrong?" she asked finally when his gaze didn't waver from her face.

"What.... ?" Cree asked, clearly confused, his head angled to one side. "No, no...was I staring? I am sorry, Laena." He looked embarrassed. "It is just that...well, you are not like the girls in...in Alaska. You look different."

"Different?"

"Not in a bad way," Cree amended, grinning. He reached out gently and took one of her long curls in his fingers. "I have never seen hair like yours, or eyes that color. And you are so tiny."

Laena heard comments about her height all the time. Being 5'2" in a sea of statuesque girls set her apart. But didn't people in Alaska have hazel eyes? Sometimes her eyes looked green, or even golden, but they couldn't be *that* unusual.

"I'm not exactly 'tiny'," Laena replied sharply, shifting away so her hair fell out of his grasp. "I'm just...petite." She busied herself pulling out her lab notebook as other students settled into their places.

"I am sorry if I insulted you—I really did not mean it that way. I think you are lovely," Cree replied, his voice sincere. "And you are obviously smart."

Lovely? Really? Laena glanced up at his face. He didn't look like he meant to make fun of her.

"Forgive me?" he pressed, smiling gently. She noticed that his blue eyes were fringed with the darkest, lushest lashes she had ever seen on a boy. And he had a stubble of growth on his face, making him look older than the other boys in her class. Laena's head swam. She could not last sitting next to this guy. She would have to ask her father to move Cree to another lab table. She nodded belatedly in response to his question, and looked up at the front of the classroom, willing her father to start the day's lecture, just so she could escape Cree's gaze.

As if reading her mind, her father cleared his throat, readying himself for teaching the class. "I'm not going to bother introducing Cree McNeil to you, as I'm sure you've all had the chance to meet him throughout the day." The class murmured their assent, and several girls looked Cree's way and giggled. "So, let's get right to work. You now know everything you need to know about genetics and heredity, so we will be starting our new chapter on evolution."

"Dr. Foster?" Tiffany Barnett had her hand raised, flailing it in the air. Laena groaned, she thought only to herself. But a sound must have escaped from her lips, because Cree glanced over at her, one eyebrow raised in question. Tiffany was not the brightest bulb on the porch, and she constantly interrupted teachers with stupid questions. Laena could anticipate what Tiffany was going to say, right down to the valley girl inflection, the last syllable of each sentence ending on a higher note, turning everything into a question. Tiffany had made it very clear in previous classes that she was a creationist, and evolution remained a problem for her.

"My father? He says I don't have to listen to this crap?" The class laughed, and Tiffany glanced around angrily, her shiny blond hair swinging. The laughter died down. "I mean, evolution is just a theory, right? And me and my family, well, we don't believe in it, see? So my dad says I should be excused?"

"Actually, Tiffany, you do have to listen. You are right about one thing, though. Evolution is a theory, just like...gravity." As he said this, Dr. Foster dropped his copy of the thick biology text on the floor, where it landed with a startling *thwack*. The class jumped, then laughed uncomfortably. "As you all know, it is called the '*theory* of gravity.' " The laughter increased, and the tension in the room abruptly eased.

Tiffany shook her head, talking over the giggles and chuckles. "No, Dr. Foster. My father says a theory is something that hasn't been proven? And if it's not proven, then what's it doing being taught in bio?" Tiffany smiled, looking quite smug with her reasoning. She began to twirl a strand of her long straight hair around her finger.

Cree slunk down in his seat, his brow creased in annoyance.

"You raise a very good point, Tiffany. Let's talk about the word 'theory.' Can someone tell me the difference between a *scientific* theory and a philosophical theory?" Dr. Foster asked, trying to be patient, but his voice belied his frustration.

Cree raised his hand quickly. "Cree?" Dr. Foster said, nodding in his direction. He looked relieved that someone wanted to take a stab at responding to Tiffany's question.

"A scientific theory is not really a theory at all, Dr. Foster. It is more like a...law. A scientific theory explains things that scientists have actually seen and observed. And evolution *has* been confirmed—over and over again." Cree spoke firmly. "The term 'theory' is not accurate when we speak about evolution, at least when most people..." Cree shot an irate glance at Tiffany, "...view theories as something that remain to be proven. In science, the term was actually abandoned...." He trailed off.

Dr. Foster, who had been nodding encouragingly, frowned slightly at Cree's last word. "Abandoned?"

"I mean, *should* be abandoned, sir," Cree modified. "It is too confusing...to certain people." Cree threw another look at Tiffany, who stared at him blankly.

"I don't get it Dr. Foster," she said, shaking her head. "A theory is something that still needs to be proven, like he said? The Bible says God created all the creatures, right? So evolution is just something that people, like, came up with that doesn't make any sense?" Her valley girl cadence became more pronounced.

The class laughed again. Laena could tell that a lot of them agreed with Tiffany, and Laena flushed with embarrassment.

"A scientific theory is accepted to be true by the scientific community," Cree said through gritted teeth. "Evolution *has* been proven, just like gravity."

"Nuh-uhn," Tiffany said, shaking her head. "What about the religious community? They believe...."

"Enough," Dr. Foster said, firmly. He had come to the end of his rope. "This is a biology class, in a public high school. Last time I checked, the United States Supreme Court agreed that evolution should be taught in science class. There is no room here for creationism or intelligent design, or discussions about the beliefs of the religious community. After all, which religious community are we talking about? Judeo-Christian? Muslim? Buddhist? Tiffany, if you and your father have a problem with this, you can make an appointment to see me in order to discuss the matter. But I would like to warn you that this material will be on upcoming tests and quizzes, and you cannot graduate from this high school if you fail biology. Do you understand?"

Tiffany slammed her book shut and slumped in her chair, staring at Dr. Foster through narrowed, angry eyes. Laena closed her own eyes, wishing she were anywhere else but here. Her father had expressed concern over dinner last night that this would happen. Every year, he said, some student would challenge his attempts to teach evolution. And each year, he had to shut them down, often after a fight with the parents, the principal, and the school board.

Laena could feel Cree fuming beside her. There were other kids in the class disgusted with Tiffany as well. She could see Mike Watson, lab partners with Sophie, head in his hands, sandy hair mussed by his frustration. Sophie rolled her eyes, peeking at Mike to ensure that he saw her shared irritation of Tiffany. Sophie had been dying to snag Mike for several months now, and she flirted shamelessly. But the vast majority of students were open to what Tiffany said. Laena glanced over at Tiffany and saw that she was deliberately ignoring Laena's father. She doodled in her notebook, as if there was no lesson being taught. Laena could imagine the conversation at Tiffany's dinner table tonight. It would undoubtedly involve her father's name and a lot of expletives. How very Christian.

* * *

Laena gathered together the books she would need for homework and slammed her locker shut. The sound of dozens of lockers banging reverberated through the halls, mingled with laughter and shouting from students happy that the school day ended. She turned away from her locker, and gasped in surprise to find Cree standing just inches in front of her. He smiled, his dimples in full force.

"I am sorry, Laena. Did I frighten you?" His voice was low.

"Just startled me, I guess," Laena replied, slinging her backpack over her shoulder. Her heart hammered.

"May I carry that for you?" Cree held out his hand for her heavy pack.

"No, I'm good," Laena said firmly. "I'm small, but I can carry my own books." She willed herself to soften her tone. "But, thanks anyway." She headed toward the school doors, and Cree fell into step next to her.

Cree laughed. "Why do I keep sticking my foot into my mouth with you?" he mused. "Can I at least walk you home?"

Laena looked at him out of the corner of her eye. What was up with this guy? What did he really want from her? He couldn't possibly be interested in her. Her heart thudded from having him close by. They exited the front door of the school together, and Laena felt Cat and Tiffany's eyes drill through them as they walked away from the school. Cree smelled like a summer day right after a thunderstorm, like the fresh smell of the air, mixed with peppermint. She gnawed at her bottom lip.

"Where do you live?" Laena finally asked, avoiding answering his offer to walk her home, and hoping maybe he lived in the opposite direction from her house.

"I am staying at Evergreen Acres," Cree said.

Laena stopped short and turned to him. "You're living at the *campground?*"

Cree nodded. "I have one of the cabins. I live there in exchange for being a caretaker."

Laena stared in amazement. Evergreen Acres was rustic, to say the least. It had electric hookups for RVs, but mostly it consisted of tent sites with cold running water and porta-potties. It was pretty, with towering white pines and very little undergrowth. There were a few one-room cabins there, but they were uninsulated and pretty run-down. The small cluster of cabins shared a common bathroom. Laena could not imagine living there for more than a week. "What about your parents? Do they live there with you?"

"No, it is just me," Cree stated. "My parents are dead."

Laena didn't know what to say. His parents were *dead*? As an 11th grader, he couldn't be much older than her—although he did look more mature than the other boys in her grade. So, he was 17, or 18 tops. How could he be living on his own?

Cree smiled gently. "I am an emancipated minor," Cree said, answering her unspoken question. "The courts gave me permission to live on my own."

"You don't have any relatives who can take you in, or help you out?" Laena couldn't imagine living without her parents. Without an adult, or at least an older sibling. Not that Laena had any siblings.

"I do not need anyone," Cree responded. When Laena snuck a glance at him, he seemed calm and relaxed. "I actually like being on my own."

"So, what made you come to Cape Cod? And how did you find Evergreen Acres?" Laena asked.

Cree shrugged. "I love the ocean," he explained, "and work disappeared in Alaska. I have always wanted to see a right whale. So, I came to the Cape, liked the town of North Bayside, and saw an advertisement for a caretaker at the campground...."

Laena had stopped in her tracks. Cree took a few steps beyond her until he sensed that she was no longer by his side. He turned to look at her. "What?" he asked. "Did I say something wrong?" Cree was smiling, his head cocked to one side. The warm spring breeze ruffled his hair, and Laena's heart seized with some feeling she couldn't name.

She started walking again, catching up with Cree. "No, you didn't say anything wrong. I mean...it's just that...the fact that you want to see a right whale is weird, because my name...." Laena trailed off.

Cree laughed. "Laena, you are not making sense."

She shook her head, as if trying to clear it. "It's just...my name. Do you know where my name is from?"

Cree shook his head, puzzled.

"The genus for the right whale is *Eubalaena*. My name is L-A-E-N-A...it's short for *Eubalaena*. My parents named me after the right whale." Laena looked embarrassed. "I don't usually tell anyone that. It's kinda...strange, I guess. The kids would torture me if they knew."

"I do not think it is strange," Cree responded tenderly. "It is a beautiful name. Unusual, and beautiful." He paused, then added, "Like you."

Laena didn't respond. This whole day had rocked her world. She could feel the earth hurtling through the universe, spinning out of control.

"Will you take me to see one?" Cree asked, interrupting her train of thought.

"To see a right whale? Cree, we can't do that, not in the U.S. It's illegal to get within 500 yards of them."

Cree nodded. "I know. I just thought maybe your parents had a research permit or something...."

Laena shook her head before Cree could finish his thought. "No, my parents don't have that kind of authority. You'd have to go up to Canada, the Bay of Fundy, to see them."

They walked in silence along the sandy road. Laena was amazed that Cree wanted to see the right whale. She herself had traveled on a research vessel with her mom, guests of a fellow CCOL scientist, to the Bay of Fundy, and they had been so close to a group of right whales, she could have reached out and touched them. But not here, not in Cape Cod Bay. You could get in big trouble if you got too close to the whales.

They had come to the end of the school's driveway. Laena lived to the left, toward the bay, and the campground where Cree lived was to the right. The General Store stood straight ahead of them.

"Well, I go this way," Laena said, pointing to the left.

Cree nodded, and did not renew his request to walk Laena home.

"Okay," he said. "I guess I will go back to my cabin and get some work done around the campground." Cree looked somewhat crestfallen, and a wave of guilt swept through Laena. *What's wrong with me?* she thought. *Here's this boy who is all alone in the world, in a new place, thinks like I do, and I'm letting him go home to a horrible little cabin by himself?* Before she could think too much,

Laena blurted, "Why don't you come over for dinner later? Say around six?"

Cree's face lit up. "Really? I mean, your parents will not mind?"

Laena shook her head. "I usually do the cooking. It's no big deal, honestly."

"I do not want to be any trouble, though. I am a vegan, so I am tough to feed." He looked worried. "Let me at least bring something."

"Nope, I'm good. I'm a vegetarian, and I can cook vegan."

Cree's smile split his face. "That would be wonderful. I will be there at six." He turned to the right and then whirled around. "See you soon!" he said, walking backwards, watching her, his bright blue eyes radiating happiness. His jeans hung low on his hips, and she couldn't help but glance at his sinewy muscles. She tore her eyes back up to his face.

Laena laughed at his boyish enthusiasm. "Um, Cree? Don't you want to know where we live?"

Cree stopped walking and laughed with her. "Yeah, I guess that might help," he admitted sheepishly.

Laena gave him her address, and directions, and Cree waved, turned, and jogged down the road toward Evergreen Acres.

What have I gone and done now? Laena thought. She hurried toward home. She only had three hours to get a head start on her homework, straighten up the house, and figure out a vegan meal to cook for dinner. *Good job, Laena*, she thought sarcastically. She walked faster.

A cloud covered the sun, and the hairs on the nape of her neck stood up. Laena glanced around. A shadow merged with the trees to her right. Was someone watching her? She glanced over her shoulder. Cree had disappeared down the road the opposite direction, toward the campground. Laena peered uneasily through the forest. Nothing there. She shook her head and continued down the road. Chided herself for being spooked. Smiling, she anticipated the evening ahead.

* * *

Laena straightened the house, hastily running the vacuum around, arranging piles of magazines in the living room, and wiping down the kitchen counters and table. She cast a critical eye around the downstairs. It was small, but cozy, an old Cape Cod with cedar shingles, and a great farmer's porch out front boasting a view of the bay. A path from the sandy front yard led down to a small rocky beach, and a dock where they kept their boat. The house was all hardwood and warm colors inside, with scattered throw rugs in oranges and burgundy. Nothing special, but a perfect house for the three of them. She went into the kitchen and started sautéing onions, garlic, and peppers for vegetarian chili.

"I'm home!" Laena's father called, as the front door slammed. "What smells so good?"

"Chili!" Laena called from the kitchen. "Take off your shoes, Dad, I just vacuumed."

Her father padded into the kitchen in his socks and leaned over her shoulder to peer into the pot of sizzling vegetables. "What's the occasion?" he asked.

"I...well, I invited Cree over for dinner. I hope that's okay."

Her father looked surprised. "Sure, no problem. His parents, too?"

Laena set down the wooden spoon on the counter and turned to her father. "He's an orphan, Dad. He lives at Evergreen Acres, doing maintenance in exchange for living quarters. I felt bad for him...you know, being in a strange place all alone...." She trailed off, feeling a little awkward, certain her father could see her heart pounding through her tee shirt.

"An orphan?" Her father opened the fridge and took out a bottle of beer. "Really? Huh," he said thoughtfully. He popped off the top with a church key, and the beer hissed softly. He took a swig of the amber liquid, and then set the bottle down on the counter. "Wow. Poor kid. He seems bright, too." He tossed the bent bottle cap between his hands, brow furrowed.

"You don't mind, then? That I invited him for dinner?"

"No, no, of course not. Anytime." He tossed the cap into the garbage and rotated his neck to get the kinks out. "Boy, am I tense...what a rough afternoon. Tiffany's father called the principal to complain about me, and I had to explain what happened. I want to teach these kids, but sometimes their parents make it incredibly difficult." He sighed. "I'm going upstairs to change. I'll be right down to help you."

"Sounds good," Laena responded, picking up the spoon and stirring the onions. As she dumped the hot peppers and the drained beans into the pot, she started getting nervous. Why had she invited Cree over? Was it because she was flattered by the attention he was giving her, and his stunning looks? And why on earth was he paying attention to her, rather than Sophie or Cat or any of the other prettier, more popular girls in school? Something was off, and Laena felt unbalanced.

Boys were generally not interested in Laena. And here was this gorgeous new boy, who could have the pick of any girl in school, paying attention to *her*. Laena shook her head. Maybe he had no interest in her as a girlfriend, though. Maybe he just wanted to see the endangered right whale, and thought she could make it happen. Laena emptied a jar of stewed tomatoes from last summer's garden in the pot, covered it, and turned the gas heat on low to allow the mixture to simmer. She wiped her hands on a kitchen towel and turned to the refrigerator to start making a salad.

Her father came back into the kitchen, wearing worn jeans and a cotton shirt. "I feel better now that I'm out of my work clothes," he said. "What can I do to help?"

Laena handed him a cucumber. "You can help me make a salad," she said. Her father grabbed a cutting board and a knife, and started in on the cucumber. Since Laena's mother worked longer hours, and had a long commute from Falmouth, Ben and Laena did most of the cooking.

"So how was school today?" her father asked.

"Weird," Laena admitted. "Having a new student is bizarre...I mean, we've had the same kids for so long, throwing someone new in the mix is really disconcerting."

"Especially someone like Cree, huh?" her father asked, smiling, scraping the sliced cucumbers into the salad bowl.

Laena looked up from ripping the lettuce into bite-sized chunks, one eyebrow raised questioningly, and said, "What do you mean, 'someone like Cree' "?

"Well, he's a pretty handsome kid. Don't tell me you didn't notice."

Laena blushed and tucked a stray strand of curls behind her ear. "It's kinda hard not to notice, Dad. But he just seems different from everyone else. I can't put my finger on it."

"Well, he is from Alaska. That's a whole different world up there," her father said pensively. "And being on his own, that would make you grow up in a hurry, I'd think. Maybe he's just more mature than the boys you know."

"You think?" Laena said sarcastically, laughing. "He's definitely more mature. But it's something else. Like he's...old-fashioned or something. Formal." She paused and then added, "He wants to see a right whale."

"No kidding?"

The front door slammed. "Who wants to see a right whale?" Laena's mother called, heels clicking as she walked into the kitchen.

"Mom, take off your shoes! I just cleaned," Laena complained.

Her mother snagged a cucumber out of the salad bowl, popped it in her mouth, and kicked off her pumps. "Who wants to see a right whale?" she asked again, mouth full of cucumber. She was slight, like Laena, and had curly brown hair that she kept shoulder length for ease. Her eyes were hazel, and radiated intelligence.

"New student at school," her father responded. "Boy named Cree McNeil. He moved here from Alaska. Laena tells me he's an orphan, so he's here all alone. And..." he paused with exaggerated drama, "he's coming for dinner."

"A new boy, hmmm? Is he cute?" her mother asked, smiling.

"Mom...."

"Judging by the way the girls were giggling around him at school today, I'd say cute doesn't really describe it," her father said seriously. "Girls were going nuts for him."

"Oooh, and he's coming *here* for dinner, Laena?" her mother teased.

"Enough!" Laena said sharply. "I swear, sometimes the two of you act like you're 13. Please don't embarrass me when Cree is here."

Her parents laughed, promising to be on their best behavior. Laena's mother went upstairs to change, and Laena set the kitchen table for dinner.

When the doorbell rang, Laena's stomach leaped. "That must be Cree," she murmured. "I'll get it."

She ran to the front door and opened it. Cree stood there, hair still wet from a recent shower, with a fresh tee shirt and jeans on. He smiled and said softly, "Hi, Laena." Her heart pounded. He wore a beautiful blue shirt which matched his eyes. She breathed in his fresh scent, and stared.

"I am sorry I am a little early...I was not sure how long it would take me to get here," he continued.

Laena stood in the doorway and nodded. "It's fine," she said. There was an awkward pause.

"Are you going to invite me in?" he said, laughing.

"Oh! Of...of course, yes," Laena stammered, backing away from the entrance and holding the door wide. "Come in."

"Thank you," he said, stepping over the threshold. Laena's parents came into the foyer.

"Cree, good to see you!" her father said, extending his hand. Cree shook it warmly.

"Thanks for allowing me to come over, Dr. Foster," Cree said.

"You know what, Cree? In school, 'Dr. Foster' is fine. But here, since my wife and I are both 'Dr. Foster,' it gets a little confusing. How about calling me Ben, and my wife Michelle? We prefer to be a little more informal."

Cree nodded. "If that is what you would like, sir," he responded, reaching out to shake Laena's mom's hand. "Ma'am," he said.

"So much for informality," Laena said, smiling.

"Please, Cree," Michelle said, laughing. "Let's drop the sir and ma'am, too," she implored, motioning Cree into the kitchen. Cree nodded his assent, and smiled. Laena thought he looked a little embarrassed.

"I understand from Laena that you want to see a right whale, Cree," Laena's mother said, pouring glasses of sparkling water over ice and handing one to Cree. "You know, you aren't allowed to get close to them in this country."

"I understand, ma'am...ummm...Michelle. But Laena said maybe in Canada.... ?"

Michelle nodded. "Yes, in Canada you can get right up to them, unfortunately for the poor whales. Whale watch boats surround them sometimes. But they are quite curious creatures...they almost seem to enjoy the interactions."

Cree's eyes sparkled. "That sounds amazing. To be able to look into the eyes of such a magnificent creature...I have never seen a whale before."

Both of Laena's parents looked up sharply at Cree. "You've never seen a whale, not even in Alaska? The waters are teeming with them there," said Laena's father. "I would have thought you'd seen plenty, at least gray whales, or belugas...or minkes, or even blues."

Cree shook his head, embarrassed. "Of course, yes. I have seen whales. I...I meant I had never seen a *right* whale. I have seen the others...lots of times," Cree stuttered.

Laena looked at him curiously. Cree looked uncomfortable, like he'd been caught in a lie.

"Where in Alaska are you from, Cree?" Laena asked, trying not to sound like she doubted him. "I've always wanted to go there."

"I lived near Kenai," Cree responded, without hesitation.

"Oh, nice," Laena's mother said, nodding. "I've heard wonderful things about Kenai from friends who traveled there. And your accent? I can't really place it."

"Is it noticeable? I did not realize." Cree responded, swirling his glass of sparkling water, ice cubes tinkling in the silence. He dodged Michelle's gaze, looking down into his drink.

There was an uncomfortable silence as they all waited for an answer to the question. When it became obvious that Cree did not plan to respond, Laena cleared her throat. "Well, dinner's ready, if anyone's hungry."

Everyone murmured assent, and Laena carried the pot of chili to the table. As they took their seats, Laena said, "It's vegan chili, Cree. No meat, no dairy."

"Great," Cree responded, smiling and at ease once again. "It smells delicious."

Laena's father passed the breadbasket around, and then the butter. Cree passed the butter on without taking any.

"Cree is vegan," Laena explained. "Dad, put the butter away. No cheese or sour cream tonight, either. No dairy products."

Cree looked up. "Do not avoid dairy on my account! Please, go ahead and have cheese or...sour cream if you want...I will not be offended." He stumbled over the words.

"Oh, you're vegan, Cree?" Michelle asked, spooning chili into her bowl. "Why is that?"

Cree once again looked uncomfortable. "It is really the...well, the impact that animal products have on the environment," Cree said. "And it is hard to get certain foods up in Alaska, so I got used to just not eating any animal products at all."

"Let's not put the poor boy on the spot, Michelle," Ben laughed. "He saved me in bio today when Tiffany started yammering on about how evolution is just a theory."

Michelle shook her head. "There's one every year, isn't there?"

The conversation became easier once Cree was off the hook, and they talked about things like the weather Cree could expect on the Cape, his classes, and things that Cree should do before the tourist season started in June. Laena contributed to the conversation, but studied Cree when he chatted with her parents. He was gorgeous, she decided, and smart. But he was odd, too, with his slightly stilted style. He seemed awkward at times, almost as if he were unfamiliar with everyday things. How could he not eat animal products in Alaska, for crying out loud? Maybe there weren't many cows in Alaska, granted, but certainly milk and cheese were available. There were McDonald's restaurants in over 125 countries...the price of globalization.

Dinner ended before she knew it, and Cree jumped up to help clear the table. Michelle stood up and put a hand on his arm. "No, no...guests do not help clear up. And Laena, you cooked, so why don't you let me and Ben take care of the dishes? You two kids go relax. In fact, it's a beautiful evening—why don't you go sit on the porch and enjoy the weather?"

"Thank you, Michelle, I appreciate it," Cree said, glancing at Laena. "Does that sound okay to you?"

Laena nodded and headed toward the front hall closet to grab a jacket. She glanced at Cree's thin tee shirt and said, "Do you want to borrow one of my dad's jackets? It's getting cool out."

Cree laughed. "I am from Alaska, remember? I will be fine."

They stepped out onto the front porch and Laena led the way to the swinging loveseat. Cree waited for her to seat herself before he sat down. They both pushed off the porch floor with their feet, setting the swing into a gentle rocking motion. Laena snuggled into her jacket against the cool night air.

"So, how was your first day at North Bayside High?" Laena asked, laughing softly. She steeled herself for negative comments about the school's tiny size, the kids like Tiffany, and the horrible cafeteria food. She complained endlessly about their tiny town and school, but deep inside, she loved living here.

"Good," Cree responded enthusiastically. Laena looked at him in surprise. "Really," Cree continued, noticing her amazement. "Everyone treated me well, and the teachers were great...I think I am going to like it here."

Laena shrugged. "There's no accounting for taste," she said, shaking her head. Cree laughed. Laena turned and looked at him, her eyes wide. "You really thought it was okay?" Her voice was incredulous.

"Yes, I really did," Cree said, his tone becoming more serious. "It is so different from Alaska, and from the...from my old town. I think this is good for me, you know? Meeting new people, seeing a whole new place. It is fascinating."

"Have you lived in Alaska your whole life?"

Cree nodded. "I have never been out of Alaska until now. Being on the east coast, seeing places I never thought I would or could see. I had only read about places like Cape Cod, and life before...." He trailed off.

"Before....?" Laena prompted. "Before what?"

Cree paused, and Laena could see the wheels spinning in his head. "You know, historically. The pilgrims and all that. The Native Americans."

"Oh," Laena said, perplexed. Had he been about to say something else? "I guess you learn about that stuff up in Alaska, too." She paused, then admitted, "We had to take a class trip to see Plymouth Rock."

"Wow. Did you see it?" Cree actually sounded excited, and Laena laughed. He sounded like a little boy talking about seeing his first fire truck.

"Yeah, we saw it. The poor rock was in a cage. So many people chip off pieces to take home as souvenirs, they had to put it in this metal cage to protect it. I felt like starting a demonstration—you know, 'Free Plymouth Rock!' Why should they put the rock in a cage? So stupid." She shook her head.

"People stole pieces of it? What for?" Cree was surprised.

Laena shrugged. "Beats me. I guess for bragging rights. To say they had a piece of Plymouth Rock. Or to sell them on eBay. The silly thing is, no one knows if that's *the* rock that the pilgrims first set foot on. It most likely isn't." She paused. "But I can take you there if you really want to see it." She said it hesitantly, afraid Cree would turn her down.

"I would love to see it," Cree said, enthusiastically. "I want to see as much as I can while I am here. I would love to see Boston, too. What is that like?"

"Didn't you fly into Logan Airport?" Laena asked. Cree shook his head. "How'd you get here? From Alaska, I mean."

"Oh, I...I came a different way."

"A different.... ? Oh! Did you fly into TF Green airport? In Providence?"

"Yes, that one. Providence," Cree agreed.

Laena looked at him curiously. Cree glanced over at her, and she could tell he read her skepticism clearly. He abruptly changed the subject.

"So, what do you do on the Cape during the weekends?"

Laena laughed. "If you're expecting any kind of nightlife, you're out of luck. The Cape is dead off-season."

"Off-season?" Cree queried. He clearly had not heard the term before.

"When the tourists aren't here," Laena explained. "The tourists descend on the Cape after Memorial Day, and don't really leave until Labor Day. There's traffic, and lines, and obnoxious people, and men wearing shorts with knee socks and sandals...." She trailed off, and Cree looked at her curiously. He had no idea what she meant. Laena finished her thought before she lost him entirely. "The rest of the year, the Cape is so quiet that there's really nothing to do. You must have that in Alaska, too, right? Not many tourists in the winter?"

"Right," Cree said. "Not many people in the winter. It is too dark and depressing."

"Exactly," Laena smiled.

"So what do you do weekends during the...off-season?"

"Well, if the weather is nice, I go to the beach, or take the boat out," Laena replied.

"You have a boat? What kind?"

"A Boston whaler." Cree looked confused, and Laena explained. "It's not much, about 18 feet long with a 150 horsepower engine...just for tooling around the bay."

Cree still looked perplexed. "Didn't you boat up in Alaska?" Laena asked.

"No, never. But it sounds great. Can you see fish, and dolphins?"

Laena nodded. "And seals sunning on rocks, and all sorts of sea birds. It's pretty relaxing, actually."

"Will you take me?" Cree asked excitedly. He turned his body to face her on the cramped swing.

"Sure," Laena replied, slowly. "But I'm sure our wildlife pales in comparison to what you have in Alaska."

Cree shook his head. "No, not really." He paused and then clarified, "I mean, there are different species down here that I would love to see. It is like a...a different world on this coast, and this far south."

"Okay," Laena said, smiling. "It's a deal. Weather permitting, I will take you boating this weekend."

"Great!" Cree smiled widely and reached out and squeezed Laena's hand. Her heart started a renewed pounding at his touch, and she pulled away uncomfortably. Cree seemed not to notice her discomfort, and instead reached out and traced the old, faded scar on Laena's cheek with his finger. She shivered as his warm skin trailed over hers. Her face burned where he touched her.

"What injured you here, Laena?" he asked gently, cupping his hand over her face. Too shocked to speak, Laena flinched at his bluntness and his touch. Just then, the front door opened and Laena's father came out onto the porch. Cree dropped his hand, but not before Ben had seen the caress. He cleared his throat. "Dishes are done," he announced. "Do you kids have homework? I know I assigned some."

Cree stood up abruptly. "I have overstayed my welcome—I am sorry."

"No, no, Cree, not at all," Ben interjected. "It's just that it's a school night...."

Cree held up a hand to stop Ben's explanation. "I understand completely. I should get back to my cabin. Thank you for your hospitality."

"Let me drive you back," Ben said. "It's dark, and getting a little chilly."

Cree smiled. "I really prefer to walk, sir. It is not a problem."

Laena's mother came out on the porch, hugging a sweater tightly to her. "Brrr, it's getting cold. That warm day we had today was just a tease, wasn't it? Winter's not over."

"What's the forecast for the weekend, Mom?" Laena asked, standing up from the swing. "We were thinking of going for a boat ride so I could show Cree the bay."

"It's supposed to be nice, but this is New England. You know the saying—if you don't like the weather, wait a minute."

Cree laughed politely. "Hopefully the weather will cooperate. Thank you all for letting me join you for dinner." He turned to Laena. "And thank you for cooking such a delicious meal." His smile was genuine, and Laena could not help but smile in return.

"Anytime," she responded. "I guess I'll see you tomorrow?"

"Absolutely," Cree said. He shook Laena's parents' hands and gave her a tight hug that made her head spin.

"Please, Cree, let me drive you...." Ben started.

But Cree had already bounded off the porch and headed down the driveway. "It is such a short distance, Dr. Foster," he called. "I will be fine. Thanks again!" Laena watched his imposing figure fade in the darkness.

"What a nice boy," Michelle said. "So handsome!"

Laena, still reeling from the brief hug he had given her, grabbed the porch railing. She could feel the warmth of his chest lingering on hers, and smell his scent. She closed her eyes and wished that he were still there with her.

"Come inside, Laena. It's chilly," Michelle insisted. Laena shook herself out of her fog and nodded. Her father closed and locked the front door behind them, and she dreamily headed up the stairs to her room. "I guess I'll finish my homework and go to bed," Laena murmured.

"Sounds like a plan. Goodnight, sweetheart," her father called.

" 'Night," Laena said, trying to figure out how on earth she would concentrate on her homework. She went into her room, and, without turning the lights on, went to the window to look down the driveway where Cree had disappeared moments ago. She sighed, wishing he hadn't left, wishing she could sit and talk to him for hours, or even just sit next to him, in silence, feeling his warm, solid presence next to her. As she gazed out the window, she saw a shadow next to a big pine shift. She leaned closer. Just like when she was walking home! Was she imagining it, or was someone out there? The shadow moved again, separated from the tree, and disappeared into the darkness. Could it be Cree, watching the house? She shivered involuntarily, and hastily shut her blind against the dark night.

Was he standing there, thinking of her the way she was thinking of him? Or was it something more sinister? Laena had a brief sense of danger, and then shook it off. She flicked on her light, booted up her laptop, and tried to put Cree out of her mind as she settled in to do her homework.

Chapter 2

THE REST OF THE WEEK passed rapidly. Laena sat next to Cree in biology every day, and they sat together at lunch. But they had little opportunity to really talk, and Laena tried to keep her distance in public. The other girls were taken by Cree—even Tiffany—and they demanded a lot of his attention. Cree treated everyone pleasantly, but Laena thought she could detect a special connection whenever he looked at her. Maybe it was all in her head. Every time she saw him, or thought of him, her heart hammered wildly, her head buzzed, and her stomach jumped.

Each day after school, Cree walked with Laena and sometimes other kids to the end of the school access road, and then Cree turned to the right toward Evergreen Acres. He told Laena he had a lot of chores to do around the campground, and on top of that, his homework. He never asked to walk her home, or to see her outside of school.

Friday morning, Cree fidgeted at his desk in English when Laena came flying in, late as usual. Cree swiveled around to talk to her as she unpacked her books. He looked pale.

"The weather looks good for tomorrow morning," Cree whispered. "Can we go out in the boat?"

Laena's heart soared. "Sure," she whispered back. She had been certain that Cree had forgotten about their date to tour the bay. But Cree looked...off. Like something wasn't quite right.

"Great. What time? Should I come to your house?"

Before Laena could answer, the teacher cleared her throat and said, "Let's get started, class. We have a lot of ground to cover today."

Laena smiled at Cree and murmured, "We'll talk later. Maybe at lunch?"

Cree nodded and turned around to face the front of the classroom.

Laena walked into the cafeteria at lunch, looking forward to seeing Cree and discussing their plans for the boat ride. She looked around anxiously as she nibbled her sandwich, ignoring the talk and laughter around her. As the minutes ticked by, and Cree did not appear, Laena's heart sank. Finally, about halfway through lunch, Sophie said, "Hey, where's Cree?" Laena shrugged, pretending nonchalance, but she worried. Where had he gone? He just seemed to disappear after math class. She thought they had arranged to meet at lunch. *Maybe there was an emergency at Evergreen Acres,* she thought, *and the owner called Cree to help.* But the more she thought about it, the more unlikely that sounded. Lunch crawled by, with no sign of Cree. She gave up even the pretense of eating, and sat at the table while her friends, and life in general, swirled around her as if nothing were wrong.

By the time Laena walked into bio, she was a wreck. Cree had disappeared, and she felt a panic build inside of her. It was irrational, she knew, but she couldn't shake this feeling of impending disaster. As soon as class got underway, Laena's father looked up and, noticing the empty seat next to her, said, "Laena, where's your lab partner today?" She shrugged in reply, unable to speak.

"Well, drag your chair over with someone else, then," he said, unconcerned. "You need at least two pair of hands for this experiment."

Laena couldn't concentrate for the remainder of the day. When the final bell rang, she got her stuff from her locker and rushed out of the school building, hoping to see Cree outside the school. But he wasn't there.

Laena walked home slowly, eyes welling with tears. She was angry with herself for getting upset, and angry at him for doing this to her. She thought they had planned to talk at lunch, to decide where and when to meet to go boating on Saturday, but maybe he simply did not understand what she had said. She racked her brain for simple explanations. Could there have been an emergency, or had Cree taken ill? As her mind tossed around the myriad of possibilities, she began to worry. He had looked off when she saw him in English. Cree had no one on the Cape—no one in the world!—to look after him. Should she call the hospital, or the police? Laena had no idea how to get in touch with him. As far as she knew, he did not have a cell phone, and the cabins at Evergreen Acres didn't have landlines. She meandered up the driveway to her house, worried. When she looked up, she was shocked to see Cree pacing anxiously on her front porch. She raced toward him, and he ran down the stairs toward her. His black hair stood up in spikes, as if he had been running his hands through it in frustration.

"Kion vi faras?" Cree yelled, desperation in his voice, grabbing her by the shoulders.

"Wha.... ?" Laena did not understand. "What did you say?"

Cree shook his head, as if to clear it. "What are you doing? What took you so long to get home?" His voice and his manner were harsh. His blue eyes bored into hers.

"What language are you speaking?" Laena asked, angry that he stood here in front of her, perfectly healthy and uninjured. Why had he left school without telling her? How dare he yell at her! He was the one who had worried her half to death. What right did *he* have to be mad?

"It is nothing," Cree said, his voice hard. "I have been waiting for you! *Mi devas fari ion!*" he went on, his face a mask of anguish.

"Cree, calm down!" Laena said, her own anger dissipating. Something was terribly wrong. "You're not making any sense. I can't understand what you're saying! You're speaking gibberish."

"Not gibberish. My language." Cree looked down at her, his eyes flashing, his mouth a thin, hard line. "I...I need your help!"

"I'm sorry," Laena said, trying to stay calm. His emotions were all over the map, and it frightened Laena. "Whatever it is you're saying, I don't understand it. Please, speak English and I will try to help you. I can't help you if I don't know what you need."

Cree took a deep breath and tried to relax. His hands, which had been grasping her shoulders with an iron grip, relaxed. He spoke slowly, in English.

"I am sorry, Laena. Please help me. There is something I need to do, and I cannot do it without your help. I will explain everything later, I promise. But right now, I need you so badly. Please...please trust me." His voice caught with emotion, and Laena nodded.

"I trust you, Cree," she said softly. "Tell me what you need."

"The boat. The Boston...whaler? Is that what you call it? We need to go out into the bay, now. Today, not tomorrow."

"The whaler? You want to go out now? Why?"

"Please, there is no time for questions!" His voice rose. Then he took another breath, and Laena could see him willing his voice to be calm. "Please," he repeated, "can you take me out in the whaler?" His black hair blew in the wind, and his blue eyes practically crackled with intensity. Laena's heart clenched with emotion.

Laena nodded. "Of course...but where? Can you show me where you need to go?"

Cree relaxed for the first time during their tense exchange. "Yes, once we get on the water, I will show you. But can we hurry?"

Laena threw her backpack on the porch, and said over her shoulder, "I just need to get the keys. I'll be right back." She ducked into the house and pulled the boat keys off the peg in the foyer. She slammed the front door and headed back toward Cree.

"Ju pli rapide, des pli bone!" Cree called, and Laena shook her head in frustration. She had no idea what he was saying, but didn't want to remind him again to speak English.

"Follow me," she called, and took off down the sandy path to their dock. As they cleared the stand of pines, Laena saw that the tide was high, which was good, and the water relatively calm. But it was cooling off as the sun sank lower on the horizon, and they were both dressed inappropriately for a boat ride. She almost suggested going back to the house to get jackets, but when she saw the expression on Cree's face, she knew that this was no time to worry about personal comfort. Something was terribly wrong, and she had to help. Their thin tee shirts would just have to suffice. But Laena had a bad feeling.

Cree followed her at a run down the dock, their footsteps pounding on the worn wooden planks, the dock swaying under their weight. When she reached the boat she leaned down and unlocked the padlock.

"Get in," she said, unwrapping the line from the hitch. Cree stepped into the boat roughly, causing it to rock wildly. "Sit down!" she ordered. "And grab a life jacket." Cree looked at her uncertainly. "The orange thing, under the bench there. Put it on and strap it tight." She pointed to the life jackets on board, and Cree complied. Laena hopped in, put on her own life jacket, started the motor on the second try, and expertly maneuvered the boat away from the dock. As soon as they were a little ways out, she opened the throttle and the boat took off.

"Gi veturas tiel rapide!" Cree called over the noise of the motor. Laena noticed that his knuckles were white as they clutched the sides of the boat.

"Cree, I have no flippin' idea what you are saying!" Laena yelled. "But, you need to tell me where we are going, and you need to tell me in a language I understand!"

Cree nodded, and pointed to the northwest.

Laena steered the boat in the direction of his finger, and opened up the throttle more. She shoved aside her apprehension. Her parents would be furious if they knew Laena had taken the boat so far out into the bay, this late in the afternoon. She knew better. Laena could not believe Cree had talked her into this wild goose chase, but she wanted to help him. He needed her, and that was enough. They rode in silence, unable to speak over the roar of the motor. Her hair kept tangling in the wind, blinding her, and she had to push it out of her face and eyes. Whenever she glanced at him, she saw him cast his eyes around the water, searching. Every once in a while he would take one of his hands off the side of the boat and put it over his nose, trying to block out the smells from the gas engine. After about ten minutes, Cree waved his arm, trying to get her attention.

"Slow down!" Cree shouted.

Laena nodded and let up on the gas, and the boat slowed.

Cree looked around wildly, then said, "Can you turn it off? Make the noise and the smell stop?"

Laena turned the motor off, and the silence was startling. The Boston whaler bobbed gently in the chop. The silence was punctuated by the slapping of small waves against the side of the boat. Cree looked around, then closed his eyes. At first, Laena thought he might be seasick, but then she realized that he was concentrating. Abruptly, he opened his eyes, and pointed to the west. "There."

Laena looked in the direction Cree pointed, but could not see anything. "Where?" she said.

"Ili venu al ni," Cree said.

"Cree!" Laena cried. "Speak English!" Her frustration brought her to the verge of tears.

"Sorry," Cree said softly, smiling. "Let them come to us."

"Let *who* come to us?" Laena asked, a shiver running down her spine. She didn't like the thought of anyone approaching them out here. The boat rocked in the water, and Laena could see only the dark blue of the cold bay, with small whitecaps from the wind. She looked back toward land and saw that they were fairly far out. Vulnerable. She started to speak, and Cree stopped her.

"Shhh," Cree said. Then he reached into the pocket of his jeans and pulled out a pocketknife.

"Cree...." Laena swallowed nervously. "Cree, what...what are you doing?" Her eyes widened as he snapped the blade open and wiped it on the leg of his jeans. The metal glinted in the sun. Her heart started pounding.

"Shhh," Cree reiterated. "Trust me, Laena. Trust me." His eyes caught hers, and held her. He smiled.

The water not ten feet away from them roiled. A huge "V" shaped blow erupted from a whale's blowhole, soaking them both from head to toe with freezing ocean water, and Laena gasped, stiffening at the shock of it. Then, the most amazing thing Laena had ever seen rose from the depths of the dark blue water alongside the boat. A right whale, the bumpy white callosities on its head clearly visible as the huge mammal floated atop the water. Scars crisscrossed its giant head, some ancient, and some fresh. The whale had to be 50 feet long—it dwarfed the Boston whaler. One slap of its fluke and they could be dead, overturned in the freezing water, smashed by the huge mammal. Laena gasped and reached for the key to the motor.

"No!" Cree cried. "No, it will be okay. Do not turn it on...you may hurt them."

"Them?" she choked, and then she saw it. The huge right whale nudged a calf toward the boat. The calf was approximately the same size as the Boston whaler. The mother pushed the calf until it hovered directly alongside the boat, inches from Cree, pinned between its mother and the boat. Then the mother whale turned her giant head, blocking the calf's escape.

"*Rimarkinda*," Cree whispered, leaning over the boat to get a closer look at the whales.

"Cree, this is so illegal, so wrong, so...dangerous. We have to get out of here. Cree! Listen to me...." Laena's heart hammered with fear. She shifted in her seat and looked at the mother whale's huge head, right next to her, almost touching the side of the flimsy boat. Laena looked into the whale's liquid brown eye and saw...warmth? Intelligence? Something. Whatever it was, it wasn't scary. Her heart rate calmed. She saw kindness, and knowledge. For a moment, she lost herself in the eye of the huge mammal. She felt something that she had never felt before—she couldn't even put words to her emotions. Laena reeled, trying to comprehend. This huge animal, ancient, probably old enough to have been hunted in this very bay by men in whaling boats, stared at Laena. She swam right next to their boat, knowing full well that the boat contained humans, the enemy. And, she had the most precious thing in her life with her, her calf. But she had no fear, and she wasn't angry. She exuded gentleness, and something more. Forgiveness?

"Look," Cree whispered. He pointed to the calf. Laena tore her eyes away from the mother's face, and saw a thick rope, once bright yellow, but now slimy and dirty, wrapped several times around the mouth of the calf. The rope dug so deeply into the flesh, blubber oozed around either side of the line.

"No...." she cried. "Cree, the fishing line...the poor thing! It can't nurse...it will starve...Cree...do something!" Laena looked back at the mother whale, and saw her watching Laena closely. The whale appeared distressed. She raised one of her flippers, and gently reached out toward Laena. Without thinking, Laena reached out her hand to the whale. The flipper touched Laena's hand, and a shiver went through her. The whale's eye shifted to the calf, and then back to Laena again.

"Oh my God, she's...she's asking for help!" Laena gasped, stunned. Freezing water from the whale's blow dripped from the seat of the boat onto the bottom. Laena glanced down. Nearly an inch of water covered the bottom of the boat, soaking her sneaker-clad feet. She knew they had to get out of the cold, and back to land as soon as possible. But they couldn't leave the whale like this....

Cree leaned over the calf with his knife. How had he known to bring the knife? He had taken that knife out before either of them had seen the whales or the entangled calf. He carefully slid the knife under the rope, and Laena grimaced. The calf wiggled in pain or fear, and the mother pushed the calf tighter against the boat to still it. Cree realigned the knife, and carefully sawed through the line until it split in two. But the rope remained so embedded in the calf's flesh, it did not come free. Laena groaned in disgust and looked away. Whales were constantly getting entangled in fishing line in Cape Cod Bay. More often than not, they either starved to death, or the wounds became infected and killed them. The non-profit animal welfare organizations in the area had permits to try and disentangle the whales, but the odds were against them. Laena couldn't watch as Cree carefully worked the rope free, struggling against the bobbing boat and the wriggling calf. Instead, she looked into the mother's eye, trying to send a feeling of encouragement. She murmured reassurances to the whale, utter nonsense, just soothing sounds. The mother whale looked at Laena, then back to the calf. Laena had looked into certain people's eyes and witnessed far less warmth than what she saw in this right whale.

Then Laena heard a sound that made her blood run cold. The sound of an airplane above them.

"Crap," she whispered and looked up at the small Cessna buzzing overhead. "Cree, we're in trouble. Hurry!" she hissed.

"I am going as fast as I dare," he responded calmly. Laena risked a glance over at Cree, and saw that the rope was almost completely unwound from the calf. With a grunt, Cree got the last of the line off the calf and out of the raw flesh.

"There," he said. "You are free, little girl," and he pulled the rest of the line out of the water and placed it in the bottom of the boat.

The calf immediately searched out its mother's nipple, and greedily started nursing. The mother extended its flipper toward Cree, and he reached out and stroked it gently. Then she gave a last glance at Laena, mouth upturned as if smiling, and serenely floated away from the small Boston whaler, the calf still feeding voraciously. Laena felt a warm wetness on her cheeks. She was crying. She looked over at Cree, and saw tears coursing down his face as well.

"We need to leave," Cree said, ripping his eyes away from the two whales.

"What?" Laena said, not understanding. She couldn't stop looking at these magnificent creatures. She had completely blocked out the plane from her consciousness.

Cree motioned up toward the plane circling them.

"Oh, crap," Laena said again, and started the motor on the whaler. She slowly steered the boat away from the whales, shivering violently, both of them soaked to the bone.

Laena headed the boat back to shore as fast as she could, but her shivering had reached an uncontrollable stage from the cold wind and her wet clothes. Her wet hair clung to her face and neck in strands that felt like frozen seaweed. Was she hypothermic? She saw that Cree was shivering, too, and cast her eyes around the bottom of the small boat for something to dry them off. There—a flash of bright red. The first aid kit! Laena yelled at Cree to get the emergency blanket from the kit.

He pulled out the square of silver Mylar, hands shaking, Cree crouched next to Laena as she steered the boat. He clutched the blanket around both of them, leaning into her, sharing body heat. The boat roared toward shore. Laena glanced up and saw the plane, still circling the two whales. She hoped it stayed there, and didn't follow the boat.

Cree saw her watching the Cessna. "Who are they?" he yelled, teeth chattering.

"North Atlantic Right Whale Association researchers. NARWA," Laena shouted back. "They saw us."

Cree nodded, grimacing. Laena kept the boat pointed toward home, numb in both body and soul.

"Are we in trouble?" he asked.

Laena nodded. "Big trouble," she answered. Then she looked into his eyes, which were filled with concern at their predicament. "But I would do it all over again," she said, and Cree rewarded her with the biggest smile she had ever seen. Warmth flooded through her frozen body, and she returned his smile.

Laena had great difficulty tying the boat back up to the dock because her hands were frozen. Cree helped, and then they both stumbled down the dock in silence, hurrying as fast as they could toward her house. When they reached the porch after what seemed like an eternity, Laena pushed open the door and tugged Cree into the foyer.

"We need to warm up," she said, teeth still chattering and body shivering violently. "We need to take hot showers and put on dry clothes." She kicked off her squelching shoes, and peeled off her sopping wet socks. Cree did the same. Laena motioned for him to follow her upstairs, and led him into her parents' bathroom. She handed Cree a fresh towel from the linen closet, and said, "Hand me your wet clothes—I'll wait here, outside the bathroom door. I'll put them in the dryer and take a shower in my bathroom." Cree, too cold to talk, nodded mutely and gave her a grim smile.

He stepped into the bathroom and shut the door behind him. Within 30 seconds, the door cracked open, and Cree passed his sopping wet jeans, tee shirt, and underwear through.

Laena gathered them up and padded to the laundry room. She left a trail of saltwater droplets on the floor. His clothes were dripping wet, and when dry they would be crusty with salt, but she did not have time to wash them. Her father's clothes would never fit Cree—Cree was much bigger—and she had to get him into something dry as soon as possible. She would just have to dry his clothes, and he would have to deal with the dirt and the salt later.

After starting the dryer, she ran into her own bathroom and turned the hot water on full blast in the shower. She stripped, and shaking with cold, climbed in. Even standing under the steaming spray, she could not seem to get warm. Her body still shook, and her mind spun out of control. Laena could not comprehend what had happened out on the bay today. The whole afternoon freaked her out, and Cree had a lot of explaining to do. First, he spoke some strange language that she couldn't even place. Her schoolgirl Spanish wasn't very good, but she did not recognize any of the words he spewed all afternoon. Second, she wanted to know how in hell he knew the whales were out there, and in trouble. And how did he find them? Or how did they find him? Third, where had he disappeared to in the middle of school? Laena turned these questions over and over in her head while standing under the painfully hot shower until she started thawing out. She turned the shower off, grabbed a towel and scrubbed her body until it was raw. Then she wrapped the towel in a turban around her long tresses, and slipped on a clean pair of panties, bra, sweatpants, and a sweatshirt. She left the bathroom and went out in search of Cree.

As she started down the hall toward her parents' bedroom, Cree appeared in the hallway at the top of the stairs, with nothing but a towel around his waist. His chest and arms were bare, and looked as hard as marble, but the color of coffee and cream. His body was amazing. He smiled at her, completely unabashed at his state of undress, and walked toward her with his arms outstretched. Cree folded her into his arms. Her towel slipped off her hair, piling at her feet. Cree murmured into the top of her head, "Thank you, Laena, for trusting me. And for helping me. We saved that baby whale together." He embraced her tightly.

Laena couldn't answer. His body felt rock solid, and burning hot. She couldn't catch her breath, yet she could smell the fresh, sweet scent of his skin. She heard his heart beating slowly, reminiscent of the pounding surf. Her heart pulsed in her throat, and her knees were weak.

"That is a very important little girl," he said thoughtfully. For a moment, Laena had no idea what he was talking about. Cree continued in a soft voice. "She will grow up to be a huge contributor to their population. She will have many babies. If she had died...well, it would not have been good."

Laena finally understood that Cree was talking about the calf. How did he know it was a female, and how did he know how many babies she would have? Laena opened her mouth to speak, but at that moment, the front door flew open, and Laena's mother burst in, Ben following at her heels. Laena tried to push away from Cree, but he held her too tightly. Laena groaned softly, knowing how the situation looked, and Laena's parents glared up the stairs at the two teens in stunned silence.

"Laena!" Michelle cried, at the same time Ben went pounding up the stairs, grabbing Cree's arm.

"Get away from her," Ben growled through clenched teeth. "Now, Cree, I mean it."

Cree raised his hands in submission, and backed away from Laena. "I can explain, Dr. Foster. Sir. Nothing happened, really. We...."

"Enough," Laena's father barked. "Where are your clothes?"

"Dad!" Laena said, sobbing. "Dad, it's not what you think. We were out on the boat, and we got so wet and chilled and...."

"I said enough!" Ben shouted, seething. "Laena, get downstairs now. Cree, get your damn clothes on and meet us in the kitchen."

Laena ran down the stairs, past her mother, who stared dumbfounded, and into the kitchen. She threw her head into her arms at the kitchen table, choking back tears of anger and embarrassment.

"Ben!" Michelle cried, as Ben stormed into the kitchen toward his inconsolable daughter. Michelle followed, grabbing his arm. "Ben, wait. They *were* in the boat. That's why I'm home early. NARWA called—they recognized our Boston whaler out in the Bay today. The kids were with right whales, Ben. You should be mad, but not for the reason you think."

Ben looked from his wife to Laena. At that moment, Cree walked in, his still wet clothes on. *He must have found the laundry room and taken his clothes from the dryer*, Laena thought. *He'll catch his death of cold. They're sopping.*

"Please, you must be mad at me, not at Laena," Cree said earnestly. "Everything is my fault."

Ben and Michelle looked at Cree, took in his wet clothes, and their distraught daughter. Ben sighed. "Sit," he said. "And explain. And it better be good."

All four of them sat at the kitchen table, Cree perching on the edge of the wooden chair in his soggy jeans. He cleared his throat. "I asked Laena to take me out in the boat," he began. "It was my idea. We...we were just sightseeing, and then we saw the whales. Laena said we must turn off the motor and wait for them to leave, because they could dive and surface too close to the propellers." Cree glanced at Laena, looking to judge her reaction to his outright lies. She nodded imperceptibly, urging him to go on. "But they came closer. And we saw the calf, she had a fishing line, a lobster line maybe, around her mouth. She looked emaciated. She could not nurse. She swam right up against the boat, Dr. Foster, and I had a knife. Laena told me not to, but I could not let her die. It was my fault. I know it was wrong, sir, but I could not let the creature die." His voice caught, and Cree looked beseechingly at Ben and Michelle. His voice sank to a whisper. "Please do not blame Laena. When we got back to your house, sir, we were so wet from the sea, we were chilled. The mother whale, she...." Cree threw up his arms in the air, simulating the blow. He did not know the word, and he gave up, describing it as best he could. "Water came out of her head, and we got soaked. Laena let me take a shower and she put my clothes in the machine to dry them." He gestured to his wet jeans. "I did not touch your daughter, sir, not inappropriately. I would never hurt her."

Ben looked at Laena, who nodded, tears streaming down her face. "Please, Dad. He is telling the truth." At least, the last part was the truth, she thought.

Michelle let out an audible sigh. "Are you two okay? Nobody is hurt?"

They shook their heads in unison. Michelle continued. "Cree, did you get the fishing line off the calf?"

Cree nodded. "Yes, ma'am. It is still in the bottom of your boat. I did not want to leave it in the water for another animal to get caught."

"Can you go get the rope for me?" Michelle asked. Cree nodded and left the kitchen. The front door opened and clicked shut. Laena heard Cree's footsteps pounding on the porch boards as he ran down to the dock.

Michelle turned to Laena. "Was the calf injured?"

Laena dried her tears with the sleeve of her sweatshirt. "The wounds were awful, Mom. The rope cut so deeply into her skin. But as soon as Cree got the line off, she started nursing, and I think...I hope she'll be okay."

There was silence as they waited for Cree to return. Ben rubbed his forehead, his eyes closed. Michelle searched Laena's face. Laena looked back steadily, hoping to reassure her mother that they spoke the truth. The last thing she wanted was to lose her mother's trust.

The front door opened and slammed shut. Cree strode into the kitchen, the scummy fishing line coiled in his hands. He offered it to Michelle, who took it and laid it on the kitchen table. He returned to his seat silently.

Michelle examined the rope carefully, then looked up. "It's the floating line to a lobster trap."

"Yes, Ma'am," Cree said. "I knew it was some kind of fishing line."

Ben and Michelle regarded the teenagers. "Cree, how could you have just happened upon a right whale and her calf in the middle of the Bay just a few short days after asking Laena to show you one?" Michelle began.

Laena and Cree shook their heads. They had no answer. At least not a believable one.

Michelle sighed. "I guess I have no choice but to accept what you're telling me. However, I'm still angry. You violated at least two federal laws, and NARWA saw you with the whales. They had been tracking that calf. I'm not sure if I can keep you out of trouble."

"What will happen, Mom?" Laena asked meekly. "We did help them, after all, so there was no harm done...."

"Unfortunately, that's beside the point," Michelle said, sighing. "Laena, I know you. I'm confident that you would never do anything to jeopardize, let alone hurt, an animal." She reached across the table and squeezed Laena's hand. "But *you* know that what you did is wrong, don't you?"

Laena nodded, her face burning with shame.

"Let me make some phone calls." She stood up, picked up the cordless phone, and walked out of the kitchen with it. They heard her dial and then a murmured conversation began.

Laena and Cree looked at each other, and then at Ben. "Sir, please. I did not touch your daughter," Cree said, his voice sincere. His eyes did not waver from Ben's.

Ben nodded, and jerked his chin toward Cree's wet clothes and the thick fishing line. "I can see you're telling the truth." He sighed heavily. "Cree, someday, when you're a parent, you'll understand. Walking into the house and seeing you half naked, with my daughter in your arms...." He trailed off, and Laena blushed.

"I understand," Cree said. "I am so sorry."

"No, no, I'm the one who should be sorry, jumping to conclusions...." He sighed again. "Cree, I think maybe I should drive you home so you can get some dry clothes on. Will you let me do that?"

Cree smiled wanly. "As long as you are not planning on yelling at me some more on the way, sir."

Ben smiled back weakly. "No, no more yelling. C'mon, let's go." Ben stood up and Cree followed his lead. But then Ben paused and looked down at Laena. "Laena, how about having Cree over for dinner tomorrow night? I'll cook...my treat." All the fight and anger had disappeared from his voice, and Laena knew he wanted to make up for not trusting her.

Laena smiled and nodded. "That would be great, Dad." Her voice sounded hoarse, and she felt completely drained. She pulled absently on the string of her sweatpants.

Ben looked at Cree with raised eyebrows. "Cree? Sound okay?"

"That would be wonderful, sir. Thank you."

Ben smiled, relieved Cree forgave him. Michelle walked back into the kitchen and clicked the phone off. "Well, I talked to NARWA, and they're going to pretend they didn't see you out there. But you kids better make sure...."

She didn't have to finish her sentence. "It'll never happen again, Mom, I swear," Laena said, standing up and hugging her mother.

"Thank you, Dr. Foster," Cree said.

Michelle patted Laena on the back, then held her at arms' length. "You, young lady, need to go upstairs immediately and get under the covers. I'll bring you some warm herbal tea and something to eat." She turned and looked at Cree. "And, Cree, I know you don't have anyone to take care of you tonight. Will your cabin be warm enough?"

Cree nodded. "There is a wood stove, so I will start a fire. And I can make myself some tea as well."

Michelle assessed him. "Maybe you should stay here so I can keep an eye on you," she murmured, more to herself than to anyone else.

Cree shook his head and held up a hand, palm outward, in protest. "I will be fine. You have done enough for one day. All I really need is a ride home, because walking in these wet clothes will be quite uncomfortable."

"Let's go, then," Ben said, starting for the door.

"Ben, wait," Michelle said, still unsure of what to do. "I really don't feel comfortable leaving him in that cabin all alone. They were practically hypothermic...he's just a child."

"I am fine," Cree reassured her. "Really, I just need dry clothes."

"He's fine, Michelle," Ben said, somewhat sharply. Laena blushed, knowing exactly what thoughts raced through her father's head. Twice now he had seen Cree touch her—the first night he was over for dinner, when Cree caressed her cheek, and then tonight, when he found them in an embrace. With Cree wearing only a towel, no less. And yet Michelle wanted Cree to spend the night. Laena shivered at the thought of Cree sleeping under the same roof, just down the hall from her. She hoped her mother would win this fight.

"I'll help him start the fire, and make sure he's comfortable. And he can always call if there's an emergency. Right, Cree? You have our number?"

Cree nodded mutely. Laena had never given him her number, but she dared not speak out. Her eyes caught Cree's, and he smiled tenderly. She smiled back, and warmth spread through her body. She had to fight the urge to run into his arms.

Michelle finally relented, and Ben drove Cree home. As soon as the front door shut behind them, Laena, drained and exhausted, slumped in her chair. Michelle helped her up the stairs and into bed, and then went downstairs to heat up some soup and tea. But by the time Michelle came back upstairs with a tray, Laena was sleeping soundly. Michelle sighed, checked Laena's temperature with her hand, and tucked the covers more tightly around her. She picked up the tray with the food, closed the door quietly, and returned to the kitchen to wait for Ben.

Laena slept deeply, but had vivid dreams of swimming alongside a huge whale in Cape Cod Bay. In her dream, the water was warm and buoyant, and the whale spoke to her in Cree's voice, saying over and over, "You have to help me, Laena. Please, help me. We have to stop them." Then the whale and Laena became entangled in what seemed like millions of slimy, multi-colored fishing lines, and were pulled toward the bottom of the ocean, where it was dark and cold.

Laena tried to scream, fighting to breathe, and then she felt warm, human arms around her. Cree's voice whispered soothingly in her ear. "Shhh, it's okay. Everything is okay." Laena snuggled into his warmth, and the horror of the dreams disappeared. She drifted off into a dreamless slumber.

Chapter 3

LAENA SLEPT LATE the next day. When she finally woke, the sun streaming in through her window, she jolted into a sitting position. The previous day came back to her in a flood of memories. Her stomach rumbled, and she remembered that she hadn't eaten since yesterday at lunch, when she had only had a few small bites of her sandwich.

Laena got out of bed, pulled on a pair of jeans, a tee shirt, and a warm sweatshirt, and ran downstairs. Both her parents were in the kitchen, nursing their coffee. Ben flipped pancakes at the stove. He heard Laena come in, turned, and gave her a big smile.

"I bet you're hungry," he said, filling up a plate with three golden, steaming pancakes, and putting them on the kitchen table in front of her. "Perfect timing."

"Starving," Laena agreed, pouring herself a cup of coffee from the carafe and sitting down. She dribbled thick, amber maple syrup on the pancakes and dug in. They were delicious. Michelle got up to get her some orange juice.

"How are you feeling, honey?" Michelle asked as she placed the glass of juice in front of Laena. "Did you sleep okay?"

"Mmmm," Laena said, nodding as she swallowed. "I slept like the dead."

"That's good," Michelle replied. "I'm sure you needed it after your...adventure yesterday." Her voice was a little sarcastic, and Laena flushed.

"Mom...." she began.

"No, no, it's okay," Michelle interrupted. "We don't have to talk about it any more. I trust, however, that you and Cree will not engage in such behavior in the future."

Laena sighed. Whenever her mother got angry, she lectured.

"No, Mom, we will not engage in such behavior in the future." Her voice mimicked her mother's.

"Don't get sarcastic with me, young lady. What you did was dangerous and irresponsible. I understand *why* you did it. But that doesn't excuse it."

Laena sighed and softened her tone. "I know, Mom. But you have to remember, we *did* save the whale. Isn't that the most important thing?" Laena didn't wait for a response. "Anyway, I promise, it won't happen again. Honest."

Michelle smiled, and a little of the tension left her shoulders. "Of course you're right, honey. The whales are important. But *you* have to remember that you're more important than the whales. Your safety and well-being. I can't stand the thought of you being in any danger. Physically, or with the law! So, while you and Cree did the right thing with respect to the animals, my primary concern is you. Got it?"

Laena nodded. "Got it, Mom."

Michelle looked at her skeptically.

"Really," Laena insisted. "I got it." She cleaned her plate and sat back, content. "Those were delicious, Dad. Just what I needed."

"Good," Ben said. "Remember, I invited Cree over for dinner tonight."

Laena nodded. "I remember," she said. How could she forget? She looked out the window at the bright sunshine. "What's it like outside?"

"Cold," her father responded. "It looks warm with all that sun, but the wind is pretty cold. Why? You have plans today?"

Laena shrugged and got up to bring her plate and glass to the sink. "I thought I'd hang out with Sophie today," she said, glad her parents could not see her face. She had no intention of seeing Sophie…Cree owed her some answers, and she was going to get them. She hated lying to her parents, but she didn't think that after yesterday, her parents would want to hear that she planned to see Cree in his cabin.

"That's fine," Michelle said absent-mindedly. "Just be home by late afternoon please, to help with chores before Cree comes over."

"I will," Laena agreed readily. "I'm just going to brush my teeth, and I'll be off." She turned from the sink and smiled. "Thanks again for breakfast, Dad."

Her parents were both absorbed in the newspaper. "No problem, kiddo," Ben replied. "Have a good day."

Laena bounded up the stairs. She brushed her teeth, tried to tame the mass of curls into some semblance of respectability, and shrugged into an extra sweatshirt. She looked at herself in her full-length mirror and sighed. She looked more like she was 12 years old than 17. Whatever. She wasn't in a beauty contest. She just wanted an explanation from Cree.

Laena stuck her head in the kitchen. Michelle was doing the dishes, and Ben was still at the table, reading the paper.

"I'm off!" Laena said, and without waiting for a response, was out the front door. She didn't feel like walking the mile or so to Cree's cabin, so she grabbed her mountain bike from the garage. She swung her leg over the seat and started pedaling down the driveway. Laena shivered in the chilly air, but riding her bike would warm her up. Her derailleur clicked and whirred as she shifted gears on a bicycle that had been sitting unused in a shed all winter long.

As she made her way to the campground, she puzzled over the events of yesterday. She didn't even know where to begin with him. But she needed to know who Cree really was, where he was from, and what he was up to. That orphan-from-Alaska story couldn't be the real deal.

Before she had figured out how to approach Cree with her questions, Laena was pedaling into the lot of Evergreen Acres. She slowed down to glance at the three cabins on the site. Only one of them looked lived in, the one on the far left. She scanned the campground. She saw someone else rounding the corner of one of the other cabins. A flash of long black hair and shapely legs in tight jeans. So there were other people living here. Laena shivered.

There were freshly washed clothes hanging from a line outside of the cabin on the left, snapping in the strong breeze, and the front door stood wide open. Laena leaned the bike against the porch and climbed the stairs to the front door.

"Cree?" she called hesitantly as she peeked into the door of the cabin. No response.

Then she saw him. Bare-chested, wearing navy blue sweatpants, Cree lay on the floor, doing push-ups. His muscles glistened with sweat, and he grunted with exertion each time he pushed his body weight off the ground. Laena felt weak in the knees as she watched him. She cleared her throat, heart thudding.

Cree turned his head and looked at the doorway where Laena stood. He nodded imperceptibly, a brief smile flashing, but kept doing his push-ups. Laena tore her eyes away from him and looked around the tiny cabin. The walls were a rough, dark knotty pine, and the floor consisted of a similar wide-planked wood, worn and pockmarked. The ancient black woodstove still radiated warmth from last night's fire. A narrow twin bed, neatly made up under a wool blanket with a Native American design, occupied a corner. The kitchen area consisted of a tiny refrigerator, and a two-burner gas stove. The counter was scarred Formica. A small wooden table with two chairs took up most of the space, and Cree's schoolbooks were neatly stacked on the table. Everything was tidy and clean, but Laena did not see any personal touches. Laena found it depressing.

Cree stood up, breathing heavily, but smiling in pleasure to see her. "Sorry, Laena. I was almost done with my set and I did not want to stop." He grabbed a towel from a hook off the back of the door and wiped the sweat off his face and chest. His body glowed.

Laena looked away, embarrassed. His body was beautiful, and she knew she was blushing. Cree stepped closer to her and peered down into her face, trying to bring her attention back to him. "Laena?"

She looked into his face, feeling the heat suffuse her cheeks. He smiled more broadly. "I am glad you are here. I wanted to talk to you. But I am sweaty...let me take a shower and I will be right back, okay?" Laena nodded, unable to utter a word. Cree smiled again, grabbed a bottle off a shelf and headed out the door of the cabin. She turned and watched him head to the communal men's room for the campground, about 150 feet from his cabin.

While he showered, Laena prowled around the tiny cabin, not wanting to disturb anything. Finally, she sat gingerly on the edge of his bed, feeling the hard, thin, mattress and wondering how he fit his large frame in this tiny bed. She closed her eyes and breathed in his scent. She struggled with her emotions. What was she doing here? She wanted answers from him, but couldn't they wait until tonight? She opened her eyes and looked around the cabin some more. Could she live in this small space? Was *he* happy here? She noticed that he kept everything immaculate—unusual for a teenage boy. A broom and a dustpan leaned in the corner, and his breakfast dishes dried in a wooden rack next to the sink. Everything in perfect order. She stared at the dying embers in the stove, and let her mind wander. She heard a sound from the back of Cree's cabin, by the window, like two rocks clinking against one another. An animal? She turned towards the noise.

"I am back," his deep voice announced from the door, and Laena jumped. She had not heard him come back in. She stood up immediately, self-conscious that he had caught her on his bed. He reassured her as if he could read her mind. "Sit, please. You can sit on my bed." Cree hung the towel back up on the hook, and put his bottle of shampoo back on the rustic wooden shelf. Still shirtless, he now wore a pair of faded jeans. His black hair was toweled dry, sticking up at odd angles. His eyes were bright and penetrating, and his dimples showed. Cree walked over to the bed and sat next to Laena, so close their thighs touched. He smelled like peppermint, and Laena breathed it in greedily. Cree smiled gently.

"How are you, Laena? Better?" He reached out and cupped her face with his large, warm hand. Laena nodded, not trusting her voice. Cree pulled her gently into his arms and gave her a hug.

"I am glad you are here," he whispered softly into her ear. He stood up, went to the door of the cabin, and shut it firmly. He came back toward the bed, towering over her.

Laena stood up shakily. "I...I just came to talk. To get some answers." She glanced at the door to the cabin, dodging his gaze. She was shut inside the cabin with him, alone. She shivered. Cree frowned slightly.

"Are you afraid of me?" he asked anxiously. "Do you want me to open the door? I thought it would be warmer if I shut out that cold wind...." He trailed off, watching Laena's cheeks burn with shame. "I will not do anything you do not want me to," he said gravely. He sat down on the small bed, grabbed Laena's hand, and pulled her down next to him. "You are my friend. What I said to your father last night is true. I would never hurt you."

"It's what *I* want that I'm afraid of," Laena blurted, and then looked away, mortified. Cree burst out laughing, and Laena glanced at him, shocked at his reaction.

"What?" she demanded. Her greenish eyes flashed. "Are you laughing at me?" Cree roared even harder, and then shook his head in disbelief.

"Don't mock me, Cree. I am *so* not in the mood to be mocked this morning." Her voice shook with self-consciousness.

"Oh, Laena. I am not mocking you. I am laughing at how blunt you are. Why would you ever be afraid of what you want?" He put his arm around her shoulders and pulled her head to his bare chest. Laena closed her eyes and groaned audibly.

"Do I make you uncomfortable? Do I scare you?" Cree asked.

Laena shook her head. "No," she whispered. "You don't scare me." In fact, she thought, she felt protected, safe in his arms.

"Then what is it?" Cree asked, lowering his voice to match hers.

She shook her head again. "I honestly don't know," she replied. It was easier to talk to him without looking into his piercing eyes. Even though his arm around her shoulders made her heart pound and her stomach jump, she could at least speak her mind. "You make me feel like I've never felt before. Weird." She so badly wanted to tell him how she truly felt, that she wanted him, wanted him fully. That she wanted to touch him and lay in bed with him and kiss him, but she couldn't make her mouth form the words.

"Weird," Cree echoed. "Well, I do not want to make you feel weird." They sat in silence for a few moments. "Listen, Laena, I have never met anyone like you. I know we only met a week ago, but you are smart, and beautiful, and so...different from all the other girls I have ever met. I do not want to make you uncomfortable, but I am drawn to you. I cannot help it. If you want me to back off, I will, but I thought we could get to know each other. Maybe we can be friends?"

He turned to look at her, and Laena's heart sank. Friends? Is that all he wanted?

"Of course we can be friends," she answered. She looked away, blinking back tears that appeared in her eyes without warning. What the *hell*? Why was she upset? A minute ago, she felt terrified because he had shut the cabin door and had sex on his mind, and now she was crying because he only wanted to be friends? She did not understand her raging emotions.

Cree started gently rubbing her arm. "Look at me," he said. Laena shook her head, keeping her face turned away from him.

"Laena, look at me. Please."

Laena took a deep breath, and turned to him. A single tear slipped out and coursed down her cheek. "What have I done to you?" Cree said, pain in his voice, lifting his free hand to wipe the tear away. Her cheek tingled where he touched her. "Why do I keep doing things wrong? I do not understand." He paused, then took her face in his hands. "What have I done to hurt you?"

"I don't know!" Laena cried, her voice catching. "I feel so weird around you...I can't explain...listen, Cree, boys don't like me. I'm different. I don't mean to sound conceited, but I'm smart, and teenagers here in North Bayside don't think smart is cool." She took a deep breath, searching for the right words. "Boys don't pay attention to me. I'm not pretty, I'm small, and I just don't fit in. Then you come here, and you're nice to me, and you're smart too, but you're so...gorgeous...." Laena paused, discomfited that she was spewing out everything that was weighing on her mind. She had come this far, and she may as well go for broke. "You'll figure out that I'm not popular, and you'll prefer one of the other girls, and there's no point, because even if we're just friends, it's not cool to hang out with me...."

Cree burst out laughing.

"Don't laugh at me!" Laena said, trying to push him away in shame. "I don't even know you, and here I am spilling my guts and you...you laugh at me!"

"I am laughing because you are so cute," Cree said. "And not as smart as you think you are." Laena opened her mouth to protest. Before she could utter a word, Cree said, "You are not very smart when it comes to assessing yourself." He paused. "You *are* pretty. Actually, you are beautiful. Yes, you are small. I think you are fascinating." He stroked her curls. "Do you really believe I care what other people think? Do you think I would be happy with a girl like...like Tiffany?"

Laena fought a smile, trying to picture Cree and Tiffany together.

"When I first saw you, standing in the doorway of English class, I felt something, Laena." He paused, and then said gently, "You have never had a boyfriend before, have you?"

Laena shook her head and looked down. He lifted her head and forced her eyes back to his. "Well, I have had girlfriends before, but I have never felt like this. Like I belong with someone. Like we were meant to be together."

Laena was in a total free fall, in completely unfamiliar territory. Cree leaned over and kissed her gently on the cheek. "Do not be afraid of me. We will take it slow, okay? We will be friends, get to know each other. And when you are ready, then we can take it further. If you want to, that is."

Take it further? Laena couldn't breathe. She buried her head in his chest, and could hear his heart beating, steady and strong, unlike her own, which felt like a frantic bird. Cree hugged her tightly.

Laena forced herself to take a deep breath. "I don't know what I'm feeling, Cree. I am so confused."

"That is okay," he replied. "It is okay to be confused." He sighed. "We will just take everything as it comes, day to day.

Okay?" Laena nodded, burrowing deeper into his warm chest. He stroked her hair softly. When she looked up, he gently traced the faint scar on her cheek.

"You never told me about this. What happened to you?"

Laena pushed his hand away, embarrassed of her flaw. "An accident. Years ago."

"What kind of accident?" he asked tenderly. His hand went back to her face.

Laena shook her head. "It was stupid. I was running on the beach. I fell, and someone had broken a beer bottle. I landed on the sharp glass."

Cree looked concerned. "How old were you? Did they stitch you?"

"I was two years old," Laena said. "I had 13 stitches, and then surgery afterwards, but the scar...it's with me forever, I guess." Cree rubbed his thumb gently across the scar.

"Do you remember it?"

Laena shook her head. "Not much. I remember the doctor at Cape Cod Hospital giving me a Popsicle to make me stop crying. A grape Popsicle. That's about it."

Cree smiled softly. "I think it makes you even more beautiful. You should not resent it. It is a part of you, like your curly hair."

She flinched. She *did* resent her scar. With perfection all around her—the other girls at school, actresses in movies and models in magazines—she had always felt imperfect. How could Cree have picked up on how she felt, when she had not even consciously known it herself?

"But, you did not come here to talk about how beautiful you are, did you? You wish to speak of something else?"

Laena had almost forgotten why she had come to see him. "I came for answers," she said hoarsely. "I don't understand what happened yesterday."

Cree nodded, resigned, as if he knew her questions were inevitable. "What questions do you have?"

She looked up into his eyes, searching. Then she stood up and walked away from the bed, and from Cree. She spoke with her back to him.

"What happened yesterday, Cree? What language were you speaking? How did you know where the whales were, and that they were in trouble? Who are you, really?"

Cree looked away from her and didn't answer. Finally, Laena turned and said, "Cree? You told me if I helped you, you would tell me what was going on. I helped you, and now I want to know what the hell happened yesterday." She swept her curls up and tied her hair in a loose knot. A nervous habit.

Cree looked down at the floor. "You said you would do it all over again," he said softly, almost sadly. "What we did together yesterday. Saving the whale."

"And I would," Laena said. "But that doesn't mean I don't want to know what's going on."

Cree grunted, rubbed his hands over his face, and finally looked at her. Unshaved stubble covered his cheeks. "Laena, I do not want to tell you. I *cannot* tell you." His eyes were sad.

"So you lied to me?" she said, stepping closer to him. "You lied? You put our lives in danger, got me in trouble with my parents? You asked me to trust you, and I did. And I trusted you when you said you would explain. But you *lied* to me?"

Cree shook his head. "No, I did not lie. I will explain...just...just not now."

"When, then? When will you explain? I don't know what to think Cree! God!" Laena pulled at her hair in frustration and whirled around. Her hair tumbled back down over her shoulders. He stood up and walked over to her.

"Laena...." He reached for her.

"No, Cree. You will not sweet talk your way out of this." She pushed his arms away in anger. "Don't touch me. I can't...I can't think when you touch me. And you...you smell like peppermint. It's...distracting."

His hands dropped to his sides. "My soap," he said, smiling. Laena looked at him questioningly. Cree pointed to the bottle of brown liquid on the shelf. "Peppermint Castile soap."

Laena exhaled noisily. "I don't want to talk about your soap! I want to know what happened yesterday! What were we involved in?"

"Listen to me," Cree said, his voice taking on a harder edge. "I cannot tell you what you want to know, not yet. But I will."

She turned to face him again. "I don't believe you," Laena said. He came toward her, but she put her palms flat against his chest to halt him. "How can I trust you if you won't trust me?" She choked back tears. She could tell she had hurt him. Cree's face was wounded.

"Laena, it is dangerous. I do not want to put you in danger."

"Don't give me that! You put me in danger yesterday."

He collapsed to the bed, head in hands. "I am so sorry...you are right," he said, his voice muffled. "I did put you in danger yesterday, and I should not have. I apologize."

"Not good enough, Cree," Laena said, regaining her composure and approaching the bed. "You'll have to do better than that. I want answers."

He rubbed his face and looked up at her in defeat. "Okay, yes. You deserve the truth." He sighed. "What do you want to know?"

Laena swallowed, nervous. Maybe she didn't want to know. But she *had* to. It was just too weird. She started with an easy question. Or what she thought was an easy one.

"What language were you speaking?" She couldn't look at him, and instead fiddled with the zipper on her sweatshirt. "It sounded like...pidgin Spanish."

"Pidgin? What does this...pidgin mean?" Cree sat up straighter.

"Pidgin is...well, it's a really simple, kind of made-up language that people use to communicate when they can't speak each other's language."

Cree's face clouded. "My language is not pidgin."

"Then what were you speaking?" Laena was exasperated.

"Not this pidgin." Cree crossed his arms across his chest. Insulted.

"Then what *was* it?"

"It is not a simplistic language that I made up. It is a real language." Cree's eyes were flashing in anger.

Laena's eyes narrowed and she jammed a hand on her cocked hip. "Then if it wasn't pidgin, tell me what it was." She paused, her tone softening. "Please. Let's trust each other, okay?"

The fight went out of Cree and he slumped. "I will tell you. But you must promise me something. You must promise that it never leaves this room. Ever."

Laena approached the bed. "Why? Why do I have to promise to keep it a secret? What's so mysterious about a language?"

"Promise me," Cree said beseechingly.

Laena sat down on the bed next to Cree, intrigued. "I promise."

"It was Esperanto," Cree said softly.

She looked at him, baffled. "*What*? What is...Esperanto?" Her tongue stumbled over the unfamiliar word.

He sighed, as if he did not want to answer, but his voice was patient. "Esperanto is a universal language. It was invented a long time ago, in the late 1800s. It is my language. It is why I speak English with an accent." He paused, and looked at her uncomprehending face. "Esperanto is my native language."

Laena shook her head in confusion. "I've never heard of it," she said. "Why do you speak it? Are you not from Alaska?"

"I am from Alaska," Cree responded. "We...my people...we speak Esperanto."

Laena observed him, head tilted to the side. "So, if I Googled Esperanto, it would say that people in Kenai speak Esperanto?"

Cree shook his head thoughtfully. "No, it would not say that."

"Dammit, Cree!" Laena hit the bed with her fist in frustration. "I want straight answers here!"

"I am giving you straight answers," he responded seriously.

"Let me get this right. You speak a language called Esperanto, which you say is a universal language, and all 'your people' speak it in Alaska, but no one knows?" Her voice betrayed her skepticism.

Cree nodded. He saw the growing anger on Laena's face, and tried to explain further. "Even though Esperanto is a universal language, people did not really accept it widely...perhaps two million people around the world spoke it originally. But now, many speak it...English is not...." He trailed off, confused.

"English is not what?" Laena asked, trying to rein her frustration in.

"English is not...not the universal language," he offered weakly. "Look," Cree said, becoming more confident, "I do not have a computer here. But if we go to the library, or your house, you can...what do you call it? Google? Look up Esperanto on the computer, and you can see I am not lying. I can even speak to you and perhaps we can translate it on the Internet."

Laena pulled her phone from the pocket of her sweatshirt triumphantly. "An iPhone," she said, holding it up. "How do you spell 'Esperanto'?"

Cree spelled it for her, and Laena typed it in. She read silently for a minute and then put the phone down. "Okay, so it is a language. But why do you speak it? Alaska is part of the United States, and English is our official language. Why is Esperanto your native tongue? You said you'd never been out of Alaska." She crossed her arms in front of her chest, challenging him to give her a reasonable answer.

Cree nodded. "You are right, of course. My parents taught me Esperanto first, English second. They believed that Esperanto would be more valuable for me...they believed it should be the universal language."

Laena looked at him with some doubt in her eyes. How could she argue with what he said? It was a real language, people did speak it...could Cree help it that his parents were weird and taught it to him before English? There was no way she was going to win this one.

"Teach me something," she blurted. "In Esperanto."

Cree smiled broadly. "Okay," he agreed. "Ummm...*Kia bela virino.*"

Laena repeated the phrase after him, and Cree corrected her pronunciation until she said it perfectly. Then she laughed. "What am I saying?"

Cree laughed with her, the mood lightening considerably. "I am not telling you."

"You have to! Cree!" Laena reached out to grab his shoulders, but he caught her hands, and brought one to her own face.

"It means, 'What a beautiful woman.' " Cree said tenderly.

Laena's cheeks colored and she pushed his hand away.

"Do you want me to teach you more?" he asked teasingly.

Laena shook her head. "Maybe later," she murmured. "I...ummm...I have more questions."

"Right," Cree said, shifting on the bed, preparing himself. "More questions." He seemed more confident now that he had Laena in a better mood.

Laena looked into his eyes. "Please tell me the truth, Cree. How did you know the whales were there? How did you know they needed help?" She searched his face, hoping that he would answer her and that she could believe him.

Cree closed his eyes and sighed. "Laena," he began.

"Please, Cree. The truth," she beseeched.

He opened his eyes and looked at her searchingly. "The truth," he finally assented. "The truth is...I sensed them. They...they spoke to me. In a way." Laena searched his eyes, but she did not pull away, or get mad, or look disbelieving.

"Go on," she said evenly.

"I have this ability," Cree continued, a little bolder. "I can sometimes communicate with animals, read their minds. I sensed the trouble they were in."

"You read their minds?" Laena asked. Her tone was still surprisingly calm, not judgmental.

He nodded. "In a way. I just...felt their pain, their fear. It started in school. I could not sit still, could not concentrate. I had to get out. I was drawn to the water, to your house. And then I felt them. And once we were on the water, the feeling got stronger as I got closer to the whales."

"I remember. You looked so pale," Laena murmured. "But how did they know to trust you?" Laena asked. "I saw it in the mother's eye...she trusted you. She *asked* us to help her calf. She...she *pushed* her calf against the boat for us." Laena's voice was full of awe, remembering how the mother whale acted. The look in her eye.

Cree nodded. "Yes. They know what I am thinking too, I suppose. She knew we meant no harm. But that is not unusual—you know that. Whales approach boats out of curiosity. They are very...human. They are advanced."

Now it was Laena's turn to nod. She had always believed that non-human animals could think, and plan, and have human emotions, such as curiosity. Anyone who ever owned a dog knew that. So, Laena wasn't surprised that the mother whale pushed her calf toward the boat. The older whale herself had scars from lines...maybe she had been disentangled by humans in the past and she knew that they could help.

"You were so *certain*, though," Laena said, almost to herself. "Like you could hear them telling you where they were."

Cree shook his head. "Laena, I truly do not understand it. Really, I do not. It is a gift, or maybe a curse, but I just knew where they were."

Laena looked up at Cree's face again. She knew he was telling the truth. She could see it in his eyes, his face, and she was overwhelmed with warmth and love for him. She reached her hand out, hesitantly, and placed it on his chest. She could feel his heart, steady and strong, beneath her fingers.

Cree placed his hand over hers and drew her to him. He rocked her gently, stroking her hair. She felt like she could stay this way forever, in his arms. Neither of them made a move to pull away.

A knock on the door of the cabin startled them. Laena jumped up and started to back away from Cree and the bed. He squeezed her hand reassuringly, and with three long strides reached the cabin door. He smoothed his hair and opened the door.

"Cree!" said a female voice Laena immediately recognized. "Hi, Cree," said another voice. Sophie and Cat pushed themselves past Cree and into the cabin. Laena was bewildered. How did they know Cree lived here? Had they been to his cabin before? She felt a twinge of jealousy.

"We just came by to see if you wanted to go out to lunch with us...." Sophie's voice trailed off as she saw Laena standing in the shadows of the cabin. "Laena! I guess I'm not surprised to see you here!" Sophie came over and gave Laena a brief hug. Laena smelled Cat's flowery perfume permeating the cabin. "You can join us, too! We were just coming to steal Cree away for lunch...."

Cat stood by the door, one hand on her slim hip. She was dressed to kill, with low-slung, tight fitting jeans, a deep V-neck purple cashmere sweater, and a tight leather jacket. A section of her flat stomach showed between the waistline of her jeans and her sweater, and something sparkly glittered in her navel. "I hope we didn't...interrupt anything?" She looked at Cree meaningfully, taking in his bare chest, wet hair, and the rumpled bed. "You are a hard man to track down. Mike told us you were living here, but we drove all around looking for your cabin." She pouted.

Laena's face burned.

"You interrupted nothing," Cree said, shutting the door behind Cat. "We were just talking. Please, come in." Cree glanced at Laena and winked, and she stiffened, hoping Sophie and Cat didn't see the gesture. If Cat thought that something was going on between her and Cree....

Cat turned toward Laena. "Why, Laena, who would have thought you'd be here with Cree, all alone? Behaving yourself, I hope?" Her voice sounded sickly sweet, but Laena could feel the venom behind the words.

"Cree and I are friends, Cat," Laena responded coldly. "I'm not sure why your mind always turns something innocent into something dirty." A giggle erupted from Sophie's mouth, and Cat colored. Cat shot Sophie a nasty look, and Sophie's laugh abruptly stopped.

Cree cleared his throat and the three girls looked at him. "Sophie, Catherine, it is really nice of you to stop by. But I already have plans today. Laena is going to take me to the beach, and then her parents invited me over for dinner. Maybe another time?"

"Cree, please call me Cat. All my friends do. But the beach? A little cold out for that, isn't it?" Cat shivered dramatically. "Wouldn't you rather be in some warm restaurant, listening to music and eating a burger and fries? Or pizza?"

Cree shook his head. "Laena promised to teach me some of the species down here on the Cape. I am pretty hopeless at it." He smiled charmingly.

"Another time, then?" Sophie asked. She grabbed Cat's arm and started tugging her toward the cabin door. Laena glanced at her gratefully.

"Perhaps," Cree responded. "And I am sure we will see each other in school on Monday."

Sophie snagged Laena's attention, put her thumb and pinky up to her ear and mouth, miming a telephone, and mouthed, "Call me!" Laena smiled and nodded briefly, and Cree shut the door behind them. Silence. Cree and Laena looked at each other in relief.

"The *beach*?" Laena queried, when it was clear they were gone.

"What is wrong with that? You do not want to take me to the beach?" Cree asked drily.

"I want to keep talking. I...I have more questions," Laena responded.

"Mmmm, questions," Cree said. He walked past Laena and pulled a tee shirt and sweatshirt off his shelf. His voice sounded muffled as he pulled the tee over his head. "Can you not ask the questions at the beach?"

"Why are you in such a hurry to leave?" Laena asked.

Cree smiled wickedly. "Do you want to stay? I would be happy to stay with you here. We can sit back on the bed, and you can ask me your questions, and I can try and distract you."

"Is that what you were doing?" Laena asked, her jaw dropping. "Distracting me?"

Cree laughed. "Relax," he said, tugging a sweatshirt on and drawing close to Laena. "I was joking. I would love to stay with you here, but I thought that if we do not go to the beach, and Sophie and Cat are watching us, we will have to answer *their* questions. Besides, Cat stunk up my cabin with that...what do you call it? That fake scent."

"Perfume."

"Right. Perfume. Why do girls *do* that?"

Laena couldn't help but laugh. She didn't like perfume, either. Plus, she knew he was right about Cat watching them. Part of her wanted to stay in the cabin with him, in his arms on the bed, but she also knew that could be dangerous. Her feelings for him were so strong, and now that Sophie and Cat had seen them together in here, she knew there would be hell to pay in school on Monday. The rumors would be flying. Laena had never been the subject of that type of gossip before, and it mortified her.

"Okay, the beach it is," she said. "I rode my bike here...do you have a bicycle?"

Cree smiled crookedly. "I can do better than that."

Cree draped a worn jacket around her shoulders. "Put this on, too. It is cold out there, and windy." The jacket was soft and warm and smelled like Cree. She zipped it up and laughed...it hung almost to her knees. But she had never felt warmer, or safer, with Cree's scent enveloping her.

"Ready?" he asked. Laena nodded. Cree grasped Laena's hand and pulled her around the side of the cabin.

"Where are we going?"

"You will see," Cree said, smiling mischievously.

A weathered barn, tucked among the towering pines, came into view. Laena smelled the horses before she saw them. Sweet hay and earth. She learned how to ride when she was nine, and took lessons at a local stable until last year. She didn't realize how much she missed it until now.

"Horses?"

Cree nodded. "Do you ride?"

"I used to," Laena said. "But I haven't in a little over a year."

Cree slid open the barn door. "Part of my job here is to care for the horses, and to exercise them," he explained, lowering his voice in the quiet of the barn. "The owner of the campground has just one horse right now, but he will be getting more. He will rent them to the campers, so they can ride on the beach."

Laena breathed in greedily as her eyes adjusted to the dim light. She heard the soft crunch of something chewing hay.

Cree paused at the first stall on the right. "Hello, buddy," he said, as a beautiful bay brought his head up. It nickered softly. "Laena, this is Zed."

"He's huge!" Laena exclaimed.

"A little over 16 hands," Cree said. "Yes, he is a big boy. But very gentle." Cree stroked the horse's velvety nose. "Want to go for a ride, Zed? Hmmm? We are going to go to the beach." The horse tossed his head and whinnied.

Cree unlatched the stall and went in with Zed. He stroked his flanks and slipped a bridle over his head, settling the noseband across Zed's nose.

"Wait, Cree...where's his bit?"

"No bit," Cree responded. "I think it is cruel. Zed and I have been working on riding with a bitless bridle."

"But...how do you control him?"

"Have you ever used a rope halter?" Cree asked. Laena nodded. "Good. Well, if you can lead a horse with a rope halter while you are on the ground, and stop him with a rope halter, then you can do the same thing when you are on his back, no? The only difference is, instead of only one lead rope, you have two reins." Cree clicked his mouth and Zed moved out of the stall and into the aisle of the barn.

"Where's his saddle?"

Cree smiled. "No saddle. We will ride bareback, okay?"

"Bareback?"

"Have you never ridden bareback?"

Laena shook her head. "No, I rode English."

"Then it is time you learn," Cree said, transferring the reins into one hand. "I will mount first, and then you can get on behind me. The trick to riding bareback is to not grip the horse with your legs. You let your legs hang loosely, and sit back on your butt. Do not roll your hips forward."

"Cree...."

Cree squeezed Laena's shoulder. "You can do this. It is fun. We will just walk. Actually, when you ride bareback, trotting is the hardest. We should walk or canter."

Cree put his hand on Zed's withers and swung up on his back gracefully. Laena looked at him skeptically.

"I can't do that," she said.

Cree laughed. "I bet you could, but you can use a mounting block for now." He pointed to a three-step mounting block hung on a peg on the barn wall. "Climb up here behind me."

Laena placed the mounting block next to Zed and scrambled easily onto the horse.

"I can feel you tensing your muscles already," Cree said. "Relax. Let your legs hang loose. Put your arms around my waist. If you are scared just hold on to me. I will not let you fall."

Laena willed her arms to stop shaking and encircled Cree's hard abs. She was tense, but it wasn't because she was on horseback. Being so close to Cree, pressed up against him, made her body tremble.

"Tighter, Laena. Do not be afraid of hurting me. Just lean into me."

Laena exhaled and leaned into Cree's broad back. He was warm and hard, and her heart hammered.

"Good," he said. "Are you ready?"

Laena nodded, and Cree made a clicking sound with his mouth. Zed walked out of the barn and into the cool sunshine. Laena breathed deeply. As they walked, Cree explained how the gentle pressure he exerted on Zed's face steered him. She gradually relaxed.

"That is it!" Cree exclaimed. "Just stay loose." He paused. "Do you want to go faster?"

Laena laughed nervously. "Cree, I've never ridden double, never ridden bareback, and never ridden without a bit. And you want to go faster?"

"I am controlling Zed," Cree responded, looking at her over his shoulder. "All you have to do is stay relaxed, sit deep onto his back, and hold on tight to me. If you get scared, or feel like you are slipping, just tell me and I will slow him back to a walk. Zed has a beautiful canter—very smooth."

Laena nodded. She was nervous, but she didn't want Cree to think she was chicken. "Let's do it," she said. "But...you promise you'll slow down if...if it's too much for me?"

"Of course," Cree said. "Trust me. Are you ready?"

"Mmmm-hmmm," Laena said, grabbing Cree tighter.

Cree squeezed his legs gently against Zed's sides and said, "Canter, Zed." The horse immediately broke into a smooth, slow canter.

"You okay?" Cree called over his shoulder.

"Fine!" Laena's hair flew behind her and she laughed delightedly.

Cree urged Zed on and they arrived at the beach in no time. He slowed the horse to a walk, and stopped him by the post fence bordering the parking lot. Cree dismounted easily, pulled the reins over Zed's neck, and looped them around the fence rail. Reaching up for Laena, he lifted her off the massive horse's back as if she weighed nothing.

"You liked that?" Cree asked with a grin, smoothing the curls out of her face.

Laena nodded happily.

* * *

By the time they got Zed settled munching happily on the grass and made their way to the small beach, Laena was freezing. The sun shone brightly against the deep blue sky, but the frigid wind chilled them. The tide was going out, and rocks were visible in the water. Laena put her arm out to stop Cree.

"Shhh!" she whispered, then pointed to one of the rocks. A harbor seal sunned himself on a large, flat rock. Cree gaped. "What is it?" he whispered.

"A harbor seal," Laena responded quietly. She glanced at him, puzzled. "You have those in Alaska. Right? I thought harbor seals were pretty much all over..."

"Right, right...." Cree said quickly, and then hesitated. "I did not see it clearly at first. I thought maybe it was a different species."

Laena sighed. She could now tell easily when Cree lied. And this was one of those times.

"How can you *not* have seen a harbor seal in Alaska?" she asked in a normal voice. The seal looked over at them, annoyed, and slipped into the water with a splash.

Cree exhaled. "It is gone," he said, disappointed. "We scared it away." He looked crestfallen.

"Cree.... ? Question number three. Why do I keep catching you in lies about Alaska? You said you've never seen a whale, you say you can't get things like dairy products in Alaska, and now you act like a harbor seal is some exotic species...are you *really* from Alaska?"

Cree's eyes scanned the water. He would not look at Laena. "Yes, I am really from Alaska," he said firmly.

"Then why does it sound like a different Alaska to me? No whales, no seals, no normal food?"

"Have you been to Alaska, Laena?"

Laena shook her head.

"Then how do you know what Alaska is like?"

"I'm not an idiot, Cree. Honestly, I've seen television programs, and read things, and I know people who have gone there."

Cree couldn't meet her eyes. "I do not get out much, there, I guess."

"C'mon, Cree," Laena said. "There's something you're not telling me. If you're really from Alaska, there must be a reason why you never saw this stuff. Were you...ill? Not able to go outside?"

Cree walked over to a large piece of driftwood jutting out of the sand and sat down. He patted the log, and Laena reluctantly walked over and sat down next to him. Years of exposure had created gentle dips that cradled them comfortably. He looked around. The view was spectacular. "This is a special place. The beach, the ocean...it is wonderful."

Laena smiled. "Yes, it is a special place. The Cape is really beautiful, but this beach is my favorite."

"I love it here. And I love being with you. Which is why it is so hard to say this." He paused, fidgeting. "Laena, you are right. I am not being entirely truthful with you."

"What aren't you telling me? Where are you from?" Laena asked. She wanted to shake him. Getting answers out of him exhausted her.

The *conk-a-reeeeee* call of a red-winged blackbird erupted from behind them. They turned, and Laena pointed out the blackbird with bright orangey-red wing patches on the cattails.

"Red-winged blackbird," Laena said. "You have them in southern Alaska, right?"

Cree shook his head and shrugged as if he had no idea, but did not speak, fascinated by the bird. He tried to mimic the call, and the bird responded, calling back. Cree laughed in delight.

"Birds will often call back like that," she explained. "If you can mimic their song well, they think you are a competitor. You know, like...another male trying to intrude on their territory. So they are warning you to go away."

"Really?" Cree asked in wonder.

"Really," Laena responded with a smile. "And it works with owls, too. It's actually fun to call them and get them to respond."

Cree called to the red-winged blackbird again, and it called back.

"Cree?" Laena prodded. "Where are you really from?"

Cree turned back toward Laena, sighing, the smile fading from his face. "I am from Alaska," he said. "I did not lie about that."

Laena exhaled noisily. "I don't understand! How can you be from Alaska and not know these simple things?"

Cree shook his head again. "I just have not seen any of those things," he said.

"And why not?" Laena leaned towards him, pleading. "Were you in...in prison? Locked up somewhere? My God, Cree, give me some answers here!"

Cree turned to look at her. Softly, he said, "Do you believe in God, Laena? That is the second time I have heard you say his name."

Laena shook her head as if to clear it. "*What?*" She was totally confused. "Don't change the subject, Cree! It's an expression! It doesn't mean anything."

"So you do *not* believe in God?" He stared at her intently.

Laena groaned out of sheer aggravation. Through gritted teeth, she said, "No, I don't believe in God. I'm an atheist. So are my parents." She took a deep breath and tried to calm down, and lowered her voice to a more reasonable tone. She wanted to explain her abrupt answer, because she knew that religion remained a touchy subject with so many people. "I have a hard time reconciling religion with science. I don't believe in God...I mean, I don't know how the first atoms came into existence, but I do think there's a scientific explanation for all of it. I don't think there is some...all-knowing man sitting up in the clouds, deciding whether the Red Sox win against the Yankees or whether someone gets hit by a car or dies of cancer...." She paused, and her voice became softer, more thoughtful. "I believe that the earth is billions of years old, not 6,000 years old. I believe that plants and animals evolved over time, and that once we all had a common ancestor. I believe that humans *do* have the power to change the climate, and cause incredible damage to the planet. And I *can't* bring myself to believe that women were created from a man's rib, or that a talking snake and a magic apple screwed things up for Adam and Eve—I don't even believe that Adam and Eve existed! And, there is *no* way that Noah collected a male and female of every one of the millions of species on Earth to put in an ark. These are all fairy tales." Laena paused again. "I think people believe all these stories because they were raised with them. They don't sound strange to most people because their parents and teachers told them those tales were the truth from the time we were born. But if you told an adult all these stories, someone who had never heard them before, they would laugh. And the problem is, with all these religions, there's no way to prove it *didn't* happen." Laena shook her head in wonder. "So, the short answer, Cree, is no, I don't believe in God. I accept science."

Cree nodded, as if things were clear for him. But his face was etched with pain.

Laena could see that Cree was tortured by something. She felt like Cree was lying to her—she couldn't see any other explanation. But about what? Her heart ached for him. She didn't know how to help him, and she didn't know how to get him to trust her.

Cree had found a stick and absent-mindedly doodled in the sand with the sharp end. Behind him, several of the red-winged blackbirds called back and forth.

"Cree?" Laena asked. He kept his head down, his brow furrowed. Laena panicked. Had she offended him? Was he religious, and her confession that she was an atheist agitated him? "Cree, I didn't mean to upset you. I may not believe in God, but people should believe in whatever they want. That's what religious freedom is all about...." She trailed off as he looked up, stunned when she saw anger flashing in his eyes.

"People should not be allowed to believe in whatever they want. Not if those things *hurt* other people," he said, his voice harsh.

"No, of course not," Laena agreed. "Hurting people is definitely a bad thing. But my atheism isn't hurting anyone. Maybe I shouldn't have said anything, but you asked me...."

Cree looked at her in surprise, and then winced. "Not you, Laena! Not you." He flung the stick into the ocean and gave her his full attention.

"I am so afraid," he said softly. "I am so afraid that if I tell you everything, if I tell you the truth, you will push me away and I will lose...I will lose it all. I will not only fail at what I came here to do, but I will lose you. And I do not want to do that. I cannot do that." He shook his head in despair, and Laena's heart clenched.

"Oh, Cree," she said, melting. "I don't understand any of this. I can't answer you...I can't reassure you that you won't lose me, because I don't know what you are going to say. I can't promise you that everything will be all right, because I don't know. I don't have a crystal ball."

"Crystal ball?" Cree shook his head in confusion.

Laena laughed bitterly. "Another stupid expression. A crystal ball is something that psychics supposedly look into to see the future." She shook her head, realizing that she was way off tangent and probably confusing the hell out of him. "Look, I can promise you this. If you haven't hurt anyone, and you aren't planning to hurt anyone...or anything...then you won't lose me. I can forgive *anything* except for cruelty and...." Laena paused, thinking carefully. "And indifference. I cannot forgive indifference."

Cree stared into her eyes silently, frowning slightly. Waves lapped on the beach with small slapping sounds, and the birds called and twittered in the cattail marsh behind them. Cree broke his gaze with her and looked up. White clouds scurried across the brilliant blue sky, carried on the cold wind, and Laena saw their reflection in the blue of Cree's eyes. She allowed the silence to persist, sensing that Cree needed the peace to make a decision.

Cree looked down, smiled and grasped Laena's hands. "I like that," he said. "Indifference is almost as bad as cruelty, is it not?" Laena nodded and smiled back, confused.

"In some ways, there is no worse sin than indifference, is there?" he asked rhetorically.

"Cree, please...." She squeezed his hands, willing him to get to the point.

"So, if I have not been cruel, and I have not been indifferent, you will not push me away? And maybe you will help me, if I want to do something that will improve the world?" Cree continued.

Laena nodded, wondering what she was getting herself into.

Cree nodded, too, as if he had come to some momentous decision. The wind ruffled his shiny black hair, and his eyes glowed with some inner force. "Then I will tell you. Please, Laena, keep an open mind."

Laena nodded again, her heart thudding with fear and apprehension.

Cree looked deep into her eyes, as the wind whipped her curly hair in a crazy halo around her head. "Laena," Cree announced, "You...you talked about a crystal ball, and seeing into the future. I can do that. Because I...I am from the future."

Chapter 4

AFTER CREE had made his astounding confession, they spent the next several hours huddled on the log, talking. Laena alternated between thinking Cree was certifiably crazy, to feeling a heart-pounding fear that his words were the truth, and they were all doomed. Cree spoke of an earth that had heated to such an extent that all coastal cities were flooded. Many animals had gone extinct. And the humans that had endured fought over diminished supplies of natural resources. Laena had begged him to tell her how he got here, to her time, but he brushed her off, claiming that the complexity made it impossible to explain.

By the time Cree and Laena rode Zed back to Evergreen Acres to get her bicycle, and she had pedaled home, it was almost 4 o'clock. The sun sank on the horizon rapidly. Laena worried that her mother would be angry—Laena had been gone all day. Although she had skipped lunch, her stomach clenched, and the thought of food made her nauseated.

Now, being away from his sincere eyes and serious voice, she questioned her own sanity. How could she, a scientist in the making, believe the nonsense he spouted? Time travel? A world where almost every place and everything she knew was gone, and only a small fraction of human populations survived?

Laena felt physically ill. She didn't know how she was going to act normally at dinner tonight with both Cree and her parents around. If it were just her parents, she could feign illness and go to bed. But with Cree coming over, and her father trying to make amends for his rash behavior yesterday, she had to do a convincing job of acting as if nothing was amiss.

Laena walked into the house and called, "I'm home!" Tantalizing smells emanated from the kitchen. She found her father at the stove, stirring something. Her mother mopped the floor.

"About time you got home," Michelle said, without looking up.

"Sorry, Mom. I lost track of time. What can I do to help?"

Michelle paused, leaning on the mop, and looked up. "Laena! You're burned!" she said, disapproval heavy in her voice. Laena's hand flew to her face.

"I am? It must have been the wind...it was so cold...I didn't think...."

Michelle sighed heavily. "Go upstairs and put some aloe or something on that. Then come down here and help me. There are vegetables to be chopped, the table needs to be set...."

"Sure," Laena said, interrupting her mother and turning heel to go upstairs. "Sorry, Mom...I'll be right down!" Laena pounded up the stairs into her bathroom. She glanced in the mirror and saw that her mother was right. The sun and wind had reddened her nose, and her cheeks were glowing. She washed her face, cringing at the hot water on her burned skin. She patted her skin gently with a towel, then slathered cocoa butter on her face and hands.

Laena moved into her bedroom to put on a fresh shirt and jeans. She felt as if she were walking through molasses—every step required effort. Her thoughts turned frantically. Could what Cree told her be possible? Was he nuts, or was he telling the truth? Part of her couldn't wait for Cree to get to the house, and the other part of her dreaded his arrival.

Laena went back downstairs and into the kitchen. She tried to put on a cheery face. "What do you want me to do first?"

Ben sliced vegetables on the cutting board. "I've got the veggies under control...why don't you set the table?"

"Okay," Laena responded. "It smells good...what are we having?"

"Vegetarian Pad Thai," replied Ben. "And we made a coconut pudding—no dairy—for dessert."

"Wow," Laena said, impressed. "Why don't you cook like this for us?" She was going for an easy banter, but unsure whether she succeeded in pulling it off. She peeked up from folding the napkins at the table, but neither her mother nor her father seemed to sense the turmoil within her. She breathed a little easier.

By the time she had finished setting the table and straightening up—and throwing in a load of laundry unasked—the doorbell rang. Laena's stomach clenched.

"You want to get that, honey?" Michelle called from the kitchen.

"Okay!" Laena called, and headed to the front door. She opened the door. Cree stood there uncertainly. She opened the door wide. "Cree!" she exclaimed heartily, and hopefully loud enough for her parents to hear. "Good to see you—come on in!" She gave him a shaky smile and he looked at her questioningly. He leaned down and gave her a peck on the cheek, and as his lips grazed her ear, he murmured, "Are you okay?"

Laena nodded and led Cree through the foyer toward the kitchen. He squeezed her shoulder, and without thinking, Laena reached back and grasped his hand.

"Cree! Welcome!" cried Ben with a big smile. Michelle went over and gave Cree a hug. Surprised, Cree hugged her back.

"What a warm welcome," he said, dimples clearly evident. "Whatever did I do to deserve this?"

Ben laughed. "I think we just feel bad for the misunderstanding yesterday. No hard feelings, right?"

"None," Cree agreed earnestly.

"So, what would you like to drink, Cree?" Michelle asked. "Laena?"

"Water is fine with me," Cree responded, and Laena added, "Me, too."

Michelle poured two glasses of water for the teenagers, and two glasses of wine for her and Ben.

"Something smells delicious," Cree said, peering over Ben's shoulder at the stove. "I think you are spoiling me."

"Sit down, sit down," Michelle urged. "Ben cooked tonight. It's vegetarian Pad Thai. Have you ever had it?"

Cree shook his head. "No. Is it an Asian dish?"

"Thai," Ben explained, bringing the steaming pan to the table. "Rice noodles with vegetables and tofu in a peanut sauce. Just a little spicy."

"It sounds great," Cree said, holding out a chair for Laena. Laena saw Michelle and Ben catch each other's eye. She could hear the silent conversation between them: *What a gentleman!*—and the unspoken response— *I know! What teenage boy does such things these days?*

Ben followed suit and held Michelle's chair out for her. When everyone sat and plates were filled, Michelle said, "So, Cree, what did you do today?"

Cree cleared his throat. "I had a lot of work to do around the campground," he said. "And I...uh...explored the area a little."

"Find anything of interest?" Ben asked, forking a mouthful of noodles into his mouth.

"Yes, sir. I saw a harbor seal sunning on a rock, and saw some red-winged blackbirds. I was at a small beach near the campground—a very special place." He winked at Laena.

Michelle laughed. "Ah, the Cape in the spring!" Michelle exclaimed. "Everything coming back to life."

The four of them ate, and Ben and Michelle talked to Cree about the Cape's natural history. Laena had to force herself to swallow her food, even though it tasted delicious. She found herself staring at Cree, trying to see through his magnificent exterior to the real person within. She couldn't wait until dinner ended, and...and what? She couldn't really think of more questions to ask Cree. Nothing she could ask would prove or disprove his story. She didn't know how to handle the situation. Normally, if she had a problem or something troubled her, she would go to her parents. She had an unusually open relationship with them, she thought, unlike most of her classmates, who wouldn't even sit down at the table with their parents. Laena told her parents almost everything, but maybe that was because she had nothing to hide. She didn't drink or do drugs, she did well in school...her friends were all leading somewhat secret lives, doing things they knew their parents would deplore. But Laena had lied to her own parents more over the past two days than she ever had in her life, and she felt herself drifting away. Or was being pulled away unwillingly, toward Cree.

When they finished dinner, Michelle suggested they all digest a little before dessert. Laena jumped up eagerly from the table. "Good idea," she agreed. "Can we go upstairs? I want to show Cree some of the field guides I have about birds in the east." Stupid excuse, but it was all she could up with quickly.

Michelle and Ben looked at each other and silently contemplated the request. "Sure," Ben said finally. "Just leave your door open, okay?" He said it casually, but Laena could feel the tension behind the question.

"Of course," Laena said, trying to reassure him.

Cree stood up. "Dinner was delicious," he said. "Thank you again."

"Anytime, Cree," Michelle said, clearing the table.

Laena jerked her head at Cree, indicating he should follow her. They walked up the stairs in silence.

"Birds?" Cree whispered when they got to her room.

"It was all I could think of," Laena whispered back. "I actually want to look at an atlas."

"An atlas?" Cree asked.

"Sit down," Laena said, indicating her double bed. She went over to the bookshelf and pulled out a big old atlas that her father had given her years ago. She lugged the book over to the bed and sat next to Cree. She flipped through the pages until she came to the map of the world. The pages of the old atlas smelled slightly musty.

"Wow," Cree breathed, dragging the book toward his lap. "It does not look like this now."

"That's what I want to know," Laena said, urgently. "What *does* it look like in your time?"

Cree's finger traveled across the pages. "This," he said, finger trailing along Florida and the Keys. "This is not here." Laena's heart sank. He pointed to the southeastern coast of the United States. "These ...islands and shorelines? Not here. What did you call them? The Outer Banks? And the barrier islands. In Maryland, and Virginia...those are gone." His finger traveled across the Atlantic Ocean to Europe. He touched Venice gently. "This is gone, too." He moved his finger over to the Halligen Islands in Germany. "Gone." Then down to the Solomon Islands and over to Tuvalu. "Gone."

"Stop!" Laena cried, trying to keep her voice low. "Gone? What do you mean, gone?"

Cree shook his head slowly. "Just ...gone. No longer in existence." He looked over at Laena. "The sea level...it has risen."

Laena swallowed past the huge lump that had formed in her throat. "Cree, what about...what about the Cape? Cape Cod?"

Cree looked at the map, his brow furrowed. He did not answer.

"Cree?" Laena murmured.

He shook his head. "I'm sorry, Laena. Between the seas and the storms...there is nothing left."

Laena emitted a strangled sound. "When, Cree? When does this happen?"

Cree closed the atlas and put it to the side on the bed. He turned to Laena and took her hands in his. "I am from the year 2217," he said softly. "It has happened over time, but things started happening rapidly in 2024."

Laena's head spun. "But...but that's so soon!"

Cree nodded. "Yes, that is soon. That is why I am here."

"What do you mean, why you are here?" Laena reached out and grabbed his shoulder. "Wait—do you mean there is something we can do? To stop it?" She felt a few fragile tendrils of hope.

"I don't know. The sea level is not the worst of it. There are other things...that happen."

"Cree, you have to tell me!" Laena was upset now. Cree smiled tenderly and reached up to cup her face with his hand.

"Does this mean you believe me?" he asked.

Laena looked into his eyes, searching for the truth. Did she believe him? She believed that climate change was real, and that if they didn't do something soon, sea levels would rise. But did she believe his story that he was from the future? She didn't know. Cree sensed her hesitation.

"I can prove it to you," he said softly but confidently.

"How?" Laena asked.

"I knew it might come to this, that I would have to prove myself to someone I trusted, so I memorized the news for this week. Not tomorrow, but on Monday. The 14th day of this month."

"What happens on the 14th?" asked Laena, afraid of the answer.

"There is a natural disaster," Cree explained. "In the Caribbean. There is an island there, called Dominica. A beautiful island. There is a large chunk of mountain that falls into the sea, causing a tsunami on the neighboring island of Guadeloupe."

"The mountain just falls into the sea?" Laena asked.

"No, no...it does not *just* fall. There is an earthquake. Dominica is a very unstable island, geologically. The island has nine active volcanoes, and the only boiling lake in the world. The most beautiful place on earth. People described it as a cross between the Garden of Eden and Jurassic Park." Cree laughed bitterly. "Two fictional places, but it gives you an idea." His face lit up. "*Jurassic Park*...do you have that film? I would love to see it. I read about it, heard about it, but...we do not have the old movies. Can you still see it?"

Laena had to smile at his eagerness. "I think we have a DVD of it. We can watch it, if you'd like. You can't see it in the movie theaters anymore."

"So, we can watch it?"

"Sure. But I have so many questions! In a few minutes, okay? Right now I want to find out more...from you."

Cree nodded, disappointment on his face. "Okay," he acquiesced.

Laena paused, struggling between her desire to give Cree what he wanted and to satisfy her own curiosity. Her inquisitiveness won. She said, "So if on Monday, there is an earthquake on Dominica, and a piece of mountain falls into the ocean and creates a tsunami that floods the shores of Guadeloupe, then I will know you are telling the truth." Cree nodded in agreement.

A horrible thought struck Laena. "Cree! Are people killed? Shouldn't we warn them?"

"People are killed," Cree conceded. "But there is nothing we can do, Laena. What would you do? Call the government of these islands and have them evacuate? On what basis? They will never believe you."

Laena slumped, knowing Cree was right. No one would listen to them. She would just have to wait...and hope Cree fabricated all of this. But then, if they could do nothing to alter the future, then why was Cree here? What good could he do? Laena looked up at him questioningly, and opened her mouth to speak.

"There are some things I can do to help," Cree said solemnly, reading her thoughts.

"How did you know what I was about to say?" Laena protested. "Can you...can you read my mind, like you do the whales?"

Cree shook his head. "I wish I could read everything in your mind," he teased, "but I cannot. You are simply easy to read. And, it was a natural question to ask."

"You mean the question I never had a chance to ask?" Laena grumbled.

Cree chuckled. "Yes. I told you we could not alter the future, at least not with respect to the events on Dominica in two days. Naturally, you would next ask why I came here if I could not change what is going to happen."

Laena laughed. "Smart ass. C'mon, let's go watch *Jurassic Park*. Why do you want to see it so badly, anyway?"

"It is legend," Cree confessed. "The movie about people and dinosaurs together. It sounds very funny."

"Yeah, well, you have to remember that in the movie, the humans cloned the dinosaurs from DNA they found. It isn't like we made a movie about humans and dinosaurs roaming the earth together naturally."

"I know," Cree said. "But some people believe that, no? That people and dinosaurs were contemporaneous? Tiffany, perhaps?"

Laena giggled. "Yes, I suppose she might. If she thinks about it." She paused, as a thought struck her. "Cree...did it ever come to be? Were we...I mean, *are* we ever going to be able to clone extinct animals, and repopulate the earth with them?"

"Yes," Cree said softly. "Humans were able to do that." He laughed as he remembered. "They had wooly mammoths roaming Alaska and parts of Asia again. Not in Europe, though. Not enough land for them."

Laena was stunned. So it *was* possible. Science had come far enough to clone sheep and dogs—but animals that had gone extinct! It was mind-boggling.

"So why is it so bizarre to you that there would be a movie like *Jurassic Park*?" Laena asked as they headed downstairs. "Do we clone dinosaurs?"

Cree shook his head. "We decided to rehabilitate—that is the word they used—animals that humans had caused to become extinct. Not the others, that became extinct from natural disasters, like meteors or volcanoes. So, we never did dinosaurs, because we did not cause their death."

Laena nodded. That made sense, she supposed, although how fascinating it would be to clone dinosaurs and study their behavior! Laena led Cree into the family room and rummaged through the television cabinet for the *Jurassic Park* DVD.

"You kids going to watch a movie?" Ben asked, peeking through the doorway.

"*Jurassic Park*," Cree replied excitedly. "I have never seen it, and I have wanted to forever. Would you like to join us?"

Ben laughed. "You've never seen *Jurassic Park*? Cree, I'm not sure I could live in Alaska. You sure are deprived up there." He paused, considering, then said, "You know what? I'd love to see that old movie again. Maybe I can talk Michelle into letting us eat dessert in here while we watch it. Laena, get the movie set up, and I'll go talk to your mom."

By the time Laena found the DVD and popped it in, Michelle and Ben were arranging a tray of coffee and coconut pudding on the table. "Dessert!" Michelle announced. Laena and Cree moved over to make room for Laena's parents on the couch, and they all settled in to watch the movie.

Cree could barely contain his excitement. He laughed uproariously at several of the scenes, and his eyes were glued to the television. He let his coffee go cold. When the movie was over he sighed contentedly.

"That was great," he said, a smile still playing on his lips.

"Glad you enjoyed it," Ben replied. "It is pretty silly, but still fun."

Cree glanced at Ben. "Do you believe that could happen? Cloning dinosaurs, I mean?"

Laena's heart started pounding out of nervousness. *Don't go there, Cree,* she willed him with her mind.

"Sure," Ben responded. "It's certainly possible. We've already cloned mammals. But the likelihood of finding a complete dinosaur DNA strand, let alone all those different species, is highly unlikely. And the whole premise of the movie is pretty silly, doing it secretly and for profit like that. And they make those Velociraptors pretty darn smart." Ben paused, and shook his head. "I don't think it will ever happen, at least not in my lifetime."

Cree nodded. "I agree...not in your lifetime."

Ben looked at Cree strangely and Laena yawned loudly to distract him. "Boy, I sure am tired," she said.

"Me, too," Michelle said, stifling a yawn in response to Laena's. "Maybe it's time to call it a night?"

"Good idea," Ben said, standing up and stretching his arms over his head. "Cree, would you like a ride home? It's pretty chilly out there."

Cree stood up as well. "No, thank you. I can walk home. It is not far at all."

Michelle nodded her approval, and Ben and Michelle said goodnight to Cree. "Not too much longer, okay kids?" Ben said sternly.

"I'll just walk him to the door," Laena promised.

"Thank you—again—for the delicious dinner. I hope I am not taking advantage of your hospitality."

"Not at all," Michelle said, and then she hugged Cree. "You're welcome any time."

Cree smiled widely, and Ben and Michelle retreated to the kitchen to finish cleaning up. Laena and Cree walked slowly toward the front door.

"Will I see you tomorrow?" Laena asked softly.

"I would like that," Cree replied. "Do you think your parents would be okay with us seeing each other again?"

Laena shrugged. "I think my father is a little nervous...you know, about...us...." She trailed off, unsure of how to finish without making Cree uncomfortable.

"About us becoming intimate?" Cree asked gently.

Laena nodded, embarrassed. Her hair hung in a curtain, partially obscuring her face, and Cree tucked her curls behind her ears.

"Well, what if we spent some time together tomorrow without becoming intimate? Then there is nothing for you to feel guilty about, or for your father to be concerned about." His voice teased.

"Good idea," Laena said, looking up and laughing. "What should we do?"

"I have some chores to do at the campground—feeding Zed, cleaning out the stall—but I can get up early and do them," Cree said. "And I have homework...."

"Me, too," Laena interrupted. "But we can do our homework together, and when we finish, we can go to the beach, or something...."

"Good idea," Cree echoed, putting his arms around Laena's waist and pulling her toward him. Warmth flooded her body and she sighed contentedly, wrapping her arms around him. "And you can tell your father we are doing homework, so he will be happy."

Cree started to release Laena but she tightened her grip around him. "No," she murmured.

Cree chuckled and caressed Laena's back. "No? You do not want me to let go of you?"

"Not really," Laena said honestly.

Cree laughed, and then whispered, "But I have to go, before your father comes out and sees us." His mouth grazed her ear and then he lowered his mouth and kissed her neck.

Laena gasped in pleasure but then pushed Cree away, glancing toward the kitchen to make sure her father wasn't there. "You're right—you'd better go."

Cree kissed the top of her head and slipped out the front door. Laena watched him. She stood at the door until she couldn't see any trace of him. She felt empty and alone. Laena shut the front door, turned the deadbolt, and trudged wearily up the stairs. Without Cree there to reassure her, the reality of the future he described weighed heavily on her.

Laena felt burdened with an impossible task as she got ready for bed. Her mind would not stop turning. Florida, the barrier islands off Maryland and Virginia, the Cape...all gone! She couldn't picture it, couldn't make it seem real to her. She tossed and turned in bed, alternating between panic and disbelief. How could what he said be true? Finally, sheets tangled and twisted around her body, she fell into a fitful sleep.

Chapter 5

LAENA HAD BEEN AGITATED all night, and never fell into that deep, restful sleep she so desperately needed. She took a steaming hot shower as soon as she woke up, hoping it would revive her. She dressed warmly and padded down the stairs. She poked her head in the kitchen. Her parents were there, reading the New York Times and the Boston Globe. Sections of paper were strewn across the kitchen table. Sunlight streamed through the kitchen window, and the room looked cozy and inviting.

"Good morning," she said, her voice thick with lack of sleep. Her parents murmured in response, their heads buried in the Sunday papers. Laena drank a cup of coffee in an effort to wake up. She nibbled the edges of a piece of toast, but couldn't make herself swallow much. She brought her dishes to the sink, stuck them in the dishwasher, and turned back to her parents.

"Well, I'm off," Laena announced, hoping that there would not be too many questions forthcoming.

No such luck. "Off? Off where?" Michelle asked, looking up from the Times.

"Cree and I are going to do homework," Laena responded, trying to sound nonchalant.

"Where?" Ben asked sharply.

"I...I don't know. His cabin, I guess."

"I don't think so, Laena," her father said.

"Why not?"

"I don't think the two of you alone in his cabin is a good idea," Ben replied bluntly.

"Dad...."

"I agree, Laena," Michelle interrupted. "It's not that we don't trust the two of you, but we don't want you to get carried away." She paused. "You're only 17."

"You obviously don't trust me, Mom," Laena retorted. "You basically said so yourself—you don't trust me to not get 'carried away.' I'm not an idiot, you know. And I'm not going to do anything stupid."

"Laena, listen..."

"No, Dad, you listen to me! Have I ever given you reason not to trust me? Do you really think I'm going to throw away my whole life by getting pregnant at 17? For crying out loud, I was raised by two biologists! I know how it all works, and I am not going to do anything to jeopardize my future!" Laena trembled with anger. She knew she was over-reacting, but the combination of sleep deprivation and Cree's depiction of the future had her on a short fuse.

Ben and Michelle looked at each other. Then Michelle said, "Laena, honey, we do trust you. And we like Cree. But you're a teenager. We see the way that you and Cree look at each other, the way he touches you...even the smartest kids, the most sensible ones, get carried away. I know we haven't really talked about this yet, but I hoped you would wait until you were at least 18 before we put you on birth control...."

"Mom!" Laena was mortified. Her cheeks burned with embarrassment. "I'm not asking permission to have sex with him! I'm asking if I can go do *homework* with him. Homework!"

Michelle sighed, and Ben stood up and walked over to Laena. He put his hands on her shoulders and looked into her eyes. "Laena. Let's be realistic here. Your mother and I aren't stupid either. We can see that you have feelings for Cree. Am I right?"

Laena shrugged her father's arms off her and nodded miserably. "Yes, but...."

"Okay. So you have feelings for Cree, and Cree obviously has feelings for you. You've hardly known each other more than a week. And he's very...mature for his age. It's scary for us as parents, watching our little girl go into a situation like this unprepared."

"What situation?" Laena cried. "Look, I'll be honest with you. Cree makes me feel...wonderful. Like I've never felt before. But it's not just hormones. He's smart, and funny, and interesting. And, he is more mature than other boys...that's why I like him. And, he actually likes me! I've never really had a boy like me." She looked away, discomfited at her outburst of emotion.

"Oh, sweetheart," her father said softly, folding her into his arms. He looked back at Michelle, still sitting at the table.

Michelle sighed. "Laena, what you said is precisely what scares me. Cree is your first love. The first time you're feeling these emotions. And they can be very powerful emotions." She paused, searching for the right words. "But by the same token, you're right. You've never really given us any reason to mistrust you. And, I have to admit, I do like Cree."

Laena pulled away from her father and looked at her mother hopefully. "What are you saying?"

Michelle looked at Ben and sighed again. "Well, if your father agrees, I guess I'm saying that we should let you go, so long as you promise to use good judgment. I want you to promise us that if you feel like you want to...get intimate with Cree, that you come to me first. And we'll go to the doctor, and we'll get you what you need. Is this something you want to talk about now?"

"Mom." Laena ran over to her mother and kneeled down next to her chair. "I swear that is not going to happen anytime soon. We're still getting to know each other. I won't do anything stupid...." Michelle reached over and gave Laena a hug.

"Ben? Are you comfortable with this?" Michelle asked over Laena's shoulder.

"Not really," he admitted.

Laena stood up. "Please, Dad," she said softly. "Please trust me."

Ben rubbed his hand over his face. "Go," he said hoarsely. "But take your cell phone, and stay in touch. When will you be home?"

"When do you want me home? Cree and I thought we'd finish our homework, and then we were going to go to the beach or something. Low tide is right around lunchtime, so I thought I could take him to explore the tide pools."

"Okay. Be home by four o'clock."

Laena nodded happily. "Four it is. Promise." She ran out of the kitchen, then ran back in. "Love you guys!" she said, a huge smile on her face.

"We love you, too!" Michelle echoed. But the front door had slammed on her words, and Laena was gone before she heard them.

* * *

As Laena walked down the access road to Evergreen Acres, her heart started thudding. She shifted her backpack containing her books from one shoulder to the other, and tried to look blasé. She wanted to drop her bag and run into Cree's cabin and throw herself in his arms, but instead she strolled casually to his door. Like yesterday, the door stood wide open. She knocked on the open door and called, "Cree?" No response. Laena walked into the cabin, put her backpack down on the small table, and glanced around. Cree's bed was made, but he was nowhere to be seen.

She headed back out the door just as he bounded up the steps to the cabin.

"I thought I heard you!" he exclaimed happily. He pulled Laena into his arms and twirled her around. She laughed. He put her down gently.

"It is good to see you, sweetie. And perfect timing, too. I just finished all my campground chores."

Laena grinned. "Great! Let's get our homework out of the way so we can go enjoy the day."

Cree nodded and headed for the stove. "I need more coffee first. Would you like some?"

"No, thanks," Laena replied. "I've already had a cup. And one is usually my limit."

"I make damn good coffee," Cree said seriously, looking over his shoulder at her.

Laena laughed. "Okay, then, I guess I can't turn down that kind of offer."

Cree lit the gas stove, put water on to boil, and took a wooden contraption with a drawer and a metal handle out of his cabinet. Laena walked over, curious.

"What is that?" she asked.

"This?" Cree asked, pointing to the wooden appliance. "It is a hand grinder. You put the beans in here...." He stopped to put a handful of beans in the top, and then screwed the metal handle back on. "Then you grind them....." Cree turned the handle round and round and the wonderful smell of fresh coffee wafted through the air. "And then, you get your ground coffee...here." Cree opened a small wooden drawer in the bottom of the machine, displaying coarsely ground coffee.

"Pretty cool," Laena said.

Cree nodded. "I try not to use electricity here when I can help it. It is easy to grind your own coffee beans."

Laena watched in silence as Cree tamped the coffee into the top of the old-fashioned percolator.

"Cree...do you have electricity...in your time?"

Cree nodded. "Of course. But not nearly as much as you do. We have mostly solar, some wind. But we use human power whenever we can. There are no fossil fuels, though. So we have no gasoline, or oil."

"How do you heat your homes?"

Cree laughed bitterly. "There is not as much need for heat where I come from. The earth is much warmer. But in places like Alaska, where it gets chilly in the winter, we rely on heat from the sun, and from good buildings."

"How much warmer is it? I mean, from now to your time. How much has the earth warmed?"

Cree hesitated before answering.

"Cree?"

"Yes, I heard you," he responded sadly. "It has warmed about 10 degrees. On average, from your time."

"Ten degrees! That's far more than they predicted."

"Laena, I mean 10 degrees Celsius. Not Fahrenheit. So, 18 degrees Fahrenheit."

Laena's mouth dropped. "But...I thought...they said it would be less than that."

"Mmmm," Cree said carefully. "It is not like you were not warned. Even the National Academy of Sciences said the temperature increase could be higher than predictions, depending on how many more fossil fuels were burned." He concentrated on making the coffee.

"So how much did the sea level rise?" Laena pressed.

"A lot," Cree responded distractedly.

"Why are you being so vague? Why won't you tell me what happens?"

Cree did not turn from the stove. "I do not want to scare you, Laena."

"Scare me? Don't you think I'm already scared? Do you really think this whole thing is meaningless to me? Without knowing the details, I am imagining the worst. I mean, how many people are left? You told me it was bad, but you didn't give me details. What about other species...what's left?"

Cree was silent, concentrating on pouring the rich coffee into two mugs. Laena got up from the table and stood next to him. "Cree? What are you not telling me?" She peered into his face, trying to read his expression.

Cree brought the two mugs to the scarred kitchen table and set them down. Only then did he look at Laena.

"I do not think you really want to know," he said grimly. "It is pretty bad...so much different than what you have now."

Laena sat at the table and motioned Cree to do the same. He sat, and wrapped his strong hands around the ceramic coffee mug.

"How different?" she asked softly. "Please explain to me so I can understand." She searched Cree's face, and noticed stress she had never seen before. His brow furrowed, and his normally bright blue eyes were clouded.

"Laena...." he began, then stopped. "I...I do not know how to tell you this."

"You've come to me for help, right? Let me try to help. If you think there is something we can do to change the course of the future, then let me help you. If you tell me how bad it is, it will only make me want to help you more. Do you think I am going to freak out and curl up into a ball and die? I'm stronger than that, Cree. I can take it."

Cree looked at Laena, his eyes searching hers. He sighed, and then began to speak. "How many humans are there now, in your time? Almost 7 billion? The earth's population reaches 8 billion rapidly. But by then the changes are already occurring—droughts, severe storms, increased temperatures, rising sea levels. Species are moving, because it is too warm for them where they normally live. Or their prey is gone. Water is the biggest problem. Fresh water, I mean. Water that is clean enough to drink. And disease, of course." Cree looked at Laena to gauge her reaction, and sipped his coffee.

"Go on." She tried to keep her voice steady, even though she felt nothing but panic.

"The sea level rise is drastic. I showed you, on the map? Many countries are lost. There is fighting, over water. And food." Cree paused.

Laena reached across the table and put her hand over Cree's. "How many people are left in your time, Cree?"

Cree shrugged. "Not many. One million, perhaps, around the world? At most. We do not really know for sure. Maybe there are less...in fact, there may be far less. One hundred thousand, maybe? We do not communicate much, and some of the groups are afraid. They do not want to be found."

Laena gasped. "Did you say one *million*? Not billion, with a 'b'?"

Cree nodded. "Like I said, not many." He tried to smile, but the smile did not reach his eyes. "There are not many non-human animals either. Many have gone extinct. Everything, all of...." His voice faded and he looked down.

"Everything? All of what? Everything can't be gone."

"No, no. Everything...." Cree sighed, resigned. "Everything in the sea, in the oceans, is gone. No life there."

"*What?*" Laena was in shock. How could the oceans be dead? They were so vast, so teeming with life. Tears of despair filled her eyes.

Cree pushed his coffee mug off to the side and patted his lap. "Come sit here, with me. On my lap. I need to hold you."

Laena got up and went to him, shaken to the core. Nothing in the ocean? No whales, dolphins, seals...*fish*? Is that why Cree was so excited to see the whales? And even the seal? Laena didn't want to believe what he said. She *couldn't* believe it. It was beyond comprehension. She refused to accept his version of the future, not until she had more proof. Nevertheless, the mere possibility that he was telling the truth horrified her. Laena clambered into his lap and twined her arms around him, laying her head on his chest. Cree sighed contentedly and they held each other silently.

Finally, Laena couldn't stand it. "What happened, Cree? To the ocean? Why is there nothing there?"

His voice was low. "It was catastrophic. A chain reaction."

Laena shook her head as if to clear it. "What happened?"

Cree sighed. "You know that our ecosystem will crash if we lose too many species, or if we lose just *one* very important species. You understand this, yes?"

"Yes," Laena responded. She learned this in ecology. They were called keystone species—one species that played a critical role in the entire ecological community. Without this one critical species, everything fell apart. She understood it in concept, but had never applied it to real life, here and now.

"That is what happened in the oceans. We lost an important species...just *one*, but a critical one, and it caused a chain reaction which led to the demise of everything that lived in the ocean."

"Oh my God," whispered Laena. She could not imagine an ocean with no life.

"A disaster," Cree agreed, stroking her hair absently. He wound one of her curls around his finger and let it spring free. "So many people depended on fish, and the oceans, to survive. It caused the human population to crash, and there were wars over what resources remained. It was...what is that old expression you use? The last straw?"

Laena nodded. Then she sat up straighter in Cree's lap, grasping his arms. "What was the species, Cree? The critical one that went extinct? Can we stop it from happening?"

Cree smiled wryly. "That is why I am here, Laena. To try and stop it."

"So?" asked Laena impatiently. "How do we stop it? What is the species, and what happened to it?"

"Krill," he said.

"*Krill?*" Laena repeated, disbelief in her voice. "Are you sure?"

Cree nodded. He reached up and stroked her neck and her face. Laena shivered in pleasure, but pushed him away.

"Cree, my mother works on krill. That is her research topic."

"I know," Cree replied, so softly Laena almost didn't hear him.

"You *know*? How can you know?" She was incredulous.

Cree didn't respond, and wouldn't meet her eye. Thoughts tumbled through Laena's mind, and then it hit her, like a physical blow. She groaned.

"Wait...you came here, to North Bayside, to *me*, because of my *mother*? Her research?" Laena pushed off Cree's lap in horror. Had he lied to her again? Was all of this, his alleged attraction to her, just a façade so he could get to her mother?

"Laena...." Cree stood up and reached for her, pain in his voice and his eyes.

"No!" she cried. "I understand now. You don't like me for *me*! How could I have been so stupid? You did this...to make contact with my mother! I'm just a...just a pawn in this game!"

Cree stiffened visibly. "It is not a game," he said coldly. "It is not a game at all. And yes, I came to North Bayside to make contact with your mother. But I did not use you. I did not know you existed, let alone what you were like, or how I would feel about you. Do you hear me? I did not know your mother even had a teenage daughter. I did not know anything about you."

"Bull!" Laena said hotly. "You are *so* using me. I am such an idiot!" She turned to flee the cabin, but Cree caught her and held her fast.

"Stop it, Laena! I swear, I am not using you. I need to feed your mother information, get her to understand what will happen without her realizing who I am, or when I am from. That is true. But that has nothing to do with you. It would have been easier if I did not feel this way about you. Do you not see that?" He swallowed with difficulty, as if there was something distasteful in his mouth. "I will have to *leave*, Laena. I have to go back to my time. Why would I get involved with you like his? Just for fun? Do you really think that is the type of man I am?"

Laena struggled in Cree's grasp, trying to free herself. Then she stopped, knowing it was fruitless. "Let. Go. Of. Me." She said the words slowly and icily.

Cree ignored her demand, holding her tighter. Then he leaned down and kissed her on the lips, hard. At first, Laena tried to turn her head out of his reach, but he held fast. Slowly, his grasp on her arms loosened, and his mouth became soft and yielding. His hands traveled down her back, ending in the hollow at the base of her spine. Despite her anger, she felt herself responding to his kisses and his caresses. She relaxed into him, and he murmured her name, trailing kisses on her neck and behind her ear. Laena groaned.

Cree murmured into her ear. "I love you, Laena. You have nothing to do with this. Our friendship, our connection, can you not feel the truth?"

Laena felt hot tears spill out of her eyes onto her cheeks. She burrowed her face into his neck. She could feel his desire for her. But how could she know what he really thought?

His hands moved to her waist, and he looked into her eyes. "Can you see my eyes?" he asked her. "Can you read what is in them? Do you think I am such a good liar? Tell me what you see. Tell me." His hands circled slowly at her sides, brushing her breasts. Insistent. Laena shivered. "What do you see?" he asked again.

Laena looked into the icy blue depths of his eyes. She saw pain, and love, and fear. Could it be that he was telling the truth? She ached inside, her own fear a physical pain. "I don't know...."

Cree laughed harshly. "You do know, Laena. Do you not? You are just afraid. Now it is your turn to tell me the truth. What do you see in my eyes?"

She looked down. "I see...love. And pain," she admitted softly. "You're right. I am afraid."

"Life is full of risks," Cree said, his voice gentler. "But if you do not follow your passion, your dreams, you will never know what could have been."

"Oh, Cree," Laena said, tears silently streaming own her face. "I'm sorry I doubted you. It's just that this is so unfamiliar to me. I don't know how to act, what to feel...."

"You feel what you feel," Cree responded. "Look, I will make you a promise. I will never lie to you again. Okay? The only lies I have told you have been to protect my identity, and to protect you. But I will not lie anymore. Do you believe me?" A smile toyed on his lips, almost hesitantly.

Laena smiled in return, her cheeks still wet from her tears. "Yes, I believe you."

"So you believe me that I am not using you?"

Laena nodded. "I might believe you more if you kiss me again." She blushed at her own boldness.

Cree laughed, and complied with her request. He took her mouth in his, and his hands held her head to him. When they finally parted, Cree asked, "How was that? Believable?"

"Yes, very," Laena breathed.

"Good." Cree took her by the hand and dragged her back to the table. "Let's finish our coffee—which is probably cold by now—and get this homework out of the way."

"I might find it hard to concentrate on homework right now," Laena mumbled, her knees still weak from his kisses.

Cree chuckled. "I am glad I have that effect on you," he replied. "But we have work to do. Once we get our homework out of the way, we have to figure out how to solve my little problem. The krill, remember?"

"Right," Laena said, sobering. "The krill."

They spent the next two hours doing homework. When they finished, Cree tipped his chair back and clasped his hands behind his head.

"So," he said seriously, "what do you know about krill?"

Laena thought before answering. She knew the basics about krill, but suspected that Cree probably knew more than she did. She shrugged and shook her head. "I don't know a lot, Cree. They are tiny crustaceans, found in all the world's oceans, and they are a vital component of the ocean's food chain. My mom says that the rising temperatures of the oceans have killed off a lot of krill in the Antarctic, and scientists are really worried about the repercussions. But beyond that, I don't know much."

Cree brought his chair back to its upright position and leaned forward. "The Antarctic is a problem, yes. Krill are so important, but not only in the Antarctic, in *all* the oceans, because they provide food for so many species. Krill feed on phytoplankton...you know these? They are microscopic—tiny, single-celled plants. The krill eat the phytoplankton, and then hundreds of species eat the krill: fish, birds, seals, and even whales. Some animals *only* eat krill, like blue whales, and birds like shearwaters. So if the krill die, these other large animals cannot just start eating the phytoplankton. They starve to death."

"What happens to the phytoplankton?"

"The phytoplankton are at the bottom of the food chain. They are plants, so they just need sunlight and nutrients to survive. So, they float at the surface of the ocean, to soak up the sunlight. But as the ocean gets warmer, the layers of the ocean do not mix as much, and the phytoplankton do not get the nutrients they need. So they eventually die, too." Cree reached out and stroked the inside of Laena's wrist absent-mindedly. She shivered in pleasure. "I wonder if your Aquarium has krill."

Laena had trouble concentrating on their conversation. "Cree...." she paused, unsure of how to continue. "I...I love it when you touch me. But I can't think straight. My mind goes somewhere else." She blushed, and glanced up at him.

Cree's hand stopped in mid-circle, and then he gave her a lopsided grin. "Maybe we should take a quick break, and let your mind go somewhere else." He encircled her wrist and pulled her out of her chair and over to him. She sat on his lap and melted into his broad chest.

Cree turned her head toward him, and kissed her deeply. She let herself dissolve into his warm mouth, her hands grasping his shoulders. Cree groaned, and Laena felt him shift beneath her.

"Maybe this was not such a good idea," he said. He shifted her weight on his lap and held her by her shoulders. "You drive me crazy," he whispered. "I want to carry you to my bed and make love to you."

Laena blushed furiously, but her heart pounded and warmth coursed through her body.

"Cree...."

"I know, I know. I should not have said that. We are not supposed to be intimate. " He raked his hand through his hair in frustration. "But it is hard for me."

"You don't think it is hard for me?" Laena asked, searching his eyes.

"Of course," he responded. "But you...you are innocent. You do not know what we are missing."

"And you do?" Laena asked sincerely. She found herself wanting to know about Cree's history. After all, he was her age. Lots of kids in the 11th grade were already having sex, but Laena was not one of them. And she certainly didn't know what it was like for teens hundreds of years from now. She was curious.

Cree hesitated. He could tell her question was not rhetorical. "You really want to know?" His voice was hoarse.

Laena nodded. Cree pulled her to him and held her tightly.

"You are asking whether I have sex with girls?" Laena nodded again into his chest.

"Yes, I do," Cree answered softly. Laena felt her chest go tight with jealousy. She stiffened, but Cree held her tightly, and she could not pull away.

"Do not be jealous, Laena. I did not know you until just recently. In my time, there are so few humans...it is difficult for women to get pregnant. When they do, it is something to be celebrated." He paused, searching for the right words. "There are so many miscarriages, and stillbirths. So much is poisoned in our time. And so many of us get sick and die fairly young. In order for humans to survive, we have to reproduce. So sex is encouraged."

"Even between teenagers?" Laena was incredulous.

"Yes, as soon as we are sexually mature, it is okay," Cree responded. "I know it is different now, in your time. And it should be. You have too many people on the earth. But in my time...." He trailed off, his voice sad. He sighed. "If I could take you back with me, we would make a baby." He paused again, and then his voice became playful. "Or at least have fun trying."

Laena didn't know how to respond. His words and his touch excited her, but she knew she wasn't ready for any of this. Cree sensed her confusion and hugged her.

"I am teasing you, sweetie," he said. "Do not worry...I will not do anything that will scare you or hurt you."

Laena pulled away and looked into his eyes. "Does that mean we have to talk about krill again instead?" she asked softly.

Cree roared with laughter. When he finally stopped, he wiped his eyes and said, "No, we do not have to...but we should, no?" His voice became serious. "The future depends on it, Laena. I must figure this out."

Laena nodded solemnly and started to clamber off his lap. "Wait," he murmured, kissing her deeply one last time. "Okay, now you can go sit in your own chair." Laena settled in, missing the warmth of his body. She felt empty without him.

"Where were we?" Cree said, thrumming his fingers on the table. "Oh, right...so are there krill at the Aquarium?"

Laena shook her head. "I honestly don't know, Cree. I'm embarrassed to say I don't know, but I don't." Laena tucked a stray curl behind her ear.

"I would love to go to there...maybe you could take me one of these days?"

"Of course," Laena replied.

"That would be great." Cree rewarded Laena with a big smile, and she couldn't help but smile back. "So, back to what happened. As the temperatures of the oceans rose, this led to a massive decline of krill in the Antarctic."

"But what about in other oceans? You said something else happened besides global warming...."

Cree nodded. "I am getting to that. Because krill are so important to the food chain, and the whole ecosystem, they can affect all the other animals in the ocean. So, once the krill died, it set off a chain reaction that led to a mass extinction, basically, and made it impossible for people to live off of the oceans. And so many people, billions of people, depended on the ocean."

Cree paused, frowning slightly, searching for the right words. "So there is a problem worse than the warming water for the krill. You know about pharmaceuticals? How they are in our water?"

Laena nodded. "You mean medicine? Drugs?" Laena had read about how most of the water that people drank had minute traces of hundreds of medicines. Everything from antibiotics to Viagra to Tylenol. Every time you filled a glass with water from your tap, you were drinking other people's medicines.

"Right," Cree agreed. "It was very bad...but it is very difficult to understand. You know, in your time, that pharmaceuticals are in our water supply, yes? Every time you take a medicine, much of it comes out when you go to the bathroom, and it gets into the rivers, the lakes. And the groundwater. No one knows how to take the compounds out of the water. So the more medicine people take, and the more antibacterial soap and cleaning products they use, the worse the contamination of the water becomes. You understand so far?" Laena nodded, but Cree hesitated.

"Is that what kills all the krill?" Laena prompted. "The drugs in the water?"

Cree grimaced. "It is not that simple. Have you heard of a virophage?"

Laena shook her head, bewildered. "A virophage? What is that?"

"They were just discovered recently, in your time. A virophage is...." Cree struggled to find the words. "I guess it is just like a virus that kills other viruses."

"Okay. But what does that have to do with the pharmaceuticals?" Laena asked.

"It is complicated, so listen closely. There is a virus that destroys krill. It kills them quickly and efficiently. Kind of like a krill flu. But the krill are safe, because there is a virophage that kills the virus. You understand? So the virophage is actually protecting the krill by harming the krill's virus."

Laena nodded. Like a war, with allies. The krill's ally was the virophage, because the virophage killed the krill's enemy, the virus.

"Okay. So, it turns out the virophage is very sensitive to an antibacterial that people in your time put in *everything*. It is in soap, deodorant, shampoo, cleaners, lotions, moisturizers, cutting boards, toothpaste...." Cree trailed off. "It is simply everywhere," he said softly. "Everywhere."

Laena's stomach clenched. "So...so this antibacterial compound in the oceans kills the virophage. And then...then the virus multiplies and kills all the krill?"

Cree nodded, clearly distressed. "Yes. So here is the whole chain of events, from start to finish. The antibacterials in the ocean kill the virophage, which allows the krill virus to flourish. The virus is everywhere now, and it kills all the krill. Once the krill die, the fish, seals, birds, and whales that feed on the krill starve to death. And everything that feeds on those fish, birds, and seals then starve to death, as well. At first, nothing is left except microscopic life, the phytoplankton and zooplankton. But the warming oceans and acidity soon kill them, too, until there is...nothing. There is nothing left."

"When does this happen?" Laena whispers.

"Now, Laena. It is happening now. Your mother is looking into the effects of these antibacterials on the ocean, and on krill, but she does not know about the virophage. "

"So...we need to stop it somehow? Or get my mother to see the effects the antibacterial has on the virophage?"

Cree nodded. "And then, of course, it will be up to your mother to get the politicians to pay attention to the problem. Or at the very least, the Environmental Protection Agency. Your mother is a prominent scientist, so I am hoping they will listen to her. She will have to get these antibacterials in soap and other products banned. And, this has to be done *without* your mother knowing who I am or why I am here. I am afraid that if people learn I am from the future, all the attention will be on me, not on the problem of the oceans. They will be so consumed with asking me questions about time travel, about the future, that the real problem will get lost. And we do not have that kind of time. How do we do this, Laena? How do we get her to see what will happen?"

Laena looked at Cree. He leaned forward on the scarred wooden table, his eyes intently searching hers. Laena shrugged. "I don't know, Cree. I just don't know. But we'll figure it out. We don't have a lot of choice, do we?'

Cree's expression was grim. "No, Laena. We do not have a lot of choice. But I am not even sure what to do next."

Laena looked into Cree's deep blue eyes. His black hair was mussed, and his dark lashes made his eyes pop with intensity. Her mind raced. She glanced around the small, bare cabin, and the paucity of Cree's belongings, considering...then she reached out and grasped Cree's hand. "I think I have an idea."

* * *

Laena and Cree ate lunch in Cree's cabin, and Laena explained her plan while they ate. If they could convince Michelle that Cree needed another job, and get her to hire Cree as a research assistant at CCOL, he could run the experiments to prove that the antibacterials were—indirectly—killing the krill. They were tying up loose ends and looking for holes in their plan, but Laena's nerves jangled. She had no idea whether they could trick her mother into doing what they wanted without exposing Cree, and opening themselves up to having Cree investigated by scientists and security experts. Laena thought his concerns were valid—if the government thought they had a real time traveler on their hands, Cree would be whisked away and questioned for a long time. They couldn't afford to risk it...the fact that Cree was from the future *had* to remain a secret. Finally, Laena wanted to get outside and walk off some of her nervous energy, and Cree agreed they should get out of the cabin. They walked hand in hand to the beach.

The sun was warm, but the wind was cool. It got windier as they got closer to the water, and Cree put his arm around Laena to keep her warm. The tide was low, and despite the cold, Laena took off her shoes and socks and rolled up her pants. Cree followed her lead. They headed toward the water's edge, leaving their socks and shoes on the dry sand by the large piece of driftwood. Laena shivered as she stepped into the firm, wet sand, an expanding oblong of dry sand radiating out wherever she stepped.

"Why does it do that?" she asked, wonder in her voice, pointing at her feet. "Look, Cree, have you ever noticed? Wherever you step at low tide, the sand looks dry around your foot. But when you lift your foot to take another step, it gets wet again." Laena shook her head. "I've been watching this all my life, but I never really figured out why it happens."

Cree laughed. "I have never seen that before," he said. "It is like your foot pushes the water out of the sand around your step."

Laena looked at him curiously. "Don't you walk on the beaches in Alaska?" she asked, almost afraid to hear the answer.

Cree shook his head, never looking up from his feet. He placed his foot in the sand, picked it up, and then put it down again, fascinated by the phenomenon. "We have no beaches," he said matter-of-factly.

"No beaches?" Laena asked in horror.

"No," he responded nonchalantly, "no beaches."

Laena grabbed Cree's wrist. "What do you mean, no beaches?"

He looked up at her frantic tone, puzzled. Then he saw her face, and frowned. "I am sorry, Laena. I forget sometimes...."

"What do you mean, no beaches?" she repeated, insistent.

"The seas...they rose, and the beaches were flooded. There is no sand, no beach like this." He paused, then added helpfully, "We have rocks."

"Rocks," Laena echoed, hollowly.

Cree nodded. "Yes, rocks. Rocky areas...I guess they are kind of like beaches."

Laena was silent. No beaches. But Cree had already moved on. He continued to examine his feet in the wet sand. "I think the pressure from our weight displaces the water from the sand, and it looks dry. Then, when we raise our feet, and the pressure is removed, the water floods back in...."

"Cree," Laena said sharply. He looked up, startled at her tone. "Yes?"

"I'm a little upset...can you help me here?"

"What?" He shook his head as if to clear it, confused.

"Are there beaches anywhere? Sandy beaches, I mean?"

"Oh." He stayed silent for a moment, reflecting. "No, I do not think so. Not that I know of, anyway...but maybe somewhere...."

Laena sighed. She couldn't wrap her brain around any of this. Could it really be true? Or was Cree just crazy? Or pulling her leg? Cree had moved out toward the water's edge, leaning over a tide pool. "Laena!" he cried excitedly. "Come here! Hurry! What is this?"

Laena walked out next to him and peered into the small pool of water. She laughed. "That's a horseshoe crab, Cree. Just a horseshoe crab."

He kneeled down, his pants getting soaked from the wet sand. "Can I touch it?" he whispered. "Can I pick it up?"

"Of course," Laena said, squatting next to him. "They don't bite, even though they look pretty prehistoric and scary...." But he hesitated, scared to touch it. She reached over and picked up the large creature by the sides of its shell. "Hold out your hands," she instructed.

Cree took the crab reverently. He had a grin on is face like a little boy, and his eyes sparkled. "It is amazing," Cree said softly. He reached out and gently poked the tail. The horseshoe crab tried to scuttle out of Cree's grasp, and he released it back into the pool. "What a strange creature," he murmured.

"Very strange. And their blood is actually blue. Not red, like ours. Blue!" Laena revealed.

"No!" Cree exclaimed. "Blue blood?" He laughed in delight.

While Cree studied the critters in the tide pools, Laena turned her face up to the sun. A movement caught her eye. Something rustled in the cattails. She peered intently, unsure. It looked like a person—a tall, slender girl with black hair. A tremor went through Laena. She'd seen this girl before—where? The girl stared at them. She made Laena extremely uncomfortable. What was she doing there?

"Cree...." Laena said, tugging on his arm.

"Mmmm.... ?" Cree did not look up.

"Cree! Do you know that girl?"

Cree's head jerked up. "What girl?" he asked.

Laena pointed to the cattails, but by the time Cree turned to see where she was pointing, the mysterious girl had disappeared. Cree looked at Laena, puzzled.

"There was someone there," Laena insisted. "I...I keep seeing her. I think...." She trailed off, unsure.

"I do not know many people here, Laena. Certainly no one that you do not already know. But tell me if you see her again." Cree went back to his explorations.

Maybe she had imagined it. Laena sighed and turned to watch Cree look at shells in the tide pool. She was still blown away about how much Cree didn't know. They spent the next hour walking the small beach, Laena identifying all the creatures for Cree. He was mesmerized. When the tide started coming back in, they retreated to their piece of driftwood, stretching out their legs to dry their jeans in the sun. There was a hint of spring in the air, and the sun finally felt warm. The red-winged blackbirds sang from the cattails, and Cree called back to them, mimicking their calls incredibly well.

Cree took a deep breath and exhaled. "Thank you," he said softly, taking Laena's hand in his and caressing it.

"For what?"

"For showing me all these wonderful things here at the beach. For bringing me back to this place...our special place. For trusting me, and being my friend."

Laena smiled. "You don't have to thank me for that...I...I love being with you." Laena looked down at the sand in embarrassment and her curls obscured her face. Cree reached over and took her face in his hands, forcing her to look at him.

"Why are you embarrassed for saying such a simple thing?" he asked gently. "Are you still uncomfortable around me?"

Laena looked into his eyes and blushed. "I am, a little," she admitted. "I'm not quite sure how to act around you, or...or what our relationship is...."

Cree pulled Laena to him and she laid her head on his broad chest. "Do we have to define our relationship, or even articulate it?" Cree asked.

Laena was silent.

"Laena?" Cree persisted.

"I suppose not," she admitted. "But I would feel better if I understood. I think."

Cree chuckled. "Okay, then. Let's see...we are friends, and you are helping me do something very important. And, we have feelings for each other, feelings that I would most certainly act upon if we lived in my time. But in your time, we must be more cautious, and therefore I must be careful with you."

Laena looked up at him. "Is that how you see it? That you have to be careful with me?"

"Yes, of course," Cree said, frowning slightly. "I do not want to hurt you, or make your parents angry."

"Sometimes...no, *most* of the time, I don't want you to be careful with me, Cree. I want you to treat me the way you would normally treat a girl." Her eyes searched his.

"Ah, Laena," he said sadly. "Do not tempt me." He sighed, stroking her cheek absent-mindedly. "I think we have to concentrate on putting our plan into effect, no?"

Laena sighed. "Yes, you're right," she said wearily. "I'm sorry to be so selfish."

Cree shook his head. "You are not selfish. It is natural, what you feel. What we both feel. I would rather spend my days with you, talking about things and getting to know you, and making love to you. But in the scheme of things, that is foolish. We need to do something much more important. Something bigger than both of us. It would be...." Cree searched for the right word. "Sinful. It would be sinful, a tragedy, to satisfy our own needs while ignoring the plight of the Earth."

Laena nodded. "No worse sin," she agreed.

Cree stood up and pulled Laena to her feet. "Then we agree. Work now, fun later. Let us put our plan in motion."

Laena smiled grimly, and they set off back toward home.

* * *

"I'm home!" Laena called, slamming the front door behind her. She dropped her backpack full of books on the floor.

"In the kitchen!" Michelle called.

Laena kicked off her sandy shoes and socks padded into the kitchen barefoot. Michelle punched down freshly risen bread dough, and the kitchen smelled of yeast.

Michelle glanced at the clock. "Right on time. Did you have fun?"

"Mmmm-hmmm," Laena said, grabbing an olive out of a bowl on the counter. Michelle nudged her hand away.

"The olives are for the bread," she explained, laughing. "If you're hungry, grab a piece of fruit."

Laena opened the refrigerator and perused the shelves. She grabbed some carrot sticks and a container of homemade hummus, shutting the door with her hip.

"Didn't you eat lunch?"

"Kinda," Laena responded, putting the food on the kitchen table. "But Cree doesn't have a lot of food in his cabin. He hardly had anything." She paused, glancing at her mother through the corner of her eyes to see if her comment had registered. "And after we finished our homework, we went to the beach and explored the tide pools. We did a lot of walking, and being outside got me hungry." Laena dipped a carrot stick in the hummus and munched on it.

"That sounds nice," Michelle said absent-mindedly. She put the bread dough in an oiled pan, pressed in the olives, and popped it into the warm oven. She wiped her hands on the kitchen towel and turned to face Laena.

"So, nothing to worry about?"

"I'm not even going to dignify that with an answer, Mom," Laena said, casting her mother an angry, sideways glance. She grabbed another carrot and munched it thoughtfully. "You know, Cree is really interested in marine biology."

"Good for him!" Michelle said, reaching over to grab a carrot for herself. "Dad says he's a good student."

"Mmmm," Laena murmured. She swallowed. "Funny, he's interested in the effects of pharmaceuticals on marine life," Laena said, trying to sound blasé. "Especially antibacterials." Her heart thudded in her chest.

"Really," Michelle murmured in response, carrot paused halfway to her mouth. "What a coincidence."

"Yeah, I thought so, too," Laena said. She chanced looking at her mother. "You should really give him a tour of CCOL. He'd *love* that. I mean, he's really into this stuff. He said he wants to work there someday. You know, after college."

Michelle was silent. Uh-oh, Laena worried. Had she gone too far? Was she being too obvious? Michelle chewed her carrot slowly, her thoughts somewhere far away from the kitchen.

"Mom?" Laena peered into her mother's face. "Are you listening to me?"

Michelle shook herself slightly. "Sorry, honey. Guess my mind wandered." She moved to the kitchen table and sat down. Laena joined her.

"So, does Cree get along okay? I mean, does the fact that he didn't have much food in the cabin mean he doesn't eat enough? Or is he just short on supplies?" She paused. "I guess what I'm really asking is whether the campground job is enough?"

Laena shook her head. "I don't know. I think it's kinda a touchy subject for him. His cabin is pretty sparse. He doesn't have much, and his cupboards were really bare. But he eats lunch at school, so he gets a full meal there." Laena wondered if she was overdoing it. She continued anyway. "He's proud, you know? Doesn't want to accept help. He...he likes to work for things. He says he's going to look for another job as soon as school lets out."

Michelle looked at Laena sharply. "Do you think I should call Social Services.... ?"

"Oh, God, Mom, no!" Laena blurted. "No, no. He's fine. He eats plenty. I mean...." Laena stammered in confusion. "He doesn't have money for extras, but he's not starving! He would hate to go live with strangers. He's an emancipated minor."

Michelle nodded. "Okay, okay, I won't do anything rash. I just want to make sure he's not hurting for anything."

"Once he gets another job, he'll be fine," Laena said. Her hands were literally shaking. Had she blown it? Was her mother going to call in the authorities?

Michelle stood up from the table. "Well, dinner is in the oven, should be ready around six. I'm going to go relax a little. Clean up your snack, will you Laena?" She swept out of the kitchen without waiting for an answer.

"Crap, crap, crap...." Laena muttered. She put the cap back on the tub of hummus, snapped the lid back on the container of carrots, and put them both back in the fridge. She hoped to hell she hadn't overdone it and ruined everything. She had no choice now but to wait and see what her mother did.

Chapter 6

FOR THE FIRST TIME that she could remember, Laena took care with what she wore to school. She tried on several outfits, discarding them disgustedly when they did not meet her standards. Finally, she decided on a pair of tight, strategically ripped jeans, a form hugging, soft, faded black Woodstock tee, and a charcoal gray zip up hoodie. She slipped into her boots, and threw some antique bangles on her wrist that her mother had brought back from Hong Kong. Laena studied her reflection in the full-length mirror. She tilted her head, examining herself critically. She sighed. She would never be as sexy as Cat, or as classically pretty as Sophie. And Sophie...lucky Sophie had finally snagged Mike. She had texted last night, telling Laena that Mike had finally made a move. Laena was happy for her, but she wasn't surprised. Sophie had never had trouble getting a boyfriend.

Today, Laena felt different. Hopeful that maybe she could find love, too. She knew that she wasn't like all the other girls, but that was okay. She went downstairs to grab her backpack with a bounce in her step.

Both her parents had already left for work, so Laena locked the front door behind her. The day held a promise of warmth to come, and Laena breathed the spring air greedily. She couldn't wait until she could dispense with her sweatshirts, and go swimming in the bay. She glanced at the time on her cell phone. She was actually early this morning. A first.

Laena got as far as the General Store when her skin tingled. She looked up, and her heart lurched as she saw Cree walk into the store's sandy parking lot. He gave Laena a huge grin. She smiled back and bounded over to greet him.

"Hi!" she said. "What are you doing here?" Her heart fluttered at the sight of him.

"I thought I would walk with you the rest of the way to school," Cree said, leaning over and giving her a soft kiss on the cheek. "Is that okay?"

"Of course!" Laena exclaimed, thrilled that he had thought to meet her. "But it's only like...100 yards down the road."

"I know. But this way, I get to hold your hand for those 100 yards."

Laena flushed and fell into step next to him.

All eyes were upon them as they walked into the school lot. Laena looked down, pretending to fiddle with the strap on her backpack, trying to hide her embarrassment at the unwanted attention from the other kids. She could almost hear them whispering and giggling.

Cree watched Laena's discomfort with a small frown.

"Why do you let them bother you?" he asked under his breath. He moved closer to her and grasped her elbow. "Are you embarrassed to be with me?"

Laena looked up sharply. "No!" she exclaimed. "No, Cree...it's not that at all."

"Then what is it?" he murmured, pulling her closer.

Laena sighed. "I can hear them...well, I can hear them in my mind. 'What's a guy like him doing with a loser like her?' "

Cree's frown deepened. "That is not what they are saying," he replied. "You are not a loser. They are probably saying...they are saying, 'Wow, what a lucky guy to have snagged Laena Foster. I wish I had her as my girlfriend.' "

Laena's heart thudded at his use of the word 'girlfriend.' She smiled and looked up at him. "Is that what I am? Your girlfriend?"

Cree didn't answer. He looked into her eyes for what seemed like an eternity, then bent down and kissed her deeply on the lips. Laena's body thrummed in response, and she twined her arms around him. She no longer heard the whispering and giggling. Instead, all she heard was the beating of both their hearts, and the blood rushing through her veins.

When Cree finally pulled away, he smiled. "No. You are not my girlfriend, Laena. You are my soul mate."

Laena melted. Cree put his arm around her possessively.

"Never let those fools make you question yourself," he said softly. "I do not care what they think, and neither should you."

Laena nodded mutely, and they walked into the school together, arm in arm. She felt the stares, but she no longer cared. As they walked down the hallway toward their lockers, Sophie approached them from behind.

"Laena! Cree!" she called. They stopped and turned.

"Hi, Sophie," Laena said, smiling. Sophie gave Laena a hug, and rewarded Cree with a big smile.

"I guess you guys had an interesting weekend," Sophie said, laughing.

Laena looked away, embarrassed, but Sophie punched her playfully. "Oh, Laena, don't be such a prude. I'm glad you guys are together. You make a cute couple."

Cree smiled at Sophie, thanking her with his eyes. Sophie put a hand on her slim hip, and looked from one to the other. "Okay, here's the deal. Now that you guys are obviously together, you *have* to come to the Spring Fling." She flipped her straight hair out of her face and smiled beseechingly. Laena groaned at the thought of the upcoming dance.

"Please?" Sophie asked.

"What is a Spring Fling?" Cree asked, confused.

"It's the spring dance. It's this Friday, right here at the school. The juniors sponsor it, but all the grades are invited. It's a semi, so you have to dress up, and we get a good DJ, and it's really fun." Sophie's eyes danced with excitement. Just then, Mike walked up and put his arm around Sophie.

"Hey, guys," he said.

"Mike, you gotta help me. I'm trying to talk Laena and Cree into going to the spring fling."

"Definitely—you have to go. It's going to be great!" Mike said enthusiastically. "I'm taking Sophie," he added, glancing at her shyly.

Cree shook his head in confusion. "I do not know what a 'semi' is, or what a 'DJ' is...."

Sophie laughed. "Cree, you are such a loser sometimes! Semi means you dress up. Not like the prom, with tuxes and full-length gowns, but a tie, and short dresses. You know...." She trailed off as the confusion on Cree's face remained.

Laena stepped in. "It just means you have to dress up a little. You know, no jeans or the stuff we usually wear to school. And a DJ stands for disc jockey, which I guess is a pretty old-fashioned term. It's just someone who plays the music so the kids can dance." She turned to Sophie and Mike. "But I don't think we're going, Sophie. Thanks anyway. You know how much I hate dances."

"Why do you hate dances?" Cree asked. "And why are you saying no? It sounds like fun. I have never been to one of these." He smiled mischievously.

"That's the spirit, Cree!" Sophie said, delighted. "Good. I'll count you two in. I'll bring the tickets to lunch today. See ya!" She grabbed Mike's hand and bounded off before Laena could argue.

Laena turned to Cree, disbelief on her face. "Cree, those dances are awful! I *really* don't want to go."

Cree smiled. "Maybe you have not enjoyed them because you have not gone with someone like me," he said. "Come on. We will have fun together."

Laena frowned. "I don't have anything to wear. And you probably don't either."

"That is a problem that is easily remedied."

"Cree...." Laena groaned.

"We are going," Cree pronounced. "It will be our first real date."

The bell rang, and Laena sighed in exasperation. "We'll have to talk about this later. We're gonna be late for class."

Cree smiled, victorious.

* * *

At lunchtime, Laena detoured to the faculty lunchroom on her way to the cafeteria. She had forgotten her lunch, and she wanted to borrow some money from her dad to get a salad at the salad bar. She had spent so much time this morning worrying about what to wear, and what she looked like, she had forgotten to pack a sandwich. Now she understood why some of her friends woke up an hour before school started. This girl stuff was time consuming.

The faculty lunchroom door stood ajar, and she knocked on it firmly before pushing it open. Her father sat at the conference table, his lunch spread out in front of him, next to two other teachers. They were all fixated on the small LCD television hanging from the wall in the corner. The television was tuned to CNN.

"Dad?" Laena asked.

Three voices said, "Shhh!" simultaneously.

Laena looked up at the CNN newscaster on the screen. Behind him were scenes of watery devastation. All Laena could see was murky ocean, muddy palm trees, and destroyed homes, streets, and cars.

Laena walked up behind her father's chair and crouched down, whispering in his ear. "What happened?" She saw his lunch, untouched, spread out in front of him.

Ben answered without taking his eyes off the television. "A tsunami in the Caribbean," he whispered back. "Horrible—it reminds me of what happened in Malaysia. And Japan."

Laena straightened up, her blood running cold. She watched the television with dread.

"The tsunami appears to have been triggered by an earthquake on the neighboring island of Dominica," the newscaster said soberly. "Dominica is one of the most volcanically active places in the world, having nine of the Caribbean's 11 active volcanoes. The earthquake that shook this sleepy island awake early this morning is what we call a 'volcanic earthquake,' and it resulted in a huge chunk of mountain crashing into the sea. The tsunami hit the neighboring beaches of Guadeloupe, killing dozens—or more—in the low-lying seaside villages. There are reports of missing American tourists. CNN will continue its coverage as we learn more."

Ben hit the mute button on the remote control as the television station moved to a commercial break. He turned to Laena. "Did you need something from me, honey?"

"I...I came to borrow some money. I forgot my lunch. And I need some money for tickets to the dance."

Ben reached silently for his wallet. Laena held up a palm up in protest. "Dad, I'm not really hungry anymore. I'm okay...I don't need anything."

"Don't be ridiculous," Ben said, handing her several bills. "You have to eat." He looked at her closely. "Are you feeling all right, Laena? You look pale."

Laena motioned half-heartedly toward the television. "The...the news. It's upsetting. I'm fine."

"You sure? Do you want to sit down for a minute?"

The other two teachers were looking at her curiously. Laena smiled. "Really, I'm fine. Thanks for the money, Dad." Laena mustered what she hoped passed as a cheerful wave, and left the faculty lunchroom. As she shut the door behind her, her knees went weak.

Laena was truly shaken. Cree was right! He could not possibly have known about the tsunami two days ago. This proved that he was telling the truth. He *was* from the future. Laena felt like she was in shock, but she was also scared. How was *she* supposed to help? How could she, a 17-year old from Cape Cod, Massachusetts, make a difference? And what did this mean for them, for their relationship? Without being conscious of where she was going, she found herself in the cafeteria. She stopped, dazed, in the doorway. Cree materialized at her side, his arm around her. She stiffened.

"Laena? What's the matter? What happened?" His voice was worried, his face etched with concern.

"The tsunami," she whispered. "It happened." Her hair fell, tangled over her face, and she pushed it to the side, bewildered. Her bracelets jangled on her wrist.

Cree relaxed. "I am sorry," he said. He shook his head. "You scared me. You looked like you had seen a ghost."

Laena looked at him curiously. "Cree...don't you understand? I am seeing a ghost. You. You don't really exist, do you? Not in my time. Not now." Her voice was hollow.

Cree grabbed her more firmly and steered her out the cafeteria door. "Come," he said urgently. "We are going for a walk."

Laena tried to resist, but she couldn't form the words, and her body did not have the strength to fight him. She felt the eyes of the other students on her, but she didn't care. Cree walked her steadily out of the cafeteria and through the front doors of the school.

"We're not supposed to leave," she protested feebly. "We'll get in trouble."

"We are not going anywhere," Cree said reassuringly. "I am just getting you some fresh air."

He brought her to a picnic table under the branches of an old oak tree next to the parking lot. Laena sank gratefully onto the bench. Cree sat next to her, his arm still firmly around her.

"How are you feeling?" he asked, peering into her eyes. When she didn't answer, he said, "I am not a ghost, Laena. I am real flesh and blood. Look...." He brought his hands to her cheeks, cupping her face. "Can you not feel that I am real? I am as real as you."

Laena shook her head. She felt numb. "You *are* from the future," she whispered. "It's real."

"Of course it is real," Cree said, lowering his voice to match hers. "But you knew that. I promised I would not lie to you, and I am not lying. I told you about the tsunami because I wanted to prove to you that I came here from the future. So...this should come as no real surprise to you." His eyes were confused and concerned.

Laena twisted her face out of his hands. "No, it is not a surprise. But I understand better now. In a way you aren't real. You can't really be here...you aren't even born yet." She felt a million emotions tear through her. "I was wrong, Cree. I don't understand." A cool wind blew, whipping her hair into her face. Cree gently pushed her hair out of the way.

"I know it is confusing, Laena. I will try to explain time travel to you better. But not now. People will be wondering what is wrong with you." He glanced uneasily toward the doors of the school. As if on cue, the doors swung open and the principal headed their way.

"Laena," Cree murmured. "You need to pull yourself together."

Laena glanced over and saw the principal, Mr. Harrison, striding toward them purposefully, his suit jacket flapping with each step. He was in his early 50s, but had a trim runner's body. He had a frown on his face that Laena could see all the way from the picnic table. "I'm fine," she said to Cree. Mr. Harrison reached them in no time.

"Laena, Cree," Mr. Harrison said, towering over them at the picnic table. "What are you doing out here?" He looked from one to the other sternly.

"I am so sorry, Mr. Harrison," Cree said, standing up. "Laena felt faint...I just brought her outside to get some fresh air."

The principal frowned even more deeply. "You may be relatively new here, Cree, and not know the rules. But Laena, I am surprised at you. If you aren't feeling well, you should go to the nurse. You cannot leave the school building before the final bell." He motioned for Laena to stand up. "I'm just giving you a warning today. Don't let it happen again."

Laena stood up. "I'm much better now," she said, her voice stronger. "I forgot my lunch and I'm just a little shaky."

"Well, go get yourself something," Mr. Harrison said crossly. "You teenagers have to learn to eat properly. Hurry now, before the cafeteria closes."

Laena nodded. "I will, thank you." Laena and Cree headed toward the school, and Mr. Harrison followed. Cree steered Laena back toward the cafeteria. Once they crossed into the cavernous room, Cree said, "Go sit down. I will get you a salad."

"I can get it myself," Laena said curtly. Then she softened her tone. "I'm sorry, Cree. Sorry to be so bitchy. But I can take care of myself. I can get a salad without your help." She walked away from him and handed the five-dollar bill to the cashier at the end of the cafeteria line. "Salad bar, please."

The cashier rung up the purchase and handed Laena her change. "Better hurry, hon. We're about to start putting things away." Laena took the change and nodded. She felt numb, and not at all hungry, but she knew she should eat something. She blindly piled things on her plate from the salad bar, and headed back to the table where Cree waited for her. All the other kids had finished lunch, and were watching her curiously. Robb Berger and Greg Nelson were snickering.

"You okay, Laena?" Sophie asked.

"Yeah, I'm fine. Just tired, I guess," Laena replied. She toyed with her fork and the food on her plate. Cree watched her, a frown on his face. She could tell he wanted to say something, but he remained silent.

"You'd better hurry, Laena. The bell is gonna ring soon," Sophie said, her voice still tinged with concern. "Are you sure you're okay?"

"Maybe...a little nauseous, Laena?" Cat asked sarcastically. When her meaning sunk in, kids at the table tittered uncomfortably. Robb roared with laughter, and Greg joined in. Cat smiled at them prettily.

Cree pushed his chair back and stood up, towering over Robb and Greg. Anger emanated from every pore. Mike stood up and grabbed Cree. "Ignore them, Cree. Don't do anything stupid. They're not worth it," he murmured. Cree was much bigger than Mike, but Mike's words had the desired effect. Cree sat back down slowly, glaring at Cat.

Laena looked coldly at Cat. "No need to worry about me, Cat. *I'm* not stupid enough to get in that kind of trouble."

Cat straightened up, her perfectly plucked eyebrows knitted together. "Are you implying that I —"

"Stop it, both of you!" Sophie yelled. "For God's sake, Cat, can't you be nice to anyone? Leave Laena alone. It's so obvious that you're jealous of her and Cree being together. Just grow up!"

Cat stood up, her chair screeching on the cafeteria floor. "Jealous? Me? I don't think so." She grabbed her books and tossed her hair over her shoulder. "Cree is a weirdo. He and Laena deserve each other." She turned and stalked out of the cafeteria. An uncomfortable silence descended on the table. Kids started gathering up their belongings and bringing their trays back to the kitchen. Mike stood up to leave and Cree reached out to stop him, his hand on Mike's arm.

"Thanks," Cree said quietly. Mike nodded and gave Cree a small smile, then walked away. Soon the only people left were Laena, Cree and Sophie.

Laena had managed to choke down about a quarter of her salad. She looked up, tears welling in her eyes. "Thanks for supporting me, Sophie, but really, I can take care of myself."

"Uh-huh," Sophie said sarcastically. "I have never seen you on such an emotional roller-coaster." She slammed two tickets to the Spring Fling on the table. "Here are your tickets. You can pay me later." She stood up and turned to Cree. "If you hurt her, Cree McNeil, you'll have to answer to me." She whirled and stomped out of the cafeteria, her hair swinging with every step.

Cree and Laena looked at each other. "Well," Cree said, solemnly, "that was a fun lunch." After a brief pause, Laena burst out laughing, and Cree joined in. They were still laughing when the bell rang for the next period.

* * *

When the last bell of the day had rung, Laena gathered her books from her locker and headed toward the main doors. Jarred from behind, Laena stumbled. Cat brushed by, her cloying perfume wafting behind her. Laena opened her mouth to say something, but decided it wasn't worth it. Cat would get bored with torturing her.

Sophie walked up beside Laena and shook her head at Cat's retreating back. "Just ignore her. Really, she's just jealous." She linked arms with Laena. "Are you feeling better?"

"I am feeling better, thanks." Laena lied. She stopped abruptly and rooted through her backpack. "Wait, Sophie. I have your money. For the tickets." She handed Sophie a $20 bill. "This is for me and Cree."

Sophie squealed and took the money. "I'm *so* glad you guys are coming!" She gave Laena a brief hug and ran off.

As Laena walked down the stairs, she saw Cree waiting. He leaned against the wall of the school, his arms crossed over his chest. He looked angry, his brow creased. She took a deep breath—even angry, he was very handsome. She watched him for a moment, until he turned and saw her. The frown disappeared, and a smile lit up his face.

"Hey," Cree said. "Want me to walk you home?"

Laena smiled despite herself. "Yours or mine?" she teased.

"Either one," Cree replied. "We can do homework. And then talk.... ?" He looked at her hopefully, and Laena knew he wanted to talk about how to reach her mother and influence her research. Her heart sank a little, wondering once again whether Cree stayed with her for her, or because of her mother. She banished the thought from her mind. He had promised her, no more lies.

"How about my house?" Laena suggested. "I probably have more food than you, and I'm starving."

"Sounds good," Cree responded. "Will your parents be okay with it?"

Laena shrugged. "You know what, Cree? I don't really care."

Cree laughed. "I am not so sure that is a good thing," he said. Laena ignored his comment and put her arm around his waist.

A few minutes later they were at Laena's house. Laena unlocked the door and stepped inside. Cree shut the door behind him, and then grabbed her from behind.

"Wait," he said huskily. He turned Laena toward him and took her in his arms. "How are you doing? You are better than before?"

Laena nodded. "A little numb, I think, but I'm okay." She paused looking into his eyes. "This is all a little...disconcerting. I'm sorry about how I acted earlier. I was pretty freaked out."

"No worries," Cree said. "You are actually handling this very well, considering how difficult it may be to grasp. I told you a lot of things that are hard to believe."

Laena nodded again. Unexpectedly, she felt a wave of sympathy for Cree wash through her. Here he was, in a strange world, trying to do something noble, and she gave him crap constantly. She reached up and pulled Cree's mouth down to her own, kissing him hungrily. He responded, and Laena pushed her body up against his.

Cree pulled away, breathing hard. "Laena...." He took a deep breath. "You do not seem numb to me."

Laena pulled him back toward her. "I don't think I'm numb anymore," she whispered, and began kissing him again.

"Wait," Cree said. He took her by the hand and led her farther into the house. They sat on the couch, and he took her hands in his. "Laena, you have to be careful with me."

She cocked her head, confused. "Careful?"

Cree nodded, and gave her a sad smile. "You are giving me mixed signals, sweetie. You do not want to be intimate with me, to really be with me, but if that is the case...you cannot kiss me like that, and rub up against me."

Laena blushed. "I'm sorry," she said, mortified.

"No, do not be sorry! I just want you to understand. When you do that, it makes me want more from you."

"But I want more, too," Laena said.

Cree sighed. "There is a point where I may not be able to turn back," Cree explained softly.

Laena ran her hand through her curls. She looked down. "I'm sorry," she said again.

"No!" Cree said. "There is no reason for you to apologize. I should be apologizing to you." He rubbed his hand across his face and stood up, and started pacing the room. "I come from a different time, a different place, where what is right and wrong is atypical for you. It is not what you have learned here. It is almost like we are from different countries."

"Different worlds," Laena said quietly.

Cree nodded his assent. "Yes, different worlds."

"How do we reconcile that?" Laena asked. "Will we ever be able to understand each other?"

Cree nodded slowly. "I think so, yes. With time." He sighed. "But right now, we are running out of time. I need to figure out how to stop the death of the krill, Laena. And I need your help." Cree pulled Laena up to her feet. "So, let's get our homework out of the way, so I can pretend that I am nothing more than a student, and then work on how to save the world." He smiled bitterly. "I would give anything to be just a teenager with you. To have no worries, no tasks, no burdens. I have dragged you into this awful world of mine, and for that I am sorry."

Laena shook her head sorrowfully. "It's my world, too, Cree. Or it's about to be." Cree took her hand and squeezed it gently.

They headed into the kitchen without speaking, Laena leading the way. Cree settled in at the kitchen table and spread out his books. Laena pulled out a fruit salad from the refrigerator, and sprinkled some walnuts and dried cranberries on top. She spooned out a bowl for each of them, then sat down at the table next to Cree. He smiled his thanks and started eating.

"Laena, I know this is a stupid question, but...what is this?" Cree peered into his bowl.

"What is what?" Laena asked, leaning over and looking into his bowl.

"This...orange fruit."

Laena would have laughed if it weren't so sad. "The orange fruit, as you call it, is a mango. It is from the tropics."

Cree tentatively placed the mango in his mouth. As he chewed, he closed his eyes and smiled. "Oh, that is good...." he said sensuously.

"My favorite fruit," Laena agreed, eating some of her own. "I suppose you've never had them...."

Cree shook his head. "No," he replied. We have apples, berries, pears and grapes."

"That's *it?*" Laena asked. "Those are the only fruits? Do you have bananas?"

Cree shook his head. "No bananas. But I have had those here. They are good, too."

"You are so deprived," Laena said.

"What do you mean?" Cree cocked his head and took another forkful of fruit.

"Deprived because you have so little variety."

"I am shocked at the variety you do have," Cree responded, a little defensively. "How do you ever make decisions, with so many choices?"

Laena didn't answer. She thought about what he said. "I guess," she said slowly, "that we choose what we like best. But the variety we have is irresponsible, isn't it? I mean, so much of our food comes from so far away...."

Cree nodded. "Yes, in my time, we can only eat what we can grow. Or what we find."

Laena had a hard time comprehending the kind of life Cree led. So few people, limited food, very little electricity, and hardly any species left...it sounded scary and depressing. She felt sorry for him, but knew her pity was misplaced. She and her contemporaries forced Cree to live that way. It was her fault! Why were humans so selfish and short-sighted?

"I feel awful that we left you with an earth that is so...limited. So polluted."

Cree put down his fork and grasped her hand. "It is not your fault." He paused, and then said slowly, "The Iroquois had a saying. They said, 'In our every deliberation, we must consider the impact of our decisions on the next seven generations.' That was not done in your time, or the years after you. People knew about climate change, about extinction of species and overpopulation, but no one had the political will to do anything about it. People said that it showed great arrogance to think that humans could alter the world so much. They thought only God had the power to do something so devastating."

Laena shook her head. "We are so ignorant...." she murmured.

"And indifferent," Cree added. "What is happening now around the world...floods in the Phillipines and Thailand, Ebola in west Africa, famine and suffering...everyone in the developed countries lives as if none of that is happening. I don't understand." He paused again. "In my time, each human life is sacred, because we are at risk of going extinct. Now our own species is suffering from the same fate we imposed on every other species."

Laena remained silent. It was so distressing! At that moment, she knew that she had to help Cree do whatever it took to alter the course of the future. If they could.

Chapter 7

LAENA OPENED THE DOOR to Cree's smiling face. She couldn't help but smile back. He had found a pair of black dress pants and a white button down shirt. She noticed that the cuffs were slightly frayed—the shirt must be used. He wore a tie, but no jacket. He had slicked back his hair, still wet from the shower. He looked gorgeous.

"Why are you smiling?" Cree asked, reaching out to take Laena's hands.

"You look very handsome," Laena responded.

Cree looked down at his clothes. "I hope these are appropriate...I did not know if this was going to be okay...." He trailed off and looked up hopefully.

"You look perfect," Laena reassured him. She knew the other boys would be wearing suits, but she didn't care. Her own dress was probably not up to par either. She wore a forest green dress, tight in the bodice, somewhat low cut, then flowing chiffon to just above her knees. Her long curly hair flowed loose except for a small braid pinned to the back on one side of her head. She even wore heels.

"And you look beautiful," Cree said, looking her up and down. "But there is one thing that will make you look even more beautiful...." He trailed off, and removed something from his pocket. Something glittered in his hands, catching the light from the hall and twinkling. He reached up and fastened a necklace around Laena's neck.

Laena gasped. "Cree...it's gorgeous!" She fingered the pendant on the gold chain. The deep green gem was cradled by an intricate gold filigree setting. It matched Laena's dress perfectly, and hung in the hollow between her breasts, radiating warmth.

"Where did you get this? How did you know.... ?"

"That you would be wearing green?" Cree finished for her. "I have my ways." He appraised her, his eyes traveling up and down her body hungrily. "You look unbelievable."

"Thank you," Laena said, warmth coursing through her body as his eyes devoured her. "I love the necklace. You know, we don't have to go to the dance. We could just walk along the beach, maybe have a picnic...."

Cree laughed. "You are a coward!" he teased. "We are going to this dance, and we are going to socialize and have fun. Okay?"

Laena sighed. "Okay," she agreed reluctantly. "But if it really sucks, can we leave?"

"I promise," Cree said solemnly. "If it really...what is the word you used? Sucks? If it sucks, I will take you home. But you have to promise me that you will try to have fun."

"I'll try."

"Good." Cree smiled, his face lighting up and his dimples showing. "Do you want to ask your parents for a ride, or shall we walk?"

"Let's walk," Laena said.

"Laena!" called Michelle from inside the house. "Is Cree here? Don't you two dare leave for the dance without letting me take pictures!"

Laena rolled her eyes. Cree smiled and jerked his head toward the inside of the house. "We should let them take some pictures," Cree whispered.

"Okay," Laena said, exasperated. "But I'm doing this for you, not for them."

"As long as you do it," Cree said, pulling her toward the living room where Ben and Michelle were waiting.

"Oh!" Michelle said, clapping her hands together in pleasure. "Don't you two look lovely!"

"A handsome couple," Ben agreed. He picked up the digital camera and started fiddling with the settings. "Why don't you stand in front of the fireplace?"

Cree took Laena by the hand and dragged her in front of the empty fireplace.

"Dad...." Laena whined.

"Oh, come on, Laena. This is your first formal dance! We need some pictures," Michelle said. "Cree, don't you want pictures?"

"Absolutely," Cree agreed sincerely. "We need to memorialize this event. After all, Laena is in a dress...I think this is the first time I have seen such a thing."

Michelle laughed delightedly. Laena threw her mother a dirty look.

"Get closer," Ben said, motioning them together.

Laena complained and grumbled through the picture taking, but in a way, she didn't want it to end. Because once the pictures were taken, she had no choice but go to the dance.

After what seemed like an eternity, Michelle and Ben released them from the impromptu photo shoot. Laena's palms sweated as they left the house. She stood on tiptoe and whispered into Cree's ear. "Do we really have to go?"

"Yes, we really have to go," Cree said, a mock sternness in his voice.

"Cree, have her home by midnight!" Ben called out from the door of the house. The warm light from the hallway silhouetted Laena's parents in the dark. Cree turned around and waved in acknowledgment. Laena longed to run back inside.

"Let's go to your cabin instead, Cree. You can have your way with me...I promise," Laena begged quietly, only half joking.

Cree laughed. "Do not tempt me," he replied. "We are going to the dance. Period."

Laena leaned her head against Cree's broad shoulder and they began to walk. She breathed his scent in deeply, peppermint soap and something woodsy. Comforting. A strong wind made her dress billow around her and she grabbed Cree tighter. The sun had set, but Laena could see huge black clouds rolling in across the moonlight. She smelled the sweet tang of ozone in the air. Was a storm approaching? Before she could become really panicked about the stupid dance, they were at the school. Kids were streaming into the open doors, freshly shaved boys in suits and girls in tight sparkly dresses showing off ample cleavage. Laena felt underdressed and out of place.

Cree sensed her discomfort. "We are going to have fun," he said firmly. "You are with me...and Sophie will be there, and Mike...."

"And Cat, and Tiffany, and all the other kids I don't really like...." Laena added. Her dress swirled around her legs in the breeze.

Cree grabbed her hand and tugged her toward the doors. "Come. Let's go have fun." He held her firmly, as if preventing her from running off.

Cree kissed her cheek and guided her into the school. Laena followed him reluctantly. Cree led her through the hallways toward the gym. Her heels clicked on the linoleum floors, echoing in the emptiness. The school looked weird at night, Laena thought, and the fluorescent lights were harsh and too revealing. The hallways looked shabbier under the artificial lights than they did during daylight hours. She hung slightly behind Cree. When they reached the gymnasium doors, Laena was relieved to see the lights inside were turned down low. She handed the two tickets to the students manning the ticket table, and they wandered in, glancing around. Music played over the sound system, but not so loud that it jarred her bones. Streamers and balloons festooned the walls, and tables were set up along one wall with soda and snacks. Students were clustered in small groups around the gym, and about 20 kids were already dancing.

Cree spotted Sophie and Mike, grabbed Laena's hand, and headed their way. Sophie squealed when she saw Laena. "You look beautiful!" she said, hugging Laena tightly. "I'm so glad you came."

Laena looked at Sophie. "You look awesome, too!" And she did. Sophie wore a deep red silky dress that hugged her curves and showed off her legs. Her silver heels were impossibly high.

"How are you going to dance in those?" Laena asked.

Sophie laughed. "I do better in heels than I do in sneakers," she confided.

Mike elbowed Cree in the side. "Laena looks great. I may have to steal her for a dance."

Cree laughed. "As long as you return her to me," he joked.

Laena's nerves rattled, and her eyes moved restlessly across the gym. A flash of brilliant blue caught her attention, and she gasped as the girl in a blue dress turned. She was stunning. Laena elbowed Sophie. "Who is that?" she whispered, gesturing with her chin.

Sophie turned and squinted across the room. She shrugged. "Oh. Her. That's Ariel. She's new. I have History with her, and gym. She's an exchange student from somewhere...Israel, maybe? I hate her."

"Why do you hate her?" Laena asked. She couldn't take her eyes off of Ariel.

"*Why?* Duh...look at her! She's gorgeous. She's perfect. In fact," Sophie paused and looked from Ariel to Cree. "She looks a little like Cree, don't you think? They could be brother and sister. Same coloring." Sophie paused. "Ignore her. She's stuck up. C'mon...let's get the guys to dance with us."

Sophie turned and whispered something in Mike's ear. Mike blushed.

Laena watched the girl from afar, feeling uncomfortable. There was something disturbing about her. Was she the girl Laena had been catching glimpses of for the past few weeks? Was she following Laena? Or Cree? Laena shook her head and told herself that her imagination was in overdrive. Sophie tugged Laena's arm, dragging her attention away from Ariel.

Cree was looking around the room, distracted. His eyes landed on someone in the crowd, and he swore softly under his breath. Laena heard him and turned toward him.

"What's wrong?" she asked, a frown creasing her brow. She had never heard Cree swear before.

Cree did not answer. Instead, he grabbed Laena by the hand and pulled her out to the dance floor. The DJ had just put on a slow song, and a number of couples were dancing. He tugged her into his arms and they started swaying gently.

"What's wrong?" Laena asked again, trying to look around the room and see what had made Cree curse.

"Laena...." Cree turned her face toward his. "Laena, I did not know this was going to happen." He looked panicked.

"Didn't know *what* was going to happen?" She searched his eyes. He looked positively frantic. "Cree, you're scaring me."

"Promise me, no matter what happens, you will trust me. Do you trust me?" he whispered.

Laena nodded, apprehensive. Did she trust him? Sometimes, the things he said made no sense. Cree pulled Laena into his arms and stroked her hair.

"Cree?" Laena lifted her head and looked into his eyes. "What's wrong?"

Cree shook his head, silencing her. Laena danced in Cree's arms, lost in his embrace, her eyes closed, shutting out everyone else in the gym. She pushed his strange mood from her mind, melding into his body, enjoying his smell, just being with him. When the song ended, they remained locked together, and then Cree said urgently, "Trust me," again. And then, Laena's world fell apart.

"Hello, Cree," said a silky voice. Laena's eyes burst open and she saw, standing before her, the girl in blue. Ariel. She was the most stunning creature Laena had ever laid eyes on. She was tall—almost as tall as Cree in her heels—with the same black hair and startling blue eyes. Her hair hung past her shoulders, straight and silky. She had high cheekbones, perfect white teeth, and skin as smooth and fine as porcelain. She had a perfect body—beautiful rounded breasts, a tiny waist, and long, lean, beautiful legs. She wore a body-skimming blue silk dress that matched her eyes flawlessly.

"Hello, Ariel. What a surprise to see you here." Cree's voice was cold. So cold, Laena shivered. She resisted the urge to throw her arms around herself for warmth.

"No hug?" the girl said, holding out her arms. Cree ignored her, his eyes icy and cruel. "And are you not going to introduce me to your...friend?" The girl's eyes raked Laena, and then settled on the gem nestled between Laena's breasts. Was it Laena's imagination, or did hatred emanate from her when she saw the necklace?

Cree disregarded both of her questions. "What are you doing here, Ariel?" Cree stiffened in anger.

"Same thing as you, Cree," she responded easily. "I am at a...dance." Her voice dripped with sarcasm.

"Go home." Cree said, seething. "You do not belong here."

"And you do?"

Cree grabbed Laena's hand and pulled her off the dance floor. The girl named Ariel fell into step with them easily, as if Cree had invited her to join them.

Cree whirled to face her, halfway off the dance floor. "Go home, Ariel," Cree hissed under his breath. "I am not going to tell you again."

"*You* do not tell *me* to do anything," she said nastily. "And I am home, Cree. I am here on an...exchange, I think they call it." Ariel turned to Laena. "You must be Laena, no? I have heard *so* much about you." She reached out and grabbed a handful of Laena's curls. "What interesting hair. I have heard of such hair...." She said the latter almost to herself, looking at Laena's locks curiously. Cree's hand flew out and grasped Ariel's wrist. Laena could see Ariel's fingers turn white, the circulation cut off. She released Laena's hair and Cree dropped Ariel's hand.

"Do not answer any of her questions, Laena," Cree said to Laena, without taking his eyes off of Ariel. "Do not even look at her." Laena was too shocked and confused to speak.

"Cree, you are being *so* rude!" Ariel laughed, a tinkling sound like breaking ice. "Can I talk to Cree a moment alone, please?" She turned to Laena, her white teeth flashing. "A private matter," she explained, smiling prettily.

"No," Cree said firmly.

Ariel leaned close, her mouth between Cree and Laena, and whispered so both could hear. "No? Then I am forced to talk in front of your *friend* here." She spat the word "friend" derisively. Cree tried to pull Laena away, but Ariel grabbed Laena's arm with a cold, dry hand. "Cree, darling, I regret to inform you that our baby did not make it. But I would be happy to try again. We really should talk, no? Perhaps tomorrow." She leaned back and stared intently at Laena's necklace. "Beautiful necklace, Laena. Cree works fast." She whirled away and was gone, striding across the gym floor toward the table of drinks and food, her hips swaying seductively with each step.

Laena gaped. She looked at Cree, who watched Ariel in horror. He turned to Laena and opened his mouth to speak.

Laena reached up and put a finger on his lips. "Shhh," she whispered. "Don't say anything. There's no need to explain." She gave him a shaky smile.

Cree almost collapsed in relief. "Laena, I have to tell you.... "

"No, you don't. Not here, and not now. Let it go."

"I cannot. I have to tell you who she is, and that.... "

"Cree, I'm not an idiot." Laena shook her head. "I think maybe we should go. I'm not sure either of us wants to stay. Not now."

Cree nodded, and silently, they grasped hands and walked toward the gym door. Laena felt eyes boring into her back, but she didn't dare turn around. She heard someone call her name, as if from a great distance, but she kept walking toward the door, toward safety and far away from that girl. The chaperone stationed at the door to the gym, stopped them. "Once you leave, you can't return, kids," he said sternly.

"Thanks," Laena said in a surprisingly steady voice. "He's going to take me home. I'm not feeling very well, so we won't be coming back."

The teacher looked at them skeptically. "If you're sure," he said.

Cree nodded, and they made their escape. Together, they ran down the hallway toward the front doors, and then out into the chilly night air. Laena still had goose bumps on her arms, but she couldn't feel anything. Without speaking, they headed away from the school. Cree started toward his cabin, but Laena stopped him.

"Cree, you have to take me home," Laena said sorrowfully. "That teacher will tell my dad what time we left, and if I'm not home really soon, I'm going to get the third degree about where we were."

Cree looked over at Laena. "Can I stay with you for a while? At your house?"

Laena nodded and smiled. "Of course." She felt strangely calm, as if the run in with Ariel was something she dealt with every day of her life.

"Thank you, Laena. For trusting me. For...everything." Cree smiled sadly, and turned toward the Foster's house.

Laena was relieved to see lights on in the house. It looked warm and welcoming, and a cold wind was picking up. She shivered.

Cree put his arm around her protectively. "What will we tell your parents?"

"I'll handle it," Laena said. "Don't say anything, okay?" She opened the front door, calling, "We're home!"

"Laena? Cree?" Michelle poked her head out of the living room. "What are you doing home so early? You just left!" Her reading glasses were perched on her nose, and she peered at them over the tops. "Are you two okay?"

"We're fine," Laena said, smiling. "The dance was kinda awful, so we decided to come home." Michelle looked at her curiously. "Is that okay?"

"Of course it's okay," Michelle said, a slight frown creasing her forehead. "I'm just surprised, that's all."

"We danced," Cree added. "But we decided we would have more fun here."

Laena went up and whispered in her mother's ear, and Michelle's face cleared. "Okay, honey, why don't you change out of that dress? Cree, come inside and sit with us while Laena changes."

Cree looked at Laena questioningly, and Laena smiled and said, "I'll be right down."

Cree walked into the living room, loosening his tie. Ben looked up from his chair and said, "Long time, no see, Cree. Did Laena chicken out?"

"Stop, Ben," Michelle said chidingly. "They just weren't having as much fun as they thought. Give the poor kids a break."

Cree sat down on the couch, loosened his tie, and glanced at the television, tuned to the Weather Channel, but muted. "Anything interesting?" he said, motioning toward the television set.

"There's a storm brewing," Ben responded. "Pretty early for hurricane season, but it looks like it might be a bad one. Ever been in a hurricane, Cree?"

"No, sir," Cree responded.

"Well, hurricane season normally runs between June and the end of November, but we've been known to get bad storms before and after the official season. It's funny, we haven't had a bad storm for so many years, Cape residents have become complacent. We're in for a big one soon. And it could be devastating."

"I think that is true all over, sir. With climate change, I mean. Storms are going to get more powerful, and the droughts will be worse as well."

Ben nodded in agreement. "I wish everyone believed that, Cree. Then maybe we would get off our asses and do something about it."

"Ben!" Michelle chided. "Language!"

Laena walked into the living room, wearing jeans and a soft cotton shirt. She had tucked the pendant inside her shirt, invisible to her parent's eyes. Her eyes darted to the television screen, taking in the telltale swirl of clouds on the radar. "Is there a hurricane coming?" Laena said incredulously. "Isn't it early?"

"We're not sure what it's going to turn into, but it's looking pretty menacing," Ben responded.

"Cree, would you like something to eat or drink?" Michelle asked.

"I am a little hungry," Cree admitted.

"C'mon," Laena said. "Let's go into the kitchen and I'll make us some tea and a snack."

"Sounds great," Cree smiled gratefully and followed Laena out of the living room.

"What did you say to your mom?" Cree whispered when they were out of earshot.

Laena blushed. "I told her I got my period and wasn't feeling well," Laena responded.

"Ach, now I have you lying to your parents." He shook his head in dismay.

"Cree, stop. It's fine. It's not your fault." Laena busied herself with filling the teakettle, taking mugs out of the cabinet, and getting teabags. Cree sat down at the kitchen table, stretching out his long muscular legs. But he looked tense. He shifted uncomfortably when Laena did not speak.

"Are you going to ask me about Ariel?" Cree said quietly.

Laena shook her head without turning around to face him. "What is there to ask? Well, except maybe why she's here.

She's obviously from your time, right? And I don't want to talk about the...the pregnancy thing." Laena's voice dropped.

"Laena...."

"No, Cree. I understand. You explained that to me already. And I can see why you'd want to...to be with her. I mean, she's gorgeous. But I can tell she doesn't mean anything to you, at least not now. And I promised to trust you, so that's what I'm doing." Laena felt almost detached as she opened the fridge to see what they could eat. She thought she would be upset, but she wasn't. She was dazed.

Cree jumped up and was at Laena's side in two long strides. He shut the refrigerator door and spun Laena around to face him. "Laena, we have to deal with this! I wish you did not have to suffer through that scene at the dance. It was wrong of Ariel. She has always been a...." Cree struggled to find the right word.

"A bitch?" Laena suggested drily.

Cree laughed hollowly. "Yes, a bitch."

"Not your fault," Laena shrugged.

"I did not expect her to show up here, Laena. You have to believe me. I had no idea. I am...stunned."

"I believe you," Laena said. She reached out and laid her palm flat against Cree's chest. She felt his heart beating, steady and strong. "What is she doing here, though? Is she going to help you? Do we *need* help? I mean, especially from her?"

Cree looked at Laena thoughtfully, shaking his head. His black hair fell over his face. "She is not here to help," he said sadly, sweeping his hair back.

"What do you mean she's not here to help?" Laena tilted her head questioningly. "Why is she here?" A thought struck her, a horrible thought, and she felt panic rising in her chest. "Cree, she's not here to take you back, is she?"

Cree laughed bitterly. "No, Laena. She does not want me to come back. She is here to stop me."

Laena opened her mouth to respond, but the teakettle started whistling, and Laena's parents walked into the kitchen. She attended to the teakettle, turning off the gas burner.

"Cree, I think you should stay here tonight," Ben said slowly.

Laena spun around. "What? Why?" Laena's heart started thudding.

"The storm is really looking awful. We don't like the thought of him in that flimsy cabin at Evergreen Acres," Michelle responded.

"I will be fine," Cree protested. "If there is a storm coming, perhaps I should leave now so I do not have to deal with it on my way home."

"I don't think you understand, Cree," Ben said. "Here, sit down." He motioned for Cree to sit at the kitchen table. Cree perched on the edge of a chair. "Have you heard of the Perfect Storm?"

Cree shook his head.

"Well, that storm hit years before you were born. But in October of 1991, a bizarre combination of weather events led to an incredible storm on the east coast. They called it the Halloween Nor'easter, but really, it was a hurricane for all intents and purposes. The storm had winds of over 100 miles per hour, and waves up to 100 feet tall."

"One hundred feet!" Cree exclaimed, incredulous. His blue eyes were wide with wonder. Laena couldn't even imagine waves that big. Incomprehensible.

"A monster," Ben agreed. "It's the spring now, of course, not the fall, but the conditions are looking ripe to create another disaster. It may not happen, but I don't want to take the chance of you being alone in that cabin if it does strike. If they evacuate the Cape, you will come with us."

"Evacuate?" Laena asked. "You mean, they might kick us out? Off the Cape entirely?"

"If it gets too dangerous to stay, yes," Michelle responded. "There's really nothing to worry about, yet, but we just want to be cautious."

"We need to go to the grocery store and hardware store, to stock up on batteries and water. We'll be right back."

Cree stood up. "But.... "

Ben stood up as well. His voice was hard. "I'm not taking no for an answer. You're staying with us. Now, you can come with us to pick up some things from the cabin, if you want." He appraised Cree. "I don't think you'll fit in my clothes."

"No!" Laena blurted. "Don't leave me here alone, Dad."

"Honey, it's not dangerous yet. We're just getting prepared," Michelle said, trying to reassure her.

"Laena, I need you to bring the boat in and put it in the boat shed. You have to stay here." Her father's voice sounded tense.

"Dad...I can't bring the boat in by myself. I need help."

"I can stay with her, sir. I can help her bring the boat in, and do whatever else needs to get done," Cree offered.

Ben looked at Cree, considering. "Does that mean you're not going to give me any flack about staying with us tonight?" he asked.

"No, sir. I am out of my league here. I will do what you suggest."

Ben laughed, the tension in the room easing. "Sounds good to me."

"I'll pick Cree up a few things," Michelle suggested. "Some sweat pants, shirts...."

"Please.... " Cree protested.

"It's not a problem, Cree. Do you have rain gear at the cabin?"

Cree shook his head.

"Then you'll be needing it anyway. "

Cree blushed. "Ma'am...Michelle...I cannot afford new things. I will not be able to pay you for them...these pants, this shirt, I got them at the thrift store. You know, the Salvation Army?" He turned to Laena, embarrassed. "I wanted to look nice for the dance, to fit in. But I cannot afford new clothes."

"Oh, you'll pay me alright, Cree," Ben said. "You and I are going to have to nail plywood up over all these windows downstairs, put duct tape on the ones upstairs. We need to clear out the yard...tables, chairs...anything that can get blown around in the wind. I'm going to put you to work, son, and it's going to be hard labor." He paused. "I need you."

Laena could see that Cree was overcome by Ben calling him "son." Cree had not had a father in years. There was silence for a few uncomfortable moments, and then Cree nodded gratefully. "Okay, thank you, sir."

Ben clapped his hands together. "It's decided, then. Let's batten down these hatches. We're taking the pick-up truck, Laena. Use the Jeep to pull the boat out of the water. We'll be back in about an hour, hour and a half. I'll keep my cell phone on in case you have trouble."

"More like two hours," Michelle said, shrugging into her coat. "Be careful, you two."

Laena and Cree murmured their assent, the front door slammed.

"Cree," Laena began. "The storm...how bad does it get?"

Cree looked at her somberly. "It is bad, Laena."

"Why didn't you tell me?"

"No need. People are forewarned. Telling you would not have changed anything. And, I did not know I would be staying here with you. I just knew that the storm hit, and it became very violent. A Category 5. We will be okay, though. But, we have a lot to do. Tell me what I can do to help you with the boat.... ?"

Laena sighed and looked longingly at her tea. "I need to pull the Jeep down to the dock and we need to hook the boat up to the trailer and drag it out of the water."

"You can drive?" Cree asked, surprised.

"I don't have my license yet, but...well, I've been driving that old truck since I could reach the pedals."

Cree laughed. "You can reach the pedals now?"

Laena pretended to hit him playfully. She turned her face away and tried to suppress her smile. Cree would be staying with her...she would have him all to herself and could keep him out of Ariel's clutches. At least for a day or two.

Chapter 8

IT TOOK LAENA AND CREE less than an hour to take the boat out of the water and put it in the boathouse. They wandered back into the kitchen where Laena made them fresh tea, and made some toast and peanut butter to go with it. Cree munched contentedly at the kitchen table.

He sighed, and said, "The only thing that would make this perfect is..." he peered into his almost empty ceramic mug, "...some brandy in this tea."

Laena laughed. "You drink alcohol?" she asked. Then something occurred to her. "Cree, how old are you?"

He looked uncomfortable. "Around your age...." he said evasively.

Laena gave him a look, raising one eyebrow, and he sighed. "Does it matter how old I am?"

"No," Laena responded truthfully. "I am just curious. You seem...older than me. And I don't know if it is because of when you are from, and your culture, or your physical age."

"I am 19 years old," Cree admitted. "Which is not much older than you! You are only two years younger."

"Nineteen!" Laena exclaimed, shocked. "Why are you passing yourself off as a junior?"

Cree shrugged. "I was not sure how much I would know of your schooling. I decided it would be better to play it safe and pretend I was younger.... "

"Nineteen," Laena mused. "So...you drink alcohol?"

"Yes," Cree replied honestly. "As often as possible."

Laena laughed again.

"Seriously, we do drink occasionally. It keeps the stress level down. And we use it for medicinal purposes."

"Do you want me to get you something?"

"No, I am teasing you," Cree replied. "I do not want to get in trouble with your parents." He paused and looked at Laena with a smile. "But you could come sit on my lap, if you do not mind that I am an older man."

Laena didn't wait for him to ask again. She sat on his lap, put her arms around his neck and nuzzled him. Cree rubbed her back languidly.

"Can I ask you something?" she said quietly.

"Yes, ask me anything."

"Why does Ariel want to stop you? I don't understand."

"Ah," Cree sighed. "It is rather a long story. Do you really want to hear it?"

"Of course," Laena replied.

"Do you remember when I asked you whether you believed in God?" Laena nodded. "Well, there is...I don't know how to explain this...kind of a battle going on in my time."

"A battle? About God?" Laena was confused.

"Sort of. There are two types of people in my time. The scientists...people like me, and you, and your parents. They are called the Brights. Then there are the people like...." Cree thought for a moment, and then his face lit up. "Like Tiffany! People like Tiffany. The people who believe the destruction of the Earth is inevitable, and good."

"But, how can they think that? It's ridiculous!"

Cree shook his head. "They say it is God's will. And that once Earth is destroyed, God will take us to a better place." He stopped and laughed bitterly. "Well, not all of us, of course. God will only save those who believe. The Righteous. We jokingly call them the Chosen."

"The Brights and the Chosen? You're kidding, aren't you? Please tell me you aren't serious." Laena searched his face for signs that he was pulling her leg.

Cree shook his head. "Unfortunately, what I tell you is absolutely true. They do not call themselves the Chosen...we do, sarcastically, of course. Although I suspect they secretly like it. They call themselves the Righteous."

"So Ariel is a Chosen?"

Cree nodded. "I am sure she came here to stop me. She wants the oceans to die, because in her mind, that will hasten the destruction of Earth and her ascension to...to wherever they think they are going." His voice was cynical.

Laena sat, stunned. How could anyone *want* Earth to die? She fingered her necklace. "Cree, Ariel looked at my necklace and said something like, 'Cree works fast.' What does that mean? Does this necklace symbolize something?"

Cree nodded. "The stone...the color...it means you are a Bright."

Laena caressed the warm stone. She was a scientist, did not believe in God, and she certainly wanted the Earth to survive. So, if she were living in Cree's time, she would be a Bright, like him. Would she be involved in the battle? She had a horrible thought.

"Are there wars? I mean, do you try to kill each other?"

Cree looked shocked. "Oh, no. Killing is a horrible crime. We are not allowed to kill...there are so few of us!" He paused. "Although, I do not know if the Chosen would kill here, in your time. Here people are not at risk. There are so many of you. And Ariel and the other Chosen...well, they would do anything to get their way."

Laena was confused. "Then how do you battle in your time? How do you try to ensure your side wins?"

Cree frowned, thinking. Laena ran her fingers through his thick, silky hair, but he seemed not to notice.

"The Brights battle with science and their brains. The Chosen...they try to scare people, telling them that they will be rewarded if Earth is allowed to die, when the end comes. They use fear."

Laena thought for a moment. "Cree..." Laena said softly.

Cree looked up at her and smiled gently. "Yes, sweetie?"

"If you and Ariel had a baby, would it be a Bright or a Chosen?"

"The baby stays with its mother in our time. So, if our baby had lived...I guess Ariel would have made sure it was a Chosen." Cree sounded sad.

"Are you sad the baby died?" Laena asked, her heart clenching.

"Of course," Cree whispered. "It would have been my son, or daughter. But, Laena, I did not want to make a baby with Ariel. She...." Cree stopped and laughed resentfully. "She got me drunk, feeding me much brandy, and...ach, it is no excuse, is it? I should never have had sex with her. And I never will again."

"I'm sorry your baby died, Cree. Truly, I am."

Cree looked up at Laena and saw a tear slip out of the corner of her eye. "Do not be sad, Laena. Please. It is for the best. I have to battle her, here, in your time, and it is best I am not distracted by a child. I have to change the future, and Ariel will do everything in her power to stop me."

Change the future. A realization struck Laena with such force that it felt like a physical blow. She gasped.

"What is it?" Cree asked, reaching for her, concern etched across his face.

"Cree.... " Laena moaned. "If you...if we change the course of the future...what happens to you?" She looked at Cree in horror, fearing the answer.

Cree grimaced. "I wondered when you would recognize there might be a problem." He paused, then said quietly, "You are speaking of the grandfather paradox."

Laena shook her head in confusion. "The grandfather paradox? What is that? It's just that if we change the future, will you...will you exist? Will you ever be born?"

Cree was silent. He pulled Laena back against his chest and rocked her gently.

"Cree! Answer me!" Her voice was muffled against his shirt. "What happens to you?" She lifted her face up and looked into his eyes. What she saw in them scared her to death. Cree's eyes were full of uncertainty. He opened his mouth to speak, but nothing came out.

"What is the grandfather paradox?" Laena asked softly. "Please tell me. I have to know."

Cree let his breath out slowly. "Laena, I do not know what will happen. Time travel into the past is very complicated. The grandfather paradox is something that people have puzzled over for years." He paused, and then went on slowly. "I am alive now. I am here, and maybe nothing can change that. So the grandfather paradox says this—if I traveled into the past and tried to kill my own grandfather before my parents were born, say with a gun, something would *have* to go wrong. He would shift slightly so the bullet misses, or I would aim badly, or the gun would jam. In other words, I could simply not kill him. Because if I *did* kill him, it would mean that I would never be born, and therefore not be alive in the future to come back and kill him."

Laena sat in stunned silence and did not answer him. If what they were about to do would change the world enough, Cree's parents may never meet, and Cree would never be born. He would cease to exist. Her heart clenched and she could not speak. Cree saw the misery on her face.

"It is probably impossible for me to change the future enough such that I will not exist," Cree said, trying to reassure her.

Laena nodded slowly. "But if that is the case, then anything we do to alter the course of the future...it wouldn't work. Because if we changed the future, you might not exist, and then you couldn't come back and help me change the future." She searched his eyes pleadingly. "So what is the point of any of this? We're doomed to fail."

Cree shook his head. "Not necessarily. What if there are...parallel universes? What if there are two equally valid universes, this one, the one you live in, and then another, where we fix the problems and the future comes to be. What if it doesn't have to be consistent? Or what if I would exist, but just not in the same context? In a world where Cape Cod and New York City are not flooded?"

Laena laughed harshly. "Cree, I am not very good at physics. I just don't see how that can be. How can there be two universes? And if there are two, which one are you in?"

"Does it matter?" he asked softly, stroking her hair.

"Does it *matter?*" Laena echoed. "Of course it flipping matters! What if...what if you're in one universe, and I am in the other?"

"Oh, Laena," Cree said sadly. "This is so much bigger than us."

"No!" Laena protested. "No, it isn't! My world...my universe, is you! I can't contemplate a world without you, Cree!" She choked on her words.

Cree shook his head. "It cannot be that way, Laena."

"What do you mean it 'cannot be that way'? It *is* that way! For me, it is that way. You can't tell me how to feel, or how not to feel! You can't just...just come to me and tell me, 'Oh, by the way, Laena, I may not exist anymore, but it's okay, because this is so much bigger than us.' "

Cree started to get angry. He grasped her by the shoulders. "What would you have me do, then? Should I not try to stop the destruction? Should I let this happen? Would you have me just go home, home to the future, so that your feelings are not hurt?"

Laena pushed him away. "Of course not!" she said, shaken. "Why can't you...can't you just stay here with me? Stay here, in my world, with me.... ?" She reached out to him then, tears filling her eyes. "Please, Cree! Please don't leave me! I love you...I can't...I can't lose you!"

Laena fell into his arms. Cree stroked her hair gently. "Oh, Laena. I love you, too. But do you not remember? We talked about this. We *agreed* that there is no worse sin than indifference. We cannot live our lives, no matter how wonderful that life together, and be indifferent to the plight of the world around us, and to the future. Could we be that selfish? Could you look at yourself in the mirror, knowing what you were doing, not even trying to help?"

Laena knew he was right. How could she live with herself? But on the other hand, how could she knowingly and willingly do something that would basically kill Cree? Or at least, make him cease to exist?

"Shhh," Cree said, trying to soothe her. "It will be okay, I promise."

"How can it ever be okay?" Laena countered, strangling on her words. She felt like her heart was being torn to shreds.

"You will be okay," he repeated. "Everything will be fine." He murmured into her ear, caressing her softly until she calmed. But Laena knew, deep in her heart, that her own personal world would never be all right again.

* * *

By the time Michelle and Ben returned, Laena had dried her tears and calmed down. But she still felt paralyzed by the realization that she might lose Cree. Cree went outside to help Ben in with the groceries, wood, and supplies. They moved all the furniture off the farmer's porch into the garage, and put the grill in the basement. They didn't leave anything in the yard that could get blown around by hurricane force winds. Michelle and Laena turned the Weather Channel on and watched the latest update on the storm. When Ben and Cree joined them, Laena noticed that Cree had changed into a pair of sweatpants and a tee shirt. The shirt still had creases from the package.

"Looking worse and worse," Ben muttered, more to himself than to anyone.

"Should we put the plywood up?" Cree asked.

"Not yet," Ben replied. "I don't want to put it up if the storm fades or passes us by."

"When will you know, Dad?" Laena asked.

Ben looked at his watch. "Well, it's 11:30 now...I imagine we'll know a lot more in the early hours of the morning." Ben looked at Cree. "What do you say we try to catch some sleep, and I'll check the weather again in a few hours? If it looks worse, I'll wake you and we can start nailing the plywood up."

Cree nodded. "That is fine, sir."

"Where is Cree sleeping?" Laena asked.

"I'll put him in the guest room," Michelle answered. "There are clean sheets on the bed, and I'll have Laena get you a towel."

"Thank you so much, Michelle," Cree said. "And for the clothes...."

"Our, pleasure Cree. You're the one helping us out, remember?" Michelle turned to Laena. "Honey, take Cree up to the guest room and get him a clean towel. You kids should go to bed soon."

"Okay," Laena agreed, and started toward the stairs. Cree followed.

"Kids?" Ben called out. They both stopped and turned. "Doors stay open tonight, right? And remember Cree, I might be waking you shortly."

"Yes, sir."

Laena threw her father a dirty look and climbed the stairs.

"Laena, he is only looking out for you. Do not be angry with him." Cree said softly as he followed her.

"Whatever," she said, embarrassed that her father treated her like a baby. She showed Cree the guest room, right next to hers. Cree looked from his room to hers. "Tempting," he said, smiling, trying to cheer her up.

Laena smiled grudgingly. Cree pulled Laena into a hug and whispered in her ear. "Shall I try to sneak into your room once your parents are asleep?"

Laena whispered back. "You tell me. Will we get caught?"

Cree laughed. "I don't know," he said honestly.

Laena looked at him in mock surprise. "What? You don't know what happens tonight?"

"I know what I would like to happen," he said huskily, his hands grasping her bottom. Laena melted.

"No, I think...." She swallowed. "I think we'd better be careful."

"Me, too," Cree said. "Unfortunate, isn't it?"

Laena groaned.

"Shhh," Cree cautioned, laughing. He released her. "Weren't you supposed to get me a towel?"

Chapter 9

LAENA WOKE in the middle of the night. Or was it morning? The wind howled outside, and her windows rattled in the dark. Something had woken her, but she wasn't sure what.

She remembered everything in a flood of thoughts and emotions. The necklace. Ariel. Cree being next door in the guest room. The storm. Before she could sit up, a hand cupped her shoulder. She stifled a scream and turned. She sighed in relief when she saw Cree, his finger to his lips, urging her to be quiet. He slipped under the covers next to her.

"Cree...you shouldn't be in here!" she whispered urgently.

"I know. I am not staying," he murmured, spooning her close to his body. "The power went out. I was not sure if your father has an alarm clock that is electric, or if I should wake him."

Laena could feel his hard, warm body next to hers, and she felt a shiver of pleasure course through her. But she also felt danger.

"You should leave. If my father walks in.... "

"I will go in just a minute." Cree's hands reached up and felt for Laena's necklace, his hand brushing her breast. She shivered. He clutched the pendant in one hand, and held Laena tight against him with his other arm. "I just wanted to tell you that I love you," he whispered. "I want to make sure you know that." She could feel his warm breath in her ear.

"I love you, too," she said, her heart clenching with an overwhelmingly powerful emotion. "Why are you saying this now? Is something bad going to happen?"

"No, no...do not be frightened. I just wanted to say that to you." He nuzzled her neck, and then got out of her bed. "Go back to sleep. It is almost 4 a.m., and the storm is getting bad. I am going to wake your father."

Laena groaned in protest, missing his comforting warmth. "Come back...."

He laughed softly. "You know I cannot. Get some sleep. It is going to be a rough day." Cree crept from the room, and

Laena heard murmuring coming from her parents' room. After several moments, she saw two male figures go down the stairs. She tossed and turned, but could not get back to sleep. Finally, she got out of bed, put on some slippers, and crept downstairs after her father and Cree. She saw the beams from two flashlights in the kitchen, and cautiously made her way there.

"Dad? What's going on?" Laena whispered.

"Go back to bed, honey. Cree and I have this under control."

"I can't sleep. What's going on with the storm?"

"We lost power, Laena. So I'm going to turn the weather radio on. But things look nasty out there. Cree and I are going outside to nail up some plywood. If you really can't sleep, sit in here and listen to the weather report, and have some tea ready for us when we come in. Or better yet, coffee."

"How the hell am I supposed to sleep if you're going to be hammering nails into the side of the house?" Laena grumbled, more to herself than her father. So she lit the kettle on the gas stove with a match, and turned the battery-operated radio on. Cree and Ben had suited up in rain gear, and headed out the kitchen door.

The emotionless voice of the NOAA weather radio announcer confirmed that indeed, the storm was bad, and it looked like it would make a direct hit on the Cape. Winds were already gusting over 75 miles per hour, and torrential rain would be arriving any minute. Evacuation had not yet been ordered, but residents should stay tuned. Laena lit a candle in the center of the kitchen table so she could see. Soon, she heard the thud of hammers against the side of the house. She wondered how her mother could possibly sleep through the racket.

Laena's thoughts moved to Ariel. God, that girl was gorgeous. She felt a twinge of jealousy when she thought of Cree being in bed with Ariel, touching her and caressing her in far more intimate ways than he had done with her. Laena's hand traveled to the pendant, and she grasped the stone. Its warmth gave her comfort. How was Ariel planning to stop Cree from his...what the hell should she call it? His mission? The gravity of the situation scared her. If Cree and Ariel were here, how many others from his time, or even later, were here? Were they overrun with time travelers, and didn't know it? And how come Cree and Ariel looked so similar...tall, black hair, bright blue eyes? Did all the humans in Cree's time look like that? Laena had so many more questions for Cree. But the most pressing question, for Laena, was what would happen to Cree after he succeeded—or failed—in what he came to do. Would he just disappear? Or could he come and go as he pleased? Could he stay here with Laena, or...could he take her back to his time with him? The thought made Laena's stomach clench. Could she leave her parents and friends behind to go with Cree? Would he let her? She shook her head as if to clear it, and got up to make the coffee.

As Laena pulled out the coffee, she thought of Cree's hand grinder. Life must be so different in his time, she thought, as she poured the ground coffee into the filter of the glass Chemex coffee urn. She and her parents tried to minimize their use of electricity—they dried their clothes outside on a clothesline in nice weather, used a gravity, drip coffee maker instead of an electric one...small things. But for Cree...not to have cars or planes, or motorboats or any of the modern conveniences...what must that be like? When she thought of the future, she thought of an even more technologically advanced society than they had now—flying cars, fuel cells, things like that. But instead, in many ways, Cree's society had regressed. Or was it progression? Maybe it was just simpler.

As the coffee dripped into the urn, Laena decided to make breakfast. She got out the skillet, and sliced some bagels. She started to spread butter on them to fry, when she remembered that Cree wouldn't eat dairy products. She rummaged through the fridge, lighting the interior with a flashlight, until she found an unopened package of soy margarine...her mother must have bought it when she invited Cree to stay with them. She hoped the soy margarine behaved the same way as butter, but she vaguely recalled reading somewhere that it didn't. Just then, a flashlight beam wavered into the kitchen.

"Laena? What are you doing up?" Michelle padded into the kitchen in her pajamas and slippers.

"Couldn't sleep," Laena said, trying to see the bagels and soy margarine in the dim light. "Mom, do you know how much of this soy margarine I'm supposed to use? Do I treat it like butter?"

"Not sure, hon," Michelle yawned. "That would be my guess. Are you done with the weather radio? We shouldn't waste the batteries."

"Mmmm-hmmm."

Michelle clicked off the radio. "Coffee ready?"

Laena glanced at the Chemex. "I don't know," she said. "Shine your flashlight on it and see if it's stopped dripping." Laena put the sliced bagels face down in the frying pan. They sputtered in the margarine.

Michelle did, and sighed in relief when she saw that the coffee was ready, steaming and fragrant. "Want some?" she asked, grabbing mugs out of the cabinet.

"Does a bear crap in the woods?" Laena responded.

"Laena!" Michelle reprimanded. She turned the flashlight on Laena and the beam caught Laena's necklace square on.

"Where did you get this?" Michelle asked, drawing closer and fingering the pendant. "It's beautiful."

Laena blushed. "Cree gave it to me. Last night, before the dance."

Michelle looked up sharply at Laena. "Honey, we need to talk about Cree...."

"Mom, don't start in on me again.... "

"I just don't want you getting your heart broken! You two are getting very close, awfully fast."

Laena shook her head and remained silent. She pulled away from her mother and turned toward the stove. She checked the undersides of one of the sizzling bagels.

"Why are you shaking your head?" Michelle asked, exasperated.

"Because I don't need you harping on me about Cree! We're fine. I'm not going to get my heart broken." As the words left Laena's mouth, she knew she was lying. She couldn't fathom an outcome here where her heart wasn't going to be broken. But she couldn't tell her mother that.

"Honey," Michelle said, her voice softening. "We love, Cree, really we do. But he's your first boyfriend, and he seems so much...older than you. I worry that.... " She trailed off.

"What? You worry what?" Laena turned to her mother, spatula in her hand like a weapon, her hair a wild mass of curls around her head. "Worry that we'll have sex? Worry that I'll get pregnant?"

"Yes, frankly, I do worry about those things!" Michelle countered. "I see the way he looks at you. And the way you look at him. He lives alone, without any parental supervision whatsoever...."

Laena rolled her eyes. "C'mon, Mom. It's not like you're here waiting for me when I get home from school, offering me cookies and milk. Kids our age don't have much parental supervision. We don't need it."

Michelle opened her mouth to respond, but the kitchen door crashed open, admitting a cold gust of wind and a sheet of rain. Cree and Ben staggered in, and Ben struggled to close the door against the force of the wind.

"Oh, my God!" said Michelle, rushing over to help. "Take those things off, gentlemen, before you flood the kitchen."

Cree and Ben yanked off their rain boots and stripped off their slickers. They were both soaked and shivering. Laena filled two cups of coffee and brought them to the table. Cree looked at her gratefully and sank into one of the chairs. Ben took a sip of coffee, then looked up at his wife.

"Michelle, can you grab the bottle of brandy for me? I am chilled inside and out."

Michelle wordlessly took the flashlight and headed for the liquor cabinet in the living room. She returned with the bottle as Laena placed the grilled bagels on the table.

"Thanks, hon," Ben said gratefully, and poured a healthy slug in his mug. He paused, then held the bottle over Cree's mug and looked at him questioningly.

"Please," Cree said, nodding. Ben poured brandy into Cree's coffee.

"Ben!" Michelle cried. "He's just a boy!"

"Pshaw," Ben replied. "He's not a boy. He's a man. We're freezing, and the brandy will help. You've had alcohol before, haven't you Cree?"

"Yes, sir," Cree replied, taking a gulp of the drink. "In Alaska, we have it quite frequently."

"There, you see?" Ben said to Michelle. "It's not going to kill him, and I'm not corrupting him."

"I'm grateful for it, sir." Cree grabbed a bagel and took a huge bite.

"But if you don't stop calling me 'sir', that'll be the last brandy you'll see," Ben said jokingly.

"Sorry," Cree said. "I keep forgetting...."

Ben clapped Cree on the back and laughed. Cree grinned in response. Laena looked at the two of them, thick as thieves. What had happened out there that brought them so close?

"After breakfast, we have to tape the upstairs windows. Then I think we have to hunker down and wait this out," Ben said.

"What if they evacuate us, Dad?" Laena asked, sitting at the table next to Cree, coffee mug in hand.

"I think we'll be okay, Laena. It's the Atlantic side that will take the brunt of the storm. Here on the bay side, we should be somewhat sheltered."

Cree nodded in agreement. "The damage from this storm will be extensive," Cree said, swallowing. "But we will be fine here."

Ben and Michelle looked at Cree curiously. Cree looked from one to the other and then grasped his mistake. "Not that I know much about these storms...but in Alaska, the bays were protected from bad storms...." He trailed off. Laena tried to change the subject and rescue Cree from unwanted parental scrutiny.

"What can I do to help, Dad?"

"You can help us tape the windows upstairs," Ben said, turning his attention away from Cree. They all finished their coffee and bagels in silence, and then Ben handed a roll of duct tape to Cree and kept one for himself.

"Cree and Laena, take the guest room, Laena's room, and Laena's bathroom. Michelle and I will do our room and bath, and the laundry room. Make a big 'X' with the duct tape, corner to corner. If you have extra tape, put another piece or two through the middle."

"What does it do?" Laena asked.

"If the window shatters, it keeps the glass from flying everywhere," Ben replied.

Cree started clearing the dirty dishes off the table, but Michelle stopped him. "I'll get it, Cree, but thank you."

"Are you sure?" Cree asked.

"Absolutely," Michelle assured him. "Go get a start on those windows. Ben, can I talk to you for a minute?"

Laena and Cree grabbed a flashlight and headed up the stairs. "What's the matter?" Cree whispered, feeling the anger emanate from Laena.

"My mother is the matter," Laena hissed. "I got another lecture about you, and sex, and getting my heart broken.... "

Just then, a branch hit the window of the guest room with a crack. Laena jumped.

"Let's get this tape on the windows before we lose one," Cree said. Laena nodded, and they worked in silence until they had all the windows in the three rooms done. They finished in Laena's room, and she pulled Cree down on the bed next to her.

"Cree, I'm so confused by all of this—your problem with the krill, and Ariel being here, and the grandfather paradox, and what will happen to us.... "

"I will always love you, Laena."

"That doesn't help if we're not together!"

"Doesn't it?" Cree countered. "The memories will not help at all? What is that old saying...it is better to have loved and lost than never to have loved at all?"

"So you're saying we *will* lose each other? For sure?"

Cree shook his head and his lips tightened into a grim line. "I do not know what will happen to us."

"But can you envision a way that we could possibly end up together? Can you give me any hope at all?" Laena looked at him pleadingly.

Cree looked at her in silence, and then said softly. "I promised never to lie to you." Cree sighed. "If I had my way, if I could dictate what would happen, we would be together forever, Laena."

"Then make it happen, Cree!" Laena implored.

"How?" he cried, his voice tortured. "How can I make that happen?"

"I don't know!" Laena whispered. "I wish I did." Cree gathered her into his arms, stroking her curls, and whispered reassurances into her ear. Cree lifted her face to his, and kissed her. Laena put her hands behind his head, tangled in his hair, and returned the kiss.

Someone clearing their throat interrupted them. Laena jumped apart from Cree, and turned toward the door. Ben stood at the door, leaning on the doorjamb, arms crossed at his chest.

"Am I...interrupting something?" Sarcasm dripped from his voice.

Cree stood up. "Sir...."

Ben sighed. "Downstairs, both of you. Please." His voice sounded resigned.

Cree and Laena walked past Ben as they headed toward the stairs. His face betrayed nothing. He looked surprisingly un-angry, Laena thought, which scared her more than anger would have.

"To the living room, please," he called.

Laena and Cree entered the living room wordlessly and sat on the sofa to await their fate. Laena sat close to Cree, fingering her pendant. She looked worn, and exhausted. Cree took a blanket off the back of the couch and tucked it around Laena. She lay on his lap, and soon, her breathing became soft and even. Cree stroked her hair absent-mindedly.

Ben and Michelle came into the room. "Is she asleep?" Ben whispered. Cree nodded.

Ben sat on the coffee table, facing Cree. Michelle sat in an armchair.

"Sir, I am sorry...." Cree began, but Ben held up a hand to stop him.

"I'm reluctant to wake her for this, Cree. But we want to talk to you about your relationship with our daughter." He spoke softly, so as not to wake Laena, but firmly.

Cree nodded mutely.

"She's only 17. I know you're the same age, but she has led a pretty innocent life here. She's never had a boyfriend, never even gone on a date. We're afraid that she's getting...swept away in the emotions here. And we don't want to see her hurt."

Ben paused, and Cree interrupted. "May I say something?" Ben nodded, looking exhausted. "I do not want to hurt her, sir. I will *not* hurt her, if it is within my power. I love your daughter."

Michelle shifted uncomfortably. "Cree," she said, exasperated. "How can you say you love her? You hardly know her. You two have only known each other for a short time...."

"Do you not believe in love at first sight?" Cree murmured. Ben and Michelle looked at each other. They themselves had a whirlwind courtship two decades ago, and they had only been 20 when they met.

"It's different when it's our daughter. We're trying to protect her...." Michelle said feebly, avoiding his question.

"Protect her from *me*?" Cree asked. He laughed. "Laena is a very strong woman. No matter what happens, she will be okay. There is no need to try and protect her from me...I am the one who loves her."

"That's just the point, Cree. She is not a woman. She is just a girl. A child," Ben said, his voice cracking with emotion.

"Where I come from, 17 is a woman," Cree said severely.

"And therein lies our problem," Michelle said. "Here, she is a child."

Laena stirred in Cree's lap, and everyone momentarily fell silent. When she settled, Cree whispered, "I am not sleeping with her. We have done nothing inappropriate."

"It doesn't matter, Cree. You are both teenagers, with raging hormones. If you're not sleeping together now, you will be soon. Or even if you don't, her heart could still get broken...."

"So you will not allow her to fall in love? To have a boyfriend? Until when? Until she's 20? Older? You cannot stop her emotions!"

Ben and Michelle fell silent. Cree stroked Laena's curls, and she smiled softly in her sleep and sighed. Cree looked back up at Ben and Michelle.

"I am sorry I have disappointed you. And I hope it is just the concept of her having a boyfriend that upsets you, and it is not merely the fact that it is me. I love Laena, and she loves me. I will do everything in my power to protect her from getting hurt, and I will never hurt her intentionally. But I cannot promise you that she will not ever be hurt...how can I?" He laughed bitterly. "We do not know what the future holds."

Michelle reached out and grasped Cree's arm. "Cree, you have to know this really has nothing to do with you personally. Ben and I are so impressed with your maturity. We love you! But it's your maturity that scares us, because Laena is not as mature."

Ben jumped in. "I'm going to ask you a personal question, Cree. Have you slept with other girls?"

Cree looked up at Ben, his eyes conflicted. "Yes, sir, I have," Cree answered slowly.

"How many?"

"Ben!" Michelle chided. "You don't have to answer that, Cree."

"Fine, don't answer it. But it proves my point. Laena had never even been kissed by a boy before you. You are...experienced. That scares me." Ben leaned back, his point made, and crossed his arms over his chest.

"I understand," Cree said. "So what are you asking of me? To break up with her? To stop seeing her?"

"No, of course not," Michelle answered. "Just...to be careful. To go slowly."

"More than that," Ben added. He paused, searching for words. "Don't break her heart. Don't do anything stupid. She's all we have...our only child. Don't take her away from us."

Cree did not respond. Laena shifted, opened her eyes, and sat up. She looked groggily from Cree to her parents.

"What's going on?"

"Nothing," Cree said. "Everything is fine. Do you want to go back to sleep?"

"Good idea," Ben said. "It's still quite early, and we've done everything we can do to secure the house. Maybe we should all try to take a nap."

Laena rubbed her neck, uncomfortable from laying on the couch in an awkward position. "Bed sounds good," she said, yawning. "I'm going up...."

"No," Cree said, forcefully.

"Why not?" Ben said.

"What I meant is, I think we should stay downstairs. Sir, when we were outside...I noticed that limb on the oak tree is very large, and very close to Laena's bedroom. If it should come down in the wind.... " He trailed off. "Maybe we would be safer downstairs, where the windows are boarded?"

Michelle looked at Ben. "He may be right. We can all stay in here. I can bring some air mattresses in."

"I cannot sleep anyway," Cree said. "No need to go to any trouble for me."

"Me, neither," Ben agreed. "But Cree, you're probably right. Laena, stay down here. You can stretch out on the couch, or we can get an air mattress."

Laena sat up straighter and pushed her hair out of her face. "I'm fine. I don't need a mattress." She leaned against Cree and he put his arm around her.

The wind howled outside, and even through the plywood, they could hear the rain slashing against the windows. Ben went into the kitchen to retrieve the weather radio. He came back to the living room and clicked it on.

The news was not good. The storm was still 75 miles offshore, but it was headed directly for the Cape. It had sustained winds of 135 miles per hour, making it a Category 4 storm. The storm had come on so suddenly that it did not even have a name. The Governor of Massachusetts had ordered the evacuation of Cape Cod, but Route 6, the only road off the Cape, was jammed with traffic and at a complete standstill. Local authorities were urging residents to stay indoors until Route 6 cleared.

Laena shivered. She had never been in a hurricane before, but she had heard of the devastation they could bring.

"Should we go into the basement, Dad?"

"No, Laena, we should be okay here. The basement may flood with the rain that's coming down."

"I don't understand why we have a hurricane so early in the season. It's eerie," Laena said, pulling the afghan from the couch around her shoulders.

Ben nodded in agreement. "It is unusual, as I said before. But weather can be wildly unpredictable. Have you ever heard of the butterfly effect?"

Laena and Cree both shook their heads.

"Michelle, this is more your area of expertise," Ben said. "Do you want to explain?"

"Sure," Michelle agreed. "It's fascinating. A meteorologist from MIT developed a computer program to simulate weather back in the 1960s. He discovered, quite by accident, that a tiny change in the atmosphere—and I mean really tiny—can *completely* transform the forecast. In other words, the flap of a butterfly's wings in Brazil can actually cause a hurricane in the United States several weeks later!"

"Wow," Laena said, stunned.

"Everything is so interconnected in nature, and not just here on Earth. Throughout the universe," Michelle continued, energized. "But so very chaotic! Totally unpredictable. As humans, we want the world to be predictable, of course. We want to believe that everything happens for a reason, and that we can identify those reasons. But, that's impossible."

"Is it...like the notion of keystone species, Michelle?" Cree asked, fascinated. "That the loss of one species can have reverberations through the entire ecosystem?"

Michelle nodded. "Yes, like that, Cree, but even on a much more imperceptible level. Infinitesimal changes to nature can have drastic impacts."

"And what about changes in space? For example, enlarging a wormhole?" Cree asked. "What might that do to things here on Earth?"

"A wormhole?" Ben interjected, surprised. "Have you learned about that in your school in Alaska, Cree?"

"Yes...a little, I guess. But, I have done some reading on my own...I find it intriguing."

Ben and Michelle regarded Cree curiously.

"What's a wormhole?" Laena asked.

"It's a theoretical shortcut through space and time," Ben replied. "Scientists think it might be used for time travel someday."

"Well, enlarging a wormhole could certainly have a huge impact here on Earth," Michelle said slowly. "Are you interested in time travel, Cree?"

Cree shook his head and shrugged. "Not in particular. I mean...it is interesting, but I do not know enough about it...."

"Why isn't this hurricane named, Dad? Don't they name all the hurricanes?" Laena tried to change the subject. Anything to stay away from time travel.

"They'll name her. It was just so unexpected. Another Perfect Storm."

And then, with the next news broadcast, they named the storm. Hurricane Ariel—an A name for the first storm of the season. Laena and Cree burst out laughing when they heard the name.

"What's so funny?" Michelle asked.

"Oh, nothing...." Laena burst into giggles once more. "We just know a girl from school named Ariel, and...well, let's just say it fits."

A huge snap and a splintering crash came from upstairs. All four of them jumped, and Laena yelped. The wind and rain were louder than before. To Laena, it sounded like a train roaring through the house.

"Stay here!" Ben yelled to Michelle and Laena, and started up the stairs, motioning for Cree to join him. Michelle and Laena ignored Ben and followed. As they crept up the stairs, they saw Ben and Cree standing in the doorway of Laena's room, perfectly still. Laena peeked around them.

"Oh, my God!" Laena whispered. A huge branch from the oak tree had crashed through the roof and landed on Laena's bed. Her pillow had disappeared, invisible under wet branches which spread off the bed and onto the floor. Rain poured through a huge hole in the house, soaking her pale green comforter. The wind roared through the hole. Cree and Ben turned around and saw them.

"Get back downstairs, now!" Ben ordered. "Now!"

Laena and Michelle ran back down, arms around each other. Laena was rattled.

"Mom, that could have been me. I wanted to go upstairs...Cree stopped me."

"Hush," Michelle said, holding Laena in her arms. "You're okay. It didn't happen."

Ben came pounding down the stairs, Cree following closely. Then in a flash, they were on their way back up, with blue tarps, hammers, nails and boards. As Laena shook in her mother's embrace they heard the pounding of hammers over the din. Finally, after what seemed like an eternity, Ben and Cree returned to the living room. They were sopping wet.

"You saved my life," Laena said, looking at Cree, her eyes wide.

"No, Laena.... "

"Let's get you men out of those wet clothes," Michelle interrupted. "Let me get some towels, and some of the extra clothes I bought you, Cree. Ben, is it safe to go upstairs to get a change of clothes?"

"I hope so," Ben said.

"I will go, sir," Cree offered. "Where are yours? What should I bring you?"

"Anything dry, Cree, thanks. My third drawer down in the dresser has some jeans. There are shirts in the closet." Cree nodded and headed back upstairs. Michelle went to the laundry room for towels. Ben and Laena looked at each other.

"Dad, I'm scared."

"It's okay, honey. We patched up the hole as best we could with tarps...just to try to keep the majority of the water out. We're safe down here. The windows are boarded, and everything is okay." He shivered.

Michelle came back in with towels, and handed one to Ben. When Cree returned, she handed him one as well. Cree gave Ben some dry clothes, and they both began to towel off. Cree stripped his wet clothes off and Laena averted her eyes reluctantly. Michelle collected the wet clothes from both men and brought them back up to the laundry room. Cree pulled on some of the new lounge pants and a tee shirt that Michelle had purchased for him. His muscles bulged through the flannel fabric.

"I'll make some tea," Michelle offered, heading for the kitchen.

"That really shook me up," Ben admitted. "Cree, thank you for your help up there. You sure are calm in an emergency."

"I am glad to be of help," Cree said. "It is a scary storm." He turned and looked at Laena, taking one of her hands in his. "Are you going to be all right?"

Laena nodded, but she looked pale as a ghost. Her hands were ice cold.

"Ben...sir? I think Laena may be in shock."

Ben approached Laena and grasped one of her hands. "Laena, are you all right? Everything is going to be okay. We'll fix your room when the storm is over. Don't worry."

Laena trembled visibly. Cree kneeled down in front of her. "Laena? Look at me. You are okay. You were not up there, and there is no harm done."

"I could have been killed," she whispered. She looked into Cree's eyes, unblinking.

"But you were not," Cree said practically. "You were down here, safe with us. Nothing happened, and nothing is going to happen. I promise."

Michelle came in with four mugs on a tray. "Valerian tea," she said. "It will calm everyone down."

Ben pressed one into Laena's hands. "Drink this, Laena."

Laena took a gulp and made a face. Cree laughed. "Does not taste good to you, hmmm? It tastes good to me." He grabbed a mug and took a drink. He smiled. "See? Drink up. It will help calm you. You are okay." Cree talked her through every sip until her mug was empty, and her shivering had subsided. Then he rubbed her back gently and murmured into her ear until she was calm and even smiling.

"Wow," Ben murmured appreciatively. "Cree, you're a master."

Cree looked at Ben and smiled sadly. "No, sir. I just love her. That is all it takes." Laena sighed and leaned against Cree, closing her eyes.

Michelle brought Ben to the other side of the living room, out of earshot of Laena and Cree. "What is wrong with her, Ben? I have never seen her so...vulnerable. So emotional!"

Ben shrugged. "Love, maybe?"

Michelle shook her head. "No...there's something else. Something is wrong."

"Well, the storm is pretty scary. And seeing that tree limb on her bed—she could've been killed."

"I disagree," Michelle said stubbornly. "Call it a mother's intuition, or whatever you want. But there is something really wrong. And I'm going to get to the bottom of it."

* * *

The storm lasted for a full day. Hurricane Ariel stalled over the Cape, reached Category 5 status, lashing the coast with massive waves and well over a foot of rain. Trees snapped like toothpicks, and beaches were swept out to sea. By nightfall, the storm started moving off, and the winds and rain dissipated. Ben, Michelle, Laena and Cree were exhausted. There was still no electricity, and dark had fallen. Ben decided to wait until morning to go outside and check for damage. All four slept in the living room. Cree slept on the couch, and Laena slept on a single air mattress on the floor. A second air mattress, a double, was pumped up for Ben and Michelle. By ten o'clock that night, Ben was snoring and Michelle's breathing was deep and even. Laena eased herself off of the air mattress and clambered onto the couch with Cree.

"Are you asleep?" she whispered into his ear.

Cree shook his head and opened his eyes. He opened his arms and Laena lay on top of him.

"I can't sleep," Laena complained in a soft whisper. "The air mattress squeaks. And it's not comfortable."

"Do you want the couch?" Cree asked, checking to see if Michelle and Ben were asleep. "I can sleep on the floor."

Laena shook her head and smiled. "No, thanks. It's my excuse to be on the couch with you."

"Ah," Cree said, a smile playing on his lips. "Silly me. I did not understand at first."

They cuddled, and Laena placed her ear over his heart. She loved the strong and steady beat in his chest. It made her feel alive. And safe. She sighed contentedly. But then all of her questions came flooding back into her mind.

"Cree," Laena whispered, "why do you and Ariel look so much alike? Almost like brother and sister. And she seemed so weirded out about my hair...."

"I love your crazy hair," Cree said, twirling a curl around his finger. He sighed softly. "You understand genetics, right?" Laena nodded. "Well, there was a bottleneck, a genetic bottleneck, in the humans that live in Alaska, at least. Blue eyes are recessive...I think the only genes left in our population are for blue eyes. And the black hair, that is dominant. We all have the same coloration."

"*All* of you"? Laena was incredulous.

"Yes, all of us." Cree replied. "That is why Ariel is so fascinated with your hair. And your eyes. We don't see people that look like you."

"How many of you are there, in the...what did you call it? Alaska population?"

"Almost 1,000 people. We are one of the biggest communities."

Laena gaped, stunned. One thousand people? That was tiny! "I...I can hardly believe it...how big is New York City? I mean, they have over eight million people now!"

"New York City is gone, Laena," Cree said softly. "I have heard there are people in New York, in the mountains, but not where the city used to be. That is all underwater."

Laena couldn't think about this now. She didn't want to. It was really too much to comprehend.

"How many time travelers are here, besides you and Ariel? And would you recognize them all?"

Cree shrugged. "I only know of me and Ariel. It takes much energy to send us here, and energy is difficult to generate, so I cannot imagine that you have many of us time travelers here. But I do not know about other countries, other places around the world. There is very little communication between us."

Laena opened her mouth to ask why there was so little communication, but Cree held his finger to her lips, shushing her. "Bed or couch?" he whispered, so low Laena could hardly hear him.

"Whaa.... ?"

Before she could answer, Cree had scooped her up in his strong arms and laid her gently on the air mattress. In a flash, he leaped back on the couch, his back toward her.

"Laena?" Ben's voice asked from across the room. "What are you doing?"

"Nothing, Dad. Can't sleep. Sorry I woke you...this mattress is so noisy.... " To demonstrate, Laena squirmed on the mattress, making the rubber squeak.

"Well, sleep on the floor, then. You're going to wake everyone up."

"Sorry. I'll be quiet," Laena whispered.

Within seconds, her father's gentle snoring filled the room. Cree turned silently toward Laena and winked. She smiled in return, and they held each other's gazes silently, for what seemed an eternity, until Laena fell asleep.

Chapter 10

CREE AND BEN woke early Sunday morning and went outside to survey the damage. They still did not have electricity, so they had no idea how the rest of the Cape had fared. Laena tried calling Sophie on her cell phone, but kept getting a fast busy signal. Laena wanted to bike down to the General Store and the school, not to mention Evergreen Acres, to see how well North Bayside had survived the storm, but Ben needed everyone's help at home.

Limbs littered the yard. Laena's room had been ruined from the huge void in the roof. Laena and Michelle salvaged what they could, moving Laena's things into the guest room. The chainsaw growled all morning, with Cree and Ben stacking the wood in the side yard. The boathouse seemed to have survived well, but the dock listed in the water, partially submerged.

The sun shone brightly in a crisp blue sky. The sky looked as if the storm had never existed. But on the ground, roads were flooded, and destruction was widespread. Finally, at 3 p.m., Ben and Cree had the yard and house in some semblance of normalcy, and they decided to go over to Evergreen Acres to see how the campsite had weathered the storm. Laena wanted to go too, but Ben asked Laena to stay behind and help Michelle.

Michelle and Laena prepared a late lunch for all four of them. As they chopped vegetables, Michelle broached the subject that had been bothering her all weekend.

"Laena, I'm worried about you. You seem so emotional. It's so unlike you."

"I'm fine, Mom," Laena responded, exasperated. "Really."

"No, you're not fine. I gave birth to you, raised you for 17 years, and I probably know you better than anyone. I know that there's something going on. Something you're not telling me." Michelle had paused in her chopping, knife poised about the cutting board. She looked at Laena intensely.

"Really, Mom...."

Michelle dropped the knife with a clatter. "Laena, please don't lie to me!"

Laena looked up at her mother. She so badly wanted to throw herself in her mother's arms, and tell her the whole story: how Cree was from the future, how the world was in crisis, and Cree was trying to stop the Earth's destruction, about Ariel and the grandfather paradox and Laena's crippling fear that she would never see Cree again...but she couldn't. Her mother would have her committed. Her mother was a scientist through and through, and Laena didn't think her mother would believe that Cree came from the future so readily. Time travel was a scientific possibility, but many scientists were still skeptical. And even if she and Cree could convince Michelle, they faced the same problem—Michelle would naively bring Cree to the authorities, and he would get lost in government bureaucracy. Laena averted her eyes.

"Laena? Please, honey, tell me."

Laena took a shaky breath. "I can't, Mom."

"Yes, you can. You can tell me anything. I will always love you, no matter what." Michelle crossed to the other side of the kitchen island and wrapped her arms around Laena. "Please, honey, let me help."

Laena could not hold back the tears. "It's just that...Cree may have to go back to Alaska." Laena blurted the best lie she could. It made sense that Cree's impending departure would make her so upset, right? Half the reason Laena was actually so upset was the thought of losing Cree.

Michelle held Laena at arms' length. "Why? He just moved here! He has no family there, does he?"

Laena shrugged. "I don't know...not really. He just said he may go back. And...well, I couldn't bear it if he did. I don't want to lose him, Mom!"

Michelle patted Laena's back. "Oh, honey! Why don't you talk to him about it? Tell him how you feel? Maybe he won't go. He likes it here, doesn't he?"

Laena nodded miserably. "I think he said he had some kind of...obligation."

"Well, there's no use getting all upset over something that may not happen. And you know that if there is anything your dad and I can do to help Cree stay here, we will. Is it money, do you think?"

Laena shrugged. She felt awful lying to her mother, but what choice did she have? "Mom, don't talk to him about it. Just let it go. If it looks like he's going to go back, or if he needs help, I'll let you know, okay?"

"But maybe I can help before it reaches a critical stage...."

"Mom, please. Don't interfere. I don't want Cree knowing I told you about this."

The kitchen door opened, and Ben and Cree walked in, grim looks on their faces.

"What?" Michelle asked. "Is it bad?"

"The cabins are pretty destroyed," Ben replied. "We looked for Mark, but I think he must have evacuated."

"Who's Mark?" Laena asked.

"The owner," Cree responded, looking stunned. "He is the one who gave me my job, let me live in the cabin. I am not sure what I will do now. The cabins have no roofs. It is a mess. I grabbed what I could find of my clothes and my things, but I lost what little I had."

"Cree! Is Zed okay?" Laena gasped. "Where is he?"

Cree shook his head. "The barn is fine. No damage. Zed is gone, but so is the trailer. I think Mark must have taken him when he left the Cape. He loves that horse—he would not have left him behind in the storm."

Michelle walked over and put an arm around Cree. "You'll stay with us, Cree. Until Mark can fix Evergreen Acres up, you can stay with us."

"No, no, I cannot impose like that," Cree protested, horrified. "You have already done so much for me...."

"Don't be ridiculous, Cree," Ben said. "Of course, we're going to have to put Laena in the guest room until we can fix her room, but you can sleep downstairs in the living room. Not exactly luxurious accommodations, but at least it's warm and dry."

"And it comes with meals," Michelle said teasingly.

"Really, I cannot...."

"You can and you will, Cree. I'm done talking about it," Ben said firmly. "Look, you are here alone, no parents, no one to take care of you." Cree started to speak, but Ben held up his hand to silence him. "I know you can take care of yourself. But you have to have a roof over your head, and you must finish out the school year. You'll stay here until Evergreen Acres is repaired. I think it's really not as bad as it looks. Mark should have that finished in a few weeks, maybe a month tops."

"I cannot pay you...."

"You don't have to pay us," Michelle said. "Please, Cree. Don't fight us on this. It's just temporary."

Laena ran over and put her arms around Cree. "Give it up, Cree. My parents are just as stubborn as I am. You're moving in. At least temporarily...face it."

Cree looked pained, but said nothing.

"What are you worried about?" Michelle asked gently.

Cree looked over at Michelle. "You are always so worried about me and Laena," Cree said hesitantly. "If I am here, all the time...."

"We can keep an eye on you," Ben finished jokingly. "Listen, Cree, it's not you we are worried about. We were teenagers once, too. Just use good judgment. And keep in mind that if you hurt my daughter, I'll hunt you down and kill you." Ben slapped Cree on the back and smiled. "Just kidding. It'll be like having the son I always wanted."

"Thanks, Dad," Laena said, sarcastically.

"This conversation is over. No more discussion." Ben turned to the sink to wash his hands. "Do you ladies have lunch ready yet? Because I am starving."

Cree released Laena and went over to hug Michelle. "Thank you, for everything. I cannot ever express to you what you have done for me...."

Michelle hugged Cree back. "Honey, it's no problem."

Ben finished drying his hands and turned from the sink. Cree held out his hand, and Ben pulled him into a hug. "You're a good kid, Cree. It will be a pleasure to have you around."

Laena could see that Cree was tearing up, and he turned away, embarrassed.

"Is everyone washed?" Michelle asked. "I'll get us lunch."

As Laena and Cree sat down at the table, Laena reached under the table and squeezed Cree's leg. He grabbed her hand and squeezed back. "Welcome to the family," Laena whispered.

Chapter 11

ELECTRICITY RETURNED sometime Sunday night, but the television said there would be no school Monday due to extensive cleanup of fallen trees. Michelle spent the night doing laundry and cleaning up the house. Laena, thrilled to have an unexpected day off from school, suggested to Cree they go into Boston to visit the Aquarium. They broached the subject over breakfast.

"Mom, can Cree and I go into Boston today? I want to show him the Aquarium," Laena asked, excitement in her voice.

Michelle hesitated.

"Please, Mom? Please?" Laena asked.

"How are you getting in? The ferry isn't running yet...." Michelle was clearly not thrilled with the idea.

"We'll take the bus. I already checked—they're running. If you could drop us off in Hyannis on your way to work...or if dad can drive us to the bus stop, we'll get off at South Station and walk."

Ben crumpled up his napkin and put it on his empty plate. "I don't see why not, Michelle. There's no school, and I'm going to spend the day trying to find some contractors who can patch the hole in the roof of our house. There won't be much for the kids to do around here."

"Michelle, it would mean a lot to me to be able to see the Aquarium," Cree chimed in. "And we won't be late...we can get home in time to have dinner ready for you."

Michelle laughed. "Okay, that clinched it. If you two will be home in time to have dinner ready, you can go."

"Awesome!" said Laena. "Can you drive us to Hyannis?"

"Sure," Michelle agreed. She glanced at the clock on her cell phone. "If you can be ready in 10 minutes, I'll drive you."

Laena and Cree jumped up from the table. "No problem!"

"Wait! Do you kids need money?" Ben asked, taking his wallet from his back pocket. "Between the bus tickets and the Aquarium tickets, it'll be an expensive day."

"Thanks, Dad," Laena said, grabbing several twenty-dollar bills from him.

Michelle swallowed the last gulp of her coffee and began rummaging through her purse. "No, wait, take our Aquarium membership cards. It'll get you in for free." She handed the cards over to Laena. "Please don't lose them."

"I won't. Promise." Laena glanced at Cree. "I'm going to brush my teeth and then I'll be ready." She brought their plates to the sink.

"I will be right up," Cree said. He turned to Michelle and Ben. "Thank you for letting us go," he said solemnly. "And for everything else."

"Anytime," Michelle said. She hesitated, then said, "Cree...."

"Yes?"

"I know you have a lot on your plate, but I was wondering if you'd like to make a little extra cash?"

Cree looked surprised. "How?" he asked, intrigued. Laena paused in the kitchen doorway to hear her mother.

"Research. For me. I'm working on a fascinating project at CCOL, and I could use a research assistant. There wouldn't be set hours, so you could fit the work in whenever you get the chance...maybe just a few hours per week, just at the beginning, to see how it works out."

Laena took a breath, relieved. Her mom must be doing this for her...she must think that if Cree has a job, he'll stick around Cape Cod rather than go home to Alaska.

Cree's face lit up. "That would be wonderful!" He paused. "I hope...are you sure you are not just doing this out of pity for me?"

"Not at all," Michelle said smiling. "I need an assistant. Go get ready, or you'll make me late for work. We can talk more about it tonight at dinner. Which you and Laena are cooking, right?"

"Right!" Cree agreed. He gave Michelle a hug and a peck on the cheek, grabbed Laena's hand, and they ran up the stairs together.

"That was nice of you," Ben said. "I didn't know you needed a research assistant."

"I really do," Michelle responded, clearing the rest of the breakfast dishes from the table. "I think Cree is bright and hardworking, and Lord knows he needs the money."

"He doesn't seem very computer savvy," Ben said thoughtfully. "I've never seen him get on Laena's laptop at all, or get on Facebook or any of those social networking sites."

"I'm sure he can handle what I give him, Ben," Michelle said confidently. "Do you think I shouldn't have offered him the job?"

"No, no," Ben replied. "Not at all. It's just that I can't always figure Cree out. He's...he's a strange boy in some ways."

"Mmmm," Michelle said noncommittally. "Maybe so, but he's smart, mature, loves the ocean, and our daughter is totally smitten with him. And he has no one else to help him out, or guide him. If I can make his life easier, then why not?"

Ben didn't reply. Michelle glanced at her phone again and said, "I'm late. Can you do the dishes, Ben?" Without waiting for an answer, she left the kitchen and called up the stairs to Laena and Cree. "I'm leaving in three minutes, kids!"

Laena and Cree came down the stairs, chatting excitedly. Michelle shook her head, laughing. "You two look like kids going to a candy shop for the first time."

Cree looked up, grinning. "That is what it is like, for me. I have never been to an Aquarium...I cannot wait to see all the species that are here on the east coast."

"Well, hurry up then, and get in the car. Laena, don't forget your phone." The three of them hustled out the front door as Laena called, "Bye, Dad! Good luck with the contractors!"

Michelle, Laena and Cree climbed into the car, Cree sitting in the passenger seat so he could stretch his long legs. The teenagers were animated, but sobered quickly as they saw the damage from the storm driving toward Hyannis on Route 6. Houses without roofs, uprooted trees, soil washed away from the torrential rains.

"Wow," Laena said, face pressed to the window. "There are so many trees down!"

"It's worse on the ocean side of the Cape," Michelle responded. "That was one bad storm. We are truly lucky we didn't get hit harder where we are."

Laena noticed that Cree clung to the door as if his life depended on it. He had probably never driven this fast in a car before. In fact, he had never been on a highway before. She grasped what life must be like for him in her time. Everything she took for granted—electricity, cars, planes, even food from other countries—was new to him. New, and perhaps disappointing. For Cree knew first hand how the choices they were making now would affect the earth in 200 years. How did he keep himself from getting angry at them? Laena leaned forward and grasped his shoulder.

"Are you okay?" she asked softly.

"Why wouldn't he be okay?" Michelle answered. "Cree, do you get carsick?"

Laena jumped in before Cree could contemplate an answer. For all she knew, Cree had no idea what 'carsick' meant. "Yes, he does," she said. "Another reason to let him sit in front."

"I'll try to drive smoothly," Michelle offered. "If you feel sick, let me know and I'll pull over."

Cree glanced over his shoulder at Laena in confusion. She put her finger to her lips and he nodded imperceptibly.

They drove the rest of the way in silence, taking in the aftermath of the storm. Michelle pulled off Route 6 and maneuvered into the bus station parking lot.

"You're sure you have enough money?" she asked, looking at Laena in the rearview mirror.

"Positive," Laena reassured her. "Thanks for the ride, Mom."

"You'll have to take a cab from the bus station home this afternoon...."

"I know, Mom. I have enough. Honest," Laena said as she unbuckled her seat belt and opened the car door.

Cree turned to Michelle and smiled. "Thank you. For the ride, and...for everything."

Michelle returned his smile and patted Cree's knee. "No worries," she responded. "Take care in Boston, now. It's not New York, but it's bigger than anything you've seen in Alaska."

"We'll be careful," Laena promised. "Cree, c'mon. Our bus is here."

Laena and Cree waved to Michelle as she drove off, and they walked over to the idling Plymouth to Brockton bus. They found two seats together and sat down. Cree looked around in amazement. "It is huge!" he whispered. His eyes were wide.

Laena laughed. "You should see the size of some of the airplanes we have," Laena whispered, not wanting to draw surrounding passengers' attention to Cree's naïveté. Cree reached out and grasped Laena's hand when the bus rumbled to a start and pulled out of the lot toward the highway. She lifted the armrest between their two seats up, and moved over until their thighs touched. She laid her head gently on his chest, and stroked his thigh with her free hand.

"There's nothing to be afraid of," she murmured, so no one else could hear. "It's just like a big car." Cree's grasp on her hand loosened slightly, but Laena wondered how he would react to the city. Had he ever seen towering buildings before? Probably not. Then she realized that she had no idea how he got here. She had asked him before, but he swept her questions aside, telling her it was too difficult to explain. But she really wanted to know—what did time travel involve? How did it work?

"Cree, how did you get here? And why did you come? I mean, who sent you?" Laena asked softly.

Cree turned away from the window and looked at her. "It is complicated," he replied thoughtfully.

Laena looked at him, waiting for more. When he remained silent, she said, "Can you try to explain it to me? I really want to understand. And I want to know how you'll get back."

Cree sighed. "I can try, but it is not easy. So much is new, having been discovered after your time."

Laena nodded, urging him to go on. "Please try," she said.

"Okay, I will try. First, you know *why* I came. I came back to try and show the scientists of your time—well, your mother—the effect antibacterials have on the krill and the oceans. But the leaders of the Alaska population sent me. They chose me because they knew they could not send someone older. Any scientist who arrived at CCOL would have to have credibility—publications, an education—we could not fabricate that. So we thought a student, someone who wanted to learn and volunteer...your mother and others might accept that."

"That makes sense," Laena said slowly. "It was a risk, of course, but I don't see what else you could have done."

"Right. The whole thing is a risk. We know there is a big chance of failure. But once our leaders decided to send me, pretending to be a high school student, we worked hard on physically getting me here. I will try to explain how we do this. Are you ready to hear? It is very complicated."

"Yes," Laena said. "I can't promise I'll understand, but I'll try."

Cree nodded. "Time does not always flow at a constant rate. It fluctuates."

Laena shifted so she could see his face better. Cree caressed her hand with his thumb. Laena nodded and said, "So time slows down and speeds up, right? It's not always the same. Got it."

"Right. Also, you know that we live in a four dimensional world, no? Three of those dimensions are obvious—length, width and depth. Something on paper is two-dimensional—it only has length and width. But you...you are three-dimensional. You have depth as well as length and width." His voice teased, and he smiled, cupping his hand around her breast. Laena gasped and pushed his hand down.

"Cree! We're in public!"

Cree chuckled. "No one can see us with these tall seats...we can fool around and no one would know."

Laena blushed and shook her head. She grabbed both his hands so they wouldn't stray. "Keep explaining...and keep your mind on time travel."

Cree sighed dramatically. "Okay, okay. So, you know the three dimensions...those are easy. Time is the fourth dimension. Time and space have to exist together...you cannot have one without the other. You understand?"

Laena nodded, even though she had always had a hard time grasping this stuff.

"Everything that happens in the universe happens in the context of time and space, yes?" Cree cocked his head, trying to ascertain whether Laena understood.

"Yes, I see that," she said. "But how do you travel through time? How do you go backwards in time, and keep your same three dimensions?"

"Ah, that is where it gets interesting." Cree's face was animated, talking about science. His blue eyes shone with a light and intensity that made them glow. He looked...stunning. Laena felt a shiver of pleasure course through her body. "Gravity not only pulls on objects, but it also pulls on time. Remember when your father dropped the book in class to demonstrate gravity? He just let it go, and it fell to the floor, because of gravitational pull. Well, that gravitational pull also operates on time. Is that not fascinating? Gravity can *actually* pull time." Cree peered at Laena to make sure she was still following. Satisfied, he went on, "So the farther you get away from the earth's gravitational pull, the *faster* time goes. Scientists have proven this, so we know that it is a fact. So...imagine a spaceship, circling the earth and approaching the speed of light. You know the speed of light? It is 186,000 miles per second. You cannot go faster than this, but if you fly just underneath this speed, time on the spaceship slows way down. Time on the spaceship is much slower than on earth. So when the spaceship lands back on earth, it is the future. But traveling backwards in time, like I did, is more difficult than moving forward in time."

Laena nodded, and tried to keep her mind on his words. She let go of one of his hands and caressed his chest, feeling his muscles beneath his shirt. Cree ignored her.

"When you look into the sky, you see stars, right? Well, the light from those stars takes *thousands* of years to reach earth. So, you may be seeing the light from a star that is already dead. In essence, you are seeing something in the past...." Cree trailed off, shifting in his seat. "Laena, what are you doing to me? I am trying to answer your question." His voice was stern, but a smile tugged at the corners of his mouth.

"I can't help it. You're so damned sexy when you talk about this stuff. So handsome. I can't concentrate. I just want to touch you...."

Cree laughed. "Okay," he said, his voice dropping and getting husky. "You want to learn about sex instead of time travel, hmmm? I can help you." He pulled Laena over to him and held her tightly. His hands ran lightly over her back, then traveled up under her shirt.

Laena gasped. "Cree! No, I...not here.... " She struggled to get his hands away from her, but he was too strong.

"Not here? Then where? When? I can teach you other things, things different than time travel. I can teach you ecstasy, like you have never known.... " Cree was whispering in her ear, and his warm breath made her moan in pleasure. "Would you like that?"

Laena nodded in a stupor. "Yes, I would like that."

Cree kissed her neck and Laena felt a warmth and wetness flood her body. "Cree," she moaned.

He removed his hands and pushed Laena gently but firmly back in her own seat. He shook his head as if to clear it. "Laena," he groaned. "You cannot do this to me. I will get out of control and I will not be able to stop myself."

"I don't want you to stop," Laena said plainly.

"Oh? You want me to have sex with you? Here on this bus? In front of all these people? I think we would get kicked off, no?"

Laena made a face. "No, not here on the bus. But...I want to be with you. I can't help it. I can't stop touching you, wanting you...."

Cree interrupted. "There is something you need to understand about men, Laena. You cannot get me all...worked up like this, wanting to take you, and then not be able to finish it. It hurts me."

"Hurts you?"

Cree motioned to his lap, and when Laena glanced down, she saw his arousal. She was mortified, and looked away immediately. "I'm...I'm sorry, Cree!" she stuttered.

He laughed at her discomfort. "Do not apologize. You just need to know the effect you have on me. We can hold hands, and cuddle, and I can control myself. But when you say those things, and moan, my body gets carried away and now.... " He looked down at his lap with dismay, "now I have to figure out some way to tell a certain part of my body to calm down, that it is not getting what it wants."

Laena giggled awkwardly. She had never had a boy speak so plainly about his body this way. "I'm sorry, Cree, really I am. Maybe if we talk about time travel it will...take your mind off of what it wants?"

Cree laughed. "You can say the word, Laena. Sex. My body wants sex." He paused and looked at her earnestly. "No, that is not right...my body wants to make love to you. Not just sex, like what I have had with other girls. I want to show you how much I love you."

Laena smiled and squeezed his hand. "We can do that someday, can't we? Show how much we love each other?"

Cree smiled wistfully. "I hope so, sweetie." He stroked her curls and looked into her eyes. "So how about we finish talking about how I got here?"

Laena exhaled deeply and nodded.

"Okay, where was I? I think I was talking about the lights from the stars when you attacked me." He grinned at her crookedly.

"I did not *attack* you," she protested.

He shrugged. "No matter. The stars, yes?"

Laena nodded, smiling. "Okay, okay, the stars. The lights from the stars."

"Yes. Some of the lights you see, the stars in the sky, are already dead, but you can still see them. Now, have you heard of wormholes? We spoke of them with your parents just a few days ago. Einstein thought of them, so really they are called an Einstein-Rosen bridge. I don't know why you call them wormholes...you have heard of them, right?"

"Yes, but I'm not sure I understand them. Physics is really not my thing."

"Okay, I will try to be simple then. Masses put pressure on pieces of the universe. If two masses put pressure on different pieces of the universe opposite each other, they could meet, and form a tunnel. Or a...a shortcut. Like a passageway from one place in the universe to another. That is a wormhole. You understand?"

Laena laughed. "I have no idea what you are saying," she said. "None whatsoever."

Cree smiled. "Yes, it is not simple. But pretend you understand that. I will tell you that there *are* these tiny little tunnels, or wormholes, that appear and reappear. They happen right now. And before I was born, scientists figured out how to stabilize them, to keep them open, and make them big enough to travel through. The government in the United States put much money into this, once they realized that the Earth was in trouble. Disaster loomed, and they needed to find a solution. One president thought maybe we could go back in time, and prevent all of our mistakes."

"So that's how you...and Ariel...got here? Through a wormhole? How do you know where they are, and how do you get back?"

"We can control them, to a certain extent. We know when they will happen, and where we have to be to enter them."

Laena's heart clenched. "So...you know when you are leaving? When you are going back?"

Cree froze, the proverbial deer caught in headlights. Grief etched his features.

"Cree? Answer me. Do you know when you are going back?"

"Laena...." he began. She could see the evasiveness on his face.

She lowered her voice to a whisper. "Do you know when you are going back to your time?"

Cree nodded miserably.

"When?"

"Laena, I do not want to tell you. If I tell you, then you will worry...."

A thought struck Laena. "I won't. I won't, I promise. You can take me back with you. Let me come back with you, Cree."

Cree had been already shaking his head. "No, Laena, that is impossible."

"Why?" she cried. "Why is it impossible? Please take me with you...."

"And leave your family, your friends, your life behind? No. I will not do that to you." He shook his head firmly.

"*You* are my life, Cree. You."

"We are not talking about this anymore," he said. His face hardened.

"Cree.... "

"NO."

"Then at least tell me when you are leaving. You have to. You can't just leave me suddenly, just...disappear."

"Oh, Laena," he said, softening. "I would not do that to you, sweetie. I will let you know. We can say goodbye."

"Great," Laena responded sadly. "Can't wait to say goodbye." She crossed her arms and turned her back to him. She knew she was being childish, but she hurt. Cree wrapped his strong arms around her and whispered in her ear. "I will be with you for a long time. It is only April, and I will be with you until the end of the summer, okay? We have many months left together."

The end of the summer? Laena felt both relieved and dismayed. The end of summer was another four months away, which seemed in one sense like an eternity. But in another sense, it was nothing at all. Only four more months left with Cree? She could not comprehend the end of their relationship. She knew, deep in her heart, that it was inevitable, but she couldn't visualize it happening. How would she go on without him? She tried to be practical. She had only met him recently, but she loved him with everything she had within her. She felt like she needed him, to be whole, to complete herself. Cree was her other half. Laena shook her head. She had always thought of herself as independent and stable and practical...and here she was, thinking that her life would be over at age 17, simply because she would not have a certain boy. But then again, Cree was not any boy. He was...he was Cree.

"Laena?" Cree interrupted her reverie.

Laena did not respond. She turned back to face him, and wordlessly sank into his arms. "I don't want to talk about this anymore," she said eventually, her voice so soft he could hardly hear her. Cree stroked her back, her hair, murmured words in her ear that she did not understand or even care to understand. The engine of the bus thrummed and rumbled beneath them, and she fell into a trance.

Cree made a strangled sound and Laena roused from her reverie. She sat up and looked out the window, following Cree's gaze. They were entering Boston, and the Hancock Tower and Prudential Building were visible from the highway. There were buildings everywhere, and cars, four lanes thick on the highway.

"Welcome to Boston," Laena murmured.

"I have never seen so much development...so many people," Cree said in awe. "It is horrifying." He could not tear his eyes away from the scenes outside his window. Laena did not respond. In a way, it was horrifying. So many people, crammed into a small space, everything living and green paved over in concrete.

"Ironic, isn't it?" Laena murmured. "All the politicians talk about is how to increase growth...build more, create new jobs...and we already have too much."

Cree nodded and turned to peer out the other window on the other side of the aisle. "And why are you so close to the sea? This is why Boston is destroyed...you cannot be this close to the sea with the storms and the sea level rise.... "

Laena felt a stab of fear go through her. She wasn't surprised that Boston would not survive, just like New York and Florida. Cree already told her the Cape had been destroyed, but Boston too? She loved Boston. And there was such history...all of that would be lost? She couldn't imagine it gone.

"Do you know the history of Boston? All the things that happened here when our country gained independence? The Boston Massacre, the Revolutionary War, Paul Revere.... ?"

"Yes, yes, of course," Cree responded, turning to her. "We learned about all that. I would love to see some of those things...the Freedom Trail, the old churches and graveyards...it is quite unbelievable that I am here, when Boston still existed.... " He trailed off. "I am sorry, Laena. I know you hate it when I speak like that, about what happens to the places you love. I keep forgetting...this is so bizarre for me to see this, when in my time it is more of a legend than anything."

Laena smiled and grasped his hand. "I understand," she said gently. "And it's okay. But for today, let's go to the Aquarium and try to see all the species that you want to see."

The bus pulled into South Station and the doors opened with a hydraulic hiss. Laena and Cree disembarked with the other passengers, and Laena grabbed Cree's hand.

"Come on," she said. "Would you rather walk to the Aquarium, or do you want to take the subway?"

"What is a subway?" Cree asked, baffled.

"It's a train that rides underground.... "

"NO. No, thank you. I would rather walk," Cree said hurriedly. "I do not want to be in a machine underground, thank you."

"This from the man who traveled here through a wormhole," she teased. "Okay, we'll walk. It's less than a mile, and we can walk along the harbor."

Laena led Cree through South Station as he looked up at the massive vaulted ceilings, paying no attention to where he was walking. Laena finally tugged him out through the doors and into the street. She turned to the right and started walking toward the Aquarium. Cree stared, open-mouthed, at the buildings.

"Laena," Cree whispered. "People go up...in those buildings? Up to the top?"

"Mmmm-hmmm," she responded. "There are elevators to take you up."

"What is an elevator?"

"It's like a really small room that you stand in, and cables pull you up—or drop you down—from floor to floor."

Cree shuddered. "Why not take the stairs? Are there no stairs?" The brilliant sun shone on his hair, and Laena realized it was so black, it was almost blue. She squeezed his hand.

"There are stairs, for emergencies, but it would take too long to walk all the way up if you worked on the 30th floor."

Cree shook his head. He stopped abruptly on the sidewalk, and people, annoyed, had to walk around them. "Are there these elevator things in the Aquarium? I do not want to ride one."

Laena shook her head. "We don't have to. The Aquarium is not that tall. We can walk."

Cree reluctantly started walking again. Laena marveled at how foreign all the technology must seem to Cree. He looked almost panicked by the people, the buildings, the cars and trucks.

"I cannot believe that all of...all of *this* is what leads to our decline. Was it worth it?" Cree shook his head in disgust.

Laena pulled him to the far edge of the sidewalk to a brick wall bordering an office building, creating a small plaza for the workers.

"Sit down," she commanded.

"What?" Cree looked puzzled.

"Sit," Laena repeated. Cree sat reluctantly on the wall. Laena stood in front of him. "Cree, there is nothing to worry about, here with me, in the city. I know this must be weird for you, but nothing is going to happen to hurt you. This is a normal day in Boston for all these people. It's a safe city, and we are here to go to the Aquarium and have fun." She paused, grabbing hold of both his hands. "I also know you must be angry at us, blithely going about our business while the world is falling apart around us. We're hastening its demise, and that must really piss you off. You probably see all this building and pollution and burning of fossil fuels and think, 'No wonder the seas rose and everything died. How can these people be so ignorant?' Well, some of us are ignorant, and others just don't know how to stop it. But we're not all bad people. There are some of us who really care, and are working hard to try and fix the problems. You being here...well, that means we failed. But it doesn't mean that we don't care, or that we want it to happen. You have the benefit of 20/20 hindsight. You *know* what's going to happen. No one here does." Laena paused and searched Cree's eyes. He watched her intently, listening skeptically. "Well, some of us suspect what is going to happen, and we try to warn others, but I guess...I guess we are just too selfish to do anything about it. No one wants to change their lifestyle to save the people in the future." Cree opened his mouth to interject, and Laena stopped him. "I know that sounds awful, and I know the future is right around the corner. I know *you* are the future. I will do everything in my power to help you. I promise. But that's all I can do. Please don't think badly of all of us. We're really not as appalling as...well, as I'm guessing you think we are." Laena paused. "And I know I've been incredibly selfish, too. I've been thinking about me...about *us*, instead of what's going to happen to the planet.

But I do know what's important here...really. I understand what's at stake."

Cree looked down, head hanging, silent. Finally, he looked back up at Laena. "I know you are not selfish, sweetie. I am sorry I have been so...judgmental. This is very hard for me, though, as you have guessed. Probably as hard for me as it is for you to hear about what the future is like."

Laena gave him a smile and tugged him back to his feet. She laughed. "I guess we're both in the same boat," she said. "C'mon...let's get to the Aquarium."

Laena pushed through the revolving doors of the Aquarium, and pulled Cree through the entrance turnstile after showing their membership cards to the Aquarium employees. The cool, dank smell of fish and seawater enveloped them as they moved toward the exhibits. Cree covered his nose and mouth.

"What is that awful smell?" he croaked.

Laena laughed. "That's fish, Cree. Just fish." Her voice echoed in the chilly chamber of the Aquarium. The whole interior of the building appeared to be bathed in a cool, dark blue, reflections from the vast tanks of water. *Like Cree's eyes*, Laena thought. Cree was astounded, and Laena grabbed his free hand and dragged him to the penguin enclosure.

"These are...penguins?" Cree said, his voice muffled through his hand.

"Yes, penguins. Take your hand off your face," she laughed, tugging his hand down. "You'll get used to the smell."

The penguins waddled around the enclosure, close enough for the viewers to touch them had they been allowed. Cree gaped. "They are so...so silly looking!" He laughed. "Oh, Laena. I have never seen such a thing!" His eyes sparkled with excitement, and Laena pointed out the different species. After several minutes, she tugged his hand.

"Come, Cree. There is so much more to see!"

"I could stay here all day, just looking at these penguins," he murmured. "Look at them!" Cree was especially enamored with the rockhopper penguins, hopping from rock to rock in perfect synchrony with their spiky black and yellow-feathered crests on their heads. "They don't look real!" he chuckled. "They look like...what do you call them? Cartoons?"

Laena tugged harder, and Cree reluctantly allowed himself to be dragged into a dim and gurgling corridor. She whisked him up the stairs to the top floor surrounding the huge central tank, and then they slowly wended their way down the ramp. Cree practically had his nose pressed against the glass.

"What's that?!" he asked, excitedly, pointing to a hammerhead shark. Laena answered him, trying to keep her voice low.

"And look at that! What is that...a sea turtle??"

"Yes," Laena answered. "That's Myrtle. Myrtle the turtle. She's famous. But Cree, you have to keep your voice down," she whispered. "People won't understand why you don't know anything."

Other people in the Aquarium were giving Cree strange glances, but he remained oblivious. He walked slowly down the ramp, face against the glass of the huge cylinder, taking everything in.

"Laena!" he shouted. "Look! There's a person in there with them!" He stopped watching in amazement as the diver fed the fish in the tank.

"They go in there to feed the animals," Laena explained in a hushed tone.

"Won't they get bitten?"

Laena shook her head. "They keep them well fed, so they are safe from the sharks. The sharks are actually intelligent animals. They know they're going to get fed by the divers." Laena took Cree's hand gently. "Do you want to go touch some animals? Starfish?"

Cree nodded. They walked the rest of the way down the ramp, Cree's eyes never leaving the tanks. When they finally reached the bottom, Cree stopped short.

"What is this?" he whispered, pointing at the Aquarium sign, his face a mask of anger.

"What is what?" Laena was confused. "The sign?"

"It is the sign of the Chosen," Cree glowered. "The sign of Jesus, of the Christians."

Laena looked at the blue and white Aquarium symbol, a blue background with a simple white fish. It did look a little like the sign for Christianity. She shook her head, trying to explain. "No, Cree, it isn't a religious sign. I agree, it looks a little like that, but it's the symbol for the Aquarium. It's their trademark."

"Trademark?" Cree was still confused, but the anger had seeped out of his body.

"Yes...a symbol that lets people recognize them. Like their own...brand." Laena struggled to explain, but Cree didn't understand.

"So it is not saying anything about God?" he whispered.

Laena smiled tenderly. "No, no, not at all. Honestly, Cree. See? It's different than the symbol for Christianity. It has this extra circle, for the gills, and an eye.... "

A velvety voice whispered in Laena's ear, and she felt a cool hand on her neck. "No, I think Cree was correct the first time. It is the symbol of God, and reminds us that he has made all these creatures." Laena whipped around, and saw Ariel standing not a foot behind them. She was dressed in tight jeans and a skimpy top that showed off her midriff and her breasts. Cree did not move, but Laena felt him stiffen.

"The Aquarium trademark," he said firmly. "God has made nothing here."

Ariel laughed and slipped her arms around Cree's back, nestling her head between his shoulder blades. "You are so naive, Cree."

Cree shrugged free of Ariel's embrace and turned to face her. "Do not touch me, Ariel. Not now, not ever again. I am done with you." His voice was calm, scarily devoid of emotion.

Ariel was not deterred. She smiled prettily and said, "You are not done with me, darling." Then she launched into an angry tirade in Esperanto, not one word of which Laena could understand. Cree stood stock-still, listening to her speak. Finally, when she paused, Cree said, "Are you quite finished?" Without waiting for an answer, he said, "Good. Laena, Ariel is done talking at us. I would like to go see the starfish now, and the jellyfish exhibit." He put his arm around Laena and pulled her away from Ariel. He looked down at Laena and smiled. "Ariel wants to join us, but I would rather have you to myself." He walked her swiftly away, propelling her firmly but gently.

Ariel stayed rooted to her spot, smiling. When they were out of earshot, Laena asked, "What did she want? How did she follow us here?"

He ignored Laena's questions. "Can we pretend that encounter did not happen? I do not want to ruin an otherwise wonderful day."

Laena opened her mouth to protest, but then thought better of it. It made no sense to talk about Ariel, or ask what she had said, especially not here where Ariel could be listening in on their conversation. The hairs on Laena's neck stood up in a primitive warning, and she glanced over her shoulder. Sure enough, Ariel walked about ten feet behind them, her eyes boring into their backs.

"She's following us now, through the Aquarium," she murmured to Cree.

"Mmmm," Cree said noncommittally. "Ignore her."

So Laena did the best she could to pretend Ariel wasn't there, and she played tour guide instead. Cree soon seemed to forget about Ariel's malevolent presence, and lost himself in the wonders of the ocean creatures. He chuckled when a starfish stirred in his hands, marveled at the spiny sea urchins and the transparent jellyfish. Laena got caught up in Cree's excitement, and before they knew it, it was lunchtime.

"I'm hungry," Laena remarked, as her stomach rumbled. "Do you want to get some lunch?"

"One more stop, please. Is there someone who works here, someone we can talk to about krill?" Cree asked.

Laena shrugged. "I have no idea. I think we just have to ask an employee." She glanced around. "There's someone." She pointed at the jellyfish tank.

Cree approached a staff member wearing the teal Aquarium tee shirt with the employee logo. "Excuse me....?"

"Yes?" The young man turned around with a smile on his face. "How can I help you?"

"I am wondering about krill...is there someone here who can answer a few questions for me?"

"Sure!" he said. "I can try to answer whatever questions you have."

"Thank you! Do you have krill here, in the Aquarium?" Cree asked.

"Mmmm, hmmm, we do. We use them to feed many of our animals—the penguins, the balloonfish, the needlefish...."

"But you don't have the krill themselves in an exhibit, for us to see?"

The Aquarium employee shook his head. "No, sorry, we don't. But you can sometimes see them when the fish are being fed...let's go take a look. Come with me." Laena and Cree followed him through the dim halls to a large tank. He peered into the depths, searching for something. "Ah! There!" he said, pointing. "See those balloonfish? They're being fed krill. They don't last long before they are gobbled up, but there they are."

The teens watched with interest as the krill were tossed into the tank. Cree turned back to face the staff member. "Where do you get them? The krill?"

"We get them from the ocean. But frankly, with all the pollution that's in the water, we're thinking about starting to use lab-raised krill. It'll be a lot more expensive, but we won't be introducing nasty stuff into our animals."

"Interesting. Thank you so much," Cree said.

"No problem," he said, nodding. "Enjoy the rest of your visit!"

Laena and Cree left the Aquarium, squinting in the bright sunshine. It had turned into a beautiful day.

Laena and Cree walked hand in hand past the Christopher Columbus Park, down Cross Street, and then turned into the crooked cobbled streets of the North End. Before long, Laena stopped in front of an old wooden building sandwiched between newer brownstones.

"What is this building?" Cree asked, gazing at it in wonder.

"This is Paul Revere's house," Laena replied. "This is where he lived when he took his famous midnight ride, on horseback, to warn all the towns that the British were invading."

Cree stared at the house, wide-eyed. His black hair ruffled in the warm breeze. "What year was that?" he asked reverently.

"1775, I think." Laena replied. "Let's go look."

As Laena pulled the door to the house open, she caught a glimpse of Ariel, standing across the street, staring at them. "Don't look now," she hissed under her breath, "but Ariel is following us!"

Cree didn't seem surprised. "Ignore her," he said. "Just pretend she is not there.

Cree and Laena entered the house, fully restored and now a museum opened to the public. The rooms smelled old and musty, and the ceilings were low. Cree had to duck his head to get through the doorways. Cree wandered around in awe, and then said, "It looks more like my time than yours. Is that not...what do you call it? Ironic?"

"In what way is it like your time?" Laena asked, genuinely interested.

Cree considered the question. "It is simple in my time," he finally replied. "No electronics or any power. A fireplace to stave off the cold. Just...back to basics, I guess."

"Which do you prefer?" Laena asked.

Cree looked at Laena and gathered her in his arms. "Do not take this the wrong way. But I like the people in my time better because we take care of the earth, or what is left of it. At least the Brights do. Your time is more comfortable, that is certain, and easier. But it is too crowded for me. Too many people, too many noises and smells. I want to sit outside at night and see all the stars, and wonder about other worlds, other universes, maybe even other beings. I do not like the lights and the noise here. You understand? I guess I am just not used to it."

Laena nodded. "I would like to be in a place where people cared about the earth, too, with you."

Cree smiled sadly. "Yes, me too. I would like to be together on a healthy planet, but with the advances you have. I hate the devastation of my time. There is so much to save here."

They left the museum slowly, arms entwined around each other, alone with their thoughts. Laena glanced over her shoulder, and stiffened when she saw Ariel walking behind them, matching their pace.

"Cree, she's still following us," Laena whispered. "She's right behind us."

Cree turned around and snapped, "What is it you want, Ariel? Just leave us alone."

Ariel smiled. "I am enjoying the tour of this beautiful city. Perhaps I could hear what Laena is teaching you if you let me join you properly."

"You're not welcome here, Ariel. Just leave," Laena said coldly. "If you don't, we'll...." She trailed off.

Ariel laughed. "You'll what, Laena? Call the police? Tell someone who I am, where I am from? Oh, no, wait. You cannot do that, can you? Because if you do...." Ariel glided closer to them and lowered her voice. "Because if you do, then I will tell them where Cree is from, too. And he will be hustled away, to some undisclosed government location, where he will be questioned until it is too late for you to fix your precious world."

Laena took a step towards Ariel but Cree grabbed her arm, stopping her.

Ariel put her hand against her cheek and opened her mouth in mock revelation. "Oh! What an idea! Maybe I should tell everyone where Cree is from!" She squealed in delight. "That would put a quick end to your plans!"

"You wouldn't dare," Laena hissed. "Because the minute you did that, you would be dragged in, too. And you would never get home to your stupid Rapture. The Rapture that will never happen."

Ariel's gaze turned icy. "I could go home before I got caught."

"No, Ariel, you could not," Cree said, laughing. "How stupid do you think I am? We know exactly when we are going home—you knew when you came here. You cannot vary from that plan. You have no way of reaching home to tell them to bring you earlier. That is why this is so risky. If we are not in the exact place at the exact time that we told them, we will be stuck here. And if I know you at all, you have arranged to go home with me. No sooner. So you will not turn me in. Just like I cannot turn you in."

Ariel lunged at Cree but he seized her by the shoulders. She let out a stream of angry Esperanto. Cree's grip tightened and she stopped talking.

"Leave us be, Ariel. You have no power over us. There is nothing you can do."

"That is what you think," she seethed.

Cree reached for Laena's hand and they started walking down the sidewalk. Laena was shaking. Cree squeezed her hand and whispered, "She cannot hurt us. Let us just ignore her. Please. Just...pretend she is not there."

Laena nodded, walked for a few blocks and ducked into a tiny restaurant with only five tables. They were the only ones in the restaurant. The tables had red-checkered table clothes, and wine jugs in wicker baskets, candle wax dripping down the sides in multitudes of colors. A waiter urged them to sit down, and brought them water and menus before heading back to the kitchen.

Laena took a deep breath, and willed herself to relax.

"Pretend it never happened," Cree murmured. "She cannot bother us if we do not let her."

Laena nodded. She opened the menu and scanned the items. Cree did not even bother looking at his. He scanned the sidewalk outside surreptitiously.

The waiter approached the table. "Good afternoon," he said, nodding.

"Good afternoon," Laena replied. "Do you have anything vegan for us, even if it is just a salad?" Laena asked.

"Yes, yes," the waiter answered. "I will bring you a nice salad with roasted vegetables, and some of our bread, fresh out of the oven, with some olive oil and cannellini beans to dip it in, yes?"

"Perfect," Laena exclaimed, smiling. "No cheese, no anchovies...."

"No, no, nothing like that," the waiter replied sternly. "I know what a vegan is. You eat nothing from animals, I understand. No problem. You wait. Not very long, I bring out to you two delicious meals."

"Thank you," Cree said, rewarding him with a dazzling smile. The waiter bustled into the kitchen and Cree looked at Laena, leaning back in his chair with his hands interlocked behind his head. Sunlight streamed through the large plate glass window, bathing the restaurant in warmth. "This is so nice...to be with you, to have you show me your world." He leaned forward, his hands on the table between them. "But I feel bad that I have no money...."

"Cree," Laena said, grasping his hand. "I have money. Don't worry about paying. It's my treat."

"But it is not supposed to be like that, no?" Cree asked, a frown creasing his brow. "I read about your time. The men are supposed to treat the women...."

"Old fashioned nonsense," Laena scoffed. "You are here trying to save my world, and you're worried about who pays for our lunch?"

"Laena, I want to court you. If you were in my world, I would be bringing you wildflowers and picking you berries and making you meals. I would be...." He trailed off, but he grinned.

"What are you thinking?" she laughed.

"Something I should not be thinking," he replied, chuckling.

"Okay, then. Let's change the subject," Laena said reluctantly. She paused, then said, "We never spoke about my mother offering you a job!"

Cree smacked his forehead with his open hand in mock exasperation. "Yes! Thank you so much...your plan worked. Now that I will be working with her, I can get access to the lab and do the experiments I need to prove what antibacterials do to the virophages. And then when she sees the results of the research, she will have to understand what is happening. Laena, you are brilliant."

Laena bowed her head in acknowledgment. "Thank you—of course I'm brilliant." She sobered. "I sure hope this works, though. Do you think you can pull it off?"

"I will have to," Cree responded grimly. "No matter what work your mother gives me, I will have to do this on the side."

"How are you going to do all of that work, and your schoolwork?" Laena queried.

"You may have to help me with school," Cree responded. "This is too important to let 11th grade homework get in the way. Especially considering I have already completed my education in my time."

Laena was about to ask what his education consisted of, when the waiter bustled over, carrying huge plates of salad with roasted vegetables, warm, crusty bread, and a bowl of dip.

"Thank you," Laena said. "It looks wonderful."

Cree murmured his thanks as well, and the teens dug into their food. Cree tore off a chunk of bread and dipped it into the olive oil-cannellini bean mixture. "Mmmm," he said, his mouth full. "What *is* this?"

"Olive oil, cannellini beans, red pepper flakes, and salt, all ground up in a blender or Cuisinart. Isn't it good?"

Cree nodded and swallowed. "Can we buy some of this to bring home? It is fantastic!"

Laena laughed. "We can make it at home...it's so easy. I'll teach you."

"We will make it tonight, for your parents," Cree said. "Yes?" He looked at her hopefully, his eyes shining with happiness.

Laena smiled. "If it makes you that happy, of course," she said. Cree reached across the table and squeezed her hand.

They finished their lunch, chattering about what they had seen in the Aquarium and in Boston. They both steadfastly ignored the run-in with Ariel, determined not to ruin the day. Finally, Laena said, "We need to get going. Our bus is at 3 p.m."

Cree nodded in agreement. "Yes, okay. This day has been very helpful. I have been thinking, what that man at the Aquarium said about the krill...he said the wild krill are contaminated with pollutants, which I know. But that means if I am going to use wild krill in the experiments, and if these krill are already full of pollutants, I need to be able to measure the level of contaminants, to remove this as a factor."

"So, is that possible? Can you measure the contaminants?"

"I certainly hope so. Otherwise, I am afraid the experiments will not work, and I will have to come up with another plan." He paused, and smiled at Laena. "But I am sad this day is over. I had so much fun with you, Laena."

"It's not over yet," she replied. "We have to cook dinner for my parents, remember? We promised. And, don't forget, you're living with us now. We'll be together all night."

Cree raised one of his eyebrows suggestively. "All night?"

"Yes, all night," she said, laughing. "But unfortunately, it's not going to be what you're thinking." She paused, then said, "I think we should cheat on the dinner. Let's buy some vegetarian minestrone soup to go, some Italian bread, and then we'll make the dip for the bread. What do you think?"

"Yes, I agree!" Cree agreed. "Do you have enough money?"

Laena nodded, and signaled the waiter for the check. When he came to the table, she asked for minestrone soup for four people to go, and a loaf of bread. The waiter nodded happily and said, "You like our food, no? It's good?"

"Very good," Laena replied.

A few minutes later, they were on the way out the door, Cree carrying the sack with the food.

Cree stopped on the sidewalk and pulled Laena into a one-armed hug, nuzzling her neck. Cree pulled back abruptly.

"Laena...where is your necklace?"

"My necklace?" Laena grabbed at her neck, patting her shirt in dismay. "Oh, no! Cree, it's gone!"

"Ariel," Cree muttered in disgust. "Did she touch you?"

"She did!" Laena cried. "In the Aquarium, when we first ran into her! She put her hands at my shoulder, my neck...she must have unclasped it!"

"It is okay, no worries," Cree said. "I will get it back for you. I *will* get it back." He reached out and embraced Laena.

Laena hugged him back, and they walked arm in arm down the sidewalk. She was distraught about the necklace, but damned if she would let anything, let alone Ariel, ruin her day.

Chapter 12

LAENA AND CREE were exhausted by the time they got back to North Bayside, and relieved they had decided to buy the soup and the bread for dinner rather than have to cook from scratch. Laena was pouring olive oil into the Cuisinart that already contained a can of cannellini beans when Michelle came home. The soup simmered on the stove, the bread warmed in the oven, and Laena was teaching Cree how to operate the Cuisinart. Cree jumped when the machine roared into action, and Michelle looked at him strangely.

"You don't use those in Alaska, Cree?" she asked, grabbing a carrot from the salad Laena had thrown together.

Cree exhaled noisily and shook his head, backing away from the machine. "No," he said loudly, to be heard over the motor. "We chop things by hand."

Laena turned the Cuisinart off and told Cree to mix in the salt and red pepper flakes that she had gotten out from the cupboard. Cree approached cautiously, peering in. "Are you sure it will not go on when I have my hand in there?"

"No, it can't go on when the top isn't locked on," Laena explained. She glanced up and saw Michelle looking at Cree with open curiosity. "Ummm, Mom, thanks so much for the Aquarium passes." Laena dug into the back pocket of her jeans and handed the passes to Michelle. "We had a great time...it was really fun."

Cree turned and flashed a blinding smile at Michelle. "Yes, thank you," he added. "It was amazing. And Laena is an excellent tour guide. We saw Paul Revere's house!"

Michelle smiled absent-mindedly. "Glad you two had fun," she said. "I'm going to go upstairs and change. I'm starved...dinner smells great. Laena, don't forget to call your father in when we're ready to eat." Laena nodded and watched her mother start to leave the kitchen. She turned back. "Oh, and Cree...I almost forgot. I brought some background material for you to look at, and then some simple research assignments. Whenever you have time to get to them...."

"Of course," Cree responded. "I will start tonight." Michelle nodded and left the room.

"Cree," Laena hissed, when her mother was out of earshot. "We have to be careful. Your...apprehension of the Cuisinart seems pretty weird. My mother noticed."

Cree looked at Laena in alarm. "Do you think so?"

"I know so," Laena whispered. "This is going to be harder than I thought, having you here all the time." Cree smiled and raised an eyebrow, and Laena blushed. "That's *not* what I meant. I mean, that's going to be hard too, but we can't be ourselves around them. You have to pretend that you know about things from my time, like this Cuisinart. If my parents find out you're from the future before we get the data from the experiment to my mother, everything will be screwed up!"

Cree looked at the machine with skepticism, but acknowledged Laena's concerns with a grunt. "Okay, okay, I will pretend. But why can't we just mash it up by hand?" he whispered angrily. "This thing is dangerous."

Laena grabbed the salt and red pepper from him. "I'll finish this up. You go tell my father to come inside and wash up for dinner."

"Gladly," Cree said, moving to the door. "That machine is like the...the devil."

Laena suppressed a laugh and called after him. "I thought you didn't believe in that stuff!"

He muttered something unintelligible. Whatever it was, it wasn't happy. Laena dosed the dip with salt and hot pepper, clicked on the top, and pulsed the machine to mix it in.

Ben came in from outside and washed his hands at the kitchen sink as Laena and Cree set the table. Michelle came downstairs in a pair of soft lounge pants and a sweatshirt. Cree carried the pot of soup to the table, carefully placing it on a trivet, and Laena placed the bread and cutting board in front of her father.

"Dad? Do you want to cut the bread, please?"

"You're putting me to work?" he chided teasingly. "I thought this dinner was on you."

Cree reached for the cutting board. "I will do it, sir.... "

"No, no," Ben interrupted, "I was teasing, Cree." He gave a tired laugh. "Sorry...just a joke that fell flat."

Cree looked confused but pulled Laena's chair out for her and they all sat down. Laena had scraped the bean dip into a large bowl, and drizzled more olive oil into it artfully.

"You can just put that in front of me," Cree said, motioning to the dip.

Laena laughed.

He looked up at Michelle and Ben. "We had this at lunch today, and it tasted so good. Now we have to see if Laena's version is as good as the restaurant's."

"Of course mine is as good," Laena responded tersely. "It's better."

Cree dipped a chunk of bread into the beans and oil, and popped it into his mouth. "Mmmm," he said, chewing slowly with his eyes closed in pleasure. "Yours is better. It is spicier." He opened his eyes and looked at Laena. "I love it."

Laena snorted. "Told you so," she said sarcastically, but she smiled at his compliment.

"I hope you two are joking," Michelle said, ladling soup out into the four bowls, "because you're starting to sound like bickering siblings, which I did *not* sign up for. I had only one child for a reason."

Laena passed Cree his bowl of soup, fingers grazing. Their eyes caught and they both smiled.

"No, not bickering," Cree responded. He struggled, searching for the right word. "We are...teasing. Lovingly."

"I'm not sure if I like that any better," Michelle said, considering his wording.

Laena blew across the surface of her hot soup, the steam eddying away. "So, Cree enjoyed Boston today," she offered, trying to change the subject.

"Tell us what you saw at the Aquarium," Ben prodded, and Cree described everything he had seen animatedly as they ate.

Before long, the soup pot was empty, the dip bowl scraped clean, and only crumbs were left on the cutting board. Laena hopped up to boil water for tea.

Ben and Michelle discussed the house repairs as they finished their tea, then shooed Cree and Laena from the kitchen. "You made the dinner, we'll clean up," Michelle said.

Laena and Cree agreed and walked hand in hand out the front door and settled into the porch swing. The sun was setting, and the air cooler. Cree put his arm around Laena's shoulders.

"Thank you again for today, Laena. It was wonderful." He laid his cheek against the top of her head, and Laena sighed and snuggled into him.

"I don't want to go back to school tomorrow," she said quietly. The storm had washed the earth clean, and the air was fresh and crisp. Laena watched the clouds scuttle low across the sky, a deep purple.

"Neither do I," Cree commiserated. "But we have to, no? And perhaps after school, we can work on the krill. I must do the work your mother has brought home...." He trailed off. "Laena, do you think she has brought me things on a computer?"

"Probably. Why?"

"I do not know how to use one," he admitted sheepishly.

"I'll teach you," Laena replied. "Don't worry...it isn't difficult."

Cree nodded his thanks. They were both silent, caught up in their private thoughts, worrying how everything would turn out. The quiet was comfortable, though, and Laena took pleasure in just being close to Cree, lost in her own thoughts. Her mind wandered, and then she felt Cree stiffen beside her.

"What's wrong?" she whispered uneasily.

Cree stood up. "Go inside, please. I will be right back." He bounded down the steps of the front porch and strode purposefully down the driveway toward the stand of trees without glancing back to see if Laena had complied with his directive. But Laena didn't move...she sank deeper into the porch swing and watched Cree's shadow merge with those of the trees.

Angry voices carried through the still night. Laena could not make out any words, but she could tell that one of the speakers was female. *Ariel*, she thought, her stomach clenching. She wanted to run down the stairs after Cree and tell Ariel to leave them alone, but she was rooted to her spot on the porch. She didn't want to move and give her presence away. The swing was in the shadows of the porch roof, and she hoped she couldn't be seen. The voices rose, then quieted. Laena caught a few words of Esperanto. She wouldn't be able to understand even if she could hear them clearly. But then, fury coursed through her. She had seen and heard enough. This was her house, Cree was her boyfriend, and she was not one to sit patiently while some gorgeous bitch huddled with Cree in the dark. Laena stood up, and silently glided down the stairs. She ran down the driveway, avoiding the gravel, hoping they wouldn't hear her coming.

But they did. Ariel looked up first, her eyes widening. Cree whirled around and physically blocked Laena from getting closer.

"I told you to go inside," Cree growled.

"And I don't always do what I'm told," Laena retorted. She looked past Cree to Ariel. "You are trespassing, Ariel. Go away. Get out of here—you're not wanted." Cree grabbed Laena's shoulders, physically restraining her so she couldn't get closer to Ariel.

Ariel stepped closer, smiling. "Do tell, Laena. I am not wanted? Are you sure?" Her hair swung loose, so black it was almost blue in the violet night sky.

"I'm positive," Laena spat. She fizzed with energy, ready to battle.

"Enough," Cree said. But Laena and Ariel were glaring fixedly each other, ignoring Cree. Laena struggled briefly in his arms, trying to break free.

"You are not welcome on my property, or in my time." Laena's voice was chilly and even. "There is nothing you can do to stop us...."

"Enough!" Cree insisted. "Do not goad her, Laena. You do not know what she is capable of. I am asking you, *please*—go inside. I will get rid of her."

"You will never get rid of me, Cree," Ariel said, sidling closer. She reached out and stroked Laena's cheek with her thumb, and Laena recoiled in revulsion. "You are interesting looking, I will give you that," she whispered seductively.

Cree pushed Laena away from Ariel. "Go inside," he repeated.

"Yes, do as he says, Laena. We need some time alone together." Ariel smiled, almost singing Laena's name, her teeth glowing white against her tan face.

"I'm not going.... "

"Yes, you are," Cree said harshly, grabbing her arm. "Go now, or I will drag you inside myself." His anger shook Laena. He was fierce. But still she did not move.

Something wild and primitive came over her, an instinct to fight for her life. Laena sidestepped Cree and got in Ariel's face. "I'll kill you, Ariel," she hissed. "Don't underestimate me. This isn't just about Cree. It's so much more. And I will not let you stop us. Do you hear me?" Laena's voice rose, penetrating the night air. "I will not let you stop us!"

In a flash, Laena's hand flew up and tried to yank the chain from around Ariel's neck. Ariel screamed, reaching out and grabbing Laena's hand.

"Give me my necklace, you bitch. Cree gave it to *me*. Not you. *Me*." Laena jerked her hand free from Ariel's clutches.

Ariel turned her body, shielding the necklace from Laena.

"You will never get this back. Cree will never be able to find you again!" Ariel taunted.

"Shhh," Cree warned, hushing them both, but it was too late. The front door opened, and warm yellow light spilled out onto the porch. "Laena? Cree? Is everything alright?" Ben stood, silhouetted against the doorway, peering into the dark.

"I will win this, Laena. Do not ever forget that. I will win," Ariel murmured, and slipped into the shadows.

Cree gave Laena a look. He was beyond angry with her, she could tell.

"Everything's fine, Dad!" Laena called, starting back to the porch. "We thought we heard something out here. But it was nothing." Cree followed slowly, glancing over his shoulder to make sure Ariel had gone. Laena walked up the porch stairs. She brushed past her father into the house, went upstairs, and shut the guest room door with a resounding bang.

Ben looked at Cree questioningly as he slowly came up the porch stairs. Cree shrugged.

"Teenage girls?" Ben guessed.

"Teenage girls," Cree agreed, smiling bleakly. "I do not think I understand them."

Ben shook his head sympathetically. "And it doesn't get any easier as they get older." The men walked somberly into the house.

Ben arched his back and shut the front door, locking it. "I think I'm turning in for the night. My old body isn't used to all this physical labor."

Cree laughed politely. "I suppose I should do some homework on the chance that we have school tomorrow."

"Indeed," Ben said. "Goodnight, Cree. Don't stay up too late." Ben trudged up the stairs, and Cree walked to the kitchen to get something to drink. As he stood at the sink, gulping water, he heard a click from the foyer. He quietly put his glass down on the counter, and peered out the kitchen door.

* * *

Laena ran noiselessly down the driveway, trying to follow Ariel. Where would she go? Laena knew the name of the family Ariel was living with, allegedly on an exchange program from Israel. But she didn't know where the family lived, and somehow, she knew Ariel would not be there.

When Laena reached the road, she saw a movement to her right, heading toward the beach. The beach? Why would Ariel go there? Laena tried to stay behind the line of trees, in case Ariel turned to look behind her. She gained ground on Ariel easily. Was it deliberate? Did she *want* Laena to follow her? Laena hesitated. Could this be a trap? She ducked behind a tree to think.

She really wanted her necklace back, especially after hearing Ariel's words when Laena grabbed for it. What had she said? Something about how she didn't want Cree to be able to find Laena again. Did the necklace have some kind of homing device in it?

Adrenaline flooded through Laena's body. So he could come back? Yes. He *would* come back to her. She knew it. But she had to get the necklace back first. Laena peeked around the tree and saw Ariel 20 yards ahead of her, walking slowly down the road. It seemed as if Ariel wanted her to follow, like she was leading Laena somewhere. Laena didn't care. She would stop at nothing to get the necklace now that she knew it could guide Cree back to her.

Laena reached the beach a few minutes later, but Ariel had vanished. The night was so dark. Laena's eyes were adjusting, but Ariel's dark clothes hid her completely. Laena stood stock-still, listening. She heard the waves lapping the shore, the granules of sand rolling over one another. Pebbles clinked gently.

There. She heard something else in the distance. Her eyes swept the deserted beach. What was that? A car door closing? Something metallic.

Laena crouched down and ran toward the cattails bordering the parking lot. There were no cars in the lot. So what had that sound been if not a car door?

Clang. There it was again!

She looked frantically around the beach. She couldn't see anything! But that sound signified something man-made. Not a car...a boat? She peered through the darkness at the small dock. There were no boats moored there. Metal. Something metal. A door....?

Laena gasped. The lighthouse! The Bass Cove Lighthouse had been out of commission for decades, and the door had been padlocked by the police to prevent vandalism. But that was the only structure close to the beach. The noise Laena heard must have come from the lighthouse. How on earth did Ariel open the door? And why?

Laena backtracked along the edge of the parking lot towards the lighthouse. A breeze picked up, and she heard the clang yet again. She peered over the vegetation and saw the door to the lighthouse swinging gently. Could Ariel be in there?

An owl hooted in the darkness. Laena ran up to the stone wall bordering the old lighthouse and flattened herself against the wall. Her hands were shaking. What if Ariel had planned all this to lure Laena into the lighthouse? Would Ariel actually hurt her—or worse? Ariel was taller and stronger than Laena, but Laena had an advantage. She knew the area—the beach, the lighthouse, the woods. She had grown up here, explored every inch of the beach and marsh. The owl hooted again, sounding eerily like a woman screaming.

Laena smiled. The wildlife. She knew the wildlife, something totally foreign to Ariel. She could use the animals to get an edge over Ariel.

Laena crept around to the southwest side of the lighthouse, and sank to her knees, looking for large crevices in the stone wall. Laena had hunted for snakes here with her father almost every spring when she was younger. They caught the snakes, identified them, and let them go. She knew it was foolhardy to stick her hand into the holes without being able to see. But she also knew that there were no poisonous snakes on the Cape. If she got bitten, it wouldn't be the first time. And worst-case scenario would be a big gash in her hand, and lots of blood.

She found a hole between some large rocks in the wall that was big enough to fit her hand. She put her hand in, cautiously. Nothing. She moved down the wall about three feet and found another crevice...this one was smaller than the last, but she thought she might be able to get her hand in...there. She felt something. It was a cool night, so the snakes would be sluggish. If she were gentle and slow, she may not get bitten. She hoped she was feeling a docile garter snake and not the irritable black racer. She wasn't in the mood for stitches tonight.

Laena grabbed the snake smoothly—it felt big—and withdrew it from the hole. Slowly. The snake coiled heavily in her hand and she brought it closer to her eyes. She couldn't believe her luck! A milk snake. Not only an easy-going snake, but a species often confused with copperheads because of the pattern on its back. She carefully brought the snake against her warm body and stood up.

"Easy, buddy. I'm not going to hurt you," she whispered.

Laena took a deep breath. "Here goes," she muttered to herself, and pulled the lighthouse door open. She pulled the door shut behind her, gently. It creaked on rusty hinges. Laena winced as the sound echoed. The lighthouse smelled musty.

The darkness was complete in the lighthouse. Not even the glitter of faraway stars. Laena paused at the bottom of the metal circular staircase, and looked up, straining. She thought she saw a faint bobbing light above her. She moved the snake gently to her right hand and grasped the metal rail with her left. She heard a faint scuff of a shoe on the stair from above. Someone was up there, climbing.

Laena carefully placed one foot on the first step, trying not to scrape her boots on the iron tread. Typical of other Cape lighthouses, the one in Bass Cove rose only 45 feet. But 45 feet was high enough when you were afraid of heights. And Laena did *not* like heights. In fact, it was her only real phobia. But it was so dark inside that the spiraling stairs and round walls did not make her dizzy. She started to climb. Silently.

Laena stopped halfway to the tower to catch her breath. She cocked her head, hoping to hear Ariel. Laena wondered why she was creeping, trying to stay silent. She knew she no longer had the element of surprise—Ariel *must* have heard the door creaking. Everything reverberated in here. She paused, thinking. If Ariel knew Laena was coming, should she call out to her? Maybe strike a deal? Laena could not think of a downside to this plan. She figured she would climb a little more and then decide how to proceed.

She took another step, but her toe caught on the metal grid in the stair and she stumbled. She went down hard on one knee with a clang. The snake started in her hand.

"Crap," Laena muttered. Well, now she had no choice. Laena took a deep breath. Exhaled.

"Ariel? Show yourself. Come out. Let's talk," Laena called. Her voice echoed off the rounded walls. She sounded surprisingly calm.

Silence.

"Ariel, I know you're in here. Answer me!"

Laena started climbing again, not bothering to cover her footsteps. She heard a groan.

"Ariel?" She stopped. "Ariel, are you hurt?"

"Laena?" Ariel's voice was weak. "I...I think I hurt my ankle. My foot. Please help me."

"Where are you?" Laena asked, suspicious.

"I am at the top. The balcony, near the glass tower. Please come. I do not think I can get down alone."

Crap. Ariel was on the balcony, or so she said. Laena knew the railing on the balcony was low, only about four feet high. It made Laena dizzy to look down from that height. She always felt like she was going to fall.

"What are you doing in here, anyway?" Laena asked, continuing to climb. She figured she should keep Ariel talking. Laena did not want to be assaulted on these stairs. The snake started writhing through Laena's hand, warmed by the heat of Laena's body. She got a better grasp of it and kept climbing.

"I...I was coming to be alone. To think. Thank God you arrived. I prayed for someone to come help me."

Laena muttered, "Oh, please."

"Did you say something?" Ariel called.

"Nope. Not me!" Laena called back. She paused to catch her breath. "Say, Ariel? I'll tell you what. I don't exactly trust you, so why don't you keep talking so I know where you are?" Laena's words were met with silence. "Ariel? Did you hear me?"

"I heard you, Laena." Ariel's voice was more forceful. "I cannot believe that I am injured and you are accusing me of lying to you!"

"Uh-hunh," Laena said, ascending the stairs again. "Go on...."

"How dare you accuse me—" Ariel fell silent.

Laena was only about ten steps below the balcony. She stopped abruptly and saw the night sky through the tower windows above her. "Ariel?"

Laena heard a creak and a clang from downstairs. That damn door must have blown open again.

"Ariel? Talk to me so I know where you are."

Silence again.

"Damn," muttered Laena. "C'mon, Ariel," she called. "Let's talk like adults. Why are we fighting? Maybe we can...reach a compromise."

Laena started up the stairs again silently. She moved her head from side to side, looking for a deeper shadow, starlight glinting off a zipper, anything to let her know where Ariel hid. She smelled the fresh ocean breeze coming in through the open balcony. Finally, she reached the top stair below the second staircase to the glass tower, where the light used to blink every night, warning ships away from the shore. She did a slow 360° turn at the top of the stairs, eyes searching the darkness.

A voice spoke softly in her ear behind her. "I am right here, Laena."

Laena gasped and jumped, retreating so the banister was against her back. Ariel moved closer. Laena could see the glimmer of Ariel's teeth in the gloom.

"I thought you were injured," Laena said, trying to keep her voice level. She shielded the hand holding the snake with her body.

Ariel laughed. "No, it is you who will be injured. I think perhaps an unfortunate accident is in order?" She reached out and grabbed a fistful of Laena's curls. "Let us move closer to the edge, shall we? We can look at the ocean together."

Ariel dragged Laena several feet towards the open-air balcony. Laena's vision narrowed. She panicked, her breath coming in gasps. She couldn't let Ariel get her to the edge of the balcony! No one could survive a fall from this height. Laena started to hyperventilate, taking big shuddering gasps of air but feeling like she wasn't getting any oxygen.

"Wait...Ariel, wait. I have something important for you. From Cree." Laena choked out, her voice rising in panic.

Ariel stopped. She looked at Laena, mistrustful. "What is this thing you have from Cree?" Her grip tightened on Laena.

"Here," Laena said. "It's right here." Laena brought her shaking right hand out from behind her back. She squeezed the snake gently and it writhed in her hand. Angry, it flicked its tail and hissed.

Ariel lost her grip on Laena, let out a blood-curdling yell and backed up against the lighthouse wall. Laena took two steps toward her, still shaking.

"Do you know what this is?" Laena asked softly, her voice catching.

"A...a serpent!" Ariel replied, crying. "Please. It is evil. Get it away!"

Laena took a deep breath, calming her pounding heart. "Yes, it is a snake. Or a serpent, as you say. Have you heard of these snakes? They are incredibly poisonous." Laena thrust the snake toward Ariel's face and she shrieked again.

"Avada Kedavra!" Laena intoned, hoping like hell Ariel had not read the Harry Potter books. She had just invoked the killing curse. At least, that's what she thought it was, but she could be wrong. It may have been the Bedazzling Hex. No matter. It was just for effect. She just wanted to scare Ariel, make her think that Laena had some malevolent power. Ariel started sobbing and sank to the floor, her arms covering her head.

"Give me my necklace, Ariel," Laena said. "Now."

Ariel reached up with shaking hands and unfastened the necklace, her eyes still screwed shut. She threw the necklace on the ground. It landed several feet from Laena.

"What were you going to do, Ariel? Were you really going to throw me off the edge of the balcony?" Laena asked, truly curious. She was calmer now that she was in control.

Ariel shook her head vehemently.

"She would not have done that," a male voice said behind Laena. Laena gasped and whirled around. Cree stood at the top of the stairs, his face hard. He knelt down and picked up the necklace and put it in his pocket.

"Cree! What...what are you doing here?" Laena asked.

"I followed you," Cree responded. "But I see you are quite okay by yourself."

Laena took a deep breath. "I came for my necklace."

Cree nodded. "And it is safe now. Perhaps you should let that poor snake go, and we should get down from here?"

Laena lowered the arm holding the frightened snake. Ariel continued to sob on the floor.

"What should we do with her?" Laena asked, jerking her chin toward Ariel.

Ariel's crying quieted. An owl hooted rather close by. She jerked her head up in fear. "What was that noise?" she whispered.

"My birds of prey," Laena responded, thinking quickly. "They are asking if I am okay. I can call them in, make them attack."

Laena mimicked the owl's call, and two owls responded immediately, calling back. All those nights, calling owls in the fields with her dad finally being put to good use.

Cree stifled a smile, remembering the red-winged blackbirds.

"Dear God, please let me go," Ariel implored. "Cree, this girl...she is crazy. She is evil. Of the devil! Please get me out of here. I would not have hurt her. I wanted to scare her. I...I wanted her to tell you to go home. Cree, please believe me." Ariel lapsed into Esperanto, taking convulsive breaths and sobbing between her words.

Cree hesitated, then nodded. "She will let you go, Ariel, if you promise to leave her alone."

"I promise," Ariel whispered. "*Me promesas. Bonvolu lasi min iri.*" She sobbed. "*Ne lasu sxin mortigi min!*"

Cree nodded curtly. "Go," he said.

Ariel pushed herself up and clattered down the stairs. Laena and Cree waited until they heard the door at the bottom creak open.

Laena exhaled. Her knees were weak. "Can we go home now? I'm exhausted."

"Yes, of course. But first ..." He reached into his pocket and pulled out the necklace, and fastened it around Laena's neck. Cree was silent, and Laena could feel his anger and disappointment in her. She had a pit in her stomach.

They walked down the stairs in silence, grasping the rail tightly, placing their feet carefully on the treads in the darkness.

When they got out of the lighthouse, Cree slammed the door tightly.

"Laena?"

"Mmmm?" she said, overcome with exhaustion. She didn't want him to yell at her. She couldn't deal with it right now.

"May I...may I see the snake?"

Laena sagged in relief. She turned to Cree and handed him the bewildered milk snake. "Hold it gently," she advised. "See the black and white checkerboard pattern on its belly? That's how you know it's a milk snake and not a copperhead. Copperheads are poisonous, and we do have them in Massachusetts. But not on the Cape."

Cree marveled at the snake and laughed as it tried to slither up his sleeve. He examined it closely, letting it coil between his fingers and glide around his wrist.

Laena watched him handle the snake, but she could no longer stand. She felt like she was going to pass out, and she sank to the sandy soil, squatting on the ground, head between her knees.

Cree glanced down at her. "I am sorry, Laena. We should get you home. You are tired." Reluctantly, he let the snake go next the rock wall where Laena had caught it.

"I take it there are no snakes in your time?" she asked softly, afraid of the answer.

Cree shook his head. "There was a bacteria..."

Laena held up her hand, palm out to stop him. "I really don't think I want to hear any more. Not tonight."

Cree grasped her hand and pulled her to her feet. They walked silently toward home. When they reached Laena's driveway, Cree stopped her, holding her by the shoulders.

"Laena, I do not want you to confront Ariel again. You won this time, and you got the necklace back. But I told you I would get it back for you. You took an unnecessary risk."

"An unnecessary risk? Really, Cree? You sound like my mother!"

"Laena.... "

"I'm tired. I'm going to bed." Laena started toward the house. But she whirled back, facing Cree, unable to contain her anger. "*You* told me she wouldn't have hurt me. *You* told me people don't kill in your time. If that's the truth, then I was never in danger, was I?" Laena desperately wanted to slam the door in his face, but knew she couldn't wake her parents up. She left the door open and ran up the stairs.

Cree sighed, following slowly. He did tell Laena that Ariel would not have thrown her off the balcony of the lighthouse. At the time, he believed it. But was he right? Or was Laena's life in danger? Cree closed the front door behind him, clicking the deadbolt firmly in place. Wishing the lock could keep her safe, but knowing it could not.

Chapter 13

LAENA SAT at the kitchen table, sipping orange juice and reading the paper. She did not look up as Cree walked in.

"Good morning," he said formally, opening the fridge to grab the juice. Laena ignored him. He poured himself a glass and brought it to the table.

"To what do I owe this silent treatment?" he questioned, sitting at the table next to Laena and peering at her over the pages of the paper. Laena did not answer. Cree pushed the paper down gently. "Laena?"

She sighed and threw the paper on the table in frustration. "I'm angry at you, Cree, in case you can't tell."

"Oh, no, I could tell," Cree said, a smile tugging at his lips. "It is fairly obvious." He tipped the glass up to his mouth and drained the juice.

"How dare you tell me what to do, order me around like some kind of...some kind of slave? And in front of Ariel no less!" The words tumbled out of her mouth, unbidden. "I did *so* not appreciate the way you treated me last night." She picked the paper back up, her eyes unseeing, her hands shaking.

"I am sorry, Laena," Cree said quietly. "I did not mean to order you around. I wanted to protect you."

Laena tossed the paper to the side with finality. "Protect me? I can take care of myself, Cree. I'm not sure what it's like in your time, but in my time women don't need to be...coddled and...and...guarded." She sputtered in anger.

Michelle chose that inopportune moment to glide into the kitchen. Both Laena and Cree glanced up uncomfortably.

"Good morning, you two." Michelle bustled around the kitchen, pouring herself a cup of coffee and popping a piece of whole wheat bread into the toaster. She glanced back at the table. "You need more for breakfast than juice. Can I make you some toast?"

"I would love some, thank you," Cree said. Laena shook her head and stood up from the table. Michelle put two more pieces of bread in the toaster.

"I'm going to go finish getting ready for school," Laena announced to no one in particular. She avoided Cree's gaze and stalked out of the kitchen.

Michelle took plates from the cupboard, and put out some jam and a butter knife on the table. When the toaster dinged, she placed two pieces of toast on a plate in front of Cree. "Things a little frosty between you two?" Michelle asked, joining him at the table.

"Frosty? You mean...cold?"

"Mmmm," Michelle agreed, chewing her toast. She swallowed. "I don't mean to pry...."

"No, that is all right," Cree responded, spreading jam on his own toast. "Yes, she is angry at me. I made the mistake of trying to tell her what to do last night," he admitted.

Michelle laughed. "Oh, yes, that is a mistake of the highest order," she said. "Ever since she was a little girl, Laena did not like being told what to do. When she was six years old, I bought her Barbie dolls, because all the other girls had them. Two days later I peeked into her room and she had dismembered all of them. She had four glass mason jars lined up on her desk, filled with colored water—blue, red, green and yellow. She had put all the heads in one jar, all the legs in another, all the torsos in a third, and the arms in a fourth...." Michelle shook her head at the memory. "A scientist from the start. She still does what she wants to do, not what others tell her she *should* do."

Cree sighed and shook his head. "I have never met a girl quite like her," he said with wonder. "I just wanted to protect her...." he trailed off. He had said too much.

"Protect her from what?" Michelle asked nonchalantly, straightening her knife next to her plate.

Cree shook his head again. "Nothing, really...we heard a noise, and I wanted her to stay back while I investigated. It was nothing." Cree adeptly changed the subject. "I read the papers you brought home for me last night. They were very interesting. I am looking forward to doing the work for you on krill."

"I'm so glad you'll be working with me, Cree. Really. It will be a treat to have you there."

"I was thinking...I want to run some experiments. Is there a budget? Do you have money to buy things we will need?"

"Hmmm, like what?" Michelle asked, sipping her coffee. "The lab is pretty well equipped. But you'll be working under a grant, so there is some money for incidentals."

"I want to use wild krill in the experiments, exposing them to the antibacterials. I think it is better than using lab-raised krill. But when we were at the Aquarium, they told me that the wild krill were contaminated with existing pollutants. So, we will have to measure the level of those contaminants before we do the experiments, in order to make sure we get valid results."

"Maybe. We can talk about it. If you present your case convincingly, I'll approve the use of wild krill, and make sure we can measure the contaminants. But I'm not convinced yet!" Michelle smiled.

"Thanks, Michelle. I am confident I can convince you." He glanced at the clock on the wall. "Ach, I am going to be late. Thank you for breakfast." He leaped up, but his plate and glass in the sink, and smiled at Michelle. "Please, leave the dishes for me. I will do them when I get home.... "

Michelle waved him off dismissively. "No worries, Cree. Off to school." Laena came thumping down the stairs, and Cree started after her. "Have a good day, Michelle," he called over his shoulder, bending down to grab his backpack by the door. He followed Laena out and had to run to catch up with her.

"Laena!" he called. "Will you wait?"

Laena slowed somewhat, but did not stop. Cree caught up with her easily and grabbed her hand, squeezing it in his. "Are you okay?"

Laena didn't answer. She jerked her hand out of his warm grasp, and kept walking without looking at him. A muscle worked in Cree's jaw as he struggled to control himself. "Laena, please talk to me. I am sorry I tried to tell you what to do last night. I just wanted to protect you. Ariel is not...she is not safe. Maybe not even sane."

"I can take care of myself." Her words were clipped.

"I know you can," Cree conceded. He reached out and grabbed her hand again, pulling her to a stop. He physically turned Laena to face him. "I know you can," he repeated softly. "But you do not know Ariel, and you do not know what she is capable of." His eyes searched hers.

Laena would not give in. "She entered *my* property, Cree, without permission. Speaking to you in a language I don't understand. She stole my necklace. She's trying to steal you away from me, too...." Her voice faded.

"Laena. She can never take me away from you." Cree pulled Laena into his arms and held her tightly. Laena slumped at his touch.

"Please don't be understanding right now. Don't be nice to me." She tried to push Cree away but he held fast.

Cree laughed. "But I do understand. I understand what you are feeling. I only have a short time with you here, and we were together, enjoying each other's company, and Ariel showed up and took my attention away from you...."

"Don't make me sound so jealous and petty!" Laena retorted.

Cree held Laena at arm's length. "You were not petty, sweetie," Cree responded gently. "Jealous, maybe, but not petty. I understand, and you have the right." He tucked some of her stray curls behind her ear.

Laena sighed. "You don't fight fair, Cree. You're supposed to be disagreeing with me. Not telling me you understand why I did what I did." The fight had left her.

Cree chuckled. "You want me to fight? Not apologize?"

"Yes," she said petulantly. "I guess that's what I want." Laena knew she sounded silly. She threw herself into Cree's arms and hugged him. "I'm sorry I'm so bitchy," she said, her voice muffled by his shirt.

"So, we are both sorry," Cree acknowledged. "This fight is over, yes? Let us get to school and forget about Ariel."

The pair walked arm-in-arm down the road toward school, knowing they should pick up their pace but unwilling to rush. "Did you read the scientific papers my mom brought you?" Laena asked.

"Yes," Cree acknowledged. "They were primarily background research on krill and population decline. Some mentioned antibacterials and their effect on krill, but no one, obviously, has discovered the virophage link. Somehow, I am going to have to make your mother not only see that the krill are protected by these virophages, but that the antibacterials in particular are responsible for harming the virophages."

"So, you'll have to show that there's a virus first, right? I mean, without the virus, the virophages wouldn't be there?"

"Right," Cree agreed. "And that's not hard. Not really. But to see the virophages, we need a transmission electron microscope." He paused, thinking. "Or maybe we can detect their DNA. And I suppose I have to help her see that the antibacterials are responsible for krill deaths, in a convoluted way."

"How do you do that?" Laena queried. They had reached the school parking lot.

"It should not be too difficult," Cree said, thinking. "I can run some experiments, exposing wild krill to the antibacterials at varying levels, and measuring mortality. In those experiments, the krill will die because the antibacterials in the ocean water will kill the virophage, which is protecting the krill from the virus. In other words, when the virophage dies, the virus is free to kill the krill. But when we use the lab-raised krill, they will be clean, with no viruses. So the antibacterials alone are not enough to kill the krill. The same amount of antibacterials given to the lab-raised krill will not cause them to die."

"That makes sense," Laena agreed. She heard the first bell ring. She sighed, not wanting to go to class, feeling like it was a waste of time. And since meeting Cree, time had become such a relative thing. She felt like she was running out of time, with Cree, time to stop the destruction of the oceans…the normal, everyday things that she used to fill her days with were now meaningless. Like school. Why should they spend their days cooped up in a classroom reading medieval literature when there was so much to do, and so little time? A warm gust of wind blew her curls into her face, and she brushed them aside impatiently. She glanced back out toward the road, the trees leafing out in bright shades of green, and she longed to just leave. Escape from the confines of school, and work with Cree, side by side, to do what they had to do.

Cree, as if reading her thoughts, took her by the hand and tugged her inside. "We will be late," he said, hurrying her down the hall. "We will have time for work later."

* * *

Laena went into the bathroom before lunch. Entered a stall and slid the lock home. She thought she heard someone else come in, and then heard an ominous metallic click from the outside door. A lock turning? No, it couldn't be. The bathroom had five separate stalls...no one would lock the door. She flushed the toilet and opened the stall door, peering out. She was on edge, but had no idea why. She couldn't see anyone else in the bathroom—maybe she had imagined the noise. Or maybe someone came into the bathroom but changed their mind and left, and the sound she heard was the door closing. She went to the sink and turned the water on, scrubbing her hands with the liquid soap. As she was rinsing the soap off, Laena's head flew up, like an animal catching a scent. She gasped. The reflection of Ariel filled the mirror over the sink, inches behind Laena. She wore a black shirt and jeans, and her intense blue eyes practically glowed in contrast with her clothes and hair.

Laena whirled around and found Ariel so close she was practically touching her. "Excuse me," Laena said, hoping her voice didn't betray her fear.

Ariel smiled but didn't move. Just then, someone tried the bathroom door, but it was locked. That *was* the sound Laena had heard—Ariel locked the bathroom door! The person on the other side pounded on the door, and when she didn't get a response, she muttered, "Dammit," and left. Laena was too stunned to call out. The two girls locked eyes.

"I need to dry my hands," Laena said as coolly as she could muster. "You're in my way." Her voice echoed in the tiled room.

"I think," Ariel said softly, "that it is you who are in my way."

Laena tried to move around Ariel, but Ariel stepped even closer, smiling menacingly. "You are not going anywhere," she sneered. "Have you been with him yet?"

"What?" Laena whispered, shocked.

"Have you slept with him yet? He is good, is he not?" Ariel leaned so close that her silky hair tickled Laena's cheek.

"Get away from me, Ariel," Laena snapped, pushing against her shoulder. "You promised to stay away."

"I promised to stay away when you threatened me with a serpent! You are evil, Laena, and I will not leave until I get what I want." Ariel reached out and grabbed Laena's upper arm, clenching it like a vise. "You—and your family—are in my way. Cree must come home. You will tell him to come with me. Tell him he will not accomplish what he wants here. It is not God's will."

Laena tried to pull her arm out from Ariel's grasp, but couldn't. She glared at Ariel. "I don't tell Cree what to do. He will do what he needs to do, and he will be successful. Why don't *you* go home, Ariel. No one wants you here." Laena shook with anger.

Ariel stared with hatred in her eyes at Laena. When she opened her mouth to speak, her voice a low, dangerous rumble. "As I said, you are in my way, as is your family. I will hurt you. How would your parents feel if you met with an accident, Laena? If you were to die, from a tree branch, or an accident in the bathroom? I can arrange that."

Laena's eyes widened.

"That is right, now you understand," Ariel mocked. "You are a silly schoolgirl, Laena, but this is not a silly schoolgirl game. This is the ultimate battle, between blasphemous *science*"—she spat—"and God's will. Do you not see what is at stake here? The earth has to die, so the Righteous can soar. We are so close, in our time. Did Cree tell you what is left? Almost nothing. Your people have left nothing worth saving. God has allowed this destruction to take place, and we must let Him finish it. We cannot stop what He wants. Try to, and Cree will die!"

Ariel was in a frenzy. Her hot breath enveloped Laena's face, her blue eyes practically sparking with intensity as she raised her hand. Laena saw a flash of metal. Ariel had a knife.

"No!" Laena roared. She hit Ariel's arm with as much force as she could muster, and the knife flew from Ariel's hand, clattering against the door of one of the stalls and then splashing into the toilet.

Ariel bellowed in frustration and launched herself at Laena, her hands going to Laena's neck. Laena instinctively dropped her chin, brought her leg up and kneed Ariel as hard as she could in the stomach. Ariel grunted and lost her grip, bent over at the waist. Laena put her fists up in a defensive stance, panting.

"No! Cree is not going to die. He will save the Earth, and he'll stay here with me!" Laena said as calmly as she could. "God is...imaginary! *There is no God.* There is no omniscient being that *wants* the world to be destroyed. Humans are just animals. Animals! We are destroying the earth, and paying the price. What's wrong with you? Would you rather wipe out our species along with all the rest?" She spoke to Ariel as if she were a child, someone too young to understand right from wrong. "As long as there is life, there is something worth saving. And here and now, we have so much...*that* is what Cree is trying to save. That is what Cree and I *will* save!"

Ariel groaned and sank down to the floor.

"Ariel?" Laena dropped her clenched fists and leaned down. Ariel lay completely still. Was she breathing? Had Laena really hurt her? "Ariel.... ?" Laena reached out to her.

Ariel exploded up and grabbed Laena by the shirt, smashing her head hard against the mirror over the sink. The porcelain sink dug into Laena's back as she careened backwards, and the mirror shattered, shards of glass tinkling down. Laena slumped toward the cold, hard floor, her head reverberating from the shock.

"How dare you!" Ariel screamed, panting. "You will regret this, Laena Foster!" In three limping strides she was at the door, unlocking the deadbolt and exiting the bathroom. Laena reached gingerly behind her head and felt a warm wetness. A triangle of mirrored glass lay on her sleeve, and Laena saw the reflection of her shocked face fragmented by the cracks. When she looked at her fingers, they were covered in sticky blood.

Laena groped for the sink's edge and pulled herself up. Her head whirled and she felt like she was going to throw up. Her feet crunched on shards of glass as she shifted, trying to maintain her balance. The door whooshed open and a girl came in and stopped short at the sight before her.

"Oh my God!" she exclaimed. "What happened?" Laena tried to speak, but the words wouldn't come out. "Hold on, hold on! I'll get help!" The girl rushed out and Laena sank back to the floor. Everything went black.

* * *

"I think we should call an ambulance," Laena heard someone say. She groaned. She opened her eyes slowly, and found herself lying on the cot in the nurse's office. Her father's face swam in front of her, and both the nurse and the principal hovered behind him.

"Laena? What the hell happened?" Her father's voice was full of concern. "Jesus, you scared me. What happened? Can you talk?"

"I'm calling 911," the principal said, turning toward the desk.

"No!" Laena croaked. "No, please don't. I hate the hospital."

The nurse was dabbing Laena's scalp with something cold and wet. "Scalp wounds bleed a lot," she reassured them. "I really think she'll be okay."

"She blacked out," the principal said. "I don't want to be liable...."

"We're not going to sue you," Laena's father said, exasperated. "Laena, what happened? Can you tell us?"

"I...I slipped," she lied. "The floor must have been wet."

"You slipped *backwards*?" Ben asked, incredulous. "The back of your head hit the mirror over the sink."

Laena looked away. "I don't know, Dad. I just slipped."

Cree blew into the nurse's office. "Laena! Laena, are you all right?" He pushed between the nurse and her father and noticed the blood soaked bandages. "Ach, what happened?" he cried. "Is she okay?" He looked frantic. He knelt beside the cot, taking Laena's hand in his. "Laena, who did this to you?"

"I slipped," Laena insisted. "I'm fine. Really."

Cree's eyes hardened. Laena could see that he knew what had happened, that Ariel had attacked her. "I will kill her," he hissed.

"I slipped!" she said, raising her voice, trying to cover Cree's words. "It was an accident. I think I just want to go home...."

"We need to take her to the doctor," Cree said firmly, turning to Ben. "Head injuries can be dangerous. Please, Dr. Foster. Please. I can carry her to the car, you can drive...." Cree trailed off.

"I agree with Cree," the principal said. "I would feel a lot better if she were checked out by a physician." He jingled the change in his pants' pocket nervously.

"You're right, of course," Ben said shaking his head. "We'll take her. I'm not...not thinking straight." Ben headed to the office door. "Cree, I'll pull the car up. Can you bring her out?"

Cree nodded gratefully. The nurse gently taped a bandage to the wound on Laena's head, and Cree scooped her up in his arms. The room swam in front of her eyes.

"Cree!" the principal called as Cree walked toward the door. He turned. "Dr. Foster has my cell number. Please...have him call me and let me know how she is. I don't care what time it is."

"Yes, sir," Cree agreed. He swept out of the room and whisked Laena through the clusters of whispering students in the hall. The principal saw them and shouted, "Get back to class! All of you. There's nothing to see. She'll be fine." Laena felt the eyes boring into her as Cree advanced down the hall. Ariel was nowhere in sight.

"I don't want to go to the hospital," Lana protested feebly.

"Tough," Cree replied.

"Cree...it was Ariel...."

"Shhh," he whispered. "Do not say a word." He paused, and then said forcefully, "I will pay her back, Laena. Do not worry. I will pay her back."

Laena closed her eyes and she felt the cool air on her as Cree carried her outside, too tired to protest. She felt Cree lay her in the backseat of the car, and then—nothing.

* * *

By the time Ben, Cree, and Laena got home from the hospital, darkness had fallen. The doctors conducted numerous tests and diagnosed her with a concussion. They prescribed at least 72 hours of bed rest, and told Ben to call 911 if she started vomiting or they could not wake her up.

Cree carried her into the house where Michelle waited. "I can walk," Laena grumbled, but everyone fussed so much that no one heard her. Michelle set her up on the couch, tucking blankets around her and bringing her buttered toast and herbal tea, which Laena pushed away. Cree crouched by Laena's head, holding her hand and refusing to leave her side.

When they had all settled into the living room, Michelle said, "I can't believe you were so clumsy, Laena! That just isn't like you. Did you really slip backwards into the mirror?"

Laena winced as she shifted on the couch. The sink had left a massive bruise on her back. The doctor had given her painkillers before they left, and they were just starting to kick in. "I don't know, Mom," Laena griped. "I'm sorry to cause you so much trouble."

"Oh, honey, it's not that...it's just strange, that's all." Michelle looked up at Ben. "Did you call the principal, Ben? He's called here three times now, wanting to know how Laena is doing."

Ben barked out a laugh. "He just doesn't want us to sue." Michelle gave him a look, and Ben relented. "I'll call him, I'll call him," he muttered as he walked out of the room, shaking his head.

"Cree, you must be starving," Michelle said. "I got some Chinese takeout for us. Is that okay? I got you tofu with broccoli."

"Sounds wonderful, thank you," Cree said.

"Hey!" Laena complained. "I want tofu and broccoli. How come he gets it and I don't?"

Cree laughed. "I will share with you, I promise," Cree said.

"I'll get some for both of you," Michelle said, heading for the kitchen. "I didn't know what your stomach could handle, Laena."

Cree and Laena were alone for the first time since the incident. Cree glanced nervously toward the living room door, and then, reassured there was no one there, whispered, "What happened? Why did she do this to you?"

The transformation in Cree shocked Laena. His muscles were taut, and his voice full of tension.

"She...she wanted me to send you home. To stop you from trying to save the world," Laena said sleepily. Her head swam and she felt almost peaceful. "I told her there was no God. And I kicked her. Hard." Laena giggled.

Cree looked at her curiously. "You told her *what?*" Then his face cleared in understanding. "The medicine, it is starting to work," he stated, smiling despite his anger.

Laena smiled back. "I love you," she said dreamily.

"I love you, too, sweetie," Cree replied. "But you have to tell me what else she said. Please, Laena. Think."

Laena's eyes widened as she remembered. "She...she threatened to hurt me. To kill me," Laena whispered.

"Over my dead body," Cree muttered.

"You won't let her do that, will you Cree?"

"Of course not. She just wanted to scare you," Cree responded gently, stroking her hair back from her face. "I will not let her hurt you again."

Michelle came back into the room carrying two plates filled with brown rice and fragrant Chinese food. She placed everything on the coffee table. Laena murmured, "Mmmm, that smells good." Laena struggled to sit up, reaching for her plate. "I am so hungry, Mom."

"I think I will feed you, Laena," Cree offered. "You are groggy from the accident. And from the medication. Let me help you."

Laena giggled and nodded. "Okay."

"Wow," Cree said, smiling at Michelle. "She complied. I think she should be on this medication more often."

Michelle laughed.

Ben came back into the room, and they all settled in to dinner. Laena ate slowly, which gave Cree time to feed both him and her. She fell asleep after eating only half a plateful of food. Ben cleared the table and brought the dishes to the kitchen while Michelle fussed with Laena's blanket.

"The doctor said we need to wake her every few hours, and make sure her pupils are the same size," Ben said softly. "We also need to make sure she isn't slurring her words."

"I hate to wake her so often." Michelle protested.

"We have to," Ben replied. "We need to make sure she doesn't get worse."

"This is so ridiculous," Michelle said, frustration apparent in her voice. "Laena has never been this clumsy. Do you think she's telling us the truth about what happened?"

"What else could it have been?" Ben asked. "The only other possibility is that someone attacked her in the girls' bathroom at North Bayside High School, and that's never happened before. We've never had that kind of violence."

Cree stiffened at Ben's speculation. He did not want them to know about Ariel. If anyone knew Ariel had attacked Laena, they would want to know why. And if they knew why, they would know about the time travel and everything Cree was trying to do would come to a screeching halt. "I will stay up with her," he offered. "She is not going to be able to go to school tomorrow, and I can stay home with her and get some rest then."

"Don't be ridiculous, Cree. It isn't your job to take care of her," Michelle said.

"Please, let me help. You both have to work, and you do so much for me. You have taken me into your home, fed me, clothed me! Let me repay you with this very small thing."

Ben and Michelle looked at each other. Cree watched them, realization dawning that they were worried about the teenagers being alone together.

"I will not do anything to take advantage of her," Cree said, anger coloring his voice. He paused and took a deep breath. "I am sorry to be frustrated, but...." He trailed off, searching for words. "I hope you would not think I would do anything to her when she is so helpless. Or even when she is well...I would not betray you or your wishes."

Ben sighed. "Why don't we take turns tonight, and then you can stay home with her tomorrow, Cree?"

Cree shook his head. "Please, Ben. There is no need for you to disturb your own sleep tonight. I will not be able to sleep anyway, worrying about her. We can stay down here, and I will watch her. That way, you can check on us whenever you want."

Ben sighed, rubbing his face with his hands. "I don't know about you, Michelle, but I'm beat. This took a lot out of me today. If Cree can watch her tonight, I'm all for it."

"Okay," Michelle said, some hesitation in her voice. "But Cree, you promise you'll wake us up if there's any change? And you will wake her up every two hours, make sure she's coherent?"

"Yes, yes," Cree replied. "Of course." He succeeded in placating Ben and Michelle, and they finally trudged upstairs to their room. Cree paced the living room, peering out the curtains every few minutes, muttering under his breath.

The fact that Ariel had attacked Laena so boldly at school frightened him. Ariel had snapped. Cree knew he needed Laena to get to Michelle, and convince her of the threat to the oceans, but he did not want to risk Laena's life in the process.

Laena slept deeply, but Cree dutifully woke her every two hours to ensure her condition was not worsening. At a little after 2 a.m., Michelle crept down the stairs and peeked into the living room. Cree looked up, sensing her presence.

"Is she okay?" Michelle whispered.

Cree nodded. "I woke her up at 1 a.m., and we spoke. She is fine." He smiled kindly. "She will be okay, Michelle. You can go back to bed. I have everything under control."

Michelle sighed. "I'm not sleeping very well," she admitted.

"She will be fine," Cree reassured her again. "There is no need for you to lose sleep."

Michelle nodded somberly and turned to go back upstairs. She hesitated and turned back to Cree. "Cree...what is going on? I mean, what is *really* going on?"

Cree rubbed his thumb against his chin thoughtfully. "What do you mean?" he asked softly, stalling for time.

Michelle cocked her head and her mouth tightened. She did not respond.

Cree expelled the breath he had been holding. "Everything will be okay, Michelle. I promise you."

Michelle's eyes searched Cree's face. "There's something wrong, Cree. I know my daughter, and I have never seen her so emotional. So fragile! I don't know what's going on, but I know it's something...big. Why won't you let me help?"

Cree shook his head, more to himself than at Michelle, eyes downcast. He could not bring himself to speak. The silence lengthened.

"I am here if you need me," she whispered, so softly he almost could not make out the words, and then he heard the soft rustle of her nightgown as she left the room and glided up the stairs. Cree laid his head down on the couch, ran his fingers angrily through his hair and swore.

Chapter 14

BEN AND MICHELLE forced Laena to stay home from school for the rest of the week recuperating, and Cree refused to leave her home alone. He feared that Ariel would come to the house and attack her again, but he couldn't admit that to Ben and Michelle. Instead, he told them that he wanted to make sure Laena did not have any lingering problems from the concussion, and that someone needed to be with her. Ben and Michelle finally acquiesced to the teenagers being home alone together when they saw how adamant Cree was about staying with her. Ben brought home their school assignments, and they worked on homework together during the long days. But spring had arrived with a vengeance, and Laena was so antsy to get out of the house that she threatened to sneak out when Cree was in the bathroom. On Friday afternoon, the doctor gave Laena permission to go back to school. Unfortunately, Laena's recovery coincided with the school's spring vacation, and there was no school at all the following week.

"I have an idea," Cree said, as Laena paced back and forth in the living room like a caged lioness. Laena ignored him. "Laena, stop. You will wear a hole in the floor with that walking." Laena threw him a dirty look. "Do you not want to hear my idea?"

She sighed dramatically, arms crossed in front of her chest. "Sure," she said bitterly. "What's your great idea?"

"Let's design our experiments today, and then ask your mother if we can go to the lab with her this week to run them. We have no school, and it will be the perfect time to do the work on krill and toxins."

Laena brightened. "Yes! That *is* a good idea, Cree! I'll go get my laptop and we can do some research and type up an experimental design." She started for the stairs and Cree jumped up.

"I will get it...tell me where it is."

Laena ignored him. "I can make it up the stairs!" she shouted over her shoulder. "Stop treating me like I'm an invalid!" She jogged up the stairs to drive home her point, and Cree sighed and shook his head. He cleared some space on the coffee table, and took out a notebook and pencil.

Laena returned with her Mac and booted it up. Cree watched with interest. "Uh, Laena? Will you teach me how to use one of these?"

Laena glanced up. "The computer? Oh, yeah, sure! Sorry, I keep forgetting you don't have these. Here, look.... " She proceeded to show him the power button, and how the mouse worked. Cree was hopeless—he could not get the subtle movements of the mouse, and he got frustrated easily. Finally, Laena took the machine away from him.

"I have an idea," she said gently. "I think it will be more efficient if you tell me what you want to search for, and I'll do the actual search. Okay?"

"It is a stupid thing, this computer," Cree grumbled. "Why do they make it so difficult? And what is with this ridiculous mouse? It even has a silly name. A *mouse*," he said scornfully. "I will stick to my paper and pencil."

Laena laughed. "Okay, you can write, and I will do the research. Tell me what type of articles you need, and I will pull them up for you."

Cree glanced up at Laena. He stared at her in silence. "Are you joking?" he asked finally.

She frowned. "Why would I be joking?"

"There are articles in there?" he asked, gesturing to the laptop. "Books?"

"Well, they're not *in* here, but I can access almost anything from the internet.

Watch.... " Laena typed rapidly and then turned the screen toward Cree. "See, I went to Google Scholar, which is a site that has all the scientific stuff, and I am just searching articles since 2010...so only the work that has been published over the past few years. I typed in 'antibacterials' and 'oceans,' and...voila!...here are some research articles on the effect of antibacterials on certain ocean fish, and another one about antibacterials getting into the ocean from wastewater treatment plants...."

Cree stared at the screen, his eyes scanning the words. "But...how do I see the articles? What the scientist wrote?"

"Just click on it...which one do you want?" Cree pointed at the first one, and Laena clicked into the article.

"Mirinda...." Cree murmured.

"What did you say?"

"Mirinda...wonderful. This is wonderful," Cree said, switching back to English.

Laena watched Cree absorbing the article on the screen. His beautiful face was intense, hungry for information. She reached over and stroked his face. Cree ignored her caress. She sidled closer and stroked his thigh. He shifted, glanced up at her, then back to the screen.

"What are you doing, Laena?"

"Trying to get your attention," she whispered. "You are so handsome. And I love it when you speak Esperanto. It is so...sexy."

He looked up at her, his eyes now fixed on her. He smiled. "Yes? You like when I speak my language?" Cree put the computer gently to the side and swept Laena into his lap. "I cannot concentrate when you do that to me, when you talk like that. *Mi estas viro.*"

"*'Mi estas viro'*...what does that mean?" Laena whispered, lacing her arms around him.

"It means I am a man," Cree said, grinning. "I cannot ignore your touch, and the sound in your voice."

"What sound in my voice?" Laena murmured.

"It is the sound of sex," Cree said huskily. "The sound of desire." He leaned down and kissed her deeply, pulling her lips into his. Laena pressed herself against him and moaned.

"Ach," Cree said, disentangling himself from her arms. "Laena, we cannot do this. Please, you must stop."

"Why?" she said softly. "Don't you want me?"

"Of course I want you," Cree said, pain in his voice. "But it is not right. I promised your parents. I cannot betray their trust. And what am I to do if you become with child? What then?"

"We have something called birth control," Laena said. "I don't have to get pregnant."

But Cree was shaking his head before Laena even finished speaking.

"Cree, I ache for you! I can tell you want me, too...I can feel it. I can see it! Why can't we be together?"

Cree held Laena's face in his hands. "No, Laena. I will not be the one to take away your virginity. I love you, but I cannot do this to you. Do you not remember? I am leaving in a few months. You should save yourself for someone who you will be with forever."

"I don't want anyone else," Laena said miserably. "No one but you. There will never be anyone but you."

Cree searched Laena's eyes. "I will always love you, too, sweetie. And I want you so badly. But we should not...we cannot."

Laena sensed his resolve weakening. "I want to have sex with you, Cree. I want to truly be with you."

Cree moaned. "Laena.... "

"How about a compromise, then?" she whispered. "Can't we...can't we love each other without actually having sex?"

Cree breathed raggedly. She saw him struggling to get control, to find a way to reject her. Her hand went to his crotch and she stroked him. He groaned louder. "We don't have to have sex, Cree. Please, let me...let me touch you, make you happy. I want to feel you give me pleasure, too. I have never been with a man before. I want to experience it with you. No one else."

Cree did not answer. In one swift movement, he picked Laena up and lay her on the couch. He straddled her, pulling off his own shirt and throwing it on the floor. He deftly pulled off her shirt, taking care not to jolt her wounded head, and she reached behind her back to unclasp her bra. The necklace Cree gave her nestled between her breasts. He eased her pants down and off and Laena reached to unbutton his jeans.

"No," he protested hoarsely. "No. This is for you, sweetie, not for me. I do not trust myself. My pants stay on." And then he was stroking her, kissing her, loving her, until she was lost in his touch and oblivious to everything but him. Laena arched her back to meet his touch, and in no time at all, it was over, and she buried her head in his shoulder, her breathing heavy. Cree lay by her side, stroking her damp hair, murmuring to her in Esperanto. She clung to him, but would not meet his eyes.

"Laena, what is wrong? Did I do something wrong? Did I hurt you?" Cree tried to lift her head, but Laena stubbornly hid her face. "Are you embarrassed, Laena?"

She nodded, her heart thumping wildly.

"Laena...there is nothing to be ashamed of. You are so beautiful...that is natural, what we did. All of it...that is the way it is supposed to be." He laughed softly. "It is a good thing we did not have intercourse, because then you would have been very embarrassed. What is the word you use...the one that means very, very embarrassed? Embarrassed almost to death?"

"Mortified," Laena mumbled into his chest.

"Yes, mortified." He sighed. "Are you unhappy with me? Or just embarrassed? If it is just embarrassment, then you are being silly. This is the fun part of biology, the drive to love each other and reproduce. Evolution has made it so it is fun, because really, being pregnant and giving birth is not a lot of fun. I have seen women in my village give birth. It looks very painful."

Laena giggled.

"That is my girl," Cree murmured. "It is a little funny, no? You should hear me when I am being pleasured." Laena laughed again and looked up at him. He caught her chin in his hand and held her gaze. "There is absolutely nothing to be ashamed of. I thought this was what you wanted? Our compromise?"

"Only half of it," Laena admitted. "What about you? I want to give you pleasure...."

"No," Cree said firmly. "I cannot control myself. I do not want to risk it...."

"There is nothing to risk, Cree. Teach me...teach me what to do, how to give you pleasure." Cree shook his head. "It's only fair, after what you just did. I promise I won't let you have sex with me. I swear...."

"No," Cree said feebly.

But Laena was already unzipping his pants. "Show me what to do, Cree. What is it you like?"

"No, no, no...." He caught her hand, but Laena pulled away easily. And then, something in his face shifted, and he helped her, easing his own jeans past his hips. Laena gasped as he sprung free, and Cree guided her hand to him and groaned, murmuring to her, instructing her and encouraging her. She helped him turn over so he was lying on the couch, and she hovered over him, caressing him, stroking him. And then he was speaking in his language, out of control, shuddering in her touch, grasping her so hard it almost hurt. She collapsed on top of him, their sweat mingling, sticky and sated. They lay together until their breathing slowed, and Laena timidly said, "Was that right?"

Cree laughed, hugging her tightly. "There is no right or wrong, sweetie. That was perfect. I loved it. I love you." And he kissed her neck and she snuggled happily into him.

After a few minutes, Cree shifted. "We should take a shower, and get back to work."

"Mmmm," Laena said noncommittally.

"I'll take that as a yes," Cree said, sitting up.

"I want to take a nap," Laena complained. "With you."

"Yes, that is what pleasure does to you," Cree agreed. "Makes you sleepy. I think there must be an evolutionary reason for that. After sex, it is best if the female stays prone, so the sperm can fertilize the egg. But we did not have intercourse, and we are not trying to get you with child. And, most importantly, it would probably not be good to fall asleep and have your parents come home and find us like this."

"Oh no!" Laena said, sitting up abruptly. "What time is it?"

Cree shrugged. "I do not know...but we should get out of this...compromising situation."

Laena laughed. She tugged her shirt on and Cree pulled his jeans on over his nakedness. They grabbed the remainder of their discarded clothes and ran upstairs.

"I do not suppose we should shower together?" Cree murmured, grabbing Laena's hand and eyeing her hungrily.

"If my father comes home...." Laena said, uncertainty in her voice.

"Mmmm, you are right. You shower in your bathroom, and I will use your parents'. Then we should get back to work." He looked at her, frowning. "This was your fault, you know," he said with a mock sternness.

"So sorry," Laena responded, amused. "I'll make sure it never happens again."

Cree laughed and pulled her into his arms. "No! Please! That is not at all what I want."

"What do you want?" Laena asked, nuzzling him.

"I want to do that as often as possible," he responded, kissing her neck.

Laena melted. "How about now?"

"No way," he said. Cree pushed her away and turned her around so she faced her bathroom. He smacked her butt gently and urged her toward the door. "Go now, before I change my mind."

They both showered and returned to the living room. Within minutes they heard Ben's car tires crunching up the driveway. Laena and Cree looked at each other in horror. "That was close," Cree whispered. "If he had come home 15 minutes ago.... " He trailed off, unable to contemplate the disaster that would have unfolded.

The front door opened and both teens looked up. "Hi, Dad!" Laena called in a cheery voice.

"Hey, kids," Ben responded, walking into the room. "I decided to come home early...I'm done with my lesson plans for the week after break." He paused, taking in the laptop and the notes Cree was scribbling. "What are you guys doing?"

"We are designing an experiment for the krill," Cree said. "Do you want to hear our hypothesis?"

"Sure!" Ben said, sitting down on the easy chair across from Cree.

Cree cleared his throat. "Okay, here it is. 'Levels of antibacterials currently found in the ocean are causing the death of wild krill.' " Cree looked up expectantly at Ben.

Ben cocked his head. "Before we get into the specifics of your hypothesis, let me ask you something...after reading those papers Michelle brought home, you still think it is the antibacterials that are killing the krill?"

Cree nodded. "Yes, I can see no other explanation." Ben opened his mouth to speak and Cree held up his hand, palm out, to stop him. "I know that they did experiments already that show that the antibacterials are not killing *lab-raised* krill," Cree said. "But I think there must be something else going on. I think if those experiments were run again, using wild krill from the ocean, we would get different results."

Ben looked stunned. "Why would that be, Cree? You think there is some physical difference between the wild krill and the lab-raised krill?"

Cree nodded. "Yes, I think there must be."

"What could the difference between the wild krill and the lab krill possibly be? If there is no reasonable explanation for the difference, there is no reason to run your experiment, which would be time-consuming and expensive. Scientists have already proven that antibacterial exposure—at least the amounts found in the ocean—does not kill the lab-raised krill."

"There could be many differences between the two populations of krill," Cree explained calmly. "For example, the wild krill may have some different genetic make-up, or perhaps a parasite...." Cree paused, hesitant to say too much and raise suspicions.

"A parasite? How would a parasite make a difference?"

Cree shook his head. "I do not know, sir. Maybe not a parasite then. Maybe something else. Like a virus. Just *something*...something that sets them apart and makes a difference. I think it is worth checking, and if it turns out that antibacterials kill the wild-caught krill, then we can figure out what the difference is."

Ben looked at Cree, puzzled. He turned to Laena. "Laena? Do you agree with this assessment?"

Laena nodded. "I do think it's worth doing the initial experiment Cree described...just doing the same exposure experiment the lab already conducted, but using wild-caught krill. If we *don't* do that experiment, then I think we're making an assumption that may be wrong. We're just assuming that the lab-raised krill are going to react the same way as the wild-caught krill, and if we're wrong...well, then, we may be missing the real answer."

Ben stared at her, then jumped up. "I need a beer," he said. "I think you two are wrong, but you should really be talking to Michelle about this." He started toward the kitchen. Then he stopped and turned around to face the teens. "I don't mean to discourage you," he said. "I think it's great that you're working on this and...thinking outside the box." He smiled half-heartedly. "But before you spend too much time going down this path, discuss it with Michelle, okay?" He headed to the kitchen.

Laena and Cree looked at each other warily. "That didn't go too badly," Laena whispered.

Cree grimaced. "Really? I thought it was pretty awful."

Ben came back into the living room with a beer and sat back on the couch. "So, what do you guys think we ought to do for dinner tonight?"

Laena glanced at her phone, surprised to see that it was almost 4 o'clock. "I hadn't thought about it," Laena responded apologetically. "I didn't realize it was so late! Cree and I were so caught up in researching stuff on Google Scholar.... " She trailed off as she saw Ben watching her, his mouth tightening into a thin disapproving line. She was puzzled, until she saw Cree's wet hair. They both had wet hair. Ben must have noticed, and assumed—correctly—that they had taken showers. "But that's not all we did," she said quickly. "I've been feeling so cooped up...we went for a walk, and then I got too tired on the way back. I was all sweaty and gross, and Cree had to carry me the last part of the way home." She forced a laugh. "It was pretty embarrassing."

Cree looked at her in surprise. This adventure they allegedly had was news to him. Laena grabbed a strand of her wet hair and curled it around her finger, willing Cree to get the clue.

Understanding flooded his face. "Right!" Cree interjected. "I should not have let you talk me into that, Laena. Too much, too soon." He shook his head at her disapprovingly, and Ben looked from one teen to the other, trying to assess the veracity of their story.

"Yeah, it was stupid of me. I was just so cranky, and I was just pacing around, and we thought a short walk wouldn't do any harm. But I guess we got carried away. I mean.... " She blushed. "We got carried away because we walked too far. And then when we got home, we were so hot and sweaty we had to take a shower. I mean, showers. Separate showers." She could practically feel Cree cringe next to her.

Ben sighed loudly and took another swallow of beer. Laena could tell he wasn't buying her story.

Cree stood up. "So, dinner, right? We need to think about dinner?"

Ben stood up as well, resigned. "I'll figure dinner out. I sure could go for some pizza, or something else easy and totally unhealthy." He smiled wanly. "But I guess that's out of the question, huh?"

"No, wait Dad! We can order from Pizza Land down at the plaza! They do a vegan calzone with no cheese. It has just veggies, sauce and dough. Cree and I can split one of those, and you and mom can have a pizza."

Ben brightened slightly. "Really? Cree, is that okay with you?"

Cree nodded. "Sure. I do not know what a...calzone? What a calzone is, but it sounds good."

"You'll love it," Laena reassured him. "It has eggplant, and peppers, onions, garlic, mushrooms...it's great."

"Okay, good!" The prospect of food seemed to have taken Ben's mind off Laena's lame story about the walk.

"I can call it in, Dad," Laena offered, trying to be as agreeable as possible. "What time is Mom getting home?"

"She said around 5, so why don't you call it in and tell them to deliver it at 5? I'm too beat to drive over there."

"Sure," Laena said, dialing her cell phone.

"And get me some onion rings, too, please. I'm feeling decadent."

Laena nodded and began to place the order. Ben wandered into the kitchen and Cree sagged with relief. When Laena hung up, she saw that he was rubbing the back of his neck in distress.

"What's the matter?" she murmured.

"He suspects something," Cree hissed. "Laena, I cannot be distracted like this. I am here for a reason, and I have a limited amount of time. I am being selfish...I am thinking of my needs, my wants, and I am ignoring what I am supposed to be doing!"

Laena bristled. "That's not fair, Cree! Ariel *attacked* me. She could have killed me! We had no choice but to take last week off. I was hardly in any shape to be doing research on this stuff...."

"No, no," Cree interrupted, impatient. "I know last week was different. But now, today, we should have come up with something better, anticipated their questions. Instead, we...we gave into our desires and wasted time."

Laena was stunned. His words tore through her like the sharp pieces of mirror that rained down on her after Ariel attacked her. "Is that what it was to you? Wasting time? Because it was a little different for me."

Cree heard the anger and hurt in her voice and looked up. "That is not what I meant," he pleaded.

"That's exactly what you said!" Laena whispered sharply. "Wasted time. Well, sorry to have *wasted your time* this afternoon, Cree." She stood up and left the room. Cree heard the front door slam, and sighed.

Ben peered out of the kitchen at the sound of the slamming door. "Everything okay?" he queried, his eyebrows raised.

Cree smiled feebly. "Who knows? I cannot seem to say the right thing."

Ben leaned against the doorjamb and laughed. "As you get older, Cree, you'll learn that you can never say the right thing to a woman." Cree shook his head and grimaced. "Hey, why don't you come in here and help me set the table for dinner? We can talk."

Cree got up and followed Ben back into the kitchen. Ben had opened a cabinet and handed Cree dinner plates.

"I am a little worried about Laena walking around by herself outside," Cree admitted, placing the plates at the table. "She is not herself yet, and she tires easily."

"Mmmm. Especially after your long walk earlier this afternoon," Ben said easily.

Cree glanced up at Ben, but Ben was fishing in the silverware drawer for forks. Cree did not respond.

Ben handed Cree four forks. "Did you have a nice walk?" He leaned back against the counter, arms crossed against his chest.

"Sir...."

Ben waited, eyebrows raised questioningly. Cree sighed in resignation.

"We...we did not go for a walk."

"No, I didn't think so."

"But it was not what you think, sir. Really. I...." Cree trailed off, out of excuses.

Ben motioned for Cree to sit at the kitchen table. Cree pulled out a chair, legs scraping against the wooden floor, and sat heavily. Ben joined him.

"Cree, I like you. I really do. But ever since you showed up, Laena is being dishonest with us. On top of that, Michelle and I have both noticed that she seems so fragile. And her 'accident'?" Ben made air quotes with his fingers. "I honestly don't believe that she slipped. What is going on here? Why can't you confide in us, let us know what is really happening? Maybe we can help."

Cree shook his head, stubbornly silent. He looked down at his hands clasped on the table.

"You can't tell me? Or you won't?"

"I cannot," Cree whispered. "I am sorry, sir."

"You don't leave me with a lot of choice, then," Ben said evenly.

Cree looked up. "What do you mean? What are you going to do?"

Ben opened his mouth to speak when the front door opened, and Michelle and Laena walked in, chatting. They stopped short at the threshold of the kitchen, sensing the tension between Ben and Cree.

"Hi, everyone," Michelle asked, dropping her briefcase on the floor and shrugging out of her sweater.

Laena looked frantically from her father to Cree. "What's wrong?"

Ben looked at Cree. "You want to take this one, Cree?"

Cree cleared his throat. "Ben does not think I am a good influence on you, Laena," Cree said mildly. "He believes that something is going on and we are keeping something from him."

Ben held up his hand. "I didn't say you weren't a good influence, Cree. You're twisting my words. I said that since you showed up, things have been...different. I don't know if here is a causal relationship between your presence and the things that have been happening."

"What things?" Laena asked, her voice tense. "What do you mean? Cree hasn't done anything wrong."

"I didn't say he's done anything wrong. I said that you've been lying to us, Laena, since he showed up, and that your accident seemed suspicious...."

"That's not fair, Ben," Michelle interrupted harshly. "Cree had *nothing* to do with Laena's accident. And Laena's just a teenager...their brains are wired differently. All teenagers lie to their parents. Did you expect to have a perfect daughter forever?" Michelle laughed, the levity forced.

"Mom...." Laena protested.

Michelle threw up her arms, exasperated. "Enough. I will not have you accuse Cree of being responsible for anything that has been happening. Laena is a teenager, and it's inevitable that her emotions get a little crazy. She says her accident was just an accident—that's all. We have to trust her. I think if someone had attacked her, she would have told us. Let's just let it go."

Ben and Michelle stared at each other silently. Laena looked in horror from one to the other, while Cree hung his head in shame. The doorbell rang, startling them all.

"The pizza...." Laena said.

"I'll get it," Michelle said, grabbing her wallet from her briefcase on the floor. "Laena, get drinks for everyone."

Cree looked up at Ben and the two men locked eyes. Cree straightened. "Ben, I am sorry if I upset you," he said quietly. "I swear to you, I had nothing to do with Laena's accident. I would never hurt her. Ever. And the things I am not telling you...it is simply because I cannot. I wish I could."

Ben nodded curtly. "You can tell me anything, Cree, and I will not judge you. If you're in trouble, I will do what I can to help. But we can't help you if we don't know what is going on. And I will do anything—and I mean *anything*—to protect my daughter."

"As will I," Cree replied firmly.

Michelle walked into the kitchen with two pizza boxes and a paper bag stained with grease. "Dinner!" she said, holding the food aloft. "Cree, I guess this will be your first experience with greasy east coast fast food." She placed the boxes on the table and looked from Cree to Ben. "Are you two men still at it?"

"No, ma'am," Cree replied stiffly.

"Dad, can we just...I don't know...call a truce here or something?" Laena looked pleadingly at her father.

Ben looked up at Laena, his eyes hard. "I don't know, Laena. Can we? Why don't you tell me what you were doing this afternoon? And what really happened in that bathroom last week?"

Laena lifted her chin defiantly. "I slipped in the bathroom, Dad. I may have been clumsy, but that's all. Really. And as for today...." She took a shaky breath. "I lied. We didn't go for a walk. I...we...we were fooling around. We didn't have sex, honestly. We were just...fooling around. And I pushed it, not Cree. He tried to stop me. He *did* stop me. He kept saying he wouldn't betray your trust. So there's no need for you to worry, because no matter what I want, or what I'm ready for, Cree won't have sex with me." She laughed bitterly. "It's me you should be mad at. Not him."

The silence was deafening. Ben shook his head as if to clear it.

"What wonderful dinner conversation," Michelle said cheerily, grabbing four glasses herself. "I think that pretty much explains everything, right Ben? So why don't we eat.... " She paused, filling the glasses with ice cubes. "And Laena and I can resume the sex conversation later, privately. And the birth control discussion." She smiled, handing the glasses to Laena and opening the refrigerator to get the seltzer water. She turned back to the three of them, who were speechless. "Sound good?"

Laena nodded wordlessly and the four of them sat down. The silence was awkward until Ben cleared his throat. "Uh, Michelle, the kids worked on the krill issue today. I told them they should discuss their ideas with you."

Cree accepted that Ben's opener was a peace offering, and he smiled at him. Ben looked up at Cree and gave a smile back.

"Yes, we have a hypothesis we would like to test," Cree said, glancing at Laena to gauge her reaction.

"Before we get into that, I have something I'd like to say," Laena said. "Dad, I'm sorry I lied to you earlier." Ben nodded silently, accepting the apology. "And Cree.... " Laena took a deep breath. "I'm sorry I got mad at you. You were right, and I was wrong, and it won't happen again."

Cree reached over and kissed Laena on the cheek. She blushed, and tucked her curls behind her ear.

"Okay, okay, everyone is forgiven," Michelle said, smiling. "Let's forget this all happened." She snagged one of Ben's onion rings from the greasy paper bag and Ben slapped her hand jokingly. "Tell me about your hypothesis." She took a bite of the onion ring and the slippery onion escaped from the fried coating and dangled from her mouth. She delicately pushed it in her mouth and looked at Cree expectantly, chewing.

Cree explained what they wanted to do, with Laena interjecting occasionally. Cree stressed that there must be a difference between the wild krill and the lab—raised krill, and raised the possibility of a virus, or a parasite. Or even a virophage. Michelle listened, chewing thoughtfully on a slice of pizza, and said at length, "So you really think this is worth doing? Repeating the experiment on wild-caught krill?"

"I do," Cree said firmly. "I think it is imperative."

Michelle looked at him, her head cocked. "Imperative?" she echoed.

"Yes, ma'am." Cree's intense blue eyes drilled into hers.

She nodded. "Okay. I'll order the krill Monday. How many do you think we'll need to get a big enough sample size?"

"I figured we would need about 100 krill per dose of antibacterials, and we have a control group and five levels of antibacterials...so...600?"

Michelle shook her head. "Let me check with the statistician to see what she suggests," Michelle countered. "You may be right, but it may not be enough. I'll have her design the experiment and we'll go from there."

"Really?" Laena said, disbelief in her voice. "That's it? You're going to run the experiment?"

"No," Michelle said, crunching on the crust of her pizza. "You two are going to run the experiment. I'm just giving approval for it." She paused, swallowing. "Laena, I want you to help Cree. It'll be good for you, working in the lab. You'll get a better taste for what it's like to be a scientist. Plus, if Cree gets a publication out of this, it'll look great on your resume for colleges."

"I'd love to!" Laena said.

"Thank you," Cree said, relief evident in his tone. "Thank you for letting me do this, for trusting me."

Michelle looked at Cree strangely. "Mmmm," she responded noncommittally. "I have a feeling, Cree, that you know more than you're letting on."

Laena stiffened, but Michelle turned away and started talking to Ben about the vegetable garden. Laena turned to look at Cree and shrugged. Cree winked at her, and they both dug into their dinner with renewed hunger. Relief flooded through Laena. They had actually done it. They were getting the chance to do the experiment. If they were successful, maybe they could save the oceans.

Chapter 15

CREE AND LAENA walked across the parking lot of CCOL behind Michelle, whose heels were clicking smartly on the pavement. Laena grasped Cree's hand and squeezed it. Michelle turned and smiled at them.

"Okay, now remember, this is your project. I'm going to order the krill as soon as I get a number from Jackie, our statistician. I want you two to meet with her, and tell her about the experiment. She will check your experimental design and make sure the data you collect can be analyzed to give you the answer you're looking for." Michelle paused. "Cree, I'm paying you for this work. You'll make $10 an hour. Laena, you're my slave. No money for you."

"Hey!" Laena protested. "No fair."

Michelle ignored Laena's griping. "Cree, I'll need your social security number to fill out the proper paperwork, okay? After you talk to Jackie I'll send you to Human Resources."

Cree looked at Laena, startled. He shook his head, baffled. Laena tried to reassure him with her eyes.

"Uh, Mom? Can't you just pay Cree under the table? Does he have to go through all the formalities?"

Michelle frowned. "Of course I can't pay him under the table. The paperwork won't take long. It's not a big deal."

Laena looked at Cree and grimaced, shaking her head. Cree understood that this number Michelle wanted would blow his cover, and he interjected. "Michelle, I do not want money," he said. "I have been living at your house, eating your food, using your water and electricity...I really cannot take money from you."

"Don't be ridiculous," Michelle said, reaching the front doors of the building. "I insist."

Cree dropped Laena's hand and reached out to grab Michelle's arm. She turned at his touch.

"I will not do this if you insist on paying me. Please. You do too much for me as it is, and I cannot take money as well." His voice was pleading.

"Cree, it's not like the money is coming out of my wallet," Michelle explained. "It's a research grant."

Cree shook his head. "No. I cannot take the money."

"Cree, you're being unreasonable. Look, you can save it for when you move back into Evergreen Acres." Laena's stomach lurched at the thought of Cree leaving their house.

"Mom, please. He doesn't want the money," Laena said forcefully.

Michelle crossed her arms and turned to face the two teens. "Doesn't want the money, or doesn't want to fill out the paperwork?"

Laena and Cree were silent. Cree opened his mouth to speak, and Laena, afraid of what would come out, said, "Cree, no."

Cree shook his head. "It is okay, Laena. Michelle, I do not have that number you speak of. The...social number?"

"Social security number?" Michelle asked, incredulous. "You don't have your social security number? Or you don't know it? Because if you don't remember it, we can call the government and they can re-issue a card. All we need is your birth date and where you were born...."

"No!" Laena and Cree said in unison.

Michelle looked at them oddly. "What is going on here?" she asked. "How did Mark pay you at the campground without a Social?"

"He...he gave me a free cabin, and gave me cash every week. I did not fill out any paperwork."

"Cree, that's illegal," Michelle said sternly.

"I know," Cree admitted. "But that is how he did it."

"Well, I can't do it that way here," Michelle responded. "This is a government grant, and I have to document every dime that I spend."

"Can't he just volunteer, Mom?" Laena pleaded.

"What is the problem here?" Michelle asked. "Cree, are you in some kind of trouble? Are you a runaway?"

Cree shook his head, and looked at her beseechingly. "Michelle, I am begging you. I have done nothing wrong. I am not a bad person. Please, can you just trust me on this? I want to do this work. I *must* do this work. But I do not want money, from you or from anyone else. Please."

Michelle stared at Cree, tapping her foot impatiently on the sidewalk. Finally, after what seemed like an eternity, Michelle nodded curtly. "Fine." She turned and opened the doors to CCOL. "In."

Laena rolled her eyes. When her mom began speaking in monosyllables, it meant trouble. But at least she had agreed not to push the paperwork. With trepidation, they entered the cool stillness of CCOL. They were in!

Michelle took Laena and Cree directly to Jackie's cubicle.

"Good morning, Jackie," Michelle said, as a young, twenty—something woman turned from her computer. She had warm brown eyes, and she had arranged her straight brown hair into a haphazard bun on top of her head.

"Hi, Dr. Foster!" Jackie replied. "Can I help you with something?"

Michelle smiled warmly. "I hope so. Do you remember my daughter, Laena? You met her last year at the office picnic."

"Of course!" Jackie shook Laena's hand. Her eyes crinkled at the corners.

"And this is Cree McNeil, Laena's friend." Jackie and Cree shook hands and exchanged hellos.

"Jackie, Cree is working—on a volunteer basis—on my krill grant. He and Laena want to run the mortality experiment again, but this time using wild-caught krill. Can you help them figure out sample size and study design so we can order the krill? I think they have some ideas already, but I want to make sure that we get statistically valid results."

"Absolutely!" Jackie said. "Why don't you guys grab some chairs and we can go through what you have?"

Laena and Cree each wheeled over chairs from an empty neighboring cubicle, and crowded around Jackie's computer. Her fingers flew across the keys as she brought up the study she had already done.

"Let's see...we were looking at how the levels of antibacterials in the ocean water affected krill mortality, and we found no statistically significant correlation between concentration of the antibacterials and mortality. So, we ruled out antibacterials as the cause of the little suckers dying." Jackie wheeled to face the two teens. "So you want to re-run this same experiment using wild caught krill? Why?"

Cree cleared his throat. "We just want to make sure that there is not something in the wild krill that would give us a different answer." He fidgeted nervously as Jackie waited for him to elaborate. "In other words, ummm, maybe there is a parasite or a virus in the wild krill that is affected by the antibacterials, and this in turn affects the krill."

"And if the lab-raised krill are free from this...thing that the wild krill have, we wouldn't get the same results," Laena added.

Jackie nodded slowly. "Okay, I hear you." She paused, and then frowned. "But how would the antibacterials affect this alleged virus, or parasite, in a way that *hurts* the krill? The antibacterials make the virus stronger or something?"

Cree shrugged. "Something like that. We do not know the mechanism, but we do know that the wild krill are dying, and need to rule out the effect of antibacterials on wild krill. The experiment that the lab already ran used lab-raised krill, and we thought we should not assume that the lab krill and the wild krill are the same."

Jackie nodded, her messy bun threatening to tumble down. "I'm not a biologist, but it seems to me that the wild caught krill would have other variables that we would have to tease out. For example, they would be different ages, different sexes, they may come from different areas of the ocean...in the lab-raised krill, all of that is standardized so you get a clean analysis. We're gonna have to increase the numbers. We can use the same concentrations of antibacterials, but our krill numbers are going to go up." Jackie turned back to the computer and her fingers tapped on the keys. "Ultimately I think we'll need to do a multivariate analysis, but for now let's just figure out what sample size we're gonna need." Her hands paused and she turned to face the teens. "No sense in you guys just sitting here watching me work. Why don't you go speak to the boys in the lab, and tell them we're going to be bringing in a bunch of wild krill? Tell them the setup will be similar to what we did last time, but with more animals. They can help you get the tanks set up, and I'll come down as soon as I'm finished and tell you how many to order. Laena, you know where the lab is, right?"

Laena nodded, standing up. "I do...thanks so much, Jackie. We really appreciate it."

Cree smiled and stuck out his hand. "Yes, thank you, Jackie."

Jackie shook his hand and laughed. "I think we're going to be seeing a lot of each other, so this isn't goodbye. By the way, you guys are gonna enter the data for me, okay? I don't do that. Take a look at the spreadsheet on the old data, and set it up the same way. Get me the file when you're done with the experiments, and I'll take it from there. Sound good?"

Laena and Cree nodded and Laena grabbed Cree's hand. "Thanks again, Jackie!"

Laena and Cree made their way downstairs to the labs. Cree stopped her on a landing in the stairwell, his eyes radiating excitement. "Laena, we are doing it. We are here, and we will soon have the data to prove what is really going on in the oceans. I cannot thank you enough. I do not know that I could have done this without your help."

Laena smiled sadly. "We're not done yet, Cree. We still have a long way to go. And what if the experiments don't work? What if we don't get statistically valid results?"

Cree shook his head. "No worries. It is there...I *know* it is there. And now, the scientists will know why the krill are dying, and they can stop it. So if we can stop the death of the krill, we can stop the collapse of the oceans. And then, who knows what will happen? We can change the course of the future, Laena!"

Cree hugged her, hard, and Laena buried her face in his shoulder. Changing the course of the future. And what will this new future hold? Laena wondered. And more importantly, *who* would it hold? She squeezed her eyes shut and clung to Cree, unable to imagine a future without him.

Chapter 16

LAENA AND CREE WORKED on the project all week. One of the research vessels offered to pick up the wild krill when the scientists on board were studying the whales in their feeding grounds. Krill were plentiful this time of year. Wherever the whales were, there were krill. It turned out to be fairly straightforward to measure the level of existing antibacterials in the wild krill, and one of the lab techs ran those tests. Jackie finished designing the study and the teenagers helped the biologists dose the krill with varying concentrations of antibacterials. The results were dramatic.

Wyatt, the ginger-haired biologist who ran the lab, beckoned Cree and Laena over. "Look at this, you guys. It's only been 50 or so hours, and almost all the krill at the two highest concentrations of antibacterials are dead."

"Dead?" Laena asked, peering into the tank. "All of them?"

"Yup," Wyatt said, nodding. "Well, almost all of them. We still have a few hardy ones holding on." He tapped the side of the gently gurgling tank.

"Are you sure the krill were not exposed to any other contamination, something else accounting for the mortality?" Cree asked.

Wyatt shook his head. "I cleaned all the tanks myself, and we used the same water in all of them. We've done water quality testing every 12 hours. In fact, the test was actually blinded. I wanted to make sure we got good results, so Jackie's the only one who knew which tank was dosed with which levels of antibacterials. When I started seeing all the dead krill, I checked the concentrations of antibacterials. Sure enough, it's the tanks with the two highest concentrations." He shook his head. "You guys are onto something here. Something big. I've never seen such stark results." He smiled. "I already told Dr. Foster what's going on...she wanted me to let you guys know immediately. She's in a meeting...but damn, I've never seen her so proud. She bragged about you two to everyone."

Laena's eyes filled with tears of gratitude. She felt like she'd been disappointing her mother for months now. Could she finally make up for all the angst? Michelle had always wanted Laena to follow in her footsteps. And she was finally making her mother proud.

"What about the tank with the third highest concentration? What's going on in that tank?" Cree asked, straightening up.

Wyatt brought them over to another tank. "Some of these guys are looking a little peaked," he said. "Not doing so great."

He pointed to yet another tank. "See that one? Krill in that tank have no added antibacterials. And look at those suckers go. They seem fine."

"Wow," Laena said. "Just...wow."

"Yeah, well, I think I'll have your data for you way before I thought I would. Actually, if you guys still have time off from school this week, you could do the counts yourselves. Pretty easy in these two tanks. I bet everything will be dead in a matter of hours. One hundred percent mortality."

Cree nodded. "I think we can do that," he replied. "Can we, Laena? Do we have the time?"

"Sure," she said. "I don't see why not."

"The tricky part isn't going to be the analysis here. What the hell is causing this? It's not the antibacterials themselves, because this didn't happen with the lab krill. There's some other factor, something that's present in the wild krill that's allowing the antibacterials to kill them. Weird."

"What do we have available to us in the lab, Wyatt? Can we do an ELISA assay?" Cree asked.

Wyatt looked up sharply. "An ELISA assay? What do you know about those?"

Cree looked sheepish. "Not very much. But I think they can detect antigens, correct? So we could use the ELISA assay to determine the levels of antigens, and therefore the amount of virus.... " He trailed off as Wyatt frowned.

"How do you know this stuff, Cree? Aren't you, like, a freshman in high school or something?"

"Junior," Laena said weakly. "We're juniors."

"You some kind of kid genius or something?" Wyatt laughed. "I'll tell you what. You tell me what it is you're looking for, and I'll figure out what type of test to use, and which of my guys is gonna do it. I don't want you kids messing with chemicals and equipment in the lab."

"But we have time, and if we promise to be very careful…"

"I said I'd do it," Wyatt said, a frown forming. "What, you don't want to tell me what you're looking for? I'm not gonna steal your ideas, man."

"No, no, I am not worried about that," Cree said, trying to reassure him. "It is just that you are so busy with other projects, and we want to help out during our vacation week.…"

"This is my job," Wyatt said stiffly. "I'll do whatever Dr. Foster wants me to. And if she wants me to put everything else to the side and figure out why your krill are dropping like flies, that's what I'll do. If she wants me to put your stuff to the side, then I'll do that. It's up to her. But you're not using the equipment in here by yourselves."

"Is there a problem?" came a voice from the doorway. The three of them turned to find Michelle staring at them.

"No, Dr. Foster, everything's fine," Wyatt said. "We have some interesting results so far, and we're just trying to figure out how to proceed from here."

Michelle nodded, but didn't look convinced.

"Mom, we just wanted to do more work, run some experiments, but Wyatt is concerned about us messing around in the lab," Laena explained.

"As well he should," Michelle said, walking toward the tanks. "Wyatt is in charge of my lab, and what he says goes. There's a lot of sensitive equipment in here, and chemicals that are no joke. If you need a certain test done, you'll have to run it by me first, and then I'll figure out if the test will be run, and Wyatt will determine who will run it. Understood?"

"Yes, ma'am," Cree said, chastened.

Michelle softened. "I have to tell you, though, how thrilled I am to see those preliminary results. I'm so proud of you two! If this works out the way I think it's going to, we may get some really interesting papers out of this! It will take some time, though, but if you can be patient...."

"But, Mom, *we* have the time right now, and—"

"Laena." Michelle's voice was sharp. "Enough. There are certain pieces of equipment that I don't want you two to touch." She sighed. "Don't get me wrong. I am so very appreciative of the work you've done so far. You're doing wonderful things! But Wyatt knows how to run this next set of tests. You don't. We have to involve him." She turned to Wyatt. "Wyatt, don't forget that we have the tour coming in at 4:30 this afternoon."

Wyatt nodded. "I remember. Everything's all set."

"Good." She turned to Laena and Cree. "Kids, we're going to leave a little early today. Want to meet me in the parking lot at 4:20?"

"Jeez, mom, what's your rush?" Laena asked.

"I need to get to the post office before 5 p.m.," she said over her shoulder.

"Can't Dad go?" Laena grumbled.

"Your father has enough to deal with fixing the hole in the roof, Laena." Michelle left the lab, her heels clicking against the linoleum floor. Cree turned to Wyatt. "I am sorry, Wyatt. I did not mean to challenge you. I am just eager, I guess, to finish this."

"No hard feelings," Wyatt said. "We'll get it done, don't worry." He glanced at his watch. "It's 3:15 now...you have an hour before you have to leave. I bet you kids can finish the counts in the two worst tanks here before you leave, and then check for any changes tomorrow. Then you can finish off the last four tanks tomorrow, okay?"

Laena and Cree nodded and Wyatt walked back to his desk. Cree sighed and whispered, "I messed things up, no?"

Laena giggled. "No more than I did. But it'll be okay."

Wyatt was right, and Laena and Cree were able to finish the mortality count in two of the tanks. The tank with the highest antibacterial concentration only had one live krill in it, and the tanks with the second highest antibacterial concentration had twelve krill left alive. They had to leave them in the tank until the experiment ended, and Laena felt guilty, knowing they may die as well. They had Wyatt check their work, thanked him for his help, and then they left to meet Michelle in the parking lot.

The sun was low in the western sky. They sat on the curb by the front doors and tossed pebbles into the road.

"Do you think we'll be able to prove there's a virophage involved?" Laena asked, leaning against Cree's shoulder.

"Well, first we have to show there is a virus, I think, and then the virophage. I will need to do some research tonight, on your computer. I keep forgetting what techniques and equipment existed in your days...I do not want to suggest something that has not been discovered yet." Cree tossed a pebble onto the road and it bounced onto the grass.

"Yeah, that would be a little hard to explain," Laena agreed, laughing.

The lobby doors opened and Michelle came out. "Ready to go?" she asked, breezing by them.

Michelle aimed her key fob at the car and clicked the doors unlocked. As Cree turned to get into the car, he stopped, and stared back at the building. Laena turned to see what he was looking at. A small group of people was entering the lobby of CCOL. One of them, a tall, slender girl with straight black hair, glanced over her shoulder. It was Ariel.

* * *

Cree agonized about Ariel's presence at CCOL all evening, and Laena did not have an answer for him. However, she could not think of anything Ariel could have done at CCOL to harm them. Cree wanted to go back into the lab after he saw Ariel, but Michelle was in a rush and said she had to get to the post office and then home.

Over dinner, Cree and Laena excitedly told Ben about the preliminary results of the experiments. He was surprised, but pleased for Laena and Cree. Michelle beamed with pride as Laena talked excitedly about the work they would do next.

The next morning, Laena and Cree parted ways with Michelle at the stairwell. Once the metal door clanged shut behind them, Cree muttered, "I have a bad feeling about this, Laena. What was Ariel doing there?"

Laena worried as well, but tried to push aside her fears. As Cree burst through the lab door, Wyatt looked up, his face a mask of concern.

"Wyatt? What is wrong?" Cree asked, stopping in his tracks.

Wyatt shook his head. "I'm afraid I have some bad news for you guys," he said. "I'm really sorry...I don't know how this happened."

"How what happened?" Laena asked, walking over. "What's wrong?"

"I don't know how it happened. I really don't. But I take full responsibility, and I'll tell Dr. Foster that."

"Wyatt. *What* happened?" Cree asked, standing in front of him.

"The krill. The thermostat went haywire. They're all cooked."

"Cooked?" Cree shook his head in confusion. "Is that an expression?"

"No. Well, yeah, it is, but not in this case. Someone set the thermostat to 100° Celsius. They're all dead. I'm really, really sorry."

Laena peered into the control tank, the one where the krill were not exposed to any antibacterials. Steam rose off the water, and all the krill were dead. "Oh, no," she cried.

Cree let off a stream of what were probably obscenities in Esperanto. Laena went over and grabbed his arm.

"What's he saying?" Wyatt asked.

Laena just shook her head. "Cree. We can't let this stop us. We'll just re-do the experiment, and make sure there's better security. We only lost a week."

"Yeah, yeah, no worries, Cree. I'm gonna call the boat and have them pick some more krill up for you today. We'll get you back on track, man. I'm really sorry. I swear this was an accident...I didn't do this on purpose." Wyatt looked miserable.

"No." Cree said. "No, Wyatt, I am sorry. I know this was not your fault. Please. I am sorry I am so upset. But I do not blame you." He turned to Laena. "It was Ariel. I *told* you she was up to no good."

"And you were right, Cree. But we just have to move forward. What's done is done," Laena responded.

"Wait. What? Who's Ariel? You know who did this? Who got in my lab?' Wyatt asked.

Cree nodded. "I have my suspicions. You had a tour group here last night, yes? I saw someone in the group...someone who does not like us being together."

"Are you kidding, man? Someone in the tour messed with my thermostats? Son of a...I can't believe I didn't notice. Cree, you gotta tell me who did this. I can call the police. Because this is destruction of property." Wyatt was livid, his face red.

"No," Laena said. "No, we can't call the police. Wyatt, is there a way you can keep the tours out of here? This girl, she's kind of crazy, and I don't know if she'll try something like this again...."

"You'd better believe it. I'm going to go talk to security right now. This lab is *off limits* to tours. Off limits to everyone." Wyatt stormed out of the lab.

"Laena." Cree's eyes were full of pain. "She is not going to stop. She will not stop until she wins."

Laena went over and threw her arms around him. He bowed his head onto her shoulder. "It's okay, Cree. This is war, and we're going to win. No matter what. I promise you. The Brights are going to win."

Chapter 17

THEY HAD WORKED HARD all weekend, and had started the experiment all over, this time under tight security. Wyatt had even installed an alarm on the thermometers, which would go off if the water got too hot or too cold. He assured Laena and Cree that nothing would interfere with their work. Michelle was horrified that someone had sabotaged their experiment, and pressured both teens to tell her who would have done such a thing.

"Mom, we just don't know," Laena explained.

"But Wyatt said you recognized someone on the tour...." Michelle protested.

"We have no proof. We can't accuse someone when we have no proof!"

Cree, realizing that they had to provide some kind of explanation, interjected. "Michelle, there is a girl at school who is jealous of Laena. We saw her with the tour, yes, but we do not know if she did this. And we cannot go to the authorities on nothing more than a suspicion."

"I can talk to the principal," Ben offered. "Maybe he can bring this girl in and talk to her. Do you want to tell me who it is?"

"No!" Laena said forcefully. "Thanks, Dad, but really...I'll talk to her myself on Monday. Feel her out. Try to patch things up with her."

"Make sure she knows that what she did is a crime, Laena. It's very serious," Michelle said.

"I will, Mom. I promise."

Neither Michelle nor Ben was completely satisfied with the proposed solution, but they couldn't get any more information out of the teens.

Laena felt almost completely normal as they walked to school the following Monday morning. It was a beautiful sunny day, and she breathed the fresh, salty air in greedily. Spring had returned with a vengeance, and it was already over 70 degrees. "I want you to take it easy," Cree admonished. "And do not go near Ariel. You are not to go to the bathroom alone. Take Sophie or someone with you...or even me. I will guard the door."

Laena shook her head, exasperated. "She's not going to try anything again."

"We do not know that, Laena. Ariel, she is crazy. And she is jealous of you. She will do anything to stop us."

"Okay, okay! I'll be careful."

"Promise?" Cree said, grabbing Laena's arms and turning her to face him.

"I promise," Laena replied, and Cree kissed her on the cheek.

They entered the school to the sounds of laughter, slamming lockers, and excited voices. Spring break had ended, but the warm weather had finally arrived and the end of school was in sight. It was going to be a long two months before school let out.

Laena approached her locker and smelled something awful—sickly sweet and cloying, yet full of decay. Several students were clustered in the area, wrinkling their noses.

"Is that coming from your locker, Laena? Whaddya do, leave a tuna fish sandwich in there over break?" Robb Berger complained. "Oh, wait! You don't eat tuna!" He put his hands up in a defensive posture, as if Laena might hit him, and the other kids laughed.

Laena ignored Robb and approached her locker slowly, a feeling of dread in her stomach. She gagged as she got closer. Cree grabbed her arm and pulled her back.

"Wait! We called the janitor, Laena," Sophie said, slipping an arm around her friend. "He'll take care of it."

"Maybe it's a gas leak!" someone said, and several girls squealed. The excitement in the crowd was palpable.

Laena heard the jingling of keys and turned to see the janitor coming down the hallway. The students parted to let him through.

"Move away, kids," he grumbled. "Nothing to see. Get to your classes." The students ignored him and moved in as close as they dared, murmuring.

The principal strode down the hall toward the group. "To class!" he said, clapping his hands together twice for emphasis. "Now!" The students dispersed unwillingly. Sophie squeezed Laena's arm in support, and left. Laena and Cree remained behind, hovering behind the janitor. The janitor yanked the lock and it fell open.

"Lock's open," he said, stating the obvious.

"Joe, can you open up the locker and see what's causing that smell?" Mr. Harrison cast a glance at Laena. "Did you leave any food in there over break, Laena?"

"Not that I remember," Laena replied. "But I left the school suddenly...after my accident." Laena glanced at Cree, confusion on her face.

The janitor opened the locker door and stepped back, retching. Laena peered around him, and stifled a scream. A dead black and white cat with a noose around its neck hung from a coat hook in her locker. The cat's mouth gaped open, as if in mid scream, its limbs splayed. Laena turned away in horror, burying her head in Cree's chest.

"Jesus H Christ!" the principal said. "What the hell?"

Mr. Harrison grabbed Laena by the arm. "Laena, to the office. Now. Cree, get to class. Joe, I trust you'll take care of this?"

"I've seen some things, working in a high school, but never anything like this." Joe shook his head, reached out and poked the cat, and it started swinging. "Unbelievable," he muttered.

"The poor thing!" Laena cried. "Who would do.... " she trailed off as Cree tightened his grip on her arm, silencing her. Of course she knew who would do such a thing—Ariel. She was the only one who could be so cruel.

"Joe, before you cut the cat down, take some pictures, please. In case the police need them. But I want that thing out of here before first period is over. I don't want the kids seeing this." Mr. Harrison turned back to Laena. "Office," he said. He pulled her away from Cree and started walking down the hall,

Laena in tow. "Cree, get to class *now*." He didn't even bother to turn around.

"Mr. Harrison, may I please come with Laena.... ?" Cree started after them.

"I'm not going to say it again, Cree. Get to class."

Laena glanced at Cree. His face froze in fury. But then his shoulders sank in defeat, and he did not follow them.

Mr. Harrison guided Laena firmly around the corner and into the main office, and Cree was out of sight.

Mr. Harrison grimly ushered Laena into his office, then turned to his secretary. "Sue, please call the police. Tell them we have an incident here. It's not an emergency, but I'd like them to come down as soon as possible." The secretary's eyebrows arched in surprise, but she nodded and picked up the phone. Mr. Harrison shut his office door firmly and moved to his seat behind his desk.

"Sit down."

Laena took the seat opposite him, grateful to get off her feet. She shook.

"What the heck is going on, Laena?" he said, his mouth a thin line. He ran his hand through his hair in frustration and then picked up a pencil, tapping it on the desk. "First, you have an 'accident' in the girl's room, get a darn concussion, then someone *hangs a dead cat* in your locker?" He pushed his chair away from his desk. "Jesus, what the heck is going on in this school?"

Laena shook her head. She didn't know how to answer him.

He sighed. "Look, Laena. It's pretty obvious that someone is trying to send you a message here. I've never had a bit of trouble with you. You're a smart girl. You're never in the middle of any of this drama. Who could dislike you so much...or be so angry at you, that they would do something like this?"

Laena shook her head again, silent.

"You don't know? Or you won't say?"

Laena looked down at her feet, stunned. It was a message—Mr. Harrison hit the nail on the head. But she could never prove it, and accusing Ariel would open up a whole can of worms that Laena could not expose. She had no idea what Ariel would say if the police questioned her, but Laena wasn't willing to take that risk. If Ariel threw Cree under the bus, and told everyone who he was and where he was from, she may never see him again. What if Ariel told everyone that Cree was from the future, and then went into hiding until she could get safely home? She doubted Ariel had the resources to disappear, especially with the government looking for her, but did she really want to take that chance? She swallowed, shaking her head again.

"Laena!" Mr. Harrison raised his voice and leaned forward over the desk. She looked up silently.

"Look, I know this isn't your fault. You're a good kid. But I also recognize that you have a better idea than anyone about who might be doing this. You need to tell me what you're thinking so this person can be stopped. Hanging a cat...that's someone with a sick mind. This person could be dangerous, Laena. Let me help you."

"I...I don't know, Mr. Harrison. I really don't."

"Well, you must *suspect* someone. You have to have an idea."

Laena shook her head in despair.

Mr. Harrison sighed and leaned back, his chair squeaking. "If you're not going to tell me, I have no choice but to think that it has something to do with Cree McNeil. These things started happening shortly after he arrived here at school...."

"No!" Laena blurted, looking up. "No, it isn't Cree! Please believe me. Cree would never do something like this, especially to me."

"Then who is it?" he asked. "Who the hell is it?"

Laena shrugged, and then her eyes widened when she heard sirens. Sirens? The police weren't coming here with sirens blaring, were they?

But they were. The secretary knocked on the door, opened it partway, stuck her head in and said, "The police are here."

"Why the hell do they have the sirens on, Sue?" Mr. Harrison bellowed, standing up. "Wait here, Laena. Don't move." He stormed past her and out of the office.

Laena blew out her breath and tried to relax. What the hell was she going to say to the police? She had to lie. No one could know the truth. She clenched and unclenched her hands.

"Laena?" someone whispered from the doorway. She stood up and whirled around.

"Cree? What are you doing here?" she hissed. "You're going to get in trouble."

He shrugged and slipped into the office, closing the door behind him. "I had to make sure you were okay," he said, his voice low and hurried. "I heard the sirens and got a pass to go to the bathroom. Are you all right? What have you told them?"

"I haven't told them anything," Laena replied, her voice quivering with tension. "What can I say? I can't blame Ariel for this, even though we both know she did it. What am I going to tell the police?" She looked at Cree beseechingly.

He shook his head. "You have to tell them you have no idea. Do not mention Ariel. If she is questioned, it could ruin everything. She is crazy...I do not know what she would say or do."

Laena grasped Cree's arms. "Mr. Harrison mentioned you. He said all of this crazy stuff started happening after you arrived."

"*Me?*" Cree was incredulous. "I would never do anything to harm you."

"I know that, Cree. I think he's just trying to scare me into saying something. Between what happened in the bathroom and now the cat, he knows someone is after me. What can I say?" Her eyes searched his urgently.

Cree winced. "He *knows* it was not me who was in the bathroom with you when you were attacked. I was in class!" He started spewing something in Esperanto, and although Laena couldn't understand a word he said, she knew he was hurling insults at Ariel.

"That's not helping, Cree. We don't have much time. In fact, the police will be here any second. You need to get back to class...."

"Too late," Cree murmured, as voices and footsteps headed toward the office door. The door swung open, and Cree and Laena looked up, caught.

"For crying out loud, Cree, what the hell are you doing in here? Why aren't you in class?" Mr. Harrison bristled with anger.

Cree was silent. He faced Mr. Harrison and glared at him.

"You know what, Cree? It's probably good that you're here. I think the police will want to talk to you, too. Both of you—in the conference room. Now."

Cree grabbed Laena's hand tightly, and walked with her out of the cramped office into the conference room next door. Two policemen were there, standing by the table.

"Officers, sit down, please," Mr. Harrison said, indicating chairs on the far side of the table. "Laena, Cree, you too." Laena's heart pounded, and she felt a headache coming on.

"This is Laena Foster. The cat was found in her locker. And this is Cree McNeil, Laena's boyfriend and a relatively new student. The school was fairly...ah...calm before Cree came into town." Mr. Harrison threw Cree a sideways glance, but Cree just stared at the table. "Kids, these are Officers Taigen and Wells. They're here to investigate the incident."

Cree looked up and nodded politely at the policemen. He opened his mouth to speak, but Laena grabbed his leg under the table.

"Officers, we have no idea who did this," Laena said, cutting Cree off. "Really. I

think...the only thing I can think of is that there's someone who's jealous of me being with Cree. I mean, North Bayside is such a small town, and...well, when Cree moved here, there were a lot of girls who were interested in him, and.... " She trailed off, blushing.

"And you got him?" Officer Wells, said, his leather holster creaking as he shifted in his chair. "You think someone attacked you and hung a dead cat in your locker because they're jealous that, uh, Cree here is dating you?"

"No one attacked me," Laena said forcefully. "No one. I slipped. There was just this one incident, the cat."

"Anyone else new in school here?" Officer Wells asked the principal.

"No," Mr. Harrison responded. "Well, except for Ariel Simone. She's an exchange student, just here through the school year. But she is very quiet, well-behaved. I can't attribute any of this to her."

Laena and Cree looked at each other. Laena opened her mouth to speak, and Cree shook his head imperceptibly in warning.

"Did anyone know your locker combination, Laena?" Officer Taigen asked. His voice sounded gravely, like a smoker's.

Laena shook her head.

"Did you always lock it properly?"

Laena nodded. "Always."

"Cree, do you know your girlfriend's locker combination?"

"No, sir. I do not." Cree said, looking straight into the officer's eyes.

"Cree wouldn't do that to me," Laena said. "We're...he just wouldn't. Never in a million years." She was flustered and angry. "Look, why are *we* being accused? I'm the victim here, right? We don't know who did it, but I do know that it wasn't Cree."

"And where were you Friday afternoon, Cree?" Officer Wells asked.

"The school was closed last week, gentlemen," Mr. Harrison broke in. "It was spring break for the kids. So the school was locked all week. Today was the first day back."

"And he was with me," Laena said. "All last week. He lives with me. With me and my parents, I mean. We were both down at CCOL working on a project for my mom. He never left my sight. We were together all last week, and all weekend, and we came to school together this morning."

"He lives with you?" Officer Taigen asked, leaning forward.

"I am an emancipated minor," Cree explained. "I lived at Evergreen Acres, and worked there, but the hurricane destroyed the cabin I lived in. Dr. Foster took me in until the cabin can be rebuilt."

"An emancipated minor, huh? How old are you Cree? You look a bit older than the typical 17 year old junior here in North Bayside."

Cree blushed. "I am 17, sir." Laena looked down when she heard Cree lie.

"Uh-hunh. So, do you have a driver's license, something like that? Something with your birthday on it?"

"I do not drive, sir. I do not have a license," Cree responded.

"What about a birth certificate? Passport?"

Laena stifled a gasp. Her heart hammered so hard she thought it would burst. She had to do something.

"Wait. Just wait." Laena stood up and pulled Cree with her. "This is outrageous. I'm sorry, Mr. Harrison, but Cree had nothing to do with the cat and you have no right to question him like this. We're not answering any more questions. If you want to interrogate Cree, you'll have to bring him down to the station and assign him a lawyer. Those are his rights."

Mr. Harrison drew back in surprise. "Laena, the officer only asked him for some identification. There's no need to get all riled up."

"Yes, yes, there is. He is implying—no, you are *all* implying—that Cree did something wrong here. He didn't. He's just...he's an orphan for crying out loud, trying to get through school. Why are you treating him like this? He would *never* do anything to hurt me, or scare me. He's all alone in the world, not from around here. He doesn't know about the law, and his rights. Just leave him alone. If you don't believe me, that he couldn't have done this horrible thing, ask my father. Go ahead! Call him, Mr. Harrison. Call him and ask. We were with Cree all week. He didn't do it!" Laena said, incensed.

Cree pulled her toward him. "Laena, it is okay."

"No, it is not okay. They're treating you like some kind of criminal. Just because they don't know you. Just because...whatever." Laena whirled around, curls flying. "Come on, Cree. We have classes to go to." She turned to the police, her eyes blazing. "I don't know who put the cat in my locker. It was awful, but it was a prank. Nothing more. It was probably some girl, jealous of me and Cree. You can investigate all you want, but no one is going to confess to doing it. It was cruel." Laena shuddered. "Cruel. The poor cat. But it's over, and there's nothing we can do. I'll...I'll keep my eye out, be more vigilant. But I'm sure nothing else will happen." She paused, and then turned to Mr. Harrison. "We're going back to class now."

Without waiting for a response, Laena pulled Cree out of the conference room and shut the door behind her. They walked into the hall and hurried down the hushed hallways toward their English class. Cree started laughing.

"What is so funny?" Laena said, eyes still flashing with anger.

Cree shook his head. "Remind me never to get on your bad side, Laena. Maybe you should consider being a lawyer instead of a biologist."

Laena fought a smile, and felt the tension leaving her body. Cree stopped her and pulled her into his arms. He kissed her deeply. "Thank you for saving my ass," he whispered.

"Anytime," Laena whispered back. "Anytime."

Chapter 18

THE SCHOOL WAS STUNNED by the dead cat incident, and word spread quickly. Almost everyone was sympathetic to Laena, and she could tell that the kids were freaked out. Ben and Michelle had questioned both Laena and Cree endlessly on Monday night, but they both insisted that they had no idea who would do such an awful thing. Michelle looked suspicious, but there was nothing she could do to get the truth out of the teens.

On Tuesday, Sophie found Laena and Cree in the parking lot.

"Oh, my God, you guys, I wanted to call you last night, but my mom took my cell phone away!" Sophie grabbed Laena's arm and searched her eyes. "What happened?"

Laena ignored the question. "Why'd she take your phone away?"

Sophie rolled her eyes. "Oh, I blew off my curfew this weekend. What the hell happened yesterday?"

"It was awful, Sophie. Someone hung a cat and put it in my locker."

"Oh, my God! So it's true! I heard there were, like, satanic symbols carved into the cat and a black rose…"

"No!" Laena interrupted. "No, those are just rumors. It was just the cat. But that's bad enough."

"That's so gross! Who would *do* that?" Sophie shuddered.

"We have no idea," Cree said as the three of them approached the front doors of the school. "Someone sick."

"Laena!" a voice called from the parking lot. Laena stopped and turned. Cat hurried through the kids dawdling outside in the sun. "Laena, wait! I have to talk to you." Cat was breathless when she reached them. "Can I talk to you alone?" She threw a look at Sophie and Cree. "This is kinda private."

Sophie shook her head. "Whatever, Cat. C'mon, Cree. Let Cat have her private moment with Laena."

Cree kissed Laena on the cheek and murmured, "Be careful." Then Sophie and Cree walked into the school building.

Cat pulled Laena away from the doors. "Listen, Laena, I just want you to know, that, like, you and me may have had our issues in the past, but I did *not* leave that cat in your locker." Cat shook her head so emphatically her earrings swayed wildly.

"What? I know you didn't, Cat...."

"Oh, thank God, because I heard kids saying that you thought I did it! And I know you talked to the police and I honestly didn't do it, and I didn't want them coming after me." Cat put her hand on Laena's shoulder and bent her head in close to Laena's ear, her voice low. "I don't know about you, but I think maybe Robb did it, you know, to piss off Cree or something?" Cat's blonde hair tickled Laena's cheek and Laena pulled back.

"Cat, don't start rumors. It wasn't Robb, and I know it wasn't you. Don't worry...I never accused you."

Cat breathed a sigh of relief, her bracelets jangling on her slender wrists. "I'm so relieved. I half expected the police to show up at my door last night, you know? But I would *never* do anything like that! Gross. Just gross. When I have a problem, I confront that person face to face, you know?"

Laena nodded. "I know, and I appreciate it, Cat. Really, I do." She smiled and tried to head toward the school doors.

"Oh, my God! Laena!" Cat grabbed Laena's arm. Her voice fell to a whisper. "Do you think it was a message for me? You know, because it's a dead *cat*, and my name is Cat?" Cat's eyes were wide.

Laena had to laugh at Cat, finding ways to make this whole thing about her. "Ummm, I don't think so, Cat."

"It could be though, right? I mean, do you *think*?"

"No. No, I don't think so." Laena glanced toward the doors. All the other kids were inside the school. "We'd better go in. The bell is going to ring any second."

Cat looked up, and then glanced fearfully at the trees bordering the parking lot. "You're right! We shouldn't be out here all alone. What if the guy after us is here, watching us?" She pulled Laena toward the door. As the doors shut behind them, Cat whispered, "Don't worry, Laena. I'll watch your back, and you can watch mine. We won't let this sick bastard get to us again."

* * *

After lunch, Laena and Cree walked into biology together. When the kids settled down, pulling out their notebooks and pencils, Ben cleared his throat.

"Listen up, kids. We're starting the chapter on Population Dynamics today. I'm going to have a *fabulous* guest speaker later this week to talk to us about a real life population dynamics issue taking place right here in our backyard." He paused, then smiled. "It happens to be my wife, so..." The class laughed. "I'm also going to ask Laena and Cree to tell us a little about the work they've been doing on this issue. That okay, guys?"

Cree nodded, but Laena frowned and slunk down in her chair. She was pissed her father put them in this position. Cree glanced at Laena. "What is the matter?" he whispered.

"I don't want to give a talk in front of the class!" she hissed.

"Why not? It is our chance to educate people, warn them about what is happening."

"But we can't really warn them. We can't let on that we know!"

Cree shrugged. "We can warn them without telling them everything. Even if we can get them to understand how fragile the ocean ecosystem is, it will help."

Ben interrupted their hushed conversation. "In particular, I would like you guys to tell the class about your hypothesis, your experiments, and then talk a little about what would happen if krill went completely extinct. What are the repercussions? Would it impact other species, other ecosystems?"

Cree nodded. "Yes, sir. That is fine."

Laena elbowed him in the side. "It's not fine," she whispered.

"Yes, it is," Cree replied out of the side of his mouth. "Do not worry."

* * *

They argued the whole way home.

"It is not going to be okay, Cree!" Laena insisted, bristling. "We're going to have to talk about what *might* happen if krill go extinct? You're living it! You're going to slip, and we are going to have a ton of explaining to do!"

"A ton?"

Laena blew her breath out, exasperated. "A lot. A hell of a lot!"

"Ach, it will be fine." Cree put his arm around Laena. "No worries."

"Yes, worries!" Laena said, pushing him away. "I think we should tell my father that we're fine explaining our research, but that should be enough."

Cree stopped in his tracks outside the house and turned Laena to face him. "I will make you a deal," Cree said, smiling slyly. "Just relax, let us do what your father wants, and I will make it worth your while."

Laena couldn't help but smile. "Worth my while how?" she asked, snaking her arms around him.

"Hmmm," Cree considered. "How about...how about I make you feel like you have never felt before?" His hands caressed her sides.

"And how might you do that?" Laena asked, her voice getting husky.

"How about I show you? We can go inside and I can convince you that we should listen to your father."

Laena laughed and they continued onto the front porch. "How is it that you can distract me so easily?"

"Because you are a teenage girl, and your hormones are running wild through your bloodstream. You have an overwhelming desire to reproduce," Cree said seriously.

"Cree!" Laena laughed. "It was a rhetorical question. You didn't need to give me the biological answer. It kinda ruins the mood."

"Does it?" Cree asked. "Is the mood ruined?" His hands ran inside her shirt and stroked her back gently.

Laena moaned softly. "Ummm, no. It's not ruined," she whispered, her head falling back. Cree leaned forwards and kissed her neck.

Laena pushed him away and fumbled for her keys. She unlocked the door and they stumbled in, slamming the door behind them. Cree dropped his backpack, ripped Laena's off her back, and swept her into his arms. He carried her upstairs to the guest bedroom and dropped her in the bed.

"Cree...." Laena whispered.

"Mmmm," he responded, his eyes full of desire.

"What...what are you doing?"

"I am convincing you of something," he replied softly. "Shhh...."

"Cree.... "

"Shhh," he reprimanded. He unbuttoned her jeans, pulled the zipper down, and pulled them roughly over her hips.

"Cree!"

He didn't bother to answer. He pulled her panties off and tossed them on the floor. He bent down, his body tented over her, raining soft kisses on her belly. She arched her back and groaned. He kissed her down her abdomen. Laena cried out and squirmed, but Cree held her firmly with his arms and his mouth. He moved lower, and Laena shuddered. His mouth was hot and moist, and soon Laena was trembling and bucking and calling out his name. She grabbed a fistful of his hair and pulled his head up, breathing hard. Cree moved up so his head was next to hers on the pillow. "Oh, my God," Laena said. She turned her face away from him.

Cree chuckled. "Laena, when will you stop being embarrassed about sex? This is natural. We still have not even had intercourse, yet you are so ashamed! It is nothing to be ashamed of."

She couldn't look at him. "Yes, it is."

"Why?" he asked. "Why are you ashamed in front of me, of all people?"

Laena shrugged.

He put his hand on her cheek and gently turned her so she faced him. "Laena, there is nothing to be embarrassed about. You enjoyed this, no?"

Laena's cheeks flamed, but she nodded.

Cree laughed. "See, now you are being honest. What is wrong with this?"

"Nothing," Laena whispered.

"Nothing," Cree echoed. "Nothing at all. And I think, maybe, I have made you feel something you have never felt before, and so you need to do what your father asks and give the talk to the class."

"Hey, wait a minute!" Laena protested, propping up on one elbow, her hair in a tangled mess around her head. "Not fair! I never agreed that if you...if you made me feel this way I would go along with the talk."

Cree laughed. "It was tacit agreement," he said firmly. He sat up on the bed. "I think maybe you should put your clothes on before I get any more bright ideas." His eyes raked her body.

Laena grabbed him and pulled him back down. "What if I have a bright idea?" she whispered.

Cree laughed. "No way. We are done here."

"Wait, Cree...." Laena's face got serious. "What about you?"

Cree smiled and shook his head, and tossed Laena her panties and jeans. "What about me? I pleasured you. That is all that is necessary. It does not always have to be equal. You do not always have to do for me what I do for you. There will be times in our lives, sweetie, when I will need something more than you, and you will give it to me. Other times, you will be the one in need, and I will provide for you. That is the way life works, the way love works."

"But...."

He kissed her on the lips. "Come on. Let us go downstairs and do our stupid homework so we can work on what is important, no?"

Laena pouted. "No."

"Yes," Cree said, grinning. He started dressing her.

"Cree!"

"What?" he asked, pausing. "You want to do it yourself?"

Laena grabbed her jeans from him, swung her legs over the side of the bed, and started getting dressed. "Yes, I'll do it myself," she grumbled. "But I don't understand why you won't let me...." she trailed off.

Cree chuckled. "Let you do what? Tell me, Laena."

Laena whipped around. "Why won't you let me pleasure you?"

"And how would you do that?" Cree asked, grinning.

"I could...I could do to you what you did to me."

"And what would that be?"

"I could...don't make me say it, Cree!"

"If you cannot say it, you are not allowed to do it," Cree responded, laughing. "You are such a strange girl, Laena. Are all girls in your time like you?"

Cree got up and walked to the door. He turned around in the doorway and watched her as she pulled her jeans on. "Laena," he said softly, "remember something. Always remember that you do not owe a boy—or a man—anything. Never let anyone use you for their own pleasure. Men and women are equal, no? If you love someone, and they love you, everything will be okay." He sighed. "Things are so different in your time. The girls do not respect themselves enough, I think. I hear Cat and Tiffany and the other girls talk about what they do with boys and...." He shook his head. "I am not explaining this well. Just promise me that you will not let men use you. You deserve pleasure, too."

"Why are you telling me this?" Laena asked, a pit in her stomach. "You sound like...like you're going away. I thought you said you weren't leaving until the end of the summer?"

"No, no, sweetie, I am not leaving." Cree held out his hand and Laena stood and walked to him. "Not yet." He pulled her into his arms and kissed her. "I just do not want to think of you getting hurt."

Laena did not want to think about other boys, about Cree being gone, or about the future. Her heart ached at the thought. She held him tight, and wished she could stay in this moment forever.

* * *

Ben got permission to bring the other 11th grade science class in to watch the presentation. The kids dragged chairs in from another classroom, and the entire junior class settled in to watch the talk. Ariel sat alone in the back of the classroom, and Laena tried to ignore her. Michelle delivered a power point presentation about krill, the threats from the warming oceans, and the important role they played in the food chain.

"Before I turn this over to Cree and Laena, I want you all to think about how important krill are to so many other animals: fish, squid, penguins, seals, and whales, even humans, to name a few." There was a smattering of applause as Michelle turned the projector off and took a seat behind Ben's desk. Cree and Laena stood up and faced the class.

Cree cleared his throat. "Laena and I have been helping Dr. Foster out with her research at CCOL," he began. "She is investigating why krill populations are decreasing, aside from overfishing and rising ocean temperatures. One of her theories was that antibacterials that get into the oceans from our medicines and cleaning products were adversely affecting the krill."

Laena could see the kids' eyes glaze over, and she knew she had to say something to get their attention. She interrupted Cree. "Did you know that when you fill a glass of water from your kitchen sink, you are pouring yourself a glass of Viagra, antibiotics, ibuprofen, and all sorts of other drugs?"

The kids laughed. "I don't need Viagra...right Cat?" shouted Robb. Cat blushed and threw a pencil at him.

"Eww, gross!" said Tiffany. "You're not for real, are you?"

Cree saw where Laena was going and jumped in. "Laena is right. Every time you drink water—whether it is from your sink or from a bottle of water you buy in the store—you are drinking other people's medicine. When you take medicine, and then urinate, the unprocessed medicine comes out in your urine, goes to the wastewater treatment plant, but does not get cleaned out. So the drugs just go back into the groundwater, and into the wells."

"And here on the Cape, we only have one aquifer for our water...and that aquifer is contaminated."

"Dr. Foster, tell me they're not serious," said Greg, making a face. "That's just rude."

"They are very serious, Greg," Ben replied.

"So," Cree said, "the antibacterials that you use, particularly the ones in our soaps, and household cleaners, and toothpaste, all of this eventually makes its way into the oceans. Even here, at North Bayside High School, the soap in the bathrooms contains antibacterials."

"Is that what's killing the krill?" someone asked. The kids seemed interested now.

"Well, that is what we are trying to find out," Cree replied. "Dr. Foster ran some experiments at CCOL that exposed lab-raised krill to varying levels of antibacterials, and there was no correlation between krill mortality, or deaths, and the concentration of antibacterials. So...."

"So perhaps you should just let it go," said Ariel from the back of the room. "If the antibacterials are not killing the krill, then there is no harm."

Cree narrowed his eyes. "I am not done explaining, Ariel. If you would listen, perhaps you would understand why we are not just 'letting it go,' as you say."

Ariel shrugged and smoothed her hair behind her ears.

Cree continued. "Laena and I are continuing the research by running the experiment again, but this time using wild caught krill."

"Why would that make a difference?" Mike asked.

"We do not know if it will," Cree responded. "But our hypothesis is that there is something different about the wild krill that makes them vulnerable to the antibacterials. Our experiment will show if this is true."

Ben nodded. "Kids, why don't you tell everyone what might happen if all the krill die? If krill went extinct, how would that impact the oceans?"

Cree nodded and responded to Ben's questions. "If krill go extinct, the food supply for many, many other species will be gone. Fish, sea birds, penguins, whales...all these species will start to starve because they all rely on krill as a food source. Krill are a keystone species—one species that is so important that it can impact a whole ecosystem. When the krill died, it started a chain reaction that resulted in the collapse of the oceans."

Laena noticed that Cree was starting to speak as if the extinction had already happened. She grabbed his arm, and he looked at her.

"*If* krill go extinct," she said, "it could have devastating effects to the entire world."

"But the ocean is so big," Sophie said. "I mean, there is so much life in there. How could the ocean ecosystem just collapse?"

"It happens," Cree said. Laena cleared her throat. Cree glanced at Laena and saw her frown. "I mean, it *could* happen. Easily." Laena saw Michelle, out of the corner of her eye, looking at Cree strangely.

"Class, does anyone know what would happen to the human population if the oceans collapse?" Michelle asked.

The class was silent. Some shook their heads.

"I can answer that, Dr. Foster," Cree interjected. "The human population also collapses." Cree responded. "Billions of people depended on the oceans for their primary food source. Probably four billion or so...about half the world's population. Once that food source was gone, they starved. Then they fought. Wars broke out, and billions more died."

The class sat in stunned stillness. Then, a slow, measured clapping began from the back of the room. "What a dramatic story, Cree!" Ariel said. "A fairy tale. But what hubris you have, thinking that man can cause such disaster."

Michelle, who had been looking at Cree with a frown, turned her attention to Ariel. "Excuse me, can you identify yourself?" Michelle asked, craning to see who had spoken.

Ariel stood up, tossing her hair over her shoulder. "I am Ariel Simone," she responded. Robb whistled, and Ariel smiled.

Michelle nodded. "Ariel, you do not believe that humans can impact their environment? We have been doing it for thousands of years."

Ariel laughed. "With all due respect, Dr. Foster, this is not true. God is the only one powerful enough to make such drastic changes on Earth."

The class started murmuring. Ben clapped his hands to restore order. "No, Ariel, you are wrong. And this is a biology class. As I have reminded you before, we do not talk about God in biology class. We talk about biology, facts. Humans are animals, and we are subject to the same evolutionary principles as other animals."

"I disagree."

"Me, too!" said Tiffany, nodding vigorously.

Ben sighed and looked at his watch. "You can disagree all you want, girls, but you are wrong. Okay, the bell is about to ring. For homework, I want you all the read Chapter 17. And how about a round of applause for our speakers today?"

The class applauded, and several came up to thank Michelle and ask a few last questions. When Laena looked up, Ariel was gone.

Chapter 19

LAENA AND CREE SPENT every day after school that they could spare at the lab. They ran the experiment again with wild krill, with no further mishaps. Jackie analyzed the data, and it became clear that somehow the antibacterials were killing the wild krill. Michelle was astounded, and asked Cree to try to figure out how the krill were dying. Cree struggled to find a way to run the experiments he needed to prove that the virophage existed without giving himself away. Laena and Cree ended up doing work surreptitiously, trying to avoid Wyatt's prying eyes.

One night, while Laena and Cree were doing their homework in the kitchen, Ben came in. "I have some news, guys," he said. Michelle trailed Ben into the kitchen and sat down.

"Good news, I hope?" Cree asked.

"Well, depends on how you look at it. I got a call from Mark today. He finished working on the cabins, and he wants you back at Evergreen Acres. School lets out in a week, and the campground is starting to fill up."

Cree glanced at Laena. She looked shocked. "Okay," Cree said slowly. "I...I guess I have taken advantage of your kindness for too long. I will move back in tomorrow."

"Dad! Can't he stay?" Laena cried. "I mean, he's working at the lab, and he's no problem because my room is fixed and he has the guest room...." She trailed off, her stomach in knots.

"Laena, you know Cree is welcome to stay. It's up to him," Ben said softly.

"Cree, we love having you here. But if you need to make money, and you refuse to take money for the work at CCOL, then I think moving back to Evergreen Acres is the best solution," Michelle said gently.

Cree shook his head. "Thank you, Michelle. You are right, of course. I made a commitment to Mark, and I must follow through. And no matter what you say, I know I am a burden here."

"No! You are *not* a burden, Cree," Laena said.

Michelle agreed. "Cree, you are absolutely *not* a burden. If you can get by without the money, we would love to have you stay. It really is up to you."

"Yes, thank you, I have made up my mind. I will go back." He stood up. "How can I ever thank you for all your kindness and generosity? I do not know what I would have done without you both."

"Don't make it sound like you'll never see us again, Cree!" Ben laughed. "I want to see you over for dinner at least twice a week. The door is open for you. In fact, we'll give you a key."

Michelle hugged Cree tightly. "Sweetheart, you're like family to us. There's no need to thank us." She looked at Ben. "I think I'm going upstairs, how about you, Ben? Are you coming?"

"Yup," he said. "Don't stay up too late, kids. School tomorrow." They left the kitchen arm in arm.

Laena reached for Cree's hand as soon as Ben and Michelle were out of earshot. "Why are you leaving? We only have a few more weeks together...."

Cree knelt by Laena's chair and caressed her face. "Do you not see, sweetie? If I go back to the cabin, I can run some of the experiments there, where no one can see. We can finish the work, prove the existence of the virophage, and I can be done."

"So you can go home," Laena said in despair.

Cree sighed. "Laena, you know I *have* to go home, whether I succeed or not. You also know that I do not want to leave you."

"Then take me with you," Laena begged.

Cree shook his head. "I am not going to have this discussion with you again. You cannot come with me."

"Oh, Cree." Laena reached for him. "Please...please don't go back to the cabin. At least stay with me here."

"Laena. Listen, if I go back to the cabin, think of how much time we will have alone together? You can come over whenever you want. You can even sleep over, and we can spend the whole night together."

* * *

Cree moved back to Evergreen Acres, and Laena felt bereft. She saw him every day, but the nights really got to her. School ended, but the campground got busy, and between the lab work and chores at the campground, she did not see as much of Cree as she wanted. She tried to go to the cabin every night, but Cree refused to let her walk or bike, because he was afraid that Ariel would attack her. So Cree walked her back and forth when he could, and occasionally gave her a ride on Zed.

One stormy Friday afternoon, Laena got a ride to the cabin from Sophie and burst in, surprising Cree.

"Laena! How did you get here?" Cree said, looking up from the kitchen table and a sheath of papers.

"Got a ride from Sophie," Laena said. "It's awful out there." She shook the rain off her coat, hung it up and walked over to the table. "How's the work going?"

"Good," Cree responded, smiling. "And because of the weather, many people cancelled their reservations this weekend. So Mark gave me some time off."

"Time off? Let's do something fun, then," Laena suggested.

Cree hesitated. "I am almost done with this.... "

Laena sighed. "Okay, well how about I help you finish, and then we can do something together?" she proposed. "Something that doesn't involve krill." Thunder boomed in the distance, and lightening lit up the sky.

Cree laughed. "I like the sound of that," he said.

The rain came down hard on the roof.

"I am going to start a fire in the woodstove," Cree said, slapping Laena's rear end gently to get her to move. "It is getting chilly."

Laena hopped off and watched Cree make the fire. He closed the door to the woodstove, waiting to make sure it caught. When the orange flame glowed through the glass door, he wiped his hands and came back to the table.

"I am glad you are here. I want to run this by you. I want you to understand this, and be able to explain it, in case...." He trailed off.

"In case you're not here?" Laena asked softly.

Cree nodded. "Yes. In case I am not here."

"Okay. Explain it to me."

Cree spent the next half an hour going through the data, and explaining the test results that proved there were both a virus and a virophage present in the wild krill population. Laena asked several questions, and Cree scrawled additional information down to make his reasoning absolutely clear.

"So, if something happens, and I am unable to get this to your mother before I leave, you must make sure she sees it. And understands it."

"Why can't you give it to her now?"

Cree shook his head. "I am not quite done. There is one more analysis I want to do. I will do it soon." He paused. "And, I am afraid when she sees the work I have done, she will suspect me. A high school student should not understand all of this virophage information. It is cutting edge in your time. So if I give it to her now, she may know I am from the future. And I cannot get caught here. I must go home and continue to work to save the Earth."

"Cree, can you tell me when you're leaving? How much time we have left?"

He sighed. "Sweetie, why do you always ask that?" His voice was husky with pain. He put his papers to the side. "I will stop the work now. Do you want to curl up by the fire and have a glass of brandy with me?"

Laena shook her head. "No brandy for me. But you go ahead."

"Listen. I am hiding these papers. Just in case. I am putting them in this tin in the cupboard. The sugar tin. See?" He stood up and placed the folded papers in the tin, replacing the lid securely. He frowned. "It is not the best hiding place in the world, but it is better than nothing."

Cree took the blanket and pillow off his bed and made a comfortable spot in front of the fire. As he poured brandy into a jelly jar, lightening cracked, making them both jump. The lights flickered and went out.

The fire in the wood stove cast a flickering, muted light throughout the cabin. Cree carried the jar over and sat down next to Laena. Laena leaned over and smelled the amber liquid. She grimaced.

"You still do not like this stuff?" he laughed, taking a sip. "It warms you inside."

"No, I don't like alcohol." She sighed contentedly. "This is cozy. I'd rather be at our driftwood log on the beach, but this is nice, too."

"Our special place?" Cree said. "Yes, I would like that, too." He took another sip of brandy.

"Don't drink too much," Laena replied, snuggling up next to Cree. "I'm going to give you two choices...we can either take our clothes off and make love—really make love—in front of the fire, or we can have a serious talk."

Cree paused. "Are those my only two choices?"

"Mmmm—hmmm," Laena nodded.

"How about if we just.... "

"No! No 'justs,' no compromises. Pick one."

Cree let out a huge sigh. "You know how I feel about making love. I do not want to do this very special thing right before...before I leave. It is not fair to you. I want you to save that for a man who you will spend the rest of your life with."

"I want to spend the rest of my life with you."

"Ah, so I guess we have chosen the serious talk?"

"I guess so," Laena said, turning to look into Cree's eyes. "Cree, take me with you." He opened his mouth to speak, but Laena put her finger on his lips. "Let me finish. I don't understand what the harm is in letting me go back with you."

"Laena," Cree responded sternly. "I will not take you away from your parents, from your world. I do not even know what would happen if I tried to get you back with me. I do not know if there is enough energy to take both of us. I will not be responsible for hurting you. You need to stay here, in your time...now that you know the truth about the future, you can work hard from your time to try and change things."

Laena shook her head. "No. Don't you see? I can't live without you!"

Cree grasped Laena's shoulders and shook her. "Do not say that! How dare you say that to me!" His voice was harsh.

Laena looked at him with shock, then withdrew at the rebuke.

Cree shook his head and gathered her into his arms. "I am sorry for yelling at you. But do you see how that makes me feel? You *must* live without me. I have no choice but to leave. I cannot bear the thought of you being unhappy, let alone not wanting to live. Please, Laena. For me...you must be happy. I will never forgive myself if I think I am responsible for your pain."

"How can I be happy without you? I love you! You are my soul mate. You're asking me not only to forget you, but to be *happy* without you? You are a part of me, Cree...I can't just pretend we never met!"

Cree leaned down and kissed her lips tenderly. Laena threw her arms around him and kissed him back, hungrily. Cree pulled away.

"Laena, every day people in love lose each other. People die, or move away, or are separated unintentionally. And they go on, and they can be happy."

Laena shook her head. "I'm not one of those people." The firelight flickered in her eyes, and Cree pulled her to him and kissed her eyelids.

"Will we ever see each other again, Cree?" Laena whispered.

"I do not know," he responded, his voice so low Laena had to strain to make out the words. He reached out and fondled her pendant. "But this necklace, the one I gave you...it can lead me back to you."

Laena sat bolt upright. "So it's true? What Ariel said? You can find me again if I'm wearing the necklace?"

Cree nodded. "The necklace, it is a stone from my time. It has a substance in it that we can hone in on. I will be able to find you. If I come back. I think...no, I *know*, that is why Ariel stole it. She does not want me to come back to you. Ever."

Hope surged through Laena. "So you *are* coming back?"

Cree shook his head in despair. "I don't know," he whispered.

"But if you *can* come back, don't you want to? Don't you love me?"

"Oh, Laena! Of course I love you. More than I have loved anyone. More than I will ever love anyone. How can you even ask me that?" His eyes and voice were ragged with pain.

"Then why," she said, "why does it have to end? I don't understand!"

Cree shook his head. "I just do not know what is going to happen, Laena," he whispered. "I do not even know what changes I have wrought by coming here." He laid her down in the blankets and enveloped her in his arms, holding on as if he would never let go.

Chapter 20

LAENA, SOPHIE AND CAT were laughing as they approached Cree's cabin. It was a Friday night, and there were only three more weeks of summer before school started. The teens wanted to make the most of it.

"Do you think you can get him to come out with us, Laena? Mike wants to keep the party small, 'cuz he has no idea if his parents are *really* in Boston for the weekend. They've never left him alone for a whole weekend before, and he can't believe his luck."

"Didn't they say they were staying in Boston for the weekend?" Cat asked, teetering on her heels on the rough ground. "Parents don't lie."

"I think I can get him to come out for a little while," Laena said. They walked up the stairs to the cabin.

"It looks dark," Sophie said. "Are you sure he's home?"

"He better be!" Laena quipped, knocking on the door and turning the knob. "Cree?" she called.

Laena swung the door open and stopped in her tracks. A small light glowed over the sink, but the rest of the cabin was dark. Then she saw the bed. Cree lay on his back, naked; his arm flung over his face, with a naked Ariel perched over him. She turned languidly as she heard the door open. And laughed.

Sophie and Cat gasped as they took in the scene. Laena slammed the door, but Cree did not stir. Ariel stood up slowly, and stretched, totally unabashed by her nakedness. She padded over toward the kitchen table, hips swaying, breasts jiggling. She grabbed her sundress off the chair and threw it on.

"Laena," she purred. "You are interrupting us. I hope this is important?"

"You bitch!" Sophie snarled. "What the hell do you think you're doing? You do *not* mess with another girl's boyfriend!"

Ariel shrugged and turned to the table, picked up two empty wine glasses and brought them to the sink. She turned her back to the girls and started washing them out.

Laena ignored Ariel. "Cree?" she said, her voice full of pain. "Cree?" She walked toward the bed and shook him. His arm fell away from his face, and she saw that he was fast asleep. Or passed out. "Cree!" she yelled. Laena yanked the sheet up to cover his naked body and turned to Ariel.

"What did you do to him? What's wrong with him?" She turned back to Cree and shook him gently.

Ariel laughed. "Oh, I suppose he had a little too much wine tonight, no? Perhaps he is drunk." She placed the clean wineglasses upside down on the washboard to dry and turned to face Laena. "We drank the whole bottle, but he drank most of it."

"A bottle of wine would not knock him out like this! What did you do to him, Ariel?" Laena frantically shook Cree. He groaned.

"Mmmm, maybe he is tired from the passion we shared. You know what that does to him, right, Laena? Or do you not know?" Ariel giggled.

Cat's mouth hung open. "Who do you think you are, Ariel? Just...just get out of here."

"Yes, yes, I am done here anyway. I just need to find the rest of my clothes...or should I leave them as a...what do you call it? Souvenir?" She bent down to pick up her discarded sweater near the bed.

Laena stood up and faced Ariel. "If you hurt him, I swear to God...."

"Tsk, tsk, Laena. You have no right to swear to a God you do not believe in." Ariel slipped her shoes on. "But I would never hurt Cree. We have a long history together. He just had a little too much fun with me." She smoothed her hair, and then picked up her purse. Ariel turned to Cat and Sophie, still standing by the door in utter shock. "Maybe you two should take advantage of the situation. Teach Laena a thing or two. Because judging from Cree's reaction to me, she has not been satisfying him."

Ariel sashayed to the door and swept past the Sophie and Cat, who stood in shock. "Ta," she said, lifting her hand in a wave. And she melted into the night.

"Is he okay, Laena?" Sophie rushed to the bedside.

"What a *bitch*," Cat said.

"I don't know! I can't wake him." Cree's eyes were rolled back in his head. "Cree! Can you hear me?"

Cree groaned and turned his head away.

"I bet she gave him a roofie," Cat said, peering over Sophie's shoulder. "Don't you think? He wouldn't be that drunk from part of a bottle of wine."

"A roofie?" Laena asked.

"Yeah, you know, the date rape drug? I bet she drugged his wine."

"Is it dangerous? What should we do? Should we call 911?" Sophie asked.

"Cree! Wake up!" Laena slapped his face and one of Cree's eyes opened a slit.

"Laena?" he mumbled.

Cat peered into his face. "He's gonna be fine, Laena. Don't worry. But I don't think he's coming to Mike's house tonight."

"Well, I can't leave him here alone," Laena said, panic tingeing her voice. "What if he vomits and chokes? Or if he goes into respiratory distress or something?"

"No, we can't leave him here, Laena. Maybe you should call your parents? They can bring him back to your house?" Sophie suggested.

"Then I'd have to explain! How the hell am I going to tell them that Ariel drugged him? And...raped him?" Laena covered her face with her hands in dismay.

"I don't think she got very far with him, Laena," Cat said. "He can't get it up in that state."

"He can't?" Laena said, hopeful.

"For crying out loud, Cat!" Sophie said, exasperated. "You're not helping."

Sophie turned to Laena. "Look, why don't you stay here with him? We'll call your mom and tell her that you're spending the night with me."

"Nuhn-uh," Cat interrupted. "That's not gonna work. Haven't you guys done this before? Look, Laena's mom is friends with your mom, Sophie. What if she calls? And you want to spend the night at Mike's house tonight, right? I think you both need to call your parents and tell them you're sleeping over at my house. Your moms hate my mom."

They all smiled. Laena stood up and looked at Cat. "You'd do that for me?"

"Of course," Cat said. "You know, I used to think you were weird, being so smart and geeky. But...you're actually pretty cool. And I think what you and Cree are doing at the lab is really interesting. And...important." She tossed her hair. "But don't tell anyone I said that."

Laena hugged Cat. "Thank you, Cat. Thank you *so* much."

Cat patted Laena's back and pushed her away. "Don't go all emotional on me, Laena. It's no problem. Call your mom now so she can talk to me if she wants to before Sophie and I head over to Mike's house."

Laena took out her cell and dialed home. "Mom? Hi, it's me. Yup. Ummm, can I sleep at Cat's house tonight? Yeah, Cat. Sophie is sleeping over, too. Kind of like a spur of the moment girls' night. Uh-huh. We're just gonna...watch movies and talk and stuff. " She paused, wincing. "Yup, her parents are home. Do you want to talk to her mom?" Another pause. Laena gave Sophie and Cat a thumbs up. "Yes, okay. I'll keep my cell on." Laena hesitated. "I will, I promise. Thanks, Mom. You're the best! Okay, love you too." She ended the call.

Laena turned to Cat. "Thanks, Cat. You saved my life."

"Are you sure you're going to be okay here, Laena? What if he gets worse? I mean, he looks terrible," Sophie said.

Cree mumbled and turned over, his eyelids fluttering.

Laena sighed. "If he gets worse, I'll have to call 911 and deal with the consequences later. Cat, should I give him coffee? What counteracts this drug?"

"I don't know, Laena! I'm not an expert. I've just heard about it. You know, people saying don't put your drink down at a party, 'cuz someone might put a roofie in it." She poked Cree and he stirred. "Yeah, coffee might work. And water. To, you know, flush it out of his system? Not that I drink water anymore, after you guys told me what's in it. Viagra? Yuck. Oh! And maybe give him some food to like, sop it up or something?"

Sophie nodded. "That's a good idea! Do you need help? Should I make some coffee or maybe order a pizza?"

"No, no, I'll be okay. You guys should go to Mike's. He's gonna wonder where you are."

"What if Ariel comes back, Laena? That girl scares me. There's something wrong with her!"

Cat gasped. "Do you think...could she be the one who put the dead cat in your locker, Laena?"

Laena shook her head. "I don't know. I guess it could have been her." She jumped up and grasped Cat's arm. "Don't say anything, you guys. *Please*. Don't say anything about Ariel and the roofie or her even being here with Cree...and nothing about her and the cat. She's crazy, and I don't want her hating me more than she already does."

Sophie shook her head slowly, biting her lip. "I don't know. She's getting dangerous

... don't you think we should tell someone? If not the police, at least your parents? I really don't like the idea of leaving you here alone. She could come back! And Cree is in no state to defend you."

"I'll be fine. I'll lock the door after you go." Laena ushered the two girls toward the cabin door.

"I want you to text me every hour, Laena, so I know you're okay," Sophie said, frowning.

"Maybe you should have a secret password? So, if, like, Ariel is here, Laena can warn us?" Cat suggested.

Laena refrained from rolling her eyes. "I don't think we need a secret password. But I'll text you every hour, Sophie. Thanks."

"If I don't get a text, I'm gonna come back here with the cavalry," Sophie warned. "And I want to hear that deadbolt click into place as soon as we're over the threshold."

"I promise I'll lock it," Laena said. Sophie gave her friend a brief hug and Laena shut the door and snicked the lock into place.

"Love you, Laena!" Sophie called from the porch. "Stay safe!"

"Love you, too," Laena replied, leaning against the door in relief. She let out a deep breath and went back to the bed. She sat down and stroked Cree's hair.

"Cree! Can you hear me?"

Cree moaned and his eyes opened slightly. "Laena."

"Yeah, it's me. I think Ariel drugged you. At least, she better have drugged you, because if she didn't, I'm gonna kill you."

"Ariel.... ?"

"She's gone. Should I make you coffee? Food? What should I do to make you recover from this?" She shook Cree's shoulder. "Cree, wake up!"

He groaned. "I do not feel well."

"No, I can't imagine you do. Do you want some coffee? Tea? Water?"

"Tea...."

Laena got up and went to the stove to boil water. She searched through the cupboard until she found some tea bags and placed one in a thick ceramic mug. "What the hell were you thinking, Cree?" she demanded, glancing over her shoulder at his prone body. "Letting Ariel in the cabin, and then drinking *wine* with her? Are you out of your mind?"

Cree just groaned.

"If you slept with her, Cree McNeil, I am never going to forgive you! Do you know what we saw when we walked in? Oh, yeah. *We*. I didn't come in alone...Sophie and Cat were with me, of all people. We open the door, and there you are, stark naked, lying on your back, under Ariel with her goddamn perfect body, not a stitch of clothes on, poised over you like she was...like she was ready to *devour* you." Laena took a breath. "You were *naked*, Cree! In bed, with another girl. Not just any girl, either. With Ariel! How could you *do* this to me?" The teakettle started whistling and Laena turned off the gas and poured the boiling water into the mug. "I so did not want to see that." Laena picked up the mug and walked back to the bed. Cree fought to keep his eyes open.

"I am sorry, Laena. I...I love you."

"Then why were you in bed with her?!"

"I do not know. I...she came in..." He swallowed and grimaced.

"Sit up," Laena said harshly, "and drink your tea." She handed him the mug, but Cree did not have the strength to hold it. Laena held it to his lips and he took a tentative sip.

"She brought wine. Said it was a...peace offering. She said she wanted to compromise."

"And you *believed* her?"

Cree scowled. "I am an idiot."

"And how did you end up naked in bed with her?"

Cree shook his head in bewilderment.

"I am so mad at you right now, Cree! How could you do this to us?"

"Laena, my data...can you check my data? Did she take it?"

Laena stared at him in shock. The data! Is that what this was all about? Ariel drugged him to get the data, not to sleep with him! She stood up. "Oh, God, did she take the data? It should be in the tin, right?"

"Yes, in...in the cupboard. The sugar tin."

Laena wrenched open the cupboard and pulled out the tin. She yanked off the lid and peered inside. Empty. She turned toward the bed. "Cree, are you sure it was in here? Because the tin is empty."

Cree groaned. "Yes. In that tin."

"Oh, no!" Laena hissed. "Well, that's just great. Not only does my boyfriend end up in bed with another girl, but she steals all of our data in the process." She slammed the cupboard closed. "I'm going after her."

"No! No, Laena, you cannot go. It is too late."

"Too late for what, Cree? Too late for us? Or too late to save the data?"

Cree looked at her beseechingly. "Laena, I did not sleep with her. At least, I do not think...I could not have...."

He turned his head and vomited on the floor.

"Great," Laena muttered. "Just great." Cree had collapsed, his head hanging off the bed. She took a deep, shuddering breath and grabbed a rag from the kitchen, and went over to clean up the mess. Cree was breathing raggedly, but Laena figured as long as he was breathing, he would be okay. When she finished cleaning the floor, she washed her hands, and went back to Cree's bedside with a clean, damp cloth. She pushed his head back on the pillow, and wiped his mouth.

"I am sorry...." he groaned. "I am so sorry."

Laena lifted the mug of tea to his lips and said, "Drink this. Slowly. You need to get some fluids in you." Cree took a few small sips obediently, and then his head fell to the side, snoring gently.

Laena did not know what to do. She thought Cree would sleep off the drug, but she didn't know if she should go after Ariel and try to get the data back. Months of work—gone! Part of Laena wondered if the loss would cause Cree to stay longer. Would they have to start all over again? Could this be considered a blessing in disguise? She chided herself for thinking that way. She knew deep inside that Cree was right, that this was much larger than the two of them. She had to think of the big picture.

"Laena," Cree croaked.

Laena turned to him and stroked his hair out of his eyes. "Do you need something?"

"I...I need to go to the bathroom."

"Do you need help getting up?"

Cree nodded. Laena supported him while he swung his legs over the edge of the bed. "Blech," he said. "I feel terrible."

"Yeah, well, that's what happens when you drink almost a bottle of wine and mix in some drugs."

Cree swallowed. "My mouth tastes awful." Laena handed him the cold tea and he drank it.

"Do you want me to make you some fresh tea?"

Cree nodded. "Yes, please. I think I will go to the bathroom and take a shower, try and get my brain working. What did she do to me?"

"We think she gave you a roofie."

"A what?"

"Roofie. A drug that makes you pass out. It's...well, some people use it to knock girls out so they can rape them. They call it the date rape drug."

Cree looked at Laena in astonishment. He shook his head. "I cannot even think about that right now. What is wrong with the people of your time?" He made a face and said, "Okay, I am ready to try and stand up. Can you get me my towel and soap? And toothbrush and toothpaste?" Laena gathered his things and helped him to the door of the cabin. She watched as Cree made his way unsteadily to the restroom.

Laena checked her phone. Almost an hour had passed since Sophie and Cat left. She texted Sophie, telling her Cree was still sick, but talking and walking around, and Ariel had not come back. She tidied up the cabin, and, fixing the sheets on the bed, she found a pair of girl's panties. She straightened up with the panties in her hand, and Cree walked in. He paused at the door.

"Laena? What are those?"

"Gee, I don't know, Cree. I think they might be Ariel's panties. Unless you had some other girl in your bed?"

Cree blanched. "I do not remember anyone being in my bed." He hung up his towel and sat down heavily on the mattress. "I am sorry, Laena. I do not remember anything." He rubbed his hands across his face and Laena could hear the rasp of his stubble. "I cannot think right now. I need to sleep." He looked up at her. "Will you stay with me?"

Laena threw the panties in the trash and turned the light off. She shimmied out of her jeans and said, "Move over." Cree laid down on the edge of the narrow bed and opened his arms. Laena crawled in next to him and he wrapped his arms around her.

"Cree, what are we going to do? She took the data!"

"I will deal with it tomorrow. Right now I just need to sleep...." He slurred.

Laena sighed, and ran her hands down Cree's hard abdomen. He murmured, but did not stir. "What a waste," she whispered. "Here we have the whole night, in bed together, and you're going to sleep through it."

Cree snored. And Laena spent the whole night tossing and turning, cursing Ariel.

Chapter 21

BY THE TIME CREE AND LAENA got to the beach, the other boys had a roaring bonfire going. The girls were sitting by the fire, chatting and drinking soda. Laena did not want to be here. August 13th, she kept thinking. School started in just two weeks. Almost the end of the summer. The end of the summer meant the end of her world. She could lose Cree at any moment. She wanted to be alone with him, not with a bunch of kids from school. People said hi to them. She smiled half-heartedly and waved in response.

Cree seemed to be behaving normally, joking around with Mike and some of the other boys. She watched him in wonder. How could he act as if nothing was happening? She had a pit in her stomach so big, she felt like she had swallowed a bowling ball. Laena watched the waves crash to the shore, and then retreat, an invisible force pulling and pushing. She dug her bare toes into the sand. She fingered her pendant, trying to take comfort in its familiarity and warmth.

"What's up, Laena?" Sophie asked, throwing herself on the sand beside Laena. "Bummed the summer is almost over?"

"Mmmm," Laena murmured noncommittally. She didn't trust herself to speak.

"Laena," Sophie said in a singsong voice. "What's wrong? You look like you've lost your best friend." Laena didn't reply, and Sophie gasped. "Oh my God! Did you and Cree break up?" Sophie clutched Laena's arm, peering into her face.

Laena smiled halfheartedly. "No, no," Laena replied.

Sophie looked at her critically. "I'm not sure if I believe you. What's up?"

Laena looked over at Cree. He had taken off his tee shirt, and his muscles glowed in the setting sun. His washboard abs were accentuated by the shadows, and Laena felt a rush of warmth through her body. "We're great," she whispered. "I love him so much."

"So you should be happy, right?" Sophie asked. She released her grip on Laena's arm. "Hey, lemme ask you something." Sophie lowered her voice and put her mouth against Laena's ear. "Have you slept with him? I mean, my God, he is so *hot*."

Laena turned and looked at Sophie in disbelief. "You're drunk!" she hissed. "I can smell it on your breath."

Sophie shrugged. "Just a little rum in my coke. You didn't answer my question. Did you?"

Laena shook her head. "I'm not going to answer that, Sophie."

Sophie gave a sharp intake of breath. "You haven't, have you? What the hell are you waiting for? You have to give it up for him. I mean, with Ariel sniffing around, he's gonna want something from someone."

"It's not like that," Laena said sharply, starting to get angry. "Please, Sophie, I don't want to talk about this. Not here, not now. In fact, not *ever*."

"Laena, I don't know what's wrong with you," Sophie said, standing up and brushing the sand from the bottom of her shorts. "I thought I was your best friend. But you're treating me—and everyone else—like dirt." Sophie turned and stalked off, her gait unsteady. Laena thought about going after her, but decided she didn't have the energy. Sophie was right, though. She had abandoned everyone since Cree came to town. She didn't want anyone but Cree, not even her family. But Cree was leaving soon, and then she'd have no one.

Cree tossed a football with some of the boys down by the water's edge, laughing and having fun. Someone offered him a beer, and he took it. Thinking, Laena watched him from the fire's edge. She was embarrassed to tell Sophie that she hadn't slept with Cree. And not because she didn't want to—he refused to be with her. She remembered what Cree had told her the night of the dance, so many months ago. Ariel had gotten him drunk with brandy, and he had slept with her and impregnated her. Is that what it would take? Could she be as manipulative as Ariel? And what if she did get pregnant...would that make Cree stay? Laena shook her head in disgust at the thoughts floating through her head. She didn't want to force his hand. She loved him so much, she ached inside. She wanted to give herself to him. But she wouldn't trick him into it. Either he wanted her, or he didn't.

The warmth of the fire made her sleepy. She gazed into the flames, mesmerized by the colors, smells, and crackling sounds of the burning wood. Cree appeared beside her, out of breath and laughing. "Laena, what are you doing here all by yourself? Come, have fun with us." Laena smiled and shook her head. Cree peered into her face and sighed, his smile fading. "Ach, Laena," he said sadly.

The beer hung loosely from his hand. Laena nodded to it and said, "Is that your first?"

He shook his head. "No. Why?"

Laena didn't answer. Instead, she straddled his lap and faced him. "I need something to numb the pain."

Cree dropped the empty bottle in the sand and wrapped his hands around Laena's waist. "There are other things besides beer that will numb the pain, but that are a lot more fun," he teased, stroking her bottom.

"Like what?" she asked innocently, settling deeper into his lap. She felt him stir beneath her.

"Hmmm, like...swimming in the ocean. Naked."

"That sounds good," Laena replied. "We call that skinny dipping, by the way. Don't ask me why, because I don't know. But let's do it."

"Now?" Cree asked, surprised, looking around.

"Yes. Now." Laena said, looking into his eyes. He didn't answer, and Laena continued, "If not now, when?" she asked. She didn't think he was going to respond. His eyes searched hers, and then he stood up, scooping her in his arms and laughing.

"Okay, now!" he said, slinging Laena over his shoulder and running toward the water's edge. Laena screamed in delight. The other kids hooted and hollered when they saw Cree carrying Laena, thinking he was going to throw her in the water. But as soon as they got ankle deep, Cree put her down gently on her feet. She was facing the bay, and Cree was facing the beach. He wordlessly peeled her shirt off and flung it to the shore where it would stay dry. He unhooked her bathing suit top, and that followed her shirt. He pulled her shorts down and off, soaking them, leaving her standing in her bikini bottoms. Then he took her hand, and led her into the ocean.

When the water lapped at Laena's shoulders, he reached down and took off his swim trunks. They floated to the surface of the water, moving with the gentle waves, like a flowered, tropical jellyfish. Cree reached down and peeled Laena's bikini bottoms off, releasing them, and letting them float to the surface as well. The two articles of clothing tangled up together, undulating with the gentle swells. Then he grabbed both, and tossed them onto the shore. Laena wore nothing but the pendant. And then Cree took her in his arms.

Laena jumped up and wrapped her legs around Cree's waist, and he groaned. She felt his nakedness, his hardness, nothing separating their bodies. His body was hot and hard, and warmth flooded her. She started kissing him, and he kissed her back. Laena knew the kids on the beach couldn't see them. It was too dark, and the light from the bonfire didn't reach the water.

"Oh, Laena," he moaned. "Wait, stop...." But she didn't. She kept kissing him, hungrily, ravenously, grinding her body into his.

"Wait," he said forcefully. "Wait." He pushed her away from him, but she still clung to his arms, her legs wrapped tightly around him.

"It would be so easy, Laena, for me to just slip inside you. So easy." His voice was husky.

She nodded. "Please...please do it." She ached for him. It was actually painful.

He looked down and cupped her breast. He looked back up at her. "*Please*, Cree." She begged him with her voice and her body.

He shook his head. "No, Laena. Please don't do this to me." She saw a tear trickle out of his eye and down his face.

"Why?" she cried. "Why won't you be with me? You say you love me, but you won't let me show you how much I love you! I want to do this, Cree. I want to give myself to you. How many times do I have to tell you?"

The water sloshed gently at their bodies. Cree shifted Laena and she knew he was right—it would be so easy. They were so close. She shut her eyes and sought him out. But somehow her legs were suddenly to the side, and Cree held her in his arms.

"Come," he said gently. "We are going back to the beach."

"Cree," Laena murmured in protest.

Cree held her tightly in his arms. "I love you. So much. You will never know how much. Which is why I cannot make love to you and leave you. I will not do that to you. You are young, Laena, younger than me, with your whole life ahead of you. You will find a man...a man from your time." He paused. "Or, if we are able to be together again...if I come back...maybe then. But not now. Not so close to when I.... " He stopped mid-sentence.

"Not so close to when you are leaving?" she asked softly.

He nodded.

"But Cree, don't you understand? That is one of the reasons why I want to do this. So you remember me, so that you have a part of me...."

"I will always have a part of you, sweetie. I have your heart, and I have the memories. Do not push me on this, Laena. I am sorry to disappoint you, but I cannot—I will not—do this." He put her gently down and they waded in silence toward shore. Cree had found their bathing suits. He put his back on, and handed Laena her bikini bottoms. He blocked her from view while she got her top on, standing at the edge of the ocean water.

Laena dressed in silence. She knew, on some level, that Cree made the right decision. She respected him for his strength, and his convictions, and for keeping his promise to her parents. But she so badly wanted to share herself with him before she lost him. Maybe forever.

Dressed, they strolled back to the fire. Robb threw Cree a towel, and he dried off, then rubbed Laena's wet curls. They sat silently in front of the fire, warming their wet bodies. They stared at the fire for what seemed like an eternity, and before long, they were dry. Kids started leaving, in groups of two and three. Soon only Cree, Laena, Sophie and Mike remained. Mike threw more wood on the fire. The bonfire devoured the dry driftwood, sending out showers of sparks and welcome heat. Sophie leaned against Mike as he threw more wood on.

"I think that's enough, Mike!" Sophie laughed. "It's going to get so hot we're going to have to leave the beach."

Laena welcomed its warmth. She felt chilled, even sitting in front of the fire, snuggled against Cree. She knew it was emotional, not physical. The empty pit in her stomach was just loneliness.

Sophie and Mike were whispering and laughing, and Laena had never felt so alone. She laid her head against Cree's chest, and for the first time since she had known him, noticed that his heart beat faster than usual.

"What is it?" she whispered.

Cree laughed cynically. "I am...unnerved," he replied.

The fire popped, and Laena jumped. Cree tightened his grip around Laena. Mike and Sophie stood up and brushed the sand from the back of their legs. "I think we're going to take off, guys," Mike said. "Cree, do you want help putting the fire out, or are you going to stay for a while longer?"

"I think we'll stay for a while. Thanks, though," Cree replied. He stood up and hugged both Mike and Sophie. "Thank you both...for being such good friends," Cree said, his voice catching.

Mike looked at Cree curiously.

Cree slapped Mike on the back.

Sophie came over and gave Laena a hug. "Talk to you tomorrow?"

Laena nodded, not trusting herself to speak. But Sophie didn't notice. Sophie and Mike wandered back toward the parking lot, arms entwined around each other, Sophie's head on Mike's shoulder.

"I am glad they got together," Cree said wistfully. "They make a good couple." Cree sat down and pulled Laena into his lap. He took her face in his hands. "Laena, sweetie. Please." Cree's voice was tortured. "This is hard for me. Can we not...just be together? Love each other tonight?"

"I don't want you to leave...." she said.

"And I do not want to leave," Cree answered. "But I have to. And I do not want to do this to you tonight, but I have to. We have to talk. About the data and how we are going to get the final information to your mother."

Laena nodded. "Okay," she whispered. "Tell me what I need to do."

"Laena, you understand, do you not, how important this is? You understand that you cannot let our relationship get in the way of doing what you must do? You cannot be afraid, Laena. Afraid of what will happen to me. This is too important. Remember the grandfather paradox. I am here now, so I *must* exist in the future, too."

Laena nodded slowly, unconvinced.

"Ariel took my data. But I had another copy. I did not tell you because I wanted Ariel to think she took the only one. I will give it to you tomorrow."

"Where is it?" Laena asked.

"Hidden in my cabin," Cree replied. "I have taken many precautions. I do not trust Ariel, and I have seen what she is capable of...."

"So you will give it to me tomorrow, and I give it to my mother...when?"

"As soon as I leave," Cree said softly, his voice coarse with pain.

"And when is that?" Laena whispered. Afraid of the answer.

"Very soon," Cree said. "Right before school starts."

"Oh, Cree," Laena said. "No.... "

She started kissing him deeply, passionately, running her hands under his shirt along his hard muscles. "I want to be with you...before you leave."

Cree groaned and responded to her caresses. He looked into her eyes, hair falling over his face, and whispered, "Is that what you honestly want? Will it make you happy?"

Laena nodded. "It is the *only* thing that will make me happy right now."

Cree searched her eyes, and she saw his resolve weaken. He sighed, shuddering. "Okay, Laena. You win. We will make love." He laid her down on the sand and straddled her, his hands roaming hungrily over her body. Laena's eyes were closed, reveling in his touches. Then he stopped and sat up abruptly, groaning. "Wait...I cannot get you pregnant. We cannot...."

"Shhh," Laena responded, brushing his hair out of his eyes. "I have something. I have a condom. I won't get pregnant, I promise." She tugged at his bathing suit, but he stopped her. "No. We will take this slowly. We are doing this my way. Open your eyes." Laena opened her eyes and looked into his. She saw love and desire. "Do not close your eyes," he whispered. "I want to watch you." Laena whimpered in pleasure as his hands caressed her.

But then she heard a sickening thud, and felt a whoosh of cold air. Cree's warm body disappeared. She heard Cree grunt, and she saw him sprawled on the sand several feet from her. Laena scrambled up on her elbows, shocked to see Ariel standing above Cree, a thick piece of driftwood in her hands. She had smashed Cree across the head with the heavy wood, and held it poised above him for another blow.

Ariel wore cut off jean shorts, her feet bare, and a cream—colored short silk tee exposing her flat stomach. She bared her teeth like a savage animal.

"Back off, Laena," she whispered, her voice rough and gritty. "Back off!" Ariel brandished the driftwood over Cree's prone form. Her hair blew in the breeze, tangled. Her icy blue eyes glowed.

"Ariel, no.... " Laena begged.

"Back off. Now. Or I will kill him." She raised the wood higher, and Laena scrambled in the sand, crawling backward away from Ariel. Ariel laid the wood down, keeping an eye on Laena. She withdrew a knife from the back pocket of her shorts.

"If you move, I will kill him. If you scream, I will kill him. And then I will kill you." Her voice was cold. Matter-of-fact.

Laena's heart pummeled her chest, and she glanced around the beach for something, anything that would help. But she saw nothing. No one. Ariel took a roll of duct tape out, and bound

Cree's wrists together. She yanked him up until he perched on his knees, head lolling forward.

"Cree!" Laena screamed. She couldn't help it. He was hurt, and she had to know if he was all right.

Ariel had grabbed Cree in an iron grip. He still knelt on the sand, woozy and unable to stand. His wrists were duct taped behind him. Ariel had the driftwood back in her hand, poised like a bat over Cree's head.

"Cree!" screamed Laena again. She sobbed and started toward them.

"Do not come any closer or I will kill him!" Ariel shrieked. "I mean it, Laena! Stay away from us!" The wind whipped Ariel's black hair around her head like an evil halo. Her blue eyes crackled with hatred.

Disoriented from the blow, Cree shook his head slowly back and forth, as if to clear it. Blood dripped down the side of his face.

Ariel pulled some papers from the back of her shorts. She dragged Cree closer to the fire, and threw the papers in, page by page.

"Say goodbye to your work, Cree," Ariel said. The fire grabbed the papers, sheet by sheet, a burst of bright flame as each page was devoured. "I found these in your cabin. Do you think I am stupid? And just in case there are more...I burned your cabin to the ground."

Laena heard sirens in the background, heading inland. Toward the campground. She looked, and saw an orange glow above the trees. Fire.

"Cree!" Laena sobbed again, torn. The data—Ariel was destroying everything they had worked for! But she couldn't save the data without jeopardizing Cree's safety. Laena was rooted in place, afraid to come closer, terrified that Ariel would make good on her promise and kill him, but horrified that he may already be mortally injured.

Cree's eyes opened. "Laena...." he croaked. He slumped forward.

"It is over, Laena! I am taking him back with me. Say your goodbyes now, because this is it!" Ariel laughed mirthlessly.

"Oh, God, Cree...." Laena cried. "Cree!"

"Oh, so now you are calling for God's help, are you?" Ariel mocked. "Too little, too late, Laena. You are not a believer. No one is going to help you."

Cree raised his head again. "Laena, do not worry...."

"Oh, Cree...." Laena moaned.

"Do not worry, sweetie. I am going to be fine." He turned toward Ariel. His voice slurred. "At least let me kiss her goodbye, Ariel. Please, do not be so heartless...."

"Sorry, *sweetie*," Ariel said sarcastically. "No kisses goodbye. I am not foolish." Ariel looked at Laena with scorn. "It has been a pleasure, Laena," Ariel said. "I so wanted to kill you, but in a way, this is better. Now you have to suffer for the rest of your life, never knowing what happens to him."

"Ariel, please! Please don't...." Laena sobbed.

"Are you wasting your last words on me, instead of saying goodbye to your lover? That is fine by me. But nothing you say is going to sway me. Get ready, Cree...we are going home!"

"No! No, I am not supposed to leave yet, Ariel. Please do not do this! It is not time for me to go. This is not what I had planned."

"Do you think I care what you had planned?" Ariel screamed. "This is what *I* planned, to take you home before you were ready to go. My people are waiting for us—they are prepared to bring us both back. You failed, Cree. Failed."

"Laena!" Cree shouted hoarsely. "Laena, listen...I love you! I will always love you! Think of me when you are sitting in our special place...think of me there. You will find all the answers you need, Laena, I promise you...*go*...you will find peace...."

Laena screamed Cree's name, her heart breaking. She heard Ariel's laugh, and then they were gone, the silence deafening. She heard nothing but the hiss of the fire and the slap of the waves on the beach. She scrambled forward in the sand to the spot where they had been. There was nothing but disturbed sand and a few droplets of blood. Laena threw herself down on her hands and knees. He was gone. Cree was gone, and she was alone. She sank prone into the sand.

Laena did not know how much time had passed, but the night air blew colder. The fire had died, just a few embers glowing a dull orange in the charred remains of the driftwood. She was numb with pain and fear. Cree was gone. She couldn't grasp that simple fact. Ariel had taken half of her, her better half, and Laena no longer felt alive.

And worst of all, Laena couldn't even remember the last words they exchanged. Cree had told her he loved her...and something else. Laena sat up, wet sand in her mouth and on her face. She brushed her hair out of her eyes. What had he said? He said he loved her. He said she would find...what was it? Answers! Answers and peace, in their special place. Laena stood up, nauseated. Their special place...could he be there? Would he be there? Was it *possible*? She ran toward the rocks. The tide was coming in, but she could scramble over them safely, if she was careful. She laughed bitterly. What did she care if she fell and hit her head and died? What a relief it would be from the pain of losing Cree. She wished she would fall.

But she didn't. Her will to live was too great. The rocks were cold and slippery—Laena wondered vaguely where her shoes were—but she made it over them without any mishaps. She cut the bottom of one of her feet on a mussel shell, but she didn't feel any pain. Only the warm blood oozing over her cold foot. She ran as fast as she could to their driftwood log.

"Cree!" she called. "Cree?" Hoping, even praying, that she would round the corner and he would be there, doodling in the sand with a stick, or trying to mimic the red-winged blackbirds.

She raced around the corner, her eyes searching in the gathering dark. She saw nothing. The cattails swaying in the wind, the hulking weathered log, and the sound of the waves on the sand. Maybe he was hiding...in the cattails? Hiding from Ariel? Laena frantically ran over to the log, calling Cree's name. Silence. Nothing. No Cree. Laena fell down to her knees again, throwing her head into her arms and sobbing into the log. He was gone! Gone! How could she ever find peace without him? And what was he talking

about.... ? Answers? Answers to what?

She raised her head slowly. Answers. Answers to her most pressing question...would she ever see him again? Had he found the answer to that? Laena glanced tentatively around the log. Had he left her something? She didn't see anything...the sun had set long ago, leaving only darkness. What had he said, exactly? "Go to our special place.... " Something like that.

"I will find the answers at our special place," Laena whispered. Her heart jumped. Could he bring her with him? If she waited here, would he bring her into the future? But that couldn't be it...he had refused her that request so many times. Laena grasped the green pendant, clutching it with all her might. As she held the warm jewel, a sort of peacefulness settled over her. Cree needed her to do something. He was trying to send her a message. She just had to figure out what he meant.

The clouds scurried across the sky, revealing an almost full rising moon. The light from the moon lit up the beach with an eerie bluish glow. And then Laena saw it. A glint...a tiny glint, coming from under the log. She got to her knees and peered at the shiny thing. It looked like the corner of a plastic bag...Laena tried to grasp it with her fingers, but she couldn't. She knew she would have to move the log to see what it was. Would she be able to? She didn't know if she had the strength.

She put all her power into shifting the log. At first, it didn't budge, but then she felt it give slightly. And then a little more. She lifted the log barely a half-inch off the sand, and used her toe to drag the plastic out from underneath. It took her several times, but she finally succeeded.

It was a Ziploc plastic bag, with papers inside it. The papers were wrapped in more plastic. Had he left her a letter? She tore open the bag and unwrapped the plastic. Yes! It was a letter! Her hands shook as she rifled through the papers. A two-page letter, handwritten, and then pages and pages of numbers...his data! They were here! Laena shook her head in disbelief. Ariel had destroyed his data—twice!—but Cree had kept another set!

She went back to the letter and tilted it so she could see the words in the moonlight.

Dearest Laena,

If you are reading this, I am gone. I am so sorry, sweetie, I know you must be feeling incredible sorrow. Please know that I feel that sorrow, too. And I know you are probably angry with me, angry that I did not find a way to keep us together. But do not give up hope, Laena. Without hope, we are nothing.

Before I talk about us, I need you to do something for me. I have enclosed my data. I had three copies, and Ariel only stole one set. There is another set hidden in my cabin, under the loose floorboard by the wood stove. This set, in this bag, is the third. You must give these data to your mother. Please tell her that I am sorry I did not get a chance to say goodbye to her, and to Ben. Tell them that there was an emergency in Alaska I had to attend to. I would write them a note myself, but I have so little time. I do not know what Ariel is going to do, but I do not think she will let me stay here long.

Give your mother these data. I have explained everything I could in these papers, and I tried so hard to put it in terms of things that exist in your time. But I am afraid I wrote some things that may give me away. I had no choice. I have to make your mother understand what is happening, and that cannot be done completely with the knowledge in your time. Please, Laena, the future of the Earth depends on you. You must convince your mother that these antibacterials will set off a chain reaction that is irreversible and devastating. You must help her to understand, and stop it. I know you will do the right thing.

Now about us. You know how much I love you. My heart is breaking as I write this. I do not know what will happen if you stop the chain of events that leads to the death of the oceans. I do not think this one thing will be enough to stop all the destruction that has led to the conditions of my time, but there are others who will come to help. There is so much more that needs to be done. And, in a strange way, this is what gives me hope. Hope for us. Hope that you and I will be together again.

Laena, if I am successful with this one small mission, perhaps they will send me on another. Perhaps I can come back. There is so much to do, and I know I can do more than just this. And you can help me.

I am not just saying this to persuade you—or trick you—into giving these data to your mother. I know and understand your fears: that if we change the course of the future, I may not exist. But remember the grandfather paradox. How can I not exist when I already do? Have faith,

Laena, not in some invisible man in the sky, who, as you once said to me, decides whether the Yankees or the Red Sox will win a baseball game. Have faith in us. In our love. And in the Earth.

I will do everything in my power to come back to you. Wear your necklace. So long as you have it on, I can find you. I will do whatever it takes to be with you. But you need to do what I ask of you, otherwise everything I have struggled for will be for nothing.

And, even if you do what I request, my plan still may not work. I promised never to lie to you. It is possible we will never see each other again. But I truly believe that we will. And I do not want you to be unhappy. I do not want you to wait for me. I want you to go out and have fun. Meet other men, go to dances, laugh. Make love to some man who truly loves you, one who will treat you right.

I know what you are thinking—I know you too well! I know you are thinking that I am going to come back to my time and make babies with other women. Not true. I am saving myself for you. If I can come back, I will come back to be with you. But I promise you this: I will not be with another woman until you are in my arms again.

I love you, Laena. You are my soul mate.

I am running out of time, sweetie. Please, do as I ask. And I will try to make it back as soon as I can. Be happy in your life. Promise me.

Cree

Laena sobbed, her tears soaking the pages. She held the letter to her chest, as if holding her heart together. She could only feel the pain wracking her body, nothing else, as if she were about to break apart into a million tiny shards. She fell, facedown, her fingers clawing the sand.

Time passed, but Laena had no idea how much time. She swallowed, a futile attempt to moisten her parched mouth, but gritty sand crunched between her teeth and all she could manage was a cough. She couldn't bring herself to move, let alone stand up and spit the sand out. A gusty wind blew off the ocean, driving even more sand into her eyes and hair. She heard the surf thudding against the shore, steady and strong, like the heartbeat of the Earth.

A distant, functioning part of Laena's brain reassured her, this stupor is okay, because her heart was broken, and she didn't want to feel the pain. She could hardly breathe, and the rhythmic pounding of the surf was the only thing that kept her heart beating, the only thing forcing the blood to course through her veins. Tears trickled down her exposed cheek.

I know I can't stay like this forever, Laena thought. *I need to get up, but I can't move.* She was doomed, no matter what she did. "This can't be happening," she whispered, and then wondered if she spoke those words out loud. How downright, unbelievably screwed up everything was.

If someone had told her six months ago that she'd be in this position today, she would have thought they were crazy. A few months ago, she was just an ordinary teenage girl. Today, she's probably the most powerful person in the world. And it was the biggest curse that she could imagine.

Here she was, 17 years old, with the ability to destroy everything for her own selfish reasons. Just what Ariel would do. She literally held the fate of the world in her hands. And all she wanted was to feel Cree's arms around her, his body next to hers...she really didn't care about anyone or anything else.

She sat up, eyes opening to the bruised and purplish night. She gagged from grief and fear. Tears tracked down her face in earnest. *Oh my God,* she thought, *I cannot possibly survive this. I will die. But then again, if I do nothing, we are* all *going to die.*

Laena forced herself to her feet and started the long walk home.

* * *

Laena walked into the kitchen, slowly and methodically, trailing sand and blood behind her. Michelle sat at the kitchen table in her pajamas, drinking a cup of herbal tea and working on papers.

"Laena!" Michelle chided, glancing at the floor. "What is wrong with you? You know better than to come in the house covered with...." Michelle trailed off as she saw Laena's face. "What's wrong? Laena? Honey?"

Michelle stood up in a flash, peering at her daughter's swollen eyes and disheveled hair. "What on earth.... ?"

Wordlessly, Laena handed her mother a crumpled stack of paper. "Cree's data," she said hoarsely. "He wanted you to have it."

"What? Where's Cree? What happened?"

"He's gone," Laena said tonelessly.

"Gone? What do you mean, gone?"

"He went home. Back to...back to Alaska."

"*What?*"

"He had to leave. Some kind of...of...emergency." Laena felt like she might collapse. Michelle pulled out a chair and gently pushed Laena into it.

"Oh, Laena, honey, I am so sorry. But maybe he'll come back. If it's an emergency that he can deal with and then return, you know he will...."

Hot tears streamed down Laena's face. She shook her head. "Oh, Mom, I'll never see him again!"

"Of course you will, Laena! Don't be so dramatic. Oh, honey. Please stop crying...." Michelle rubbed Laena's back gently. "If he doesn't move back here, it's not the end of the world. He can visit, and maybe you can go visit him! And you can email, and write, and speak on the phone...."

"You don't understand, Mom," Laena said, choking on her words. "It doesn't work like that."

"You can make it work like that. Laena, I know you feel like your heart is breaking, like your world is over, but it's not. I promise you."

"You don't understand," Laena whispered.

"Then make me understand. Explain it to me, so maybe I can help." Michelle looked into Laena's eyes, willing her to open up. Laena stared back, unblinking, wishing she could throw herself in her mother's arms and tell her everything. But she couldn't. There was nothing Michelle could do to bring Cree back. Except...except carry out Cree's plan.

"Let me help, Laena," her mother whispered, her own eyes filling with tears at her daughter's pain.

Laena pushed the papers across the table to her mother. "This is how you can help, Mom." Laena looked up, her eyes pleading. "Cree's data. It was...is...so important. Please, Momma. Can you look at it? Can you read what he has here, and see what you can do?"

Laena had not called Michelle "Momma" since she was a little girl, and Laena's sudden vulnerability scared her. "Now?" Michelle looked down at the sheath of papers in confusion.

"You asked how you could help, and that's how you can help. If his data are useful, maybe he can come back and do some more research...*please*, Mom."

Michelle looked skeptical, but she picked up the papers and straightened them out. "Are you sure? Are you sure you want me to do this *now*?"

"Yes!" Laena said emphatically. "Yes, I want you to do it now. I can help explain it. They mean everything to him, these data. He worked so hard...sacrificed so much...." Laena's voice trailed off.

Michelle took one last nervous glance at her daughter, and then turned her attention to the papers. She read through the tables, Cree's explanations of the experiments and the data analyses. She spread the papers out, getting absorbed. Laena sat silently, tears spilling down her cheeks in a steady stream. Time seemed to slow, and each second felt like an hour. Laena just sat at the table, miserable, crying. After what seemed like an eternity, Michelle spoke.

"Oh my God," she whispered breathlessly. "I don't believe it...."

Laena watched her mother closely with swollen eyes. Michelle looked up at Laena. "Did he...did Cree tell you what this says?"

Laena nodded. "Kind of," she murmured, her voice husky, heavy with the lie. "It's bad, right? The antibacterials, killing the virophage?"

"Very bad." Michelle shook her head in amazement. "He's right. There *must* be a virophage," she murmured, talking to herself. Michelle stood up, pacing the kitchen restlessly. "The antibacterials...they kill the virophage, and the krill are vulnerable to attack from the viruses. The krill...oh, God. The oceans...how did he know? How could he have.... ?" She collapsed back in her chair.

Laena could tell her mother had put it together. At least some of it. Michelle could see the fate of the earth unfold in her mind. Doomsday around the corner.

"Laena...." Michelle stood up jerkily, her chair clattering to the floor. She didn't even seem to notice. "Laena, call your father. He's at the school, at a meeting. Tell him it's urgent. I don't want to leave you alone. But I have to go to work...I have to drive to CCOL. I have to call our Senator. The EPA. We have...an emergency."

"I know," Laena whispered. "I know, Mom. Can you stop it?"

Michelle looked at Laena curiously. "I don't know, honey. But I'm sure as hell going to try." She kissed Laena on the cheek and ran out of the room, calling over her shoulder, "Phone your father *now*!"

But then Michelle rushed back in and grasped Laena by the shoulders. "Laena," she whispered. "Where is he? Really? Where is Cree?"

"He...he went back," Laena stuttered. "Oh, Mom, he went *back*!" Her voice rose into a wail and Laena felt so fragile that if someone touched her she would shatter.

"Back," Michelle murmured. "Back...home?"

Laena nodded miserably.

Michelle's eyes drilled into her daughter's. "Laena, this is important. Can he...can he get here again? Back to us?"

Laena's mouth dropped open. Did her mother *know*? Could she possibly? "You mean back to Cape Cod?" Laena whispered hoarsely. She wasn't thinking clearly, and didn't know if she understood what her mother asked.

"No, honey," Michelle said, shaking Laena gently, trying to rouse her back to reality. "Back to *now*. Back to our time."

"You know?" Laena cried. "You *know*?"

Michelle shook her head impatiently. "I just figured it out," she said, her voice raw with emotion. "Can he?"

"I don't know," Laena admitted, crying silently now. "We don't know."

Michelle nodded curtly. "You should have told me. Maybe I could have helped."

"Would you have believed us?" Laena murmured. "And would you have turned him in to the authorities?"

Michelle sighed, staring into space. "I don't know. Oh, God, I don't know *what* I would have done." She turned to Laena. "Call your father," she said. "You can't be alone in this state. And, Laena?"

Laena turned and looked at her mother, her face a mask of despair.

"I think he can get back to us. I think he *will* be back, honey," she whispered. "And I won't turn him in."

Laena nodded.

Michelle flashed a tremulous smile, and she was gone.

Laena stood up at walked robotically to the kitchen phone. She punched in some numbers. She heard the phone ring dully, as if a long way off, and then a voice answered.

"Dad?" Laena said, her voice cracking with emotion. "It's me. I...I need you home. I need you, Dad. Please. Mom said you have to come home. Now." Laena heard her mother's car peel out of the driveway. She barely registered her father's voice on the other end of the phone, but she knew that he was on his way. She hung up and sat back at the kitchen table, waiting for her father to come home to take care of her. She thought about her mother, racing to CCOL, trying to stop a tragedy from happening. Trying to change the future, to save the oceans. And in that coming world where ocean life survived, everything would be different, including the people who lived there. And she thought of Cree, wherever he was, whenever he was—*if* he was—and felt a small wisp of hope that someday, maybe, she would see him again. Despite what she had just done. She clutched her pendant. And then Laena cried like she had never cried in her life, knowing that maybe, just maybe, she had just killed the man she loved.

More books from Harvard Square Editions

People and Peppers, Kelvin Christopher James
Gates of Eden, Charles Degelman
Living Treasures, Yang Huang
Close, Erika Raskin
Anomie, Jeff Lockwood
Transoceanic Lights, S. Li
Nature's Confession, J.L. Morin
A Little Something, Richard Haddaway
Dark Lady of Hollywood, Diane Haithman
Fugue for the Right Hand, Michele Tolela Myers
Growing Up White, James P. Stobaugh
Calling the Dead, R.K. Marfurt
Parallel, Sharon Erby

CPSIA information can be obtained at www.ICGtesting.com
Printed in the USA
BVOW05s1843220115

384211BV00006B/1/P